Blvnp Incorporated
A Nevada Corporation
1887 Whitney Mesa DR #2002
Henderson, NV 89014
info@blvnp.com

ISBN:_**978-1-68030-951-5**

DISCLAIMER
This book is a work of fiction. The characters, incidents, and dialogue are drawn from the author's imagination and are not to be construed as real. While references might be made to actual historical events or existing locations, the names, characters, places, and incidents are either products of the author's imagination or are used fictitiously, and any resemblance to actual persons living or dead, business establishments, events or locales is entirely coincidental.

Praises for Catching Genesis

Humor, Thrills, Suspense, Drama, Romance...what else can you ask for in books? This is honestly the best Lycan book I've read so far. I had to share this book on Wattpad with all my classmates here in Nigeria. It was that good. This is nothing close to cliché and being published is really a great deal for everyone who came across this book. I honestly can't wait to have a paperback
-Sharon Obeya, *Goodreads*

The main thing that has made me feel so connected with this book is the spirituality of the characters. I fell in love with their decisions, their actions, and their hearts. Throughout this book I have cried, laughed, and swooned at the beauty of these words. I never knew how inspiring words could be until the meaning of these words related to my own life. And for that, I can't thank the author enough.
-Elena C.

This is the first book I've ever read by this author on Wattpad, I can't say that I've read it when she first posted because I didn't, I didn't even know it existed. What I can say though, is that when I ultimately found it and read it, I could not put it down, it's just one of those stories. The characters are all well developed, funny and have a depth to them; the story is beautifully crafted and a must read, I have read it twice already and I do intend to buy the published version of the book when it becomes available. If you're a lover of werewolf stories, and ultimately romance (like I am) this is definitely the book for you.
-Kiana Yarde, *Goodreads*

This book helped me start reading and wriring again. I happened upon ot on wattpad, and it was such a refreshing change. The plot is amazing, and this book is just so great. I love it to bits amd can't wait for Fighting Darius and Trapping Quincy(the sequels) to finish. If you are new to the Werewolf/Lycan genre, this is an amazing start.
-Kimberly Chambers

Catching Genesis was my introduction to the werewolf genre after a long absense from Wattpad, and I was hooked from the first chapter. As the cast of dynamic characters developed, I emoathized with them at every twist and turn. The pack society and plotlines were fascinating, and I found myself riveted at any given moment. Maybe it's because I'm new to the genre that I'm so intrigued, but the story was something special from start to finish. If you're a sucker for romance, or just a wild ride in general, Catching Genesis is perfect.
-Nicole S., *Goodreads*

CATCHING GENESIS

NICOLE RIDDLEY

BLVNP

My bae, Peter,
for the best life and putting up with an absent-minded partner in crime.
Always.

CHAPTER I
Worst Birthday Ever

"Happy birthday!!!" They chorus as soon as I step into the kitchen.

Mom is beaming, carrying a stack of pancakes dripping with maple syrup to the breakfast table. A single candle is burning right on top of it. Dad is already sitting at the table, smiling wide.

"Hyaaaahhhh!!!" I hear my sister yells as she bounds down the stairs behind me.

I huff the candle out before she even reaches the bottom of the stairs.

"Genesis! Damn it!!!" she yells in frustration.

"Autumn Harmony Fairchild! Language!" Mom admonishes her.

I flash my sister a victorious grin before I turn back around and give mom and dad an angelic, innocent smile.

My sister Autumn is two years younger than I am. Last week was her birthday, and I blew out the candle on her special birthday pancakes. I knew she would try to seek revenge. Unfortunately for her, I came downstairs early today, and just like that, I've foiled her evil plan of revenge.

Mom disappears into the living room and I give my sister another mischievous grin. She takes her seat beside me at the breakfast table and scowls at me.

Not only are our birthdays close together, Autumn and I look almost the same. Sometimes people thought that we were twins. From our light hazel eyes to our red hair. The only difference is that Autumn's face is a little bit rounder than mine and my red hair is a darker red, closer to Auburn, while Autumn is more of a strawberry blond. I'm also a bit taller than she is. I'm 5'11" which is just a little over the average height of most she-wolves, and Autumn is 5'9".

"Happy Birthday, by the way," says Autumn "Are you excited yet?"

"Excited about going to school on my birthday?" I ask back, sharing my stack of pancakes with her. Mom gave me too much.

"No, silly! About possibly meeting your mate today!" she replies, looking at me as if I've lost my marbles.

"I don't know...I'd be more excited if I don't have to be stuck in school the whole day on my birthday." I am, but I'm not going to admit that to her.

Yeah, we're the regular werewolf family, and as werewolves, we get the gift to sense out our mate as soon as we turn eighteen. That means for me, sometime during lunchtime today, if my mate is already eighteen and he's living somewhere around here.

"I had to go to school on my birthday too," she reminds me. "I can't wait to turn 18 so I can meet my mate already." She sighs. "Oh, I bet he's so hot. Hotter than your mate. The hottest guy in the whole pack."

"My baby girl might be meeting her mate today!" mom exclaims as she comes back from the living room where she hid my birthday gift. She places my gift on the table and says, "You're excited, right?"

I'm going to be asked this question over and over again today, it seems.

"No, she's not. She's not going to let any boys near her until she's at least 40," announces dad.

I resist the urge to roll my eyes at both of them as I rip open the wrapper. I already knew what's inside. It's a new airbrush paint set and mediums. I'd been giving obvious hints about wanting it for months.

"Thanks, mom, dad! I can't wait to try it out." I give them both a hug.

Actually, I am very excited about meeting my mate. I can feel my wolf, Ezra, being restless and excited the whole night.

My Ezra is excited, which makes me even more excited. That's why I'm all dressed up today. Well okay, so I'm dressed the same way I always dressed for school every day. Jeans and t-shirt. Nothing special, but yeah, I am very excited about possibly meeting my mate today. Not that I would ever admit that to my parents. Goddess, no! That would be so embarrassing.

Autumn and I walk to school. It's just a 15-minute walk. The weather is mild and I always enjoy the short walk.

When we get to school, Autumn heads off to where her friends are waiting, while I stroll inside to where my friends usually hang out.

Penny, Reese, and River are hanging out by our lockers as usual. Reese and River are mates. Penny hasn't turned 18, so she hasn't found her mate yet.

"Happy birthday, girl!" yells Penny as soon as she spots me, drawing the attention of most other students loitering the hallway.

She pulls me into a hug and soon after, Reese and River do the same.

"You're going to have to wait until after school for your gift," says Reese excitedly.

"You're going to be 18! Finally. Are you excited?" asks Penny.

"I don't know. I think I'm a bit nervous," I admit.

3

"Yeah, I'd probably be nervous too, meeting our mates for the first time...but it's exciting too!" shrieks Penny, clapping her hands excitedly.

"Don't be nervous, Genesis. It'll be okay," soothes Reese.

"It's better than okay. It's the best thing that's ever happened to me," says River, wrapping his arms around Reese.

"Awww...isn't he sweet?" coos Reese with that look in her eyes as she stares up at River. "Anyway, we'll see you losers at lunch!" she says as River pulls her away.

"Later, bish!" says Penny. I just give them a little wave before I start digging my locker for my books.

"Boy, I wish we can mate with one of those hotties." she suddenly whispers as she stares dreamily over my shoulder.

I turn around to the sight of three male lycans walking down the hallway. They are so tall, about 6'5 or more.

You see, lycans are different than us regular werewolves. For one thing, they are known to be the direct descendants of the moon goddess, so they are treated like the nobility in the werewolf world. In fact, our king is a lycan.

Second, they are bigger, faster, fiercer, smarter, stronger and more powerful than any werewolves, even the alphas. They are like killing machines when provoked. You don't want to mess with them.

Third, in their human form, they are better looking and more attractive than us regular werewolves who are considered to be better looking than most humans...like way more. So, lycans are god-like smoking hot.

Fourth, they don't have to belong to a pack. They can travel anywhere alone and not be considered a rogue.

And fifth, they don't have mates chosen for them by the moon goddess like us regular werewolves. They get to choose their own mates, either another lycans, regular werewolves or even humans they're attracted to. They would form a bond, much like a werewolf's mate bond, or even stronger if they're both attracted to

4

each other, to begin with. Once, I heard a story about a lycan who took an already mated she-wolf, leaving her mate broken since there's nothing anybody could do about it.

There are only three male and two female lycans in our school of over six hundred students. Only 10 percent out of those six hundred students are humans. All the teachers and the administration of this school are werewolves too.

The three lycans who are heading this way right now are Lazarus, Caspian, and Constantine. The female lycans who are not around right now are Serena and Milan. I haven't seen those two around for a few days now. They are, of course, drop-dead gorgeous.

I think Serena is mated to Lazarus, and Milan may or may not mated to Caspian. There are rumors that those three boys are closely related to our ruling king, but we don't know for sure. There's not much else that we know about the lycans in our school. Not even their last names. They keep to themselves and pay no attention to us mere werewolves and humans. That makes them so mysterious and much more attractive to the female population here.

So yeah, those three god-like looking Adonis are drop-dead gorgeous. Jaw dropping. Panty melting. And I so would be making a fool of myself if I don't stop drooling over them—like Penny— and all the other un-mated she-wolves around us right now.

I quickly turn back and start pulling books that I need from my locker. There's no way a lycan would be interested in an Omega like me. Lycans are attracted to strength, intelligence, and beauty. Besides, I might be meeting my mate today. Flutters of excitement start in my tummy at the thought. My wolf Ezra is getting excited. We've been waiting for this for years.

I grab Penny's hand and drag her along to get to our class before the bell rings. We share English lit class together.

"I can't wait to be out of this place soon. Thank goodness we only have a few months of school left." I inform Penny.

"Oh, I don't know...I don't mind school. There are lots of hot guys around, like those lycans." she says. " Or like those boys...too bad they're such jerks and man-whores," whispers Penny in my ear as we pass the popular group in our school.

Logan Carrington, our future Alpha is kissing or rather shoving his tongue down the throat of Mia Brown, the head cheerleader. They're together, but everybody knows they're seeing other people on the side. Zeke Walker, future Delta has his arms around Elle Johnson and Marie Jacobs, while talking to Hunter Stevens, the future Beta. I think Hunter isn't so bad. He doesn't seem like a player like the other two. He talked to me once or twice before and seems pretty nice.

"I wonder if he's digging for hidden treasure down her esophagus," I whisper back and Penny starts laughing.

Hunter turns to look at us, then his eyes shift to me, looking amused. I think his lips twitch a bit like he's trying not to laugh. Cuddly bunny and fuzzy slippers! He must have heard me.

I practically push Penny into our English lit class, while trying to hide my flaming face.

Yes, I do think that those boys are pretty hot. There's no way in hell would I admit it to anyone, though.

Logan and Zeke have this class with me and Penny. They enter the class ten minutes after the teacher started teaching. Not that she would say anything.

Logan slides into a seat in front of me and my wolf stirs. I stare at the back of his golden head for a bit. Logan is about 6'2", well-muscled; has high cheekbones and sharp features like a model; bright blue eyes and golden blond hair. When he smiles, wow. His straight white teeth and those adorable dimples are simply to die for. Well, maybe I have a bit of a crush on him. Just a little bit. I think a lot of the girls here do.

The rest of the classes went pretty well —boring and uneventful. Art is the only subject I look forward to. Did I mention that my mom is an artist? Well, she is, and I'm very proud of her.

Lavinia Fairchild is quite well known. Every werewolf household here has at least one or two of her prints or originals. My dream is to go to an art school and be as good as her.

We are sitting at our regular table during lunchtime when I suddenly smell that wonderful smell that I can't describe. Whatever it is, it smells awesome! Ezra, my wolf is fighting to be let out and take control. I guess I was born during lunch time. I stand up and start to follow my nose to identify where that smell comes from. I can't help it. I have to find it. I vaguely hear my friends calling my name, but I can't seem to focus on anything else but that smell.

My nose brings me to the popular group table. Oh no, I can't seem to bring my feet to stop. Ezra's taking control. Everybody stops talking. Logan Carrington? My mate is Logan Carrington? No no no no.

His beautiful blue eyes widen as he looks up at me. His eyes softened as they roam my face. I can see lust and hunger flitting across his face briefly as his eyes move up and down my body. But then he looks away quickly. His breathing ragged. My wolf howls with joy and my first instinct is to jump on him and stake my claim.

"Follow me," he says gruffly, and swiftly walks out the cafeteria through the back door.

I follow him across the lawn to an Oak tree. The tree provides us a bit of privacy from prying eyes.

"What's your name?" he finally asks. His beautiful eyes are not even looking at me. I can't seem to tear my eyes away from his perfect face. The sun is glinting in his golden hair. The shadows fall across the planes of his sharp features.

"Genesis... Genesis Fairchild," I finally answer.

"Fairchild? You're an Omega, aren't you?" he says. "I can't have an Omega as my mate. My pack needs a stronger luna, not someone weak like you. Besides, I love someone else. Mia makes a better Luna than you ever could." Each word is like a knife slicing through my chest. Ezra whimpers.

7

Oh no, suddenly I know what's going to happen. My heart starts to race, my breaths come out short and shallow. I don't know what's happening to me. All I know is that my heart is breaking.

"I, Logan Carrington, future Alpha of Shadow Geirolf pack, reject you, Genesis Fairchild, as my mate and future luna of my pack," he utters coldly, not looking at me once.

My wolf cries and howls in pain. She doesn't understand. Why is our mate hurting us so?

"Hey baby, what's going on?" says Mia, wrapping her arms around him. Where did she come from?

"Nothing to worry about, sweetheart," he answers.

She looks me over with disdain. She pointedly pulls Logan's head down and plants her lips on his for a claiming kiss. He wraps his arm around her waist, and then they turn and leave. I watch her whispers something in his ear and they both laugh.

I watch them laugh as I fall to the ground, clutching at my chest. Oh, goddess, it feels like he just plunged a knife deep into my chest and twisted it. Then he just keeps yanking the knife up and down, left and right over and over again until there's nothing left of my heart but a bloody, twisted ugly gash in my chest. Ezra curls up in pain then goes silent.

*   *   *

I'm lying on my bed now. Everything was a blur after I fell. I remember seeing my friends Penny, Reese, and River running to me, calling my name in panic. They were asking me what was wrong. River carried me to his car. Then I don't remember anything else. The three of them must've brought me home.

"Talk to me, honey. Tell me what happened," says mom gently, pushing my hair from my forehead.

"He rejected me, mom. My mate rejected me." My eyes are tearing up again. I still find it hard to believe that this is really happening to me. I was wishing that it was just a horrible nightmare.

There are a thousand different emotions chasing across mom's face. Disbelief, anger, pain, sadness....

All the pain comes back. I start twisting in my bed and mom wraps her arms around me. Even mom's comforting loving arms can't stop or ease the pain away.

"It hurts so bad. Make it stop...make it stop. Mom, please make it go away." I sob, clawing at my chest. "I'd do anything...just make it stop." Goddess, it hurts so much, I want to die.

"My baby. My poor baby girl," cries mom. Tears running down her face as she hugs me close, willing my pain to go away.

After what feels like hours, I calm down, or maybe I'm just too exhausted to even shed a tear. Only my chest is moving up and down. Sleep doesn't come easily. In the middle of the night, all alone in the darkness, tears leak out again, falling down my face silently. My wolf, Ezra, is completely silent now, but I can feel her crushing pain, as well as my own.

I had been looking forward to meeting my mate since I was four. Mom told me about it like it's the best thing to ever happen to a werewolf. I had been waiting for someone who would love me and protect me and be by my side no matter what.

All werewolves look forward to meeting their mates. It's very rare that a mate gets rejected, but it happened to me. What is wrong with me?

All werewolves know you only got one chance of having a mate. What now? Will I ever be loved and have a family? Will my wolf, Ezra, ever comes out and be the same again? A werewolf without his or her wolf is only an empty shell. Most would eventually die or go crazy after they lost their mates. Their wolves decide to disappear when the pain gets unbearable. Now I understand how very painful it is, and we're not even mated yet. Will I die or go crazy too? I hope Ezra is strong enough to stay.

How could the moon goddess do this to me? What did I do to deserve this? I didn't ask for an Alpha. She could've matched me to another lowly Omega and I'd still be happy. As long as I am loved, I'll be happy.

How did this day turn out so bad? Worst. Birthday. Ever.

CHAPTER II
How Do I Reject Thee?

After that first day, I never cried in front of my parents again. Mom and dad, and even Autumn, looked very upset when they saw me crying and in pain. When he first heard about it, dad got really angry. That was the angriest I've ever seen him. He's usually a very laid back and easy going kinda person. That day, I learned that my daddy could be very scary when he's angry. Mom had to calm him down to stop him from changing and go charging into the pack house.

Now I cry in the shower. I make sure to muffle my sobs with my hands. Also that second night, I felt the pain so intense that I had to bite my pillow to swallow the sound of my scream. It lasted almost an hour. I knew right away what my mate was doing then.

Some say it's a gift, but I think it's a curse that you can feel it when your mate is cheating on you after that first meeting. It's very painful.

He's having fun with some other female, probably Mia, while I'm feeling the pain. How is that fair? My wolf Ezra howled in pain, sadness, and rage. Oh, I can feel her rage now, and that's better than her silence. My wolf is strong. I'm glad she's still here. At least she hasn't abandoned me yet.

My friends Penny, Reese, and River now know the whole story and are very pissed off. Reese had to calm River down who looked pissed enough to kill somebody. They come to visit me after school almost every day to cheer me up. I don't know what I'd do without my loyal friends.

I never thought being an Omega is that bad. I mean, my parents taught me that everybody is equal. Even the humans should be treated with the same respect. I guess not everybody thinks that. Now, I'm conscious of my status as an Omega.

My father was actually in line for an Alpha in his old pack. I think my dad and my mom are hippies at heart. He's too carefree to be an Alpha, much to my grandpa's endless chagrin. His younger brother, my uncle Ashton, took over while dad followed mom to this pack. His old pack, Canis Gunnolf Pack, is one of the strongest in the world.

We never talked about this to anyone. I think the only people who knew about my dad being an alpha in line for Canis Gunnolf are Alpha Carrington (Logan's dad) and his beta.

I think Alpha Carrington was worried that my dad would challenge him for the title as an alpha when he first made a request to join this pack. My dad is quite a big man after all. He relegated my dad to an Omega level, which my dad didn't at all mind.

Today is Friday, the third day after it happened, I decided that I've wasted enough time. I'm not wasting any more time mourning over a useless jerk of an ex-mate. My wolf Ezra hasn't left me. I can live without a mate. I'm determined to make it without a mate.

However, I'm not ready to go to school yet. I'm not ready to see *him* and Mia eating each other's face and laughing and being happy together. But I'm going to show him that I'm strong; that he doesn't have the power to break me.

I go to our Art Supply Store instead—Fairchild's Kraft & Art Supply Store—the sign says in bold colorful letters up the front above the entrance. We own this store, and we're the only art supply store in town. Mom sometimes offers painting lessons as well.

"Hey, baby girl!" says dad, looking surprised but happy to see me there. "Just the girl I want to see. I have a good news for you." he announces, looking enthusiastic as he arranges the pastel boxes on the shelf. "You just sold your very first painting this morning."

"Really? Which one?" Wow, that *definitely* lifts my spirit up a little.

"The rundown hut by the lake in oil," he answers as he moves behind the counter. "Here you go, honey." He hands me the money. Pride shines in his eyes.

Five hundred dollars. It wasn't even a big painting.

"You're a rich woman now. What are you going to do with all that money?" he asks me teasingly.

"Wow! I don't know, dad. So many possibilities. I might buy myself a Porsche, and a fancy condo and ditch you guys."

"Smart-aleck." Dad laughs, ruffling my hair. I think he's relieved that I'm out of my self-imposed imprisonment and sound almost like my old self again.

My phone beeps with an incoming text message.
Queen Penny: Whatcha doing? Daytime tv any good?
Me: Nope. At art store. Whatcha doing? Chem any good?
Queen Penny: Ha Ha Ha....bored. kill me now.
Me: Ha Ha...Sold my painting today. $500 Woo hoo!
Queen Penny: COOL! Be my sugar momma, you rich woman you! We're going shopping after school. Pizza & ice-cream your treat.
Me: NOOOOOO!!!
Queen Penny: YESSSS!!! Will let Reesey know. Got to go. See ya! Love ya!

I know my friends would drag me to the mall by my ankle, kicking and screaming, if they have to.

I enter the studio at the back of the store. I pick a big blank canvas, put an apron on, then I attack the canvas, pouring every anger and frustration and sadness into it. And, it is only after I'm done when I realize that my cheeks are wet with tears.

I stare at my work—it's a semi-abstract, with layers and swirls of colors of demons and angry lines of heartbreaks. A single white dove is flying alone. Its fluttering wings are almost translucent. The dove is ethereal, too exquisite for its surrounding. My hope and strength. I am good enough.

"Oh, honey," says mom from behind me. "That is...absolutely amazing." She gasps. Tears are filling her eyes as she stares at the painting.

After school, my two friends show up looking excited. They both drag me to shop for some new outfits and get my hair trimmed up a bit and add a few very bright red highlights. Oh, joy, retail therapy.

*   *   *

"You guys suck! Why are we watching this movie again?" complains Penny as she throws some popcorn on my head.

"Hey, Reese voted for this movie too," I argue, flicking some popcorn back at her.

For someone so sassy and looking so tough, Penny's a scaredy-cat when it comes to horror films. Reese, who's always looking like a sweet Disney princess, can't seem to get enough of them. I'm stuck in between them.

It's Saturday evening, and we are currently watching Annabelle: Creation on Netflix in my bedroom and Penny is hiding behind a big pillow on her lap.

Mom and dad are still at the store and Autumn is out with her friends.

"Come on, Penny, it's not that scary," says Reese, shoving a big scoop of Ben and Jerry's in her mouth.

Penny scowls and throws another handful of popcorn onto our heads. Reese giggles and picks another bowl to empty it over Penny's.

"You are so helping me clean my room before you go tonight," I warn them laughing, throwing more popcorn at the both of them.

All of a sudden the familiar pain starts at the base of my stomach, knocking the wind out of me.

"GenGen, what's happening?" asks Reese in alarm as I writhe in pain.

"Nothing," I gasp. Oh no, I don't want them to see this.

"Should I call your mom?" asks Penny, panicking.

"NOOO.No," I yell, clutching my stomach. "Don't.. tell my mom." I choke out. Tears are starting to run down my cheeks.

"What's wrong? What's happening?" asks Penny again.

"I think I know what's happening," answers Reese, gripping my hands on my stomach. "That manwhore Logan is doing some nasty things with some slut," she continues coldly.

Penny lets out a string of curses.

The pain is excruciating. I think I passed out after a while. *Thank goddess for that.*

When I open my eyes again, Reese and Penny are still there. Reese is still holding my hand tightly in hers with tears on her face. Penny is fuming and walking around the room as if she wanted to kill someone.

"Hey, you're still here," I smile, feeling exhausted.

They both snap their heads to look at me. Penny is looking totally pissed, and Reese is staring at me with sadness, pity and also some anger. I don't think her anger is directed at me though.

"How many times had this happen, hon?" asks Reese.

"I bet this is not the first time," says Penny, looking at my belly now exposed from my t-shirt that has ridden up from my twisting and squirming.

My stomach is black and blue. The bruising came from me clutching my stomach so hard when the pain gets too much.

"This is the fourth time so far," I decided to be truthful. They had seen me in pain, after all, there's nothing much else to hide.

Penny starts cursing all over again. "It's not fair! He can't do this!" yells Penny.

"Now where are you going, Penny?" asks Reese when Penny jumps to the door.

"Where else? I'm gonna go and kick his ass off to the moon!" Penny wails hotly. Her chocolate brown eyes turn even darker, showing that her wolf is close to the surface.

"No, you're not," announces Reese, dragging her back into the room.

"Oh, hell yes I am!" argues Penny, trying to get out of Reese's firm grip on her arms.

"We're not kicking anyone's ass today. We're going to do even better," Reese declares. That makes Penny stop struggling.

"He's hurting one of us and we're beyond pissed. Girls, we're getting even. It's operation payback," announces Reese.

What did I do to deserve such awesome friends? "I love you guys," I say as I hug my two besties.

Penny writes down our plan for Operation Payback on paper. If that's not a commitment, I don't know what is.

Most of the ideas come from Reese and Penny. I just scrunch up my nose at most of them. Well, maybe all of them.

There are a few phases to our Operation Payback:

The first one is for me to look awesome and get the attention of un-mated boys at our school. Umm...I think that needs a lot of work, but maybe that can be done. Maybe. I don't know.

The second part is for me to flirt with some guys to make him jealous. According to Reese, all werewolves, especially the Alphas are very possessive of their mates...even with the ones they've rejected. We'll have that theory tested soon. I kinda doubt that he cares. He has the beautiful Mia and all the other girls anyway.

The third phase is for me to get a boyfriend since I don't have a mate anyway.

The third phase would lead to phase four, and this is the toughest one for me...lose my V-card so that he can feel the pain he causes me when he's with someone else. I'm not sure if I'm on board with this one.

"It's not like you're saving yourself for your mate anymore," argues Penny when I disagree with the fourth stage. Ouch!

"GenGen, you have to commit to this. Promise me you're going through with this. He made you suffer, he's gonna pay. He should feel at least a fraction of the pain he put you through. You're gonna show him what he's missing. You're going to show him that you don't need him. He needs you," commands Reese spiritedly. "Doesn't he know that an alpha needs his true mate to be really strong? This pack is going to the wolves...like literally.

"I'm getting an ulcer just thinking about him and Mia leading the pack." Reese shudders.

The thought of the two of them together is less painful now. Maybe because I haven't been around him in a while. I don't think I'm good enough to be a luna, but I don't know what I'll do when the two of them become the alpha and luna of the pack.

"You think they'll kick me and my family out of the pack once they become alpha and luna?"

"They can't do that, can they?" asks Penny.

Yes, they can. The three of us sit in thoughtful silence for a few minutes before I suggest that we let our wolves out and go for a run.

It's a great relief to let Ezra out. I feel light and feel almost normal again. I should let my wolf out more often.

Penny ends up spending the night at my house. Reese has a date with River later that night and has to leave. Both of Reese and Penny are coming for a sleepover again tomorrow night.

After Reese left, Penny wants to watch Deadpool and drools over Ryan Reynolds. I've drooled over him like a thousand times, so I decided to butcher Elizabeth Browning's beautiful sonnet, *How do I Love Thee* , changing the word love to reject and tape it on my wall.

How do I Reject Thee?
How do I reject thee? Let me count the ways.
I reject thee to the depth and breadth and height
My soul can reach, when feeling out of sight
For the ends of being and ideal grace.
I reject thee to the level of every day's
Most quiet need, by sun and candle-light.
I reject thee freely, as men strive for right.
I reject thee purely, as they turn from praise.
I reject thee with the passion put to use
In my old griefs, and with my childhood's faith.
I reject thee with a love I seemed to lose
With my lost saints. I reject thee with the breath,
Smiles, tears, of all my life; and, if God choose,
I shall but reject thee better after death.

Penny thinks I'm nuts. I think it's funny in a sick, twisted and sad kinda way.

Original Poem:
How do I love Thee? (Sonnet 43) by Elizabeth Barrett Browning.
How do I love thee? Let me count the ways.
I love thee to the depth and breadth and height
My soul can reach, when feeling out of sight
For the ends of Being and ideal Grace.
I love thee to the level of everyday's
Most quiet need, by sun and candlelight.
I love thee freely, as men might strive for Right;

18

I love thee purely, as they turn from Praise.
I love thee with the passion put to use
In my old griefs, and with my childhood's faith.
I love thee with a love I seemed to lose
With my lost saints,—I love thee with the breath,
Smiles, tears, of all my life!—and, if God choose,
I shall but love thee better after death.

CHAPTER III
Operation Payback

Today is Monday. Last night, the girls had a sleepover at my house so that we can get ready for school together. We're starting Operation Payback—phase one.

"So, tell me why are we wasting our time doing this again? We agreed that he's a worthless jerk anyways," I ask, as Reese pulls and tugs at my hair.

"Well, reason number one, he's gotta pay for what he put you through. Number two, isn't this fun? I'm excited to do this!" answers Penny.

"And reason number three, it stops Penny from going crazy ninja on Logan and getting herself thrown into the dungeon," adds Reese.

"I still think we're just wasting our time. No amount of work will get me noticed around school when all the other girls are so gorgeous."

I stare at Reese in the mirror. Reese looks like a doll in her yellow gossamer sundress, a white cardigan, and a pair of bright yellow sandals. Her golden curls are in a high ponytail, tied with a white filmy ribbon.

"Genesis," sighs Reese, turning me around to face her. "Even without all the makeup and the makeover, you're easily the prettiest girl in school."

"Boys are always staring at you, you're just too dense to notice," adds Penny, dabbing some color to her eyelid. Penny is rocking her new sleek hairstyle with black shorts and dark blue crop top paired with high top black sneakers and also a black leather jacket. Truly, Penny is so gorgeous, she looks like a model to me.

"Hey! I resent that," I complain. "If you think I was already pretty why do we need to do all this then?"

"Honey, the makeover and all this is just to boost your self-confidence...plus, you finally agreed to let us dress you up. It's like having a real-life Barbie doll to play with," replies Reese gleefully. "Oh, I can't wait to have a baby girl with River...well, not yet, but in a few more years."

"You'll make a wonderful mother, Reese," I smile, imagining her with babies.

"Yeah, she will. And I'll probably be the worst mother ever. I'd probably forget where I left my pup when I'm too busy playing Crashlands or something," confesses Penny.

We start laughing at that because Penny does tend to forget things when she plays her games.

Checking my reflection in the mirror, I have to admit, I like how I look in the small purple top and a white skater skirt. The top follows the contours of my body like a glove, the V-neckline just skimming over the rise of my creamy skin, making my boobs look bigger...sort of. The skirt makes my legs look long and endless. I have a pair of white converse on. My hair is in big loose curls.

"I envy your long legs." Reese sighs. She really has no reason to envy my anything.

"My goddess, you girls look stunning!" exclaims my mom when we get to the bottom of the stairs.

"Thanks, Lavinia," reply Reese and Penny.

Mom hugs all three of us with tears in her eyes. I think she's thankful for my friends for getting me up and about again. Ready to get back to school again too.

21

We join dad and Autumn in the kitchen for breakfast. Mom has made lots of pancakes for us.

Later, Autumn joins us in Reese's car for a five-minute drive to school. I know Autumn enjoys spending time with my friends too. She's known them since she was in diapers. They're more like big sisters to her.

"I'd like to do my hair like yours too soon," says Autumn, pulling at a lock of my hair before she jumps out of the car and disappears into the crowd.

"That's the closest to a compliment I've ever gotten from her," I inform Penny and Reese.

"Sisters," mumbles Penny, shaking her head. "Sometimes I'm glad I'm an only child."

I notice we draw a lot of attention as we exit the car. I wonder if it's because they know about what happened between me and Logan, or because of our new looks.

Some students stop and stare. I hear whispers here and there. My strong werewolf hearing catches the word "Logan's mate" and "rejected" several times. I hear some guys lewd comments too. "Damn she's hot, I'd tap that." I catch a girl's bitchy voice saying clearly, "Gosh, who gets rejected by their own mate? How pathetic and embarrassing. I'd kill myself if I were her." Either way, I can't say that I'm enjoying it.

Remembering our mission, I hold my head up high, paste a smile on my lips and defiantly add a sway to my hips. Reese gives me a smile and a wink before her attention is taken by River who is jogging over to meet us.

"Atta girl," whispers Penny.

I see Logan's blond head facing away from us when we get nearer to our classroom.. Penny's grip tightens around my arm. Logan is talking to Zeke and Hunter. He seems relaxed, leaning against one of the lockers. Well, at least he doesn't have his tongue down Mia's throat this time.

My wolf Ezra perks up and seems more restless the closer we get to him. I think she can't decide whether she wants him or is furious with him for treating us like trash. His delicious smell is messing with me even when I'm very determined not to feel anything towards him anymore. The mate pull is still very strong.

Zeke's wandering eyes find me and flicker up and down my body. His blue eyes darken even more when I give him a tiny smile.

I find Hunter also staring at me and I give him a bigger friendly smile. Didn't I tell you I think Hunter's a nice guy?

Logan sniffs and looks around. His eyes widen as soon as they land on me. I let my smile go slack, my eyes go cold and look away. Penny tugs at my arm and whispers something so low, but it sounds like "Phase one a success, moving on to phase two."

Penny and I slip into our English lit classroom and take our regular seats near the middle, next to each other. The room is only half filled, and a steady stream of students are still coming in.

"Did you see how he was staring at you?" whispers Penny excitedly, bringing her chair closer to mine.

Before I could answer, the door bangs open and Logan walks in looking intently at me. Boy, he's still so good looking. It's killing me. I lean back in my chair, trying to be as far away from him and his delicious smell as possible.

He slides into his seat in front of me, facing backward, staring at me while I pretend not to notice.

Zeke takes a seat beside him, surreptitiously glancing at me from time to time.

"This should be fun," whispers Penny, gleefully. She's having too much fun with this.

I flip my hair and turns around to face Zeke with a smile.

"Hey," I whisper softly but loud enough to make sure that he can hear me. I smile coyly at him before lowering my eyes to Julius Caesar in front of me.

"Hi," Zeke answers and he gives me that slow smirk that melts so many girls' panties as I peer up at him through my eyelashes. His eyes travel down the length of my legs underneath the table.

A growl beside him interrupts Zeke. The future delta straightens up and snaps his head around to look at his future alpha.

Logan is staring at us with a clenched jaw and dark eyes. His nose flares in anger. Even now he's looking hot. Well, hotter actually. I can feel Ezra's anger though as well as her attraction towards Logan and his wolf.

Well, well, well…theory tested. Steeling my resolve, I decided to ignore Logan.

A buffed looking boy enters the classroom seconds before the teacher does. I can tell from his smell that he's a human. I smile when his eyes land on me and his eyes widen comically. Then he cockily makes his way over, sitting in an empty chair on the other side of me.

"Hey," he says, smirking. I smile flirtatiously at him once before deliberately ignoring him. I hear another growl and swallow the laughter that tries to escape my lips.

"So, how's it going?" the boy asks. I smile but keep my eyes trained on the front since the teacher has started teaching. I can see Logan clenching his jaw, his whole body is stiff. Oh I know, I'm feeling like jumping at him right now too…even after he rejected us. Sad really. Pathetic.

Not wanting to be pathetic, I focus my attention on annoying him instead.

I stretch my legs to the side, giving the human and Zeke a clear view of my long legs. The human boy doesn't disappoint, but Zeke stares straight ahead, looking flustered.

"My name's Kevin. You're Genesis, right?" He keeps trying.

"Yep, you got that right," I mumble softly under my breath, but he must have heard me because Kevin shifts his chair closer to mine.

24

Logan is gripping the side of his desk tightly. So tightly, I wonder if he's going to break the table soon.

Wow, this is actually a lot of fun.

I wonder if he's even listening to a word our teacher was saying for the last fifteen minutes or so.

Then an idea strikes me. I rip a page of my notebook, making it obvious, and start writing. Then I make a show of passing the note to Penny.

The paper is ripped away from my fingers before Penny has the chance to grab it, not by our teacher, but by Logan Carrington.

He scans the note once, crumples it, then throws it on the wall. His desk scraps back noisily and his chair almost toppled over as he stands up and angrily stomps out of the room.

The whole class, including the teacher, are left staring at the door that he disappeared through.

In the note to Penny I wrote: Don't you think Zeke is hot? I think he is super hot!

When I manage to meet up with the rest of my friends during lunch, Reese is bursting with excitement. Apparently, Penny had been busy the whole morning, texting Reese about the development of our plan.

"I wish I were there," moans Reese, as we wait in line to get our food.

"You should've seen her. I think we've created a monster," gloats Penny.

"Remind me not to cross you, girls," says River, laughing.

"As long as you're not hurting Reese, we're good, buddy," Penny pats his arms playfully, but the look in her eyes warns him that she's very serious.

"I wouldn't dream of it," he smiles dreamily into Reese's eyes.

"Those two make me sick sometimes," quips Penny as we walk to the table with our tray of food.

25

"You're just jealous," responds River.

"Wow, if looks could kill," says Penny.

Most of the people at the popular table are staring at us...or me right now. Logan is nowhere to be seen, and Mia is giving me a deathly glare.

I choose to look the other way and ignore them.

*   *   *

"So now, all you have to do is get yourself a boyfriend," states Penny like she's stating the weather.

"Yeah, as soon as you can tell me where to buy one at the mall," I retort.

"Does it really matter to whom you lose your V card to?"

"Yes it does," Reese and I answer in unison.

We are currently in Reese's car on the way to school the following day, arguing about phase 3 of our Operation Payback.

"You know what? I think we approach this one all wrong. We shouldn't rush you looking for a possible guy to lose your v-card to. That's too much pressure. Mated or not, it should be with someone special." Reese reasons. "Revenge is not a good enough reason to lose your virginity for. It should be when you're ready."

"I hate it when you make sense," complains Penny. "I so want that jerkface to taste his own medicine, but I think Reese is right." She sighs. "However, it wouldn't hurt to find you a boyfriend."

Both Logan and Zeke didn't show up during English Lit. I feel both disappointed and relief at the same time: disappointed because some stupid part of me still want to be around him; relief because I don't have to fight the pull I have towards him whenever he's around. It's stressful, not to mention exhausting trying to fight the feeling.

Kevin, the buffed human boy, shows up though. He sits beside me like yesterday and keeps glancing at me throughout the lesson. I try to avoid looking at him and pretend to be very fascinated with Shakespeare the whole period.

He manages to catch me after the class, waiting for me by the door when I exit the classroom.

"Genesis, can I talk to you for a minute?" he asks hopefully.

"Yeah, okay..." I reply as he pulls me to the side, away from other students. I see Penny rushing out to her next class, probably thinking I'd already left.

"Would you go out with me this Friday?"

Huh? "Uh...I'm flattered that you asked, but I'm sorry, Kevin. I can't." I hate saying no to people, but I'm not interested in him that way and it would be a kindness not to lead him on.

"What about Saturday?"

"Uh...nope."

"Sunday?"

"No, sorry."

"Listen, Genesis, I like you. I've liked you since the beginning of the school year, but you never looked at me."

"Uh, okay...thank you?" What do you say to somebody who just confessed to like you when you don't share the same feeling?

"I know you like me from the way you smiled at me yesterday. You're shy, I get it." he says, cockily.

Huh? What? "No, Kevin. I'm not shy. I just don't want to go out with you."

"Ahhh...you're playing hard to get. That's okay. I like that. You know I won't give up that easily. I'll work hard at winning your affection, my lady." He winks, then he walks away with a swagger and a smile like he's just won a lottery.

Wait! What? What had just happened?

I walk to my next class in a bit of a daze, still wondering what had just happened. He won't give up? What does that mean? Should I be worried?

CHAPTER IV
Let Me Count The Ways

"Kevin asked me out," I announce during lunch time.

"Kevin? Kevin who?" questions Penny, her fries suspend in mid-air.

"He's the human who sat on the other side of me yesterday, and again today in English Lit?" How can she not know this? Duh!

"Well, we shouldn't discriminate. You definitely should go out with him," Reese says encouragingly.

"But I'm not interested in him like that, I don't want to lead him on. Besides, I just smiled at him yesterday, and he's convinced that I liked him. Imagine if I agreed to go out with him...he might think we're getting married and ready to have babies by noon tomorrow or something."

Reese, River, and Penny seem to think that's funny.

Penny starts singing. "Genesis and Kevin sitting in a tree, K-I-S-S-I-N-G! First, comes love. Then comes marriage. Then comes baby—"

"Genesis, can I talk to you?" Logan Carrington cuts in, looking murderous.

Oh boy, it seems like he's been walking around with a frown these days.

I can feel my wolf Ezra getting excited and annoyed at the same time. That heavenly scent that only Logan Carrington carries is driving my wolf insane even when I'm still furious with him.

My three friends are staring daggers at Logan, but he returns their death glares with his own, which is quite impressive, given that he's the future alpha and all. Then he turns and walks away without a backward glance, expecting me to follow him. Wow, this seems familiar.

I reluctantly get to my feet.

"You know you don't have to go with him, right?" says River, looking miffed.

"You know if I didn't, he's just gonna get madder and comes back here and makes me go with him anyway, right?"

"I could kick him in the nuts," mutters Reese heatedly.

Penny blows her bangs off her forehead. "I could cut off his nuts."

"Okay, enough talking about his nuts already," I interrupt. "See you guys soon. If I didn't make it, tell my parents I love them, and there's some money in my underwear drawer."

River's lips twitch and look as if he has some lewd comments he wants to share, but I walk away quickly before he opens his mouth.

"Took you long enough," snaps Logan when I reach the oak tree where he rejected me over a week ago.

"Who's Kevin?" he growls.

His sea blue eyes are just so gorgeous. Gosh, what am I thinking?

"That really is none of your business. So what's up?" I look away from his gaze.

Despite all the pain that he put me through, he still gives me butterflies when he's near me. When he looks into my eyes, I get lost in his gaze. I hate that I'm feeling this way.

"That's not the way you should be talking to me, Genesis. Everything you do is my business. So, who's Kevin?" He sounds so possessive.

"Does it matter? Like I said, none of your business."

"Like I said, everything you do is my business. So, is he your boyfriend now?"

"Why do you care? You're not my mate. You're nothing to me."

As soon as the words left my mouth, his lips slam on mine. I feel the roughness of the tree bark on my back as I'm being pushed against it.

It takes me a few seconds to comprehend what's happening, but my body is already responding to his kiss and his touch. Ezra is close to the surface, taking some control. I feel the delicious sparks breaking all over my body as he leans in further, pushing his body flush against mine.

Fireworks.

Our bodies fit perfectly together. *This* is supposed to be wrong but, damn, it feels so right. It's impossible for me not to respond to his touch. My lips are moving against his and his warm hand is touching, traveling up and down from the sides of my breasts, moving to grip my waist, down to my thighs, then up again. Another hand is in my hair, holding my head still for his onslaught.

My hands move up to his neck, then move up some more to grip his hair. He pulls back just to have his lips move across my jaw and down my neck, kissing, licking and biting.

"Goddess...you smell so good." He groans, breathing in deeply before he latches onto the base of my neck and starts sucking. The feel of his sharp canine against my skin suddenly brings me out of my lust-filled haze. I push him roughly off me.

The pain! No!

We're staring at each other, breathing hard and raggedly. Even now, he looks so hot to me; lips red and swollen; his usually blue eyes, now dark and dangerous; golden hair in wild disarray.

31

"You feel that? We're mates whether we like it or not." he barks out.

"No, you've rejected me. We're nothing. No, not mates," I deny.

"Well, too bad if you think that...but you're still mine. You're not going to see this Kevin guy or any other guys."

"No, you don't get to tell me what to do, and I'm not yours," I wail at him.

"Look, here's the deal, sweetheart. I've changed my mind. I'd like to keep you...and I get to keep you since you're my true mate." He moves dangerously close again. "You. Are. Mine."

"I am not yours! Stay away from me," I yell as I run back into the building.

I want to be with him, of course, I do, but I'm still very hurt by his rejection and the pain he caused me and my wolf. A big part of me and my wolf feels wary. We don't want to feel the pain that we felt that first time he rejected us. It was the most painful experience in my life.

I sit quietly in my seat and my friends look at me questioningly, but none of them say anything. I'm grateful for that. However, I've lost my appetite. I get up to throw away the half-eaten sandwich as my eyes are slowly drawn to the popular table. Mia is sitting on Logan's lap. They're eating each other's face again. All of those at the table is staring at me. Most with glee, but some with sympathy and looking a bit uneasy...like Hunter. Mia's eyes open to look at me and she smirks, taunting me, as she pulls Logan's mouth onto hers again. I feel Ezra's fury.

"Bitch!" Penny spits as she notices what I'm staring at.

Why is he doing this to me? Is it because I said no to him or has it been his plan all along?

Is it possible to break the already broken heart? The answer is yes. Not like I'm going to give them the satisfaction of knowing that. I force the tears down.

I flip my hair haughtily and sashay out of there with my three friends close behind me.

How do I reject thee? Let me count the ways.

*   *   *

Last night I felt it again. Logan was with somebody, probably Mia. They did it over and over again. My healing stomach is decorated with new bruises. I woke up tired and cranky this morning.

"Genesis!"

Oh no, I know that voice. Kevin. He's been bugging me today. He's serious when he said that he's not giving up.

"Here comes your admirer." Penny giggles. She finds it funny. I find it very annoying, but I've been trying really hard not to be rude to him. I know too well how it feels like to be cruelly rejected.

"Well, I'll leave you two lovebirds alone." She winks at me, then makes a kissy-kissy face before leaving me with Kevin in the hallway.

"So much for being a loyal best friend!" I wanted to shout after her. "What's up, Kevin?"

"What kind of flowers do you like? Do you like red roses?" He's been asking me random questions like that all day today.

"Yeah, sure. Why not?" I'm getting increasingly annoyed every time he stops me in the hallway or in a classroom to ask questions.

"Would you go out with me this Saturday?" He always ends it up by asking me out, and I'm so getting tired of it. How many times do you have to say NO?

"No. What part of the word no are you not getting, Kevin?" I finally snap at him.

The look of shock to crestfallen on his face makes me feel really bad and guilty.

"I'm sorry...I'll leave you alone now. It's just stupid of me...I just like you...I'm sorry to bother you." He walks away with his shoulders slumped and head down. Goddess, I'm a monster!

"Kevin! Wait!" I run after him and grab his arm. "Look, I'm sorry okay?"

"No, I'm sorry. What was I thinking? You're way out of my league —"

"No, I'm not out of your league. Pssshh..that's just silly."

"Yes, you are, but my friend Justin said if I keep asking, you'll say yes....eventually. So I kept trying. A girl like you would never go out with a guy like me."

Oh, goddess...don't say it, don't say it. "Okay, I'll go out with you."

Gah! I suck!

His eyes get really big. "Really?"

"Yeah..." I sigh. What did I just do?

Kevin's face split into a big smile, and then I'm engulfed in a big suffocating hug. "Thank you. You won't regret it."

I already am.

He lets me go, and I realize that we're the only people in the hallway. I am so late for my next class. Then I smell the scent that I both crave and dread. Logan is close by.

"Gosh! I'm late for Gym," exclaims Kevin. "I'll pick you up at six on Saturday, okay? I'll text you."

"Yeah....okay." How did he get my number?

"We'll have a great time together, I just know it." He grins. His blue eyes are shining. All of a sudden he gives me a peck on the cheek, then off he goes with a big smile on his face.

"Well, well, well...for an Omega, you don't take instructions very well, do you? I told you not to do one thing. You're either too stupid or too stubborn to listen. Either way, I'll enjoy breaking you, my sweet." I hear Logan's voice from a corner before he comes into view.

I tear my gaze away from his golden good looks and his blazing blue eyes. His looks and his scent are messing with my senses. His words are drawing fury out of me and my wolf, Ezra. Usually, I don't mind, but this time my chest is growing hot, that's how angry Ezra is for being called an omega. It reminds me of the strong alpha blood that is coursing through me.

"I'm not yours, Logan. You don't own me. I'll go out with anyone I want when I want."

In less than a second he's on me. He pushes me against the locker. His lips grind against mine roughly. His hand closes around my throat, holding me in place. Even like this, sparks are still flying between us. I can't stop from responding to his rough kiss, and pretty soon he moans into my lips, and his hand on my throat moves to roam my body.

His lips trail across my jaw and down my neck, sucking and biting. "I hate that you're my mate, but I want you.." he groans against my throat. That pulls me out of my lust-filled stupor.

I push him off me as hard as I can. "Leave me alone. Go have fun with Mia like you did last night!" I yell at him.

"Oh, don't worry about Mia. I've promised her she'll be my luna. She's strong. I'll mark her, and she will be luna. That'll keep her happy. While you, my little omega, I get to keep. Just keep me happy, and you will be very well taken care of."

I feel sick. This is another form of rejection,worse actually, it's an insult, and Ezra recognizes it too as such. I'm his mate, but he's treating me like a common whore.

I attend classes with pent-up emotions. No tears. I'm not sure yet whether that's a good thing or bad.

At the end of lunchtime, somebody else approaches me.

"Genesis, I need to talk to you," says Hunter, the future beta. Just what I need. I can't catch any break today.

"I'll catch you guys later," I wave to my friends who watch me walk away with worried expressions.

35

Hunter leads me outside to an empty football field. There are five minutes left till our lunch break.

"I don't really understand what had happened, but Logan was in a very bad mood yesterday. He picked fights with everyone and now he barely talks to Zeke," he explains. "Alpha Carrington now knows about you and Logan."

"What do you want me to do Hunter? He rejected me," I say dejectedly.

He sighs and runs his fingers through his brown curly hair. "I know. I'm sorry. He's being a stupid idiot. He must've put you through a lot these past few days."

You have no idea. However, I'm surprised that he called the future Alpha a *stupid idiot*.

"You know that an Alpha needs his true mate to be a strong leader right? This pack needs you, Genesis. I know I'm asking a lot from you, but could you...give him another chance?"

I suddenly burst into a mirthless laugh. Once I start, I can't seem to stop. Tears falling freely down my cheeks. I wipe the endless stream of tears while still laughing uncontrollably.

Hunter stares at me, looking lost at what to do, probably disturbed by my laughing and crying like some crazy woman.

"I'm sorry." I gasp-sob between the giggle. "Yeah, about that...umm.." I clear my throat and wipe my eyes after I manage to get it together finally. "So, yeah...Logan already had that talk with me." I almost choke in another fit of laughter again, but I bit my lip, stopping it before it starts.

"Uh...that's good. You two have it all figured out then." He sounds unsure.

I blow my breath out heavily. "Yeah, he wants us to be together. But he's going to mark Mia so she'll be the next luna. Logan and I...he wants us to be together, but on the side, you know..." I bit down hard on another bout of hysterical laughter about to erupt. Wow, it feels ridiculous just to say it out loud like that.

Hunter stares at me as if I've just told him that clouds are made of cotton candies and chocolate milk actually came from brown cows. Then he runs his hands through his hair and over his face, blinking hard in disbelief a few times.

"Oh goddess, Genesis..." he mutters. "I'm sorry. I'm so sorry. Nobody deserves that from their mate. Nobody. That's...messed up...even for Logan."

"Yeah...and to think that I've been saving myself for my mate. This is what I'm getting," I mumble, not caring if I'm giving off too much information to a guy I barely know.

"Look, Genesis, I think Logan messed up big time," he says. "For what it's worth, I think you're smart, kind, and beautiful, and funny, any guy would be lucky to have you as his mate. I know, I would've been very happy if you were mine. I was hoping that you were my mate before...I'm sorry, that's probably an inappropriate thing for me to say." His cheeks tinged with pink. His liquid brown eyes fixed on his black biker boots.

"No. Thank you for saying that, Hunter, that's....the nicest thing anybody ever said to me," I smile at him sadly.

*　　　*　　　*

"Genesis!" hisses Mia. Oh goddess, really? "You and I, we need to talk."

I'm really starting to hate that word, *talk*. Nothing good happens when people tell you they want to "talk". Especially not today. Not for me.

Her two minions grip my arm on each side and push me into an empty classroom behind me.

No, no, no..."Sure, what's up?" I flash her a big fake smile while the two bitches shove me hard against the wall.

"What's that? Well, well, well...look at here," Mia pulls the collar of my jacket down, revealing the hickeys Logan gave me yesterday and this afternoon. "I see you've been whoring around. Not so pure after all, are we?" She smiles like a cat that just ate a canary. Then she sniffs.

"Wait, is that Logan I smell on you???" she yells. "It's Logan, isn't it? I thought I smelled you on him yesterday. You're all over him again today weren't you? You whore!"

"No, he's all over me." I can't resist smirking.

"Aaarghhh!!!" she screams. Her palm smacks on my cheek hard. Her sharp nails graze my skin. Bitch!

"Listen, bitch." she says as she grips my hair and pulls it back roughly. "Stay away from Logan. He's mine, you hear? Touch him again and the next time, and I won't be so forgiving."

"Trust me, I don't want him, but...maybe you're not good enough, that's why he keeps coming back for me." I give her another big fake smile.

Mia loses it then, she has her minions holding me still as she kneed me in the stomach several times before she leaves.

Ughh..me and my big mouth!

Oh wow! Lucky me. I feel so popular today. Everybody seems to want to "talk" with me. I'm missing one class already. I'm currently hiding out in the washroom. Cowardly, I know, but I need a minute to myself. If another person wants to talk to me today, then I'll lose it for sure.

I examine my face by the mirror above the sink. My makeup is mostly all gone. Some stain of mascara and eyeliner smudges underneath and at the corners of my eyes. Very attractive. My left cheek is red and a bit swelled with scratches and dried blood from Mia's nails.

I lift my shirt up and softly trace the bruises already forming on the bruises I had before when Logan was having his *fun*.

I wash my face and fix the jacket so that nobody can see the red blotches that Logan gave me. Then the bell rings. Ughh... I need to get to class. But what I really want to do right now is go home and hide from the world.

When I walk down the hallway to my chemistry class later, I'm almost positive that I see all the three lycans, Lazarus, Caspian, and Constantine turn their heads to look at me. Only briefly. Then they're looking away again as if I didn't exist. But then, maybe I was mistaken. Maybe they were looking at something behind me.

I shrug it off as I slip into Chemistry and spend the next 40 minutes trying to understand and figure out the Henderson-Hasselbalch equation.

CHAPTER V
Anyone Ever Died Of Embarrassment?

"Okay, now spill," orders Penny. We're sitting on her queen size bed while Control by Halsey is playing softly in the background on her I-pod dock on her study table.

My friends managed to corner me at the school parking lot before I could run off. It's not like they don't know where I live, anyway. We're here at Penny's to talk.

"Who did this to you, Genesis? Did he do this?" asks Reese. When she touches my cheek, I wince.

Penny is fuming.

I feel guilty for avoiding them since after lunch yesterday. They've been there for me through thick and thin. I shouldn't keep them in the dark.

"Did Logan do this to you?" asks Penny. She looks like she's about to lose it.

I sigh and start telling them about what happened between me and Logan yesterday and again today.

"He kissed you?" Penny croaks, gawking at me.

"Yep, and he gave me this." I remove the jacket collar off my neck to show them the bite marks.

"Oh goddess." Reese gasps. "At least he hasn't marked you yet."

"I don't know if he ever would. He said he's marking Mia and will make her Luna. He's keeping me on the side...like his personal whore," I explain heatedly.

"The bastard!" explodes Penny.

"Then he hit you?" asks Reese looking appalled.

"No, this is from Mia." I point to my red cheek. "She and her minions cornered me to warn me to stay away from Logan. She smelled Logan on me, then she went nuts and slapped me and also gave me this," I lift up my tank top and show them the bruises on my stomach.

"Okay, here's what we're gonna do," states Reese calmly. Too calmly. "We're gonna grab the shovels, and dig a hole in my backyard where my new flower bed is going to be. Genesis, you're gonna lure Logan into the woods where Penny and I are going to be waiting. I'm sure the three of us can take him, especially if he's not expecting it. Then we're gonna get Mia. We'll bury them in the flower bed. I know some herbs that can mask their scent."

She looks totally serious that Penny and I look at each other, then we stare at her worriedly. Wow, angry Reese is totally scarier than angry Penny. Where has my best friend, the sweet and angelic Reese, gone to?

"You're not serious are you?" asks Penny warily.

"Oh, but I totally am," counters Reese. "They're killing her! Can't you see?" Then she turns to me, and says, "Do you know how long you're going to last if that keeps happening? Do you, Genesis? Look at your stomach now. How much more of that can you take, Genesis? Huh?" Her eyes glisten. I put my arms around her, truly touched by her concern. Penny wraps her arms around the both of us so that the three of us are in a tight group hug.

"I'm grateful that my friends are willing to kill for me. I swear I love you guys like family. You two are my sisters, but we're not killing anybody." I declare. My voice is muffled against Penny's shoulder, but I think they can hear me.

41

"I went to the pack's house library and did some research on that yesterday after lunch," I confess. Yeah, the first time I ever sneaked out of the school.

"So, that's where you disappeared to," says Penny, releasing us.

"I went through recorded incidences throughout werewolves history and found that I need to...uh, mate and be marked by another werewolf to sever the natural mate bond...or move far far away, preferably join another pack to not to feel the pain anymore," I explain.

Both Penny and Reese are quiet for a while after what I said.

"You're not moving away from here, so we need to find you a mate," announces Penny.

"That can be done, but that might take some time," says Reese.

Actually, "might take some time" is an understatement. What are the chances of finding a male werewolf my age without a mate who would like me? The three of us know this, but none of us are willing to say it aloud.

"Well...I agreed to go out with Kevin this weekend," I announce casually.

"You did what?" asks Reese, clearly shock. "Didn't we agree that you didn't want to lead him on or something like that?"

"Yeah, about that..." I grimace.

"You need to lose your v-card ASAP," interrupts Penny.

"Penny.." Reese groans. "Not the v-card again."

"No, listen! I have my reasons," explains Penny. "First, Logan needs to know what it feels like when your mate is mating with someone else. Maybe it'll slow him down a bit...who knows," she says as she rolls her eyes. "Secondly, you really don't want to lose your v-card to your asshole ex-mate, Logan, do you?"

If she puts it like that, no, I don't want my first time to be with someone who has no respect for me; someone who regards

42

me as a cheap omega whore; good enough to be his dirty little secret, but not good enough to be a proper mate. I don't want to be with him. Period.

Gosh! How did we get from planning to kill someone, to losing my virginity? Can my life and my friends get any crazier?

"Maybe it's a good thing that you're going out with Kevin this weekend then." Penny wiggles her eyebrows.

"Nope. Not happening," I quickly disagree. "It's gotta be with someone I like...that way, you know.."

"Then who?" asks Reese.

"I don't know...but I know it's not Kevin."

"Come on, Genesis. There must be someone that you like. Like really really like in our school," says Penny.

One person quickly comes to mind, but I squish it down. "Nope, none," I reply.

"You know that's not normal, right? I bet even Reese can think of one other than River."

"Hey!" protests Reese.

"The fricking school is full of hot men!" argues Penny, lifting her hands up in defeat. "You must have at least one crush. Think of one name," she urges.

Constantine.

"Nope, nobody," I repeat.

Constantine. That one name keeps going on repeat in my head. Strong, sharp angular face, dark silky sexy hair, his unusual silver-gray eyes, long thick eyelashes, firm pink lips...

But he's a lycan. Untouchable. I know how impossible that is.

"Aha! There must be someone. You have that look on your face," exclaims Penny.

"What look?"

"That dreamy, mushy, soppy...oh, I-so-wanna-do-you look...you know, that look," says Penny.

43

"I was just thinking about my English essay I'm supposed to hand in tomorrow," I lie.

"You can't be thinking about English essays when you have that look on your face," protests Reese.

Penny stares at me with narrowed eyes. I quickly look away and says, "Nope, nobody."

"You'd better start liking someone pretty quickly, you hear?" demands Penny, pointing her finger at me sternly.

*   *   *

I can't seem to stop thinking about Constantine tonight as I lie down flat on my bed, staring at my boring white ceiling. I blame it on Penny.

I first met Constantine at the end of a summer break when I was 15. I never told a soul about it. Not even my two besties. I was at our Art Supply store by myself that afternoon. Dad went to the next town over to deal with something, and mom was meeting a client for a portrait commission.

The delivery guy just delivered boxes of newly shipped merchandise and left them in the hallway. Lazy man. They were too heavy for me to lift to the back storage.

I was standing behind the counter, scowling at the boxes when the bell chimed, indicating a customer at the door. I looked up and there he was.

I stared up at him, and he just stared at me staring at him.

He was so big and tall, radiating with such power and authority and....so beautiful. I had never seen a man so beautiful before, it's almost unreal.

His shoulders were so broad they almost fill out the door. He's wearing black jeans that followed the contours of his well-muscled legs. A white t-shirt that stretched tightly across his well-defined chest and six-pack abs. His tanned golden skin looked as smooth as honey. A few silky locks of that thick, lustrous dark brown hair fell carelessly across his forehead and his strong arched dark brows.

He had perfect symmetrical features with prominent cheekbones, a high bridged straight nose, and a sharp angular jaw that led to a strong chin. What captured me the most was his silver-gray eyes that were surrounded by amazingly thick and long eyelashes. They were so piercing and were regarding me with such intensity that I couldn't look away from even if I wanted to.

I kept staring at him, yet I had no idea when he got so close. One moment he's standing by the door, the next thing I knew, he's standing so close with only inches between us. This close, I can see how unusual his silver-gray eyes were; the pupils were so black, the Irises were actually the palest blue-silver with black rim surrounding them.

"Hi," I said shyly, trying to look away as I felt my cheeks warming up.

"Hello," he replied and smiled back. Then I was lost again, staring at his smile. His smile made him looked even more breathtaking. His pink lips looked surprisingly full and sensual. His teeth were straight and white. His canines a little bit prominent, but that only made him look even more dangerous and attractive.

He looked amused, and his lips twitched as if he was trying hard not to laugh.

My cheeks were burning, and my heart was racing.

Oh goddess, I must be looking like a crazy girl in front of this gorgeous god-like creature. What is wrong with me? I never looked at a man this way before.

I cleared my throat and said in my most professional voice. "Hi, how can I help you, sir?" Sir? Oh goddess, really? I felt like banging my head against the wall. He looked about 17 or 18 at the most.

He told me that he needed some painting supplies, so I told him that he could take a look around and just ask if he needed any help.

He kept asking me about the merchandise so that I had to follow him around even though what I really wanted to do was to hide or lie down and die from my embarrassment.

He wasn't even looking at the paint or the medium he was asking me about. His silver-gray eyes were fixed on my face the whole time. My heart stuttered, and my cheeks kept burning up every time I looked up to meet his steady gaze.

Once, I thought he took a sniff of my neck when I was reaching in for a jar of Gesso at the back of the shelf, but when I straightened up, I found that he was staring at rows of oil paints in front of us.

I cursed myself for my wild imagination. Only mates sniff each other like that. At least that's what my mom told me.

He bought a lot of stuff that day. I mean a lot! Including an expensive wooden studio easel, an easy to carry French easel, a studio table, oil paints, acrylics, pastels, canvasses, brushes—a lot. My dad was impressed with the sales that I made that day.

I couldn't stop thinking about him that summer. I felt as if there was a connection between us that day. Then school started, and I found out who or what he was. He was a sophomore even when he looked older than sixteen and had one class with me that year. I guess the feeling was one-sided. He never even looked at me once. I doubt that he even knew I existed. It was foolish of me to think that he might even remember me at all, let alone having a connection.

I was crushed. I tried to pretend that I didn't notice him at all, though I think I still have a crush on him, even now. I just ignored it the best I could. I pretended that I didn't see him around even when I took a little peek at him every once in a while. Just a little.

Well then, if he doesn't even remember me, maybe I can go up and talk to him. But then again, no werewolf nor human ever dared approach or talk to the lycans before. Even those girls who keep looking at them with openly lustful stares. They might talk about how hot those lycans are and how they wish the lycans would pick them as mates, but none of them dared breathe a word to those lycans. The lycans are very aloof and mysterious and intimidating.

If I were to go up to him, what would I even say? "Excuse me, your lordship, your gorgeousness...would you please take my v-card?" Then I'll die of embarrassment for sure.

Or maybe say, "Excuse me, Constantine...you gorgeous creature you, would you take my v-card? Please? Here are five hundred dollars...uh, a hundred and twenty-three dollars and fifty cents, actually. Sorry, I went shopping with my buddies. So yeah, would you?" Then I'll double die.

Arrgghh...I groan into my pillow.

Maybe I should just ask him if he wanted to be friends. Yeah, that's a better idea. I mean, even a lycan could use a werewolf friend, right? You can't have too many friends, as dad said to me a few times.

Okay, that's it. That's what I'll do tomorrow. Once we're friends, we'll see what will happen...or more likely, what will never happen.

Well...whatever. I'm a grown, brave and strong woman. I can so do this. Yeah!

Easier said than done because I was nervous the whole day. Penny kept asking me what was wrong.

It's at the end of school hour when all students are leaving that I gather enough courage to approach him. I figure, if he said no to my offer of friendship, I don't have to bump into him again, thus avoiding anymore embarrassment...for the day at least.

I look frantically around, determined to do this before I lose my courage. Students are rushing past me when I catch a

47

glimpse of the three lycans. It's not that hard to catch them actually since they're way taller than the rest of the student body.

They are walking casually like they have nowhere important to get to while other students are scurrying out the exit door.

When the hallway is almost clear, I briskly walk up to them from behind. Before I lose my courage, I tap him on the shoulder. "Excuse me, Constantine? Can I talk to you for a minute?" Wow, I sound so strong and confident.

He turns around, and words died in my throat.

Oh goddess, he's so beautiful and perfect and big...and intimidating. What was I thinking?

He raises an eyebrow in question when I stand there gaping at him with my mouth open. I'm sure I look like a fish. A dying fish.

I gulp. "Uh...forget it. Never mind... Sorry. Umm...bye!" Then I turn and run.

Idiot! Idiot! Idiot!

Has anyone ever died of embarrassment? Because that's what I'm about to do...go die.

CHAPTER VI
Lycans Are Confusing

I can't believe I left Constantine standing there. I left a lycan standing there after I went up to him and asked him if I could have a talk with him. Who does that? Me, a crazy person, that's who.

I've been lying here on my bed for over an hour now, replaying every embarrassing second in the school hallway. Goddess, I hope nobody else saw me making a huge fool out of myself. I groan and beat the pillow.

Why? Why? Why?

Way to go, Genesis. Now you can add another to the list of embarrassing and sad accomplishments in your life. As if being rejected and insulted by alpha jerkface isn't enough.

That's it! No more thinking. The more I think, the more amazed I am at my own stupidity. I'm letting Ezra out. I'm going for a run.

"Now where are you going?" asks Mom from the kitchen.

"I'm just going for a run, mom. Do you need any help?"

"No, you go on, sweetie. I'm just making chicken casserole for tonight. Be back before dinner though."

"Okay, I won't be long."

"Everything is okay though, right?" asks my mom with concern just before I step out through the back door.

"Sure, everything's fine," I give her my best smile. Well, I'm adding more to the list of things that I can't tell my own mom.

*   *   *

It's almost lunch time and so far, I've been doing a great job avoiding certain people: my ex-mate, Logan Carrington; his girlfriend the queen of all bitches, Mia Brown and her group of minions; Kevin, the human who's convinced that he has a crush on me; and the lycans, especially Constantine. It hasn't been easy mind you, not to mention a little tricky since there are quite a number of them. I have to use all my stealth ninja skills.

"What is the matter with you today, Genesis?" exclaims Penny, looking peeved when I failed to answer her for the tenth time today since I was too busy scanning the area for any threat, while also marking my escape route and identifying possible hiding corners.

"I'm sorry, what?"

"You're not even listening to me." She wails. "I feel like I've been talking to myself for the last ten minutes."

"I'm sorry, Penny. I'm just a bit occupied today. You know...lots of stuff to think about..." I hedge vaguely.

We were let out early from our Social study class since the teacher wasn't here today. Penny and I have that class together too. Now we're both waiting for the next class by our lockers before we go our separate ways to our different classes while other students are coming out of their classrooms and filling up the hallways briskly..

"Are you looking for somebody?" She narrows her eyes, looking at me quizzically.

"No," I reply, looking around. "Oh gosh! Look at the time. Gotta go. Good talking with you." With that, I jump over a guy who's kneeling down, tying up his shoelace, then down the hall I go...straight into the girls' washroom.

Phew! Lucky escape. I thought I saw the lycans. All three of them were looking at me, or maybe they were looking at something behind me. I'm not taking any chances though.

I sit at the very back of the library munching on an apple all by myself during lunch time. My stomach growls. An apple is not enough for a werewolf with a high metabolism like me. At least nobody sees me. Lucky!

My phone beeps with messages from Reese and Penny asking me where I'm at. I text back, saying that I'm finishing some homework that I forgot to finish last night. However, my luck runs out right after lunchtime because I spot the lycans standing across the hallway as I dig into my locker for books for my next classes. They're looking right at me...or maybe at something behind me.

"Oh my gosh." A girl giggles beside me to her friend. "Look at the lycans. You think they're staring at me?"

"Uh...maybe...but they never looked at anyone like that. Oh my goddess, what did you do?" asks her friend enviously.

"They're so hot. You're so lucky," says another one.

"What do I do? Should I go and say hi? What do I do?"

I would have laughed if I'm not panicking a bit inside. Maybe they are looking at something behind me, or they are staring at the girl beside me, either way, I'm not taking any chances. I scram as soon as I grab everything that I need from the locker.

I make it halfway across the hallway when I almost bump into a figure in front of me.

"Where'd you think you're going?" That smooth, deep sexy voice.

Constantine.

He's leaning against the wall with his well-muscled arms crossing over his chest, looking completely relaxed.

"Have you been avoiding me? It's rude you know...to say that you wanted to talk to me one moment, then the next, you ran off like that. After that, you went on avoiding me." His voice is playful, but his piercing silver-gray eyes are blazing through me.

51

Oh, my goddess. Kill. Me. Now.

Every time I come face to face with this god-like creature, I lose my brain function. I'm struck stupid by the sheer beauty of him and the power that radiates off him. My stomach is now filled with crazy drunken butterflies and my heart is racing.

"What? Nothing to say for yourself?" He lifts one exquisite eyebrow.

Gah!!! Get a hold of yourself! Say something...anything! Come on, think!

"Uh...n-nothing. I'm s-sorry for bothering you. Nothing really...okay. Bye." I stammer, quite relieved when I reach the end of my short speech. I twirl around to make another escape, completely forgotten that my Chemistry class is the other way.

"Oh, no you don't," He appears right in front of me in a flash. I blink in surprise. "You're not escaping again until you tell me what you really wanted to talk to me about." He sounds mildly amused.

Wow, yeah. Lycans have amazing speed. There's no way I can get away from him if he refuses to let me go.

I sigh as I tear my eyes away from his mesmerizing gaze. I can't think when I'm looking at him...or when he's looking at me...or when he's anywhere near me.

Even when I'm not looking at him, I can feel the heat of his eyes burning through me. "Can you like...uh...look away or something?" I ask him as I stare fixatedly at my plain brown flats.

"I'm sorry?" He sounds puzzled.

"Uh...never mind." I sigh. It's a stupid request anyway. I do, however, take a few steps backward, away from him.

"What are you doing?" he asks me suspiciously.

"N—nothing," I answer, still staring at my shoes as if they're the most interesting objects in the whole wide world.

I quickly look up when he takes a few steps closer to me.

"What are you doing?" I blurt out.

"Moving closer to you so that we can talk," he answers, looking thoroughly amused by now. His full sensual lips curl up into a tiny smile, his eyes hold the most wicked glint. "Also, to make sure that you're not getting away from me again."

I gulp noticeably. Why does it feel as if he's talking about something more than just about me running down the hallway away from him?

It's all in your head, idiot! I scold myself.

"So...do you like standing here the whole day?" he asks again, sounding like he's totally enjoying this.

I can see no way out of this other than asking him what I wanted to ask of him in the first place.

Gathering up my courage, I blurt out quickly, "I just thought...uh... I just thought that maybe we could befriends," I say, finally. Phew! I look up and grin.

He looks amazed and confused, then dazed for a second. "What?" he finally asks again.

I sigh. Wow. I just confused a lycan. I guess he never met anyone as crazy as I am before...or as stupid. I curse myself for even putting myself into this situation.

Taking a deep breath, I try again. "I just thought that maybe...uh... maybe we could be friends?"

A smile slowly forms on his lips while my cheeks are slowly burning red.

"You want us...you and I... to be friends?" he clarifies.

"Y yeah." I nod, looking away.

"You and I can't be friends, sunshine." he drawls.

Huh?

"Don't you think that skirt is too short for you to be walking around in?"

What? That's so totally random.

Why the hell did he care if my skirt is too short if he doesn't even care to be my friend? So, does he think that I'm too lowly to be his friends? Well, okay...so he's a lycan..and I, a she-wolf

53

who's been rejected by her own mate, who can't even utter a word without embarrassing herself in front of a certain lycan, who would lose all brain function when he's near her, but still.

I'm still too deep in my confusion and slow-burning rage when I feel his hand reaches into my jacket pocket and pulls out my cell phone.

He then starts typing something in it without even asking for my pin number. His phone rings once, then he cancels the call.

He smiles and slowly slides my phone back into my pocket. "Now I have your number," he says. "You're late for Chemistry, sunshine." Then he's gone.

What? What had just happened? What does that mean? What does anything mean anymore?

I walk around school the rest of the day today in deep confusion.

By the time I reach home, my head hurts. I give up trying to make sense of everything. Are all Lycans so confusing?

CHAPTER VII
My Date Has Gone To The Wolves

It's 11 am. Saturday morning and I'm still in bed. The pain was unbearable again last night. Thank you, Logan! I woke up to the pain around midnight, and I had a pillow over my face, trying to muffle the sound of my cries. I think I passed out for a bit. I must've fallen asleep again after that; I'm not sure what time, but now I'm still exhausted.

My wolf Ezra is in agreement with me that our mate is no good for us. The only thing that's between us is the mate pull and attraction that I'm determined to fight.

I spend a good half an hour thinking about my ex-mate Logan as my heart squeezes in pain. I push it aside and spend another half an hour thinking about the confusing lycan named Constantine. He doesn't even want to be friends with me. Why can't I stop thinking about him?

I really should stop obsessing over men who don't want me.

I truly don't feel like getting up, but my stomach growls in hunger. Besides, I smell bacon, eggs, pancakes, and coffee wafting up from the kitchen. I hear voices talking and laughing, the plates and cutlery clinking and clunking together. My sensitive werewolf senses are working against me this morning.

After washing my face and brushing my teeth, I walk down to the kitchen.

"Good afternoon, sunshine!" sings my dad cheerfully.

That stops me on my track. Constantine called me *sunshine* yesterday.

"Good morning!" Everyone choruses. Everyone is here. By everyone, I mean River, Reese, and Penny who are at the breakfast table with my family. They're stuffing their faces with bacon and eggs and Mom's special pancakes.

"Boy, you look awful." Autumn observes.

"Gee, thanks." I return grumpily, taking my seat between Reese and my dad.

"Why are you looking so tired? Are you sick? Have you been staying up late? You shouldn't stay up too late, sweetie," advises Mom, shoving a plateful of scrambled eggs, bacon, and pancakes with a drizzle of maple syrup. My mouth waters.

I steal a glance at my friends who are giving me knowing sympathetic looks.

"Didn't sleep well, that's all," I answer vaguely. "Thanks, mom. This looks yummy."

"At least she's not hungover," remarks dad, to which he gets a smack on the arm by mom.

My friends laugh as my dad winces and rubs at his arm.

"So, we're thinking, maybe we'll go see Fantastic Beasts and Where to Find Them today," begins Reese.

"And everybody is okay with this?" I ask curiously, looking at Penny.

"Yeah, I love JK Rowlings, so I'm okay with it," answers Penny happily. Penny's usually very picky with movies.

"Then we'll head off to the beach later," announces River with a big grin.

"It'll be fun! But don't worry, we'll make sure you'll be home before four this evening, so you can get ready for your date tonight," says Penny.

I groan...just great Penny.

"You have a date tonight?" questions mom excitedly. Yep, just as I suspected, now mom's all excited.

"With who?" interrogates Autumn and dad at the same time.

"His name's Kevin," Penny eagerly answers for me.

"Kevin? Do we know him?" inquires dad again.

"He's a human," answers Reese.

"Oh.." says Autumn, looking unimpressed and suddenly losing interest.

"Well, if he's a good kid, then that's great, sweetheart," says mom, patting my shoulder.

"It's not like that, mom," I try to explain. "He's just a friend."

"Oh, he likes to be more than her friend." Penny reveals, sounding as excited as my mom. "He wouldn't stop asking her out until she said yes."

"Oh, a persistent admirer," exclaims mom. "I'd love to meet this young man."

Reese and River are about to burst out laughing while my dad is pretending like he didn't hear anything.

I'm wishing that I could strangle Penny to be quiet.

*   *   *

It's great to be spending time with my friends. We had a good time at the movie and the beach. The only problem is, I can't stop thinking about Constantine. I don't understand why I can't get him out of my head.

I just had my shower, and now I'm sitting in my bed with Penny doing my nails. She insists on helping me get ready for my date tonight. Reese and River took off somewhere after dropping us off at my house.

"You know this date is not anything special, right?" I ask Penny just to be sure that she understands. I have no interest like that at all in Kevin. I intend to tell Kevin that we're going to stay friends and nothing more.

"I know, but you should always look great. Give it a chance, you might have a good time tonight. You never know. Besides, Kevin is way better than Logan jerkface,"

"Everyone is better than Logan, right now," I state. "You're sounding just like my mom. Have you two been discussing this?"

"Well...your mom's been worried about you, Gen." Penny's smile looks guilty. So the two of them have been plotting together. My mom and Penny are a bad combination. Dangerous, even.

Penny insists that I wear a deep purple dress that she found at the back of my closet. I bought that dress two years ago. I've grown quite a bit since then. It was meant to be a bit loose and fell just above my knees. Now it's quite figure hugging and reaches a few inches above my knees.

I let my hair air dry to its natural wave.

Penny does my makeup, eye lining my eyes really dark to enhance my light hazel eyes. Then she adds some purple to my eyelids and some pink shiny lip gloss to my lips.

"Put these babies on, and you're ready," she announces as she hands me a pair of black pumps.

Just then the doorbell rings. He's right on time.

Mom is already at the door when I get downstairs. She smiles widely at me as she opens the door wider for Kevin.

"Wow! You look really good, Genesis," says Kevin after he picks his jaw off the floor. Boys!

Kevin is looking nice in his light blue button-down dress shirt and dark jeans. He looks nervous as he hands me two dozen red roses.

Mom looks giddy as I hand her the roses to be put in the water. I almost roll my eyes at her.

Kevin is being really sweet, opening the car door for me and everything, making me feel bad about what I'm about to do.

"You told me the other day that you like Italian, so I made a reservation at Toni Marino's. I hope that's okay," he inquires as he makes a turn, blending into the traffic.

"Yeah, that's fine." I smile.

Kevin is not the smartest guy, but he's nice. He's not bad looking and he treats me like I was precious. Like I matter.

I stare at him as he tells me about how his dad made him clean out their garage so that they can work on a 1970 Dodge Challenger they found. His blue eyes shine as he talks about what they're planning to do with it.

His reddish-brown hair is cropped really short. He has a smattering of freckles across the bridge of his nose and a bit on his cheeks. I find that kinda adorable.

Maybe I can make this work. Maybe I can learn to like him if I just give us a chance.

As soon as we step inside the restaurant, I know something is about to go wrong. I can smell Logan and his friends.

I look around, but I can't see them anywhere. Maybe they were here earlier, I reasoned with myself. The scent is still very strong, so they can't be that far.

We are shown to our seats and our waitress promptly brings out a basket of warm breadsticks.

"This is nice, Kevin." I smile at him warmly. It is a very nice place. The ambiance is amazing, and the smell of food is mouthwatering.

I sense most of the people here are werewolves.

"Hello, Genesis. What a surprise to see you here," says a familiar voice.

Logan.

Kevin frowns as he notices the group of popular boys from school are here, crowding around our table.

"Good choice, Kevin. This is a nice place. The food is good too. You don't mind us joining you, do you?" Logan says as

59

he pulls another chair from a neighboring table. He slides in and pulls his chair closer to mine. Our thighs are touching.

"Logan," I growl warningly.

"Yes, sweetheart?" Logan smiles, casually popping a piece of breadstick into his mouth. He sits back comfortably, while his eyes are looking at me and Kevin lazily.

"You know what Kevin? Let's go somewhere else," I say to Kevin. I grab his hand in mine, trying to get him out of there.

Logan grabs my wrist tightly, almost painfully. "Stay, sweetheart." He is smiling, but his tone is commanding. The smile doesn't reach his eyes. I grit my teeth while staring at him defiantly.

"This table is too crowded," I announce.

"If you haven't noticed, Genesis and I are on a date. So if you'll excuse us, " declares Kevin, putting his other hand on top of mine.

"Is that so?" Logan smiles wolfishly. "There must be some mistake. You see Kevin, this one here is mine. She knew she's not supposed to go out on a date with anyone else." He curves his arm possessively around my neck.

I try to squirm out of his arm, but he's too strong.

"Screw you, Logan!" I burst. I can't take it anymore. He just has to go and ruin everything. "I'm not yours. Just leave us alone!"

His patience seems to snap at my outburst. He grabs me by the back of my neck roughly and smashes my lips against his. His canines graze my lips, so I know his wolf is not far above the surface. His wolf must be going crazy wanting to mark me. It's natural for his wolf wanting to mark its mate especially when there is a threat of other males around.

Tears pooling in my eyes. This date is over. I can taste my own blood on my lower lip where his canines puncture it.

"Take her home," he instructs one of his boys.

"I'll do it," offers Hunter.

Two of his other boys are holding Kevin by his shoulders.

Kevin is well muscled, but Logan and his friends are werewolves. It's not going to be a fair fight. They could kill him pretty easily.

"Let her go!" yells Kevin, but nobody's listening to him.

Hunter tries to pull me out by my waist, but Logan pushes his hands aside and drags me out to the car himself. I struggle in his hold.

We're drawing attention, but he doesn't seem to care.

"No! No! No! Let me go!" I smack his chest and his shoulders ineffectively. "Don't hurt him. You hear me? Logan! Don't you hurt him!"

I sit quietly in the car, trying hard not to cry. Hunter drives silently. I'm thankful that he doesn't say anything or ask any question. However, halfway through the thirty-minute drive, my dam breaks. I cover my face with my hands and sob the rest of the way quietly.

After he parks the car in front of our house, Hunter quietly gathers me into his arms and lets me cry it out. It's nice to be in his arms, but he'll get into trouble if Logan smells me all over him.

"Why is he doing this? He doesn't love me. Why can't he just let me go?" I ask finally.

"No...he doesn't love you," agrees Hunter with a sigh. "But werewolves are very possessive of their mates, especially the alphas. Logan is also having a problem with his father. They are both very stubborn. Logan has been arguing and rebelling against his dad at every turn since he was very young. His father wants him to mate with you, so that makes him even more determined to mate with Mia."

I just nod. So I'm just a pawn between Logan and his father. He's putting me through all this pain so he can win this fight he has with his father.

"I'm sorry, Genesis. You deserve so much better." His voice is heavy.

I pull back and look into his chocolate brown eyes. I see regret in his eyes and something else.

"Thank you, Hunter. Thank you for taking me home and for telling me this...for everything. Oh, can you please make sure they don't kill my date?" I fumble with the door handle.

Hunter looks disappointed, but he nods his head and smiles gently.

"You're a good person, Hunter." Impulsively I lean forward and quickly peck his cheek. I jump out and then stagger inside the house.

I sneak in as quietly as I can. When the light hit me in my bedroom, I'm thankful that nobody saw me when I sneaked inside. Smudges of black eyeliner and mascara are running down my cheeks. My hair is a mess. There's some trace of dry blood on my lower lip.

My date had gone to the wolves.

Poor Kevin. He doesn't deserve this.

CHAPTER VIII
My Erasthai

I hear a beep of an incoming message on my phone at six thirty the next morning. Who would be sending me a text message at six thirty on a Sunday morning? I pull a pillow over my head.

But then I wonder if it's Kevin. I called him so many times last night, wondering how he's doing. All of my calls went to his voicemail. I wonder if he's okay.

Don't do it! Don't do it! Just close your eyes and go back to sleep! Gah!!! I suck! I open one eye and sneak a peek. Then I have both my eyes wide open in surprise.

Constantine.

My heart races just by seeing his name on the screen. I'm wide awake now. How can one person have such power over me? He's not even my mate.

Constantine : Had a busy night last night?

How did he know? I struggle with what to write back to his text.

Me : What are you talking about?

Better fake ignorance rather than confess, or outright deny. I wait with a racing heart for his reply, biting my lips in agitation and anticipation. Not even a minute later my phone beeps again.

Constantine : You know what I'm talking about, sunshine.

What's with him calling me sunshine now?

Me : What's it to you? We're not even friends.

63

There! Let's see what he has to say to that!

Constantine : No. We're more.

What??? I fell off the bed.

Owww. I think I broke my butt.

So far I think I've been pacing the floor of my bedroom almost forty times. Back and forth, back and forth, back and forth. I'm getting dizzy.

"Meet me 7 am at the park behind Carson Hill's Public School," said his last text. I know where the park is. It's near the wooded area where not many people go to anymore, especially on a Sunday morning like this.

It is now 6.47 am. Should I go? It's not like I don't have enough on my plate right now. I have no business getting anywhere near a lycan.

Ezra is quiet. No help there. She's been quiet since Friday night when I felt the pain. She was quiet even when we were around Logan last night. I wonder if that means she's sticking to her guns about staying away from the mate who keeps hurting us.

I shouldn't go meet with Constantine. I should stay away from him. At least that's what the rational part of my brain is telling me. Since when did I listen to my brain anyway?

I rush to the bathroom, wash my face and brush my teeth in a hurry. Then I run a brush through my hair very quickly and tie it up in a ponytail. I dash back into my bedroom and stare at my phone. Five minutes left. I really should stay away. Lycans are not to be messed with. Werewolves are deadly, but we're nowhere near as powerful as the lycans.

Nope, I shouldn't go. Lycans are a whole new level of danger. However, something powerful inside of me rebelling against the idea of me not going. It's pulling me to go. It's like the pull of a mate and it scares me as well as excites me.

Arrgghhh....

I throw myself on my bed and pull the cover over my head. I pull my hair tie off and hug my knees to my chest under the cover. I close my eyes, and all I can see is Constantine's mesmerizing silver-gray eyes, his beautiful face that's being carved by the hands of a god..or goddess...his smile, his lips.

Goddess, I'm so going to regret not going and find out what he has to say. I know that for certain.

I screech and spring out of my bed in alarm when my warm comfy blanket is being stripped off of me.

Constantine.

Right here in my bedroom.

Constantine in my bedroom? I'm not dreaming, am I?

But he's standing there not five feet away from me. His eyes slowly travel the length of my body. His sexy lips curve up into a tiny smile.

What? How? I'm standing there with my mouth opening and closing without a sound coming out. Then I notice my bedroom window wide open. The curtains are blowing in the wind. Right. He came in through the window.

"Nice. Though I prefer to sleep in nothing at all, I like your pajama choice," he drawls.

I automatically look down at myself, even when I already knew what I put on for bed last night. A baby blue boy shorts pajama bottom with a matching tank top that says, EYES UP HERE across the chest.

They don't cover much at all. His eyes clearly show how much he's enjoying the view.

I yelp in horror and dive into my closet for cover. My face, without a doubt, is flaming red.

He laughs lowly. The sound is deep and sexy. Goddess, even the sound of his laughter is making me weak in the knees. How am I going to function around him?

"What are you doing here?" I squeak, trying to sound angry. It's easier to talk to him when I'm hiding out in my closet.

"You didn't come to me, so I came for you."

He came for me? The lycan is messing with my head.

I quickly changed into a pair of gray yoga pants and a black short sleeved v neck t-shirt.

I peek out slowly through the doorway. It's surreal to have him in my room.

It doesn't seem like he belongs here, but he's now lying on my bed with his back against the headboard. His arms folded behind his head, looking completely at home. He has black jeans and a tight black t-shirt on. The fabric stretches against his broad chest and flat stomach. His sexy well-muscled body takes over my whole twin bed.

I try to be mad. I should be mad. He shouldn't be here.

But oh goddess, isn't he gorgeous? His dark brown hair is tousled and has slight curls in it. His silver-gray eyes always have intensity in them, even when he looks totally relaxed. His sharp chiseled features are out of this world.

He's studying my room. The pictures of me with my family, and my friends scattered all over the memory board beside the bed.

He turns his piercing gray eyes on me as soon as I step out of the closet. To have such attention on me is somewhat unnerving. I force down the urge to smooth down my shirt and tuck away any stray hair on my head.

"A shame." He smiles playfully. "I much prefer what you had on before."

My heart stutters and my cheeks are blazing red again. It annoys me that I feel like everything is out of my control where this lycan is concerned.

It feels as if he's undressing me with his eyes as they raked me from head to toe.

"Stop looking at me like that." I finally snap, looking away.

"Looking at you like what?" It's clear from the sound of his voice that he finds me amusing. That's another thing that riles me. Me, embarrassing myself at every turn every time he's near, and him, finding me amusing.

"Like a perv," I answer him, showing my annoyance.

"Not a perv when I'm looking at something that belongs to me."

My head snaps back up to look at him. He must be joking, right?

He's gotta be joking. Yet, he doesn't look playful or amused now. His eyes are challenging me to deny his claim.

"What do you mean?" I manage to squeak out instead.

"What do you think I meant, sunshine?" he taunts me. "I mean, you're mine so I can look at you anyway, anyhow, anywhere I want to," he announces. His eyes are watchful.

My heart flutters crazily at his words.

No! I shouldn't be happy about this. I should be getting tired of being treated like an object. Logan said that I belong to him, and treats me like garbage. I'm not having another male, treating me like that. I'm a person, damn it! A respectable, strong she-wolf! I have to show him that I deserve to be treated with respect.

Yeah!!!

Satisfied with the pep talk I'm giving myself, I steal a glance at the lycan sitting comfortably on my bed. His biceps taut with muscles. His well-defined chest and abs almost visible underneath that tight t-shirt. His hair mused sexily like he just rolled out of bed, well, he's still in bed—my bed. His eyes, his lips...

Oh for goodness sake! Focus, Genesis!

I quickly avert my eyes. "Well, you don't own me."

"Sure I do...and you know it. You've known that for three years now."

What?

"Now put your shoes on, sunshine," he continues.

"You can't just tell me what to do," I protest. "I do what I want to do. Just because you're a lycan doesn't mean you can make me do things you want me to do." I think I'm blabbering. I do that when I get nervous.

He pushes off the bed and lithely gets to his feet. His movement is so quick yet so quiet.

"You have no idea what I want to do to you," he mumbles under his breath. "When did you become such a little spitfire, sunshine?" His eyes narrows as he stalks closer.

I gulp nervously. The way he moves reminds me of what he is. He's a lycan, the ultimate hunter. It scares me and excites me at the same time.

"Careful, I might like it. I might enjoy bending you to my will." His breath teases my ear. My heart flutters in my chest. My head fills with the image of him— *bending* me to his *will*. My stomach clenches and my toes curl at the image.

Oh, cuddly bunnies and fuzzy slippers! When did you become such a hussy, Genesis?

My cheeks turn fiery red.

"I wonder what delicious thoughts are playing in that pretty little head of yours, sunshine," he muses wickedly. "Whatever it is, I would love to oblige, but we don't have time for that now."

He effortlessly picks me up and in a blink of an eye, sets me down on my bed.

"What are you doing?" I manage to squeak. He's kneeling down beside me. His fingers are caressing my ankle, sending jolts of electricity up my leg. He easily slips my feet into my old sneakers.

He smells wonderful. All male and woodsy...somewhat sweet and reminds me of summer and raindrops and sunshine. Like a crazy creeper that I am, I lean in and breathe in his scent deeply. I could breathe him in all day.

The back of his head is so close to my nose, my fingers itch to comb through the silkiness of his hair.

"Your family is waking up. I'm taking you away, where nobody can interrupt us."

Interrupt us? Interrupt us doing what exactly?

He turns and smiles as if he knew what I was thinking. My cheeks turn red. His smile widens, showing his straight white teeth.

His amusement at my expense is back. He's turning me into a little hussy. I blame him for all the dirty thoughts that pop into my head just now.

Before I can answer him, he grabs me by the waist and hauls both of us up, and out of the window. My arms instinctively wrapped themselves tightly around his neck. His agility amazes me. We reach the ground without any sound.

As a werewolf, I've done that a few times myself, jumping in and out of the window of my own bedroom but, never have I been as quiet or as graceful.

"Would you like to walk or do you want me to carry you there?" he asks me huskily. His breath fans my ear. Sparks shoot through me. Our bodies flushed together. My arms still wind up around his neck, and his arms are wrapped tightly around my waist. His lips inches from mine. My wolf Ezra is purring at this closeness to him.

I quickly unwrapped my arms from around his neck. I step back awkwardly as he slowly let go of my waist. Ezra is protesting. She wants to stay close to the lycan. *I* want to stay close to him. There's a wicked glint in his eyes as he observes my movement.

We walk in silence into the woods through my parents' backyard. All the werewolves' houses here have their backyards that lead into the woods. It makes it easy for us to change into our wolves' form and go out for a run or hunt. We also love nature. Having an untouched natural ground is important to us even in our human form.

Surprisingly, I enjoy the walk. He seems to be careful not to be touching me.

We reach a clearing with grass and wildflowers and rocks protruding from the ground. Further ahead is a cliff of over 70-foot drop to the greenery below. From here, we get a nice view of the East side of the town. This is one of my favorite spots.

He sits on the rock, at the edge of the cliff. I sit further away from him. I need that space to be able to think clearly. He notes the distance with a small smile playing on his lips.

We sit there looking out at the scenery below. I feel his eyes on me. He's observing me, while I'm looking straight ahead pretending to be engrossed with the view.

"How much do you know about us, lycans?" he asks suddenly, still studying me.

"Uh… not much at all," I admit. "You guys are so full of mystery," I complain.

"Yeah, we are a secretive bunch." he agrees. "But I bet you knew that we don't have mates given to us by the moon goddess like werewolves. We are governed by our instincts. The only way for us to have mates is when we feel the attraction…or when we meet what we call our *erasthai*. It only happens once for every lycan, because when we find our erasthai, we claim them. Our erasthai could be anyone, a mated or unmated werewolf, a human, married or not, another lycan, or a fae. What we don't do is let them get away. Ever." His unusual silver-gray eyes never leaving my face.

I nod, showing that I understand, but what I don't get is why he's telling me all this. I can feel his burning gaze. Still, I refuse to look at him.

"I remember the first time I saw you," he continues. "You're so young, and sweet, and beautiful….and fascinating."

Huh?

I finally turn to look at him. That's not how I remember it. That first time I saw him I was too busy staring and being stupid, so in awe of his presence, so awkward, and embarrassing.

I gulp. "Are you sure? I mean the first time you saw me was at the art store, right?" I have to be sure.

"Yes, the art supply store," he affirms with a little smile. "We just arrived here. I left everything in Russia. I needed all the supplies for my studio."

Okay. So, that explains why he bought so much stuff that day.

"I didn't expect to meet you there. Everything about you, your look, your voice, your scent, the way you moved...was captivating. I knew right away then. So I marked you."

What?

"What?"

"You are my *erasthai*."

I blink a few times. No, there must be some mistake. "Are you sure? How can you be sure? Marked me? What do you mean marked me? How?"

I must be dreaming. I'm still lying in my bed, right? I'll be laughing so hard when I wake up in the morning and remember all this.

"Oh, I'm very sure, Genesis. I've been sure for three years. When a lycan meets his erasthai, he knows," he assures me confidently. "I haven't marked you physically... not yet." He is silent for a while as if letting the word sink in. "I just marked you through your wolf. She knows me by now. I've started our bond by marking you through your scent and aura so other lycans who might be interested would know right away that you're mine. You don't want fights between lycans. It'll leave a city like this in carnage and destruction within hours."

I scramble up to my feet to clear my head. This is not what I expected when I woke up this morning.

How do I feel about all this? You know, if by any slim chance that this was all real? Well, I don't know yet. This can't be real. I mean, I've been thinking and dreaming about this unattainable lycan for three years. Now, he's telling me I'm his "erasthai"?

It's like when you wanted something that you thought impossible to get. You dream about it for a long time. You've even resigned yourself that you'd never get it. But when you suddenly get it, you just don't know what to think of it or what to do with it.

71

However, I don't know how I feel about another male claiming me like a caveman. I've had enough of that with Logan so far.

Yet, this is *Constantine*. The lycan I've been dreaming of for three years. Oh, I'm so conflicted.

I stare at the beautiful creature in front of me. I can't be his, and he can't be mine, right?

He is now standing in front of me, watching me curiously. "What are you thinking?" he asks.

"If I was your erasthai, how come you never talked to me once after that day at the store three years ago?"

"I couldn't bring myself to get close to you without taking you. You were too young, and you were waiting for your mate."

"So if my mate had claimed me, you would have backed off?"

Constantine growls. "The thought of you being claimed by another is enough to make me want to destroy everything in my path," he mutters fiercely. "But that's what I had been telling myself to do... the right thing. Wait for you to grow up. Give you the chance to meet your mate. Lazarus and Caspian think I was being stupid. They wanted me to just claim you right away," he explains. "If I was being honest with myself, I don't think I would be able to ever let you go. I wouldn't have let him claim you. I've been around, waiting for you for three years...not that it's an issue now. The moment he rejected you, he lost any tiny chance he had to keep you."

"So you've marked my wolf, and you've started our bond...now all you have to do is mark me physically?" I squeak. I'm surprised my brain still works.

"Yes."

"How?"

"Almost like the way a werewolf mark his mate...by biting her neck. Only lycans can bite and mark their mate anywhere they choose to." His intense silver-gray eyes roaming my body as if deciding where to mark me.

I swallow hard. My breath hitches at the thought. "So I don't have any say at all in this?"

An emotion flicker in his beautiful eyes before his thick dark eyelashes sweep down and the flash of emotion is gone.

"Sure you do...you can say yes." He stalks closer.

I take a few steps back. My heart is hammering against my rib cage by the way he is looking at me.

"Uh...can I have time to think about all this?" I don't know why I said that. Well, maybe I'm trying to buy time because the way he's looking at me now is giving me a heart attack. Not even Logan has this effect on me.

"Of course, my sunshine. Whatever you wish." He smirks.

Why do I get the feeling that he's just saying that to humor me? Like he's just giving me the time that I want...but not too long.

CHAPTER IX
Of Sweat Pants And Baggy Shirts

The atmosphere between us changes after that. I think Constantine makes an effort to make me feel more at ease and relaxed around him. We play stupid games like twenty questions as we walk through the woods. It's surprising how I'm able to talk freely with him. I seem to be able to make him laugh with my ability to say stupid things. After a while, I forget how formidable he could be. Every now and then, when I glance up at him, my breath hitches at how perfect he looks. However, I don't feel like the power that he radiates is intimidating anymore. In fact, it strangely feels as if that power is enveloping me. It makes me feel powerful and protected. Makes me feel as if I'm part of him.

"Okay, my turn. How old are you?" I ask him.

"Very old," is his answer.

"Oh come on, I'll tell you how old I am, if you tell me how old you are." I tempt him. I'm very curious. He looked like he was 18 three years ago. He still looks like he's 18 now.

He chuckles. "I already know how old you are, sunshine. Why don't you ask questions that normal people usually ask? Like what my favorite color is."

"Lame! Don't normal people ask how old you are? Besides, I already know your favorite color. Black. You're always wearing black."

"Polite, normal people don't ask questions about other people's age. Besides, you're wrong. I like red. Like the color of your hair."

"I like Blue. Okay, so color was your question. Now it's my turn."

"Again?" he groans.

"So, when were you born?"

Constantine bursts out laughing. The sound of his deep laughter sends the whole army of butterflies going crazy in my tummy.

"You don't give up, do you sunshine?"

"Nope, I'm pretty stubborn," I announce proudly.

"Alright then, I was born in the year 1703 in Bucharest, though my parents aren't Romanian," he says casually. His eyes are regarding me carefully as if gauging my reaction.

"That wasn't so hard, was it?" I grin up at him. "So, where are your parents now? Where were they from?"

"Nope, I think it's my turn now." He grins. "You didn't run for the hills after I told you my age. Why?"

I shrug. "I don't know...I think I sorta expected that. I know lycans live a long time...much longer than werewolves."

"We don't age like werewolves." He nods.

"Why do you call me *sunshine*?" I ask him, truly curious.

"Because the evening sun was shining through the glass window that first day I saw you. It hit your face and your hair. It made your face glow and your hair fiery red." He takes a lock of my hair between his fingers. His face is full of wonder as he stares at it. Then his eyes shift to my face. "You're the most fascinating thing I've ever laid eyes on. I could look at you, listen to you, and breathe in your scent all day and all night and still can't get enough. You're on my mind every single minute of every day. You're the most important person to me even when you don't know it. I don't understand the power you have on me, but I can't fight it."

75

I arrived back home just after 11 am. Our hands brush once, sending delicious sparks shooting through my entire body. By the third time our hands touched, Constantine takes my hand in his.

Oh, cuddly bunnies and fuzzy slippers!

My poor heart. We walk with our fingers entwined that last few minutes together and now I'm on cloud nine.

We part ways reluctantly. So much for me wanting more time to think things through. Are we going too fast or three years too slow? I have no idea. The only thing that I know now is that I'm on cloud nine.

I take my shower, brush my hair, and put on my outfit for the day in a daze.

I must be dreaming. This is too perfect to be real.

I walk downstairs to join my family for brunch, still on cloud nine.

"How's your date with Kevin last night?" asks mom, looking strangely worried.

I crash back down to earth. Oh gosh! Does she know? Did anybody tell her about my doomed date last night?

I slide down my seat at the breakfast table trying to look nonchalant. First and foremost, look innocent. Then ask vague questions to find out how much they really know. These steps have served me well throughout my eighteen years of living.

"Why?" is my first vague question before biting into my toast.

"Honey, we have an invitation to dinner at Alpha Carrington's house tonight," mom informs me.

Huh? "What? Why?" I almost choke on my toast.

Dad sets his coffee mug down and looks at me seriously. I'm not liking where this is going.

"Well, sweetie, Logan seems to have changed his mind and decided to accept you as his mate and luna after all," explains my dad.

Logan did what? Must be the alpha's decision. Last time I heard, Logan still wanted Mia to rule the pack by his side.

"Does Logan know about this? I mean...how'd you know about this?" I look at both mom and dad.

"Alpha Carrington himself called this morning," says dad. "He invited us to dinner to apologize and to discuss plans for the future."

My heart sinks to the bottom of my shoes. I want my cloud nine back. I just want to be drunk on Constantine's presence again.

"Isn't it great honey? He must've realized that he can't live without his mate. The mate's attraction is too strong to resist. Soon you'll have your mate." Mom smiles.

I try to smile back, but I think my smile looks forced.

"I understand that being a luna is a big responsibility, but you'll be great at it, Genesis. I know you would," says mom, misunderstanding my reluctance and troubled look.

I notice my parents looking at each other in puzzlement and concern as my mom pats my hand soothingly. They must be wondering why I'm looking so down.

"Tell you what, let's go shopping and find a dress for tonight," suggests mom, trying to cheer me up.

"Okay," I agree slowly, even though that's the last thing I want to do. I just want to sit at home and dream about Constantine all day.

*   *   *

Half way through our shopping expedition together, I get a text from Constantine. My heart speeds up at the sight of his name as usual.

Constantine: Hey sunshine, what are you doing? Thinking of me? ;)
Me: Nah, too busy stripping ;P
Constantine: ?

Me : In changing room at the mall. Shopping with mom.

Constantine : Don't tease me.

Constantine : If I knew shopping involves you stripping, I'd take you shopping myself.

Me : Perv :P

Constantine : What did I say about perv?

Constantine: When you're not too busy stripping, can I see you soon?

Me : maybe tomorrow?

Constantine : why not tonight?

Me : Can't. Have dinner tonight.

His next reply comes very quick.

Constantine : With who?

I hesitate for a second, but then I reply truthfully.

Me : Alpha Carrington's house.

Constantine : W-why?

Constantine : Never mind. I'm coming to see you soon.

Me : Soon tomorrow?

Me : Tomorrow right?

Me : Constantine?

"Are you done, sweetie? You're taking a long time in there." Mom's voice urging me to change quickly.

My mom is feeling generous today. We each get a dress and a few beautiful tops. Mom gets a pair of black sling back heels, while I get a pair of nude color pumps. It's after four that we manage to get out of the mall. Dinner is at 7 pm.

Constantine never replied to my last text.

Now, here I am in my room trying to get ready for dinner that I don't really want to go to.

"You look beautiful, sunshine." I suddenly hear a familiar voice.

I jump, almost falling off my chair. "Are you trying to give me a heart attack?" I gasp, turning around to look at him.

Constantine is leaning against the window sill with one hand at the top of the frame, while the other at the side of it. My

78

breath catches and my heart stops for a beat. Will I ever get used to how good this god-like creature look? The muscles of his arms bulge. His dark brown hair is sexily messy with slight curls at the end.

He slowly stalks further into the room and I stand up facing him. He walks like the predator that he is, but he doesn't scare me or intimidate me. Not anymore, I note in surprise.

"Are you all dressed up like this for him?" There's something dangerous lurking in his silver gray eyes. His thick long dark eyelashes sweep down as he scans my body slowly.

I'm wearing a dark red spaghetti strap dress that follows the curves of my body. It ends a few inches above my knees. The deep red looks good against the paleness of my skin.

"No, but I have to dress up for dinner. My mom bought this dress for tonight," I whisper softly, not wanting my family to hear us.

He moves in closer until there are only a few inches between us. He raises his hand up and he trails the back of his fingers softly against my cheek. His touch sends sparks down my body. His closeness is affecting my breathing. I sway in his touch. His delicious scent clouding my senses.

"Change." He breathes against my ear. His warm breath fans my skin.

I find myself wanting to please him. I move into the closet and take another dress off the hanger.

What is wrong with me? I don't usually let guys boss me around. Didn't I have that talk with myself this morning? Well, I've never been anyone's erasthai before either.

I change into a green halter dress. The green brings out the color of my eyes and complements my red hair. The top part of the dress hugs my curves and the bottom flares out in a flirty soft fabric. It's an inch longer than the first dress, so I should be good.

I walk out of the closet feeling quite proud of myself.

"No," he growls as soon as he sees me.

"What? Do I look ugly in this dress?" I whisper yell, feeling frustrated.

He groans. "Sweetheart, I want you to go looking ugly for this dinner," he replies.

What?

"What do you want me to do? Wear my pajamas there?"

"No, especially not the pajamas you had on this morning," he answers quickly. "Don't you have sweat pants and a baggy shirt or something?"

"Know what? You're funny," I laugh softly.

"No, I'm serious," he counters.

"Honey? Are you ready? We don't want to be late," hollers mom from downstairs.

"In a minute, mom!" I holler back.

"I have to go," I whisper to him.

He sighs. "If you must." He relents broodingly, looking very unhappy. "Before you go...can I do something?"

"What?"

He steps in closer, and I freeze. With just a few inches gap between us, he moves my red curls off my shoulder and neck and leans in. His fingers graze my skin.

Oohh... goosebumps.

His nose and lips touch my neck and my hands grip his solid rock hard arms.

"What are you doing?" I slur, feeling drunk by the touch of his skin on mine.

"I'm strengthening our bond," he whispers against my skin, then he breathes in deeply. I feel his warm lips brushing my neck softly.

My breath catches. Then I involuntarily breathe his scent in as well.

I feel his power enveloping me, like a warm blanket. I feel powerful and protected.

"Now you remember that you're mine," he says with satisfaction.

CHAPTER X
Dinner Disaster

We arrive at the massive pack house just in time. We are promptly ushered to the Alpha's wing of the house by the beta, I'm assuming Hunter's dad and another man.

Luna Catherine greets us just inside the door and we are met by Alpha Carrington and Logan in the living room. By the looks on their faces, both father and son seem like they've just had a disagreement.

Our parents seem to get along fine. Luna Catherine is a very beautiful lady with blond hair and blue eyes just like Logan's. She's very friendly and gets along with mom very well.

"My, you must be Genesis," she greets me happily. "You are stunning, my dear," she gushes, giving me a quick hug.

Out of the corner of my eye, I see Logan giving me a head to toe survey. He keeps staring at me as if willing me to look at him. I ignore him while plastering a smile on my face, looking at everyone and everything except for him. I'm still very mad at how he ruined my date with Kevin yesterday night. I wish I could ask him how Kevin is doing.

Luna Catherine announces that we should all go into the dining room. As everybody is making their way there.

Logan steps in front of me. "Genesis," he begins, but I step around him.

I walk in with everybody else, completely ignoring him. I can feel his anger, but I couldn't care less. I still feel the attraction, but somehow the thought of Constantine is consuming me more. Ezra is completely silent.

All of a sudden, Mia makes an appearance. Mia looks exquisite in her dark blue sleeveless dress that reaches her mid-thigh and five inch high heels. She steps right in front of me and takes a seat right next to Logan, beside my mom. I was assuming the seat was for me.

Mia's hand quickly grabs onto Logan's as if staking her claim and Logan stares at me as if gauging my reaction.

Mia's father, Gamma Brown, looks at the couple approvingly. The atmosphere in the room, however, changes drastically. My mom's demeanor changes so does my dad's. Alpha Carrington looks furious, while the rest in the room looks embarrassed and uneasy.

I know this is supposed to be embarrassing for me and my family, but strangely, I'm feeling just fine. I feel powerful and safe. *Constantine.* Just remembering the feel of his lips on my neck this evening makes me feel all tingly inside.

"Hello, Mia." I smile politely and take a seat next to Autumn near the end. I look at Alpha Carrington who avoids my gaze. His jaw clenched, and his face is turning red. He's furious and embarrassed. His golden son is disrespecting his guests and defying him in front of everybody.

Dinner is a strange experience for me. While everybody else seems uneasy, I'm feeling strangely detached from the whole situation. The meal is awkward and tense. Poor Luna Catherine is trying to lighten the mood with no success. My usually happy easy going mom and dad barely utter a word. Mia is hanging onto Logan, looking desperate. Logan keeps staring at me as if he couldn't take his eyes off of me. Overall, the tension is so palpable that I think not a single soul is sorry when dinner is finally over.

When the last plate of dessert is served and eaten, Alpha Carrington suggests that we all move to his office. It's a massive room with books lining the walls from floor to ceiling. At one end of the room is a dark red leather chair behind a heavy mahogany table. That's probably where he usually conducts his business. A huge stone fireplace is at the other end of the room, and a thick dark red Turkish carpet is dominating the floor.

He ushers us to where a big comfortable sofa and chairs cluster around a big chunky coffee table, in front of the fireplace. More chairs are being brought in by the helps so that there are enough chairs for everybody.

Mia openly glares at me while I notice my sister Autumn is glaring deadly daggers at her.

While coffee is being served, Alpha Carrington announces his plan for me and Logan. "I want to announce Logan and Genesis, Alpha and Luna before the next full moon. I expect her to be marked and mated before then," he declares.

The next full moon is in less than a week! *No!*

"With all due respect, Alpha Carrington, my family and I would like some time to talk about that," says my dad before anybody else can say anything. *Thank you, daddy!*

"What is there to talk about? They are mates; my son Logan should've marked her by now. We've given them enough time. I want my son to take over the pack as soon as possible," objects Alpha Carrington.

"Still, it's a big decision, and in the light of a certain situation—" my father quickly glances over to Logan and Mia who are sitting in a corner "—We as a family would like some time to talk things over," continues my dad politely yet firmly.

Alpha Carrington seems to disagree. "There is nothing to talk about. I am being reasonable enough—"

Dad stands up and in his Alpha's voice, he says, "Enough. I said my family needs some time to talk. We'll continue later." His voice vibrates with such full force Alpha dominance. Most in the room instinctively lower their heads, except for Alpha Carrington, my mom, and myself.

The room falls into a complete silence. Everybody seems shocked. I hide a smile. Nobody would've expected a lowly omega to emit such power and authority. Never have I been prouder of my dad. I see my mom's lips curve up slightly into a proud smile as well.

"Alpha Carrington, luna Catherine, thank you for dinner. My family and I must take our leave now," states my dad politely. His tone of voice invites no arguments.

My mom and my dad, and even Autumn are silent the whole drive home. I sit at the back thinking about Constantine.

The silence continues as we get into the house and get into our respective rooms to change.

I shower, and brush my teeth, then change into my pajama shorts and a comfy tank top.

After a short knock, my mom enters my room. She stares at me with sadness and some other emotions that I can't quite decipher. Then, without any warning, she lifts the bottom of my tank top up to reveal my stomach.

She gasps at the blotches of colors decorating it. Dark purple for the newer bruises, lighter purples, blues, pinks and finally greenish to yellowish hues for the healing older ones. Then she sobs into her hands uncontrollably. It breaks my heart.

"Mom..." I put my arms around her, trying to console her. "It's okay," I hush softly.

"Why didn't you tell me? Why?" she cries. "He could've killed you...my poor baby."

My dad and Autumn rush in to see what happen. Dad's face looks grim, and Autumn's face looks like she's about to cry herself.

Do I think now is the right time for me to tell them about Logan's plan to keep me as his kept whore while marking Mia as his Luna? I think not.

"Get packing. We're going back to my family's pack. We're going back to Cannis Gunnolf," says dad firmly.

*   *   *

I wonder if Constantine is coming tonight.

I'm lying in my warm, comfortable bed, staring at my phone. It's almost 11 pm. I need to talk to somebody. I suppose I could call or text Penny or Reese, or River, but it's kinda late to call them now. Besides, the person I really want to talk to right now is Constantine.

I suppose I could call or text him too...but I know I'm not gonna.

My dad felt totally insulted and furious tonight. Rightly so, I think, but I don't want to move away from here. I don't want to leave my friends especially Penny, Reese, and River. I don't want to leave Constantine.

I try to stay awake, but my eyes feel heavy, and my eyelids are drifting shut. Just when I'm losing my battle with sleep, I feel cold air blowing in through the window.

"Constantine," I whisper heavily.

"Shhh.. sweetheart. I just want to say good night," he whispers back above me.

"...need to talk to you..." I mumble sleepily.

"You can talk to me tomorrow. Sleep now, sunshine."

I feel his warm lips brushing my forehead before I drift off.

CHAPTER XI
Call Me Juliet With Mad Ninja Skills

As I'm getting ready for school, I realize that there are a lot of things that I don't know.

Apparently, I don't know my bra size, because right now it feels like my girls are spilling out of my B-cups. Whoa! My jeans are a bit tighter around my bottom area too, though my waist is still very tiny. What happened? Did I gain weight?

Another thing I don't know is, how to break it to my friends that we're moving away from here.

I don't know if Kevin is still alive. If he still is, does he hate me now?

I don't know how I'm going to behave around Constantine today as well. Should I be with him like we were yesterday? Should I pretend I didn't know him like I always did before?

If I am with him, I'll be the latest gossip in school again. Not to mention all the girls, werewolves and humans would definitely hate me.

I really don't know what to do, so I end up trying to avoid him around school. Using my crazy ninja skills again, of course.

I manage to avoid the lycans and the populars all morning, much to my friends' annoyance. They think I'm behaving weirdly. Reese is starting to worry about me. I feel sorry that my friends have to put up with someone like me.

At lunchtime, though, it's hard to stay hidden. I notice that other female lycan, Serena, is with them today.

And I haven't told my friends about my dad's decision to move. They're going to freak. I'm such a coward.

"Did you do something different with your makeup today, GenGen?" asks Reese as she studies my face closely.

"Nope. In fact, I just wore my lip gloss today. Nothing else."

"Hmm...maybe that's it," comments Reese skeptically. "Whatever it is, keep doing it. You look better without makeup I think."

"Are the lycans looking at us?" questions Penny suddenly in a hushed voice.

"Nope, they're looking at something behind us," I answer quickly even before I begin to look.

Yep, all the lycans including Serena are looking our way. Even I can't pretend they're looking at something behind us anymore. Maybe I should leave the lunch room now. I'm still so hungry, though.

"Are you sure they're not looking at one of us? How can you be so sure?" asks Penny again suspiciously.

"Nope. Not looking at us," I confirm.

"Oh, but I think Penny's right. I think they're looking at this table," announces Reese. "Don't you think so, River?" She nudges River's side.

"Why would they be looking at us?" I interrupt before River gets the chance to answer. I get up and dump the rest of my food in the dumpster except for an apple. My stomach growls in protest.

I sneak a quick peek. Yep, the four lycans are still staring at us—or me. My heart thuds faster in my chest. Better run.

"See you guys later... got somewhere to be, things to do, people to see and all that. Ciao!" I wave at my friends as I make my quick escape. I'm such a coward.

I stumble upon Kevin walking with a friend in the hallway. Guilt consumes me. He has black eyes. His lips are busted. One cheek is swollen. One arm is in a cast. One plaster over his eyebrow. There is a huge plaster over his nose too. Other than that he seems okay. I mean, it could be worse, right? I was worried that he might be dead last night.

"Kevin," I call out.

He stops in his track when he hears me.

"Genesis," he says in dismay. "I can't be seen with you." His eyes frantically scan the almost empty hallway.

"Excuse us." I address his friend as I grab his uninjured hand and drag him into one of the empty classrooms. Then I notice that he's walking with a limp too. Poor Kevin.

I pull out a chair for him to sit, then I sit on the other side of the table across him.

"You weren't in English lit this morning," I state. I was looking for him the whole morning actually.

"Well, yeah...I just got here," he answers, scratching his arm just above the cast.

"I'm so sorry, Kevin," I apologize.

"I thought Carrington's with that cheerleader or something. Why didn't you tell me that you're with him?" he asks me.

"Well, I'm not with him."

"Oh," says Kevin looking confused.

"It's complicated," I explain.

"He said he's going to kill me the next time he sees me near you. I know it sounds crazy, but I believe him. He and his friends looked really scary that night," says Kevin.

Oh, I believe him too. I'm surprised that he let Kevin off this easily.

"Look, Genesis, I don't mean to upset you. I mean, I know you like me. I do like you too, but I'm sorry, we can't be together."

As I look into his serious blue eyes, I thought, oh what the heck. If this is the only time I get to play Juliet in an epic tragic love story, I'll take it.

"I understand, Kevin...but I'll never forget you." I take his uninjured hand in mine and sorrowfully look deep into his eyes.

Kevin lifts my hand up to his busted lips at the same time the door bursts open.

Constantine is standing there taking in the scene before him with narrowed eyes. His piercing silver-gray eyes zoning in on my hand in Kevin's near his lips.

Somebody clears his throat, and I instantly aware of the other three lycans standing silently behind Constantine.

Wow. This is awkward.

Kevin's eyes are big with surprise and fear. He raises his hands up as if in surrender.

"I didn't touch her. I swear, man," Kevin declares.

Constantine's eyes are now fixed on me.

Kevin scurries out of there as fast as his limping feet can carry him. I don't blame him. I want to do the same—only I don't think I can get away with it now.

Lazarus pats Constantine's back while Serena smiles softly at me before they both leave. Caspian looks at me in amusement, a slow panty-melting smile growing on his lips. He winks at me playfully before he thumps Constantine's back once and leaves as well.

Constantine never takes his eyes off of me the whole time. We're all alone now.

"Hey?" I say awkwardly. My fingers are fidgeting with the hem of my cardigan.

He looks so good today. Black jeans and a black t-shirt that fit him like gloves. A black leather jacket, thick dark silky hair all mussed up. He looks dangerous and seriously hot. My fingers itch to touch a lock of dark brown hair that curls at the nape of his neck. "Say something," I plead finally, no longer able to take the silence much longer.

"What do you want me to say, Genesis?"

"I don't know...anything."

"I seriously don't know what to say. You've been avoiding me the whole morning today. When I found you, you're with another man," he states calmly and somehow that makes it more threatening. "Alone. With his lips kissing your hand. What am I supposed to think, Genesis?" There's hurt and anger and jealousy in his silver-gray eyes.

Now I'm feeling like a heel. Constantine has always been upfront about his feelings for me. As hard as it is for me to believe that this beautiful, powerful creature feels that way for someone like me. He's not the one being childish. He's made it clear about what he wants. I'm the one being wishy-washy.

What do I want?

"Constantine," I breathed softly.

He takes a quick sharp intake of breath. It's as if just hearing his name on my lips takes his breath away.

"I'm sorry. I think I just got scared...the way I'm feeling for you...it's overwhelming. It's all-consuming. Nobody ever made me feel like you do. Not even my ex-mate. I don't know how to deal with it," I tell him.

We're both staring into each other's eyes. Trying to figure out and read each other's thoughts.

The bell rings. The class is starting. A student enters the classroom we're in. Her big owlish eyes are staring at the both of us with curiosity.

We both ignore her. Constantine grabs my elbow and pulls me out of the school through the cafeteria door. We walk past the oak tree and stop not too far into the woods.

I'm not fully aware of my surrounding. All I can see is him.

"Do you want to be with me?" he asks me suddenly.

"Yes," I whisper softly, but I've never been so sure of what I want until that moment. I truly want to be with him.

"Then be with me," he says. "I want you, Genesis. All I want is you."

He's looking at me as if waiting for me to do something. Expectant look on his beautiful face as he stares at me. His arms open. For a minute, I don't understand what he wants.

He lays it all out there. He states what he wants. Now it's my move. I take a step up to him, and a second later I'm in his arms. Jolts of electricity shot through me. His warmth, power, and scent envelop me. I feel weak and strong at the same time. This is where I want to be. In his arms.

"You are mine, Genesis. There's no turning back. I don't share, and I don't let go of what's mine. I won't give you up." His lips brushing against my temple.

I swallow nervously. The thought of me being his scares me and excites me. It brings delicious shivers down my spine.

*   *   *

Constantine and I decided to skip school after that. Well, I suggested it. Constantine seems to be happy to go along with it. I've been so bad lately. With the number of classes I've skipped just this past couple of weeks, I'm surprised they haven't called my parents yet.

Constantine takes my hand in his and I'm on cloud nine...again. I see rainbows and unicorns when we're together like this. Well, okay...not really, but you get what I mean. At school or everywhere else, he seems cold and aloof, but he seems so different when he's with me. I don't think I ever saw him smile much before. He seems to be playful, and mischievous when we're alone. His smile and his laughter, my goddess, so amazing, it makes me weak in the knees.

"Come on, sunshine. Get on my back," he coaxes.

Right now, he's trying to persuade me to get on his back so he can jump to the other side of the raging river. The river is very wide. The rocks are wet and slippery. Even the strongest werewolf wouldn't be able to make a jump to the other side.

"Nope," I refuse, shaking my head and taking a few steps back away from him.

"Sunshine..." His tone is a warning as he saunters towards me menacingly. Mischief in his eyes.

"Costa.." I fire back in the same tone.

"Costa?" He stops in his track. He raises an eyebrow. Then his lips curve up into a little smile and his eyes glint with humor. "Is that your new nickname for me?"

"Yeah, Costa...Constantine is a mouthful," I declare. "Why? Would you prefer me to call you Pooh bear? Cutie pie? Sweetpea? Studmuffin? Chunky monkey?"

"Chunky monkey?" His eyebrows rise. His lips twitch as if he's trying not to laugh. He shakes his head as if he can't believe I would think of calling him with any of those names. "I wouldn't mind you calling me Stud Muffin." He winks.

"Now, get on my back, my sweet pea," he says as he hauls me onto his back. And before I can say *Chunky monkey* we're on the other side of the river.

We stop by another cliff this time. We lie on our backs close to the edge, next to each other. This cliff has a 50-foot drop to the river below. We both seem to have a thing for cliffs.

It's a beautiful day. A soft breeze is blowing. The sky is blue and white fluffy clouds drift slowly in different shapes. I swear I could see ones that look like a bunny and fuzzy slippers.

Constantine entwine our fingers together. His thumb is drawing circles, caressing my hand. It's funny how his simple touch can make my toes curl, and my heart speeds up.

"Constantine?"

"Hmmm..?"

I decide to tell him what's been bothering me since last night. "My father decided that we're moving away from here. He's taking us back to his old pack, Cannis Gunnolf Pack."

Constantine raises himself up on his elbow to look at me. "You think your moving away can separate us, sunshine? You are mine. No matter where you go, I'll find you."

*　　*　　*

When I reach home, there are boxes in the living room. Some stuff is already packed, ready for moving, but a lot of things are still where they usually are. I'm surprised that my parents only got this far. I'd thought the house would at least be partially empty by now.

When I get into the kitchen, I'm surprised to see mom sitting at the table. She's sipping tea, staring out the window absentmindedly.

"Mom?"

"Oh, honey, you're home." She smiles brightly. Her smile seems forced. Something isn't right.

"Mom, what's going on?"

Her smile falters. "Nothing to worry about, honey. Do you want some tea?" She gets up to put the kettle on the stove.

"Mom, please. If it concerns me, I need to know."

Mom sighs. She looks worn. We both take our seat at the table, and she wraps her hands over her mug tightly.

"The alpha called your dad for a meeting today," she says. "They declined our request. Our application to leave the pack is rejected."

"Okay...can't we just take off and get Uncle Ashton or Grandpa Quentin to send the paper works later?" I ask. Let them deal among the alphas, it's easier. Some werewolves do that when they travel and find their mates in a different pack.

"Honey, our application is not only rejected, we are prohibited from leaving the pack," explains mom. "As of now, the border patrol is also aware of our position. I think they even send pack scouts to keep watch, to make sure we don't leave the territory."

My eyes widen at this information.

"Why?" I blurt out even when I can guess the reason why. This is not a normal thing to happen. They don't make this huge a deal of a family leaving the pack to join another.

Mom sighs heavily as she stares at me sadly.

"Alpha Carrington wants you to mate with his son, Logan," she states gently as she tucks a piece of stray hair behind my ear.

"But he rejected me, mom. He made it clear he didn't want me."

"I know, honey." Mom sighs softly. "But he decided that the party is going to be in three days. You are to be mated and marked by Logan before then."

"I will not let Logan mark me or touch me, and they can't stop us from leaving," I cry out in frustration, completely forgetting that I don't want to move out in the first place. "They can't force us. It's not fair!"

"No, it's not fair....but the elders would completely agree with them. It's within their right to prohibit us from leaving. You're Logan Carrington's true mate. You're rightfully his."

My chest grow hot when I hear this. The heat grows and spreads throughout my body. My vision is turning red. Ezra is protesting at being called Logan's. My whole being is rebelling against it.

"I am not his! " I spit out in a voice that doesn't sound like mine.

Mom Gasps in shock. "Genesis?"

A screeching sound makes me look down at a pair of hands that don't look like mine. My nails are long and sharp. They just made deep scratches across the dinner table.

"Genesis, your eyes..." whispers mom in fear. "What's happening?"

I withdraw my hands from the table and run. Not a second later, I'm in my room. What's happening? How did I get in my room so fast? My senses are ten times sharper than even when I'm in my wolf form. For a few seconds, my senses are overload.

I look in the mirror and my eyes are all black. No whites at all.

Oh, my gosh! Oh, my gosh! Don't freak out. Don't freak out. I'm freaking out!!!

What's going on? Even when I'm changing into my wolf, my eyes usually still have some white in them.

"Genesis?" Mom knocks on my door hesitantly.

"In a minute!" I call out. That doesn't sound like my voice. My fury is forgotten as I stare at my elongated fingers and the thick, sharp, long nails in curiosity. I'm growing taller as my limbs elongated. I'm still changing.

"Genesis?" mom calls out. The door handle turns. I jump out through the window.

CHAPTER XII
How To Stay Out Of The Spotlight

"Where did you go?" asks mom worriedly as soon as I climb in through my window a couple of hours later. She must be worried sick. The smell of brownies and chocolate chip cookies waft strongly through the air. Mom bakes when she's stressed. So, she must've been really stressed.

"I'm sorry, mom. I just needed to go for a run," I explain, which isn't a complete lie.

I did go for a run, but not in my wolf form. Not fully in my human form either. It's almost somewhere in between wolf form and human form. I was running on two legs, instead of on all fours. It left my hands free to fling myself upwards and grab onto trees. I felt like I was flying. I was so fast, the border patrols didn't even sense me up there. I was moving so fast that I think I might have reached the Canadian borders in such a short time. It's kinda weird, but I loved it! I felt so powerful and free like nothing can touch me.

I don't know what is happening to me, but selfishly I want to keep it to myself. Besides, telling mom about it would probably add more to her stress.

"It must be all that stress. It's good that you clear your head by going for a run," says mom, smiling in relief. "Your friends are waiting for you downstairs, by the way."

Reese and Penny are sitting in our kitchen, busy shoving mom's chocolate chip cookies and brownies into their mouths.

"What are you guys doing here?"

"Well, it's good to see you too!" scoffs Penny. "This is an intervention," she announces seriously. It's hard to take her seriously when she's talking with her mouth full of cookies.

Reese rolls her eyes. "It's not an intervention, Penny," she says. "We want to know what's going on with you. You've been acting weird, and you haven't been answering our calls or our texts."

I grab a few cookies and some still warm pieces of brownies on a plate before going up to my room.

Boy, I'm hungry!

"What aren't you telling us?" asks Penny as she and Reese follow me up to my room.

I closed the door, and the three of us sit on my bed.

"So...are you going to tell us what's happening? Or don't you trust us?" asks Reese, looking hurt.

"It's not that I don't trust you. I just don't want you two to be worried. I always end up in trouble...one way or another. Aren't you tired of it? Don't you just want to live a peaceful life?" I ask them.

"I love living in your drama, Genesis. I crave it. I yearn for it. I live for it. I need your drama to entertain my boring existence," yells Penny. The three of us go quiet for a second before we simultaneously burst out laughing uncontrollably.

I laugh so hard I have tears in my eyes. I'm actually very glad that my friends are here. I'd probably be driving myself nuts thinking about what's going on right now if I were by myself.

So I tell them everything. Well, almost everything. I tell them about the dinner at Alpha Carrington's, about dad wanting to move away, about the party that's about to happen in three days. I also tell them about Constantine.

"You and Constantine??? A lycan?" Penny shrieks.

"Shhh..." I shush her, worried if mom could hear us. I'm not ready to break it to my parents yet. They are under a lot of stress lately. I don't know how they are going to take the news about me and Constantine.

"So...you and Constantine, huh? A lycan." repeats Reese in disbelieve.

"Wow, I didn't see that one coming," says Penny, looking dazed.

I can't believe my friends! Of all the things I just told them, that's the only thing that they heard?

"But guys, what about Alpha Carrington's plan to have me mated to Logan soon? The announcement is in three days!"

I'm freaking out a bit.

"I think you should tell Constantine about it," suggests Reese.

"Yeah, you should tell him," agrees Penny. "So, you and Constantine, huh? Wow, do you know how seriously hot he is???" she exclaims while she grabs another one of my cookies.

"No, she doesn't Penny," Reese deadpans, before she rolls her eyes. "When we told you to get a new mate, we didn't mean a lycan. But, wow! You don't do things half-assed do you, GenGen?"

"I can't wait to see how Logan's going to take this," states Penny, smiling evilly. "I can see it now. You'll be the talk of the school soon...again. Not that they've stopped talking about you yet."

I groan. That's what I'm afraid of.

"Great job, Penny. You really know how to make a friend feels better," says Reese sarcastically.

*   *   *

Something is puzzling me. Do I look different? Does my skin look softer and even more dewy than usual? My features definitely look sharper: my nose; my cheekbones; my lips look fuller and redder; my light hazel eyes seem brighter. The green and the gold at the centers and the bluish-gray around the rims are more vivid. My eyebrows are more prominent, and eyelashes are thicker and longer too. My hair seems fuller and shinier; the red seems richer than before.

My body is curvier as well. Not too much of a difference, but when I pull the jeans or the skirt up over my bottom, I can feel it. My girls are spilling over. There's a cleavage now above the neckline of my tank top.

What is wrong with me? Whatever it is, I know I'm changing.

I sigh and throw the hairbrush back on the dresser. This is ridiculous. My life is in chaos and I'm staring at my reflection in the mirror.

I know Constantine dropped by last night. His scent lingers in the air. I wish I wasn't such a heavy sleeper. I miss him. The need to be with him spurs me to get dressed for school faster. I'm not putting any makeup on today, not even a lip gloss.

Reese shows up in her car with Penny in the passenger seat. Autumn and I climb in. "You look a bit different, did you do something with your makeup today?" asks Penny, turning around.

"That's what I said yesterday!" exclaims Reese. "You look even better today," she adds, staring at me thoughtfully through the rearview mirror.

So it's not just me imagining stuff then.

"Whatever it is, girlfriend...you look hot," announces Penny with a giggle.

Autumn rolls her eyes. "She's probably just gained weight!"

"Hey!" I protest. "I did not!" Well, I might. I don't know. I didn't check, but I'm not going to admit that to my annoying little sister.

Reese drives the car so fast that the ride doesn't even last five minutes.

I can feel the attention we're getting as soon as we step out of the car. There are a few catcalls from the boys while the girls glare at us.

"Morning girls," greets River, wrapping his arm around Reese's shoulders. Even River is looking annoyed by the attention we're suddenly getting. I shake my head. When are they going to stop paying attention to us?

I can feel *his* eyes on me even before I see him.

Penny nudges me so hard, I think I break a rib cage. "That's him! That's him!" she whispers excitedly.

Constantine is standing with three other lycans at the bottom of the steps leading up to the school entrance. This time, I'm pretty sure they're not looking at anything behind us.

He looks so incredibly hot today in his dark wash jeans, a gray t-shirt, a black leather jacket, and black leather biker boots. I still can't believe that this gorgeous creature is *mine* and that he's standing there waiting for *me*.

I look up and smile. His eyes lit up. Then all I can see is him. My heart picks up, and I hasten my steps.

"Constantine," I whisper as I get a few feet away from him.

He doesn't hesitate to close the gap between us. He steps up and pulls me right into his arms and places his lips and nose right at the base of my neck, nuzzling me there. Jolts of electricity shoot through me and I tighten my arms around him to stay upright.

Oh, wow!

"What are you wearing, sunshine? I thought we've established that you're not going to wear anything too revealing and skirts that are too short," he whispers in my ear.

I didn't try to dress slutty or anything, but with my new curves, everything that I own seems to fit sinfully snug in certain places.

"We did?"

"Yes, we did. Those male werewolves and humans are staring at you. They're looking at what's mine. It makes me want to rip their heads off." He growls.

101

"But I wore this for you." I blurt out softly. My face turns bright red as soon as I realized what I just said, but Constantine stops scowling. The anger in his eyes is replaced with something else as he stares at me. A slow sexy smile is growing on his lips.

Wow. I guess that's the right thing to say to cool him off.

"Did you now?" There's a mischievous gleam in his silver eyes. "I'd much prefer you in nothing at all," he growls wickedly.

He's expecting me to blush and look away in embarrassment. Two can play this game. My cheeks flush beet red, but I smile naughtily back. "Maybe I can show up in nothing at all to school tomorrow."

He growls deeply in his throat. The sound sends delightful shivers down my spine.

"Don't test me, my love," he mutters. "If you want the school to be still standing tomorrow, I suggest you'd better not, my little imp," he murmurs in my ear. His teeth nip my earlobe gently.

Oh, flying cows, cuddly bunnies and fuzzy slippers!

When I pull back, I notice how everybody is staring. Everybody is frozen in their spots. Even Reese, River and Penny are staring with their mouths open.

Wow, I guess this is not the way to stay out of the spotlight.

CHAPTER XIII
How Not To Piss Off A Lycan

I'm in English Lit again with Penny. The lycans walked us to our classroom, and so far Penny hasn't stopped talking about what happened between me and Constantine.

"Oh my gosh! I knew you said you're with him, but...whoa, you know?" she prattles. "I've never seen a lycan like that with anyone..like ever. Wow! You two look so cute together. He's sooo into you," she whispers dreamily. "I think you two make a beautiful couple."

My cheeks flush red again. I can't believe how everybody was staring at us. I guess nobody ever seen anything like that. The lycans never ever talked to anybody outside their little circle, let alone showing any emotions.

The teacher has been in the classroom for over ten minutes when the door swings open with a bang and Logan and Zeke walk in. Logan is looking furious. He's staring at me the whole time.

I inwardly groan. It's been almost twenty minutes since he entered the classroom but Logan is still facing backward, staring at me, or rather glaring at me challengingly. I ignore him the whole time. Or at least I'm trying to. I pretend that he's staring at something behind me. I stare straight ahead, pretending to be engrossed with the lesson. Isn't the teacher going to do anything at all? I know he's the future alpha, the golden boy and all that, but this is ridiculous.

I glance at Penny who rolls her eyes before she looks at Logan, then quickly shifts her gaze back down to her fascinating Julius Caesar. Never have I seen Penny so interested in Shakespeare before.

We seem to be the focus of the whole class, even though everybody is pretending to be looking at something else.

Coward! Well, so am I. I can't wait for this class to end.

What a jerk. Why is he doing this to me? He really should just leave me alone. I still feel him in the evening sometimes when he's having his *fun*. The pain isn't as intense anymore. I don't know if it's because of my bond with Constantine getting stronger or because mine and Logan's bond is getting weaker.

I gather my things into my school bag very quickly even before the bell rings. I can't wait to get out of there. But Logan has another plan in mind because as soon as the bell rings, his hand wraps around my upper arm.

"Just where are you running off to, mate?" He pulls me out into the hallway with him and pushes me up against the wall. His whole body is pinning me against it.

"I am not your mate." I spit out. "You rejected me, remember? We're nothing."

"Well, I changed my mind. Didn't I tell you that? What's this I hear about you and a lycan?" His grip on my arms tightens. His other hand grips my hair and pulls my head to the side, baring my neck to him. "You are mine," he growls against my neck. "I will mark you, and I will mate with you." I feel his teeth grazing my skin. His canines sharpen.

Wait. Is he marking me? Here? Now?

"NO!!!" I struggle and push him as hard as I can. I feel him harden against my upper thigh. All my squirming only excites him. I start to struggle wildly.

I push with all my strength. I hear a loud bang and in the next instance, I realize that I'm free.

Logan is slumped against the opposite wall with Constantine standing over him. One of Logan's arms bent the wrong way. The lockers behind him have a big dent in them.

Constantine is looking positively dangerous. His eyes are all black, which reminds me of my own eyes yesterday. He's breathing hard as if trying to calm himself, but his stance is threatening. Dangerous power is emanating from him in strong waves. Even the crowd shrink back.

His hand reaches down to grip Logan by the neck and drag him back up with ease. Logan winces, his arm is dangling uselessly at an awkward angle.

Three lycans easily push through the student body. Lazarus and Caspian grip him on his shoulders and arms. Serena walks over to my side to hold my shoulder and touch my face gently.

"You okay?" she asks softly.

I nod, staring at the scene before me nervously. I now realize how serious this is and how ugly this could turn out to be.

"Go to him. Only you can calm him down now," she whispers calmly.

I nod again and walk on unsteady legs to stand in front of him. He's staring down at Logan. I can see how hard he is struggling to hold on to his form and stay in control.

"Constantine," I whisper. He doesn't seem to hear me.

"Costa.." I try again. This time I cup my hands on his cheeks and turn his face towards me. His eyes are two black shiny soulless holes, regarding me coldly. Dark blue veins decorating the surface of his skin, spreading from his eye sockets down across his cheeks, snaking down to his neck. I can feel his power. Dark and dangerous. My heart speeds up, but not from fear. His dark, strong power excites me, I realize.

I stroke his face gently and he closes his eyes. He releases Logan with a loud thump as he leans in closer to me.

"She's my mate. She's mine," says Logan defiantly.

105

Is he kidding me right now? I'm trying to save his sorry ass. No sane werewolf in his position would say anything now.

Constantine's head snaps down. His dark focus is once again on Logan.

"She's mine now. She belongs to me, mutt." His voice is unrecognizable.

I feel, rather than hear a deep rumble in his chest. I don't know what that means, but I quickly grab his face in my hands again and pull it to me. When I get his eyes back on me, I tug at his hands trying to pull him away just in case Logan decides to open his big mouth again. He stares at me, but refuse to budge.

"Costa...please," I plead. I tug again, and this time he lets me. The crowd parts as I pull him away. I don't know where I'm leading him to, all I know is that I need to get him away from there.

We end up at the back door of the school. I push open the door and pull us out with a deep sigh.

As soon as we're out the door, he grabs me by my shoulders and presses his face into my neck.

"You are mine. Mine. All mine". He repeats as he breathes me in. His nose flaring, eyes still black.

Then he pushes me back. "You smell like him," he growls fiercely. Dark blue veins once again appear on his face. He doesn't look much like a human now.

"But I don't want him...I'm only yours," I whisper urgently, clutching his muscular arms tightly.

"Say that again. Tell me that you're mine."

"I'm yours. Costa, I'm only yours."

*   *   *

Once Constantine regained control of himself, he drove me to this mansion not too far out of town, but very well hidden by mature trees and the long winding driveway.

Even now, I'm not sure how much control he has over himself. Once in a while, I catch him clenching his jaw or balling his fists around the steering wheel till his knuckles turn white.

He opens the massive door to the sight of an impressive grand foyer. The foyer has a high ceiling with a dome skylight. It opens up to a grand staircase. The gleaming marble floor reflects the light from the skylight as well as the huge crystal chandelier that hangs in the middle of the room. Everything is in cream, accented with black and gold. Either side of the staircase opens up to other areas of the house. This is even more impressive than the pack house.

"Is this your house?"

"It belongs to all of us, though Caspian makes most of the decision regarding the house. The rest of us couldn't care less. Caspian likes everything lavish," remarks Constantine as he leads me up the staircase.

We walk past several doors on the second floor until we reach the end of the hallway. He opens the last door to our left and waits for me to get in.

"This is my room," he informs me as we step in. His room is easily four sizes bigger than my bedroom. The walls are gray. Everything else is in black and white with little splashes of red here and there. There's a massive king size bed in the middle of the far wall with a huge red, black and white abstract painting behind it. A sitting area, with a sofa, chairs and an ottoman is at the front, facing a big screen TV.

"You can have a shower in here. There are fresh towels in the bathroom," he says as he pushes his en-suite bathroom door open. He hands me some clothing items.

"You want me to take a shower?" I ask, incredulous.

He leans against the wall with his head back, and his eyes closed, looking tortured. "Every time I smell him on you, I feel like my control is slipping away. I'm trying very hard not to go to him now and rip his heart right out of his chest," he growls.

107

He sounds like he's really struggling to keep in control, so I quickly grab the garments and step into the bathroom, locking the door behind me.

His bathroom is impressive too. There's a deep claw foot tub right in the middle, but it's the shower that draws my attention.

The glass-enclosed shower has a granite bench and nine shower heads including the biggest rain shower at the top. Aahhh, yes. If I had a shower like this, I'd never leave my bathroom. I use his shampoo and soap too. I think I smell like Constantine now.

After drying off with a thick fluffy towel, I put my underwear back on. There's no way I'm going to walk around without any underwear on. His white shirt comes down just a few inches above my knees. His boxer shorts disappear underneath his shirt. It makes it look like I'm not wearing any pants.

When I open the door, he's sitting on the sofa with his MacBook on. "Are you finally done?" he asks with a lift of his eyebrow. He's looking much more relaxed now. An amused smile tilts the corners of his lips.

I just poke my tongue out. I did stay quite a long time in there. I stayed until my skin turns pruney. I blame it all on the shower heads.

"I think I'm in love with your shower heads," I announce.

"Are you now?" he drawls lazily as he gets to his feet. "Didn't think I would have to compete with shower heads."

His eyes zone in on my bare legs as soon as I step out of the bathroom. His eyes smolder, and his face grows serious.

"You look so sexy in my shirt," he says as he steps in closer. "Now you smell like you're supposed to...like you...and my shampoo and soap."

"What do I smell like?"

His hands grip my waist as he playfully, but roughly, pulls me closer, making me gasp. My heart is hammering in my chest. His thick dark eyelashes sweep down over his cheeks as he closes his eyes and his nostrils flare when he takes a deep breath close to my neck. It sends shivers up and down my spine.

"Delicious," he murmurs. His warm breath fanning my neck. "Now tell me again that you're mine."

"I'm yours."

He opens his eyes and I'm mesmerized. His beautiful gray eyes are so piercing—and hungry.

"Goddess, you are beautiful," he whispers huskily. "And all mine." His voice sounds so possessive. His intense gray eyes studying my features, then his sooty black eyelashes sweep down as they focus on my lips.

His breathing quickens, so does mine. He leans down slowly as if waiting for my reaction. My lips part, my eyes flutter shut, and suddenly his lips are on mine. Soft and warm at first, but electricity and fireworks explode through me, and he deepens the kiss. His arms circle my waist, pulling me flush against him. My arms go around his neck. My fingers tangle in his silky hair. My heart feels like it's about to explode in my chest.

We both pull back for air at the same time, staring at each other. Breathing hard.

I pull myself up on a tiptoe and he eagerly leans down for more kiss. Our lips touch and move together. His lips grow more urgent and his tongue finds entrance into my mouth. Our tongues tangle and slide together. Teasing, tasting each other. Oh, goddess, I'm drunk on his taste.

"Mine..." he mouths against my skin as he moves his mouth across my jaw and down my neck hungrily, kissing nipping and licking.

"Constantine..." I bite my lip, but a moan escapes. He slams his lips back on mine and presses my body tighter against his. I roll my hips, making him moan against my mouth. Then he rips his mouth off of me. His breathing ragged. I can hear the rapid beating of his heart along with my own.

My lips are red and swollen, and my heart is still beating fast. I know my hair is all over the place.

Hunger is still evident in his silver-gray eyes as he stares at me. "Oh, goddess..." he groans as he closes his eyes and runs his fingers through his very tousled hair.

"Unless you want to get marked and mated right here and now, we'd better get out of here," he says gruffly. "Are you hungry? Let's go get you some food." He sounds desperate to get out.

He walks in front of me and lead me downstairs and into a massive modern kitchen. All granite with built-in appliances, and white cabinets.

There's a woman, perhaps about two or three years older than I am, wiping the kitchen counter. Human, by the smell of her.

Her eyes light up when she sees Constantine. I recognize a massive crush when I see one.

"Mr. Constantine. I didn't know you're home this early," she says breathlessly. She pushes her chest up and smiles flirtatiously up to him. I can hear her heartbeats speed up.

Her smile falters as soon as she notices me. Constantine pulls me closer and wraps his arm around my waist. "Yeah, we skip school. Found something better to do today," he remarks carelessly, not taking his eyes off me. "Genesis, this is our cook, Lora. Lora, this is my girl, Genesis."

"Hi," I flash her a friendly smile as I wrap my arms around Constantine. That's right, I'm marking my territory. She doesn't look too happy. Her eyes assessing me coldly.

"I'm hungry, let's get something to eat," he murmurs into my ear with a wicked smile that says he knows what I'm doing.

"I'd like my dessert first," he mumbles against my skin before he kisses and licks and nips me along my jawline and down my neck. Oh, goddess, what his sexy mouth can do to me. My brain stops working.

"Costa.." I sigh as I run my fingers through his silky hair.

110

Lora clears her throat loudly. "Would you like me to prepare you something for lunch?"

"No...we'll make a sandwich or something," says Constantine against my neck. "You can go, we'll order pizza for tonight."

She's very annoyed and she's making sure that we know about it. I can hear her stomping her feet and banging the door shut on her way out.

"Do you know that she has a crush on you?"

"Yeah, I don't want her to get any more ideas. I don't want to deal with unwanted attention." His lips begin teasing me behind my ear. That feels so good. I clamp my mouth to stop myself from moaning. His mouth is magic.

Oh, fuzzy bunnies...cuddly slippers...or whatever.

"You smell so good," he murmurs huskily, nuzzling my neck.

I try to think straight. "If you don't want any trouble like that, why'd you hire a young woman?"

"Caspian did," is his only answer as he runs his hand over my hip and pushes me against the kitchen counter. He grinds his body into mine. Delicious chills run up and down my spine.

"Costa..." I moan breathlessly. He groans deep in his throat as his other hand goes into my hair. He tilts my head at an angle to his liking and slams his lips onto mine hungrily. I lose all thoughts as I grab his hair and pull while my other hand moves over his solid wide shoulder and back. His lips are hot and demanding. His hand moves down to stroke my bare thigh.

"We should stop," he mumbles against my lips before he covers them with his again.

"Umm… yeah," I agree as I draw deeper into his kiss.

"Now," he says again before his tongue delves inside my mouth.

Our bodies strain to get closer. Our tongues tangle together.

111

"Mmm... hmm…" I agree as he sucks my bottom lip.

Constantine tears his mouth away from mine with a deep groan. His breathing is uneven. He places both hands on the counter on either side of me and he closes his eyes for a second. Then he opens them again and without turning, he calmly says, "Hello guys."

I try to regain my heartbeat before I slowly peek around him to see three other lycans standing by the entrance of the kitchen with various levels of amusement on their faces.

CHAPTER XIV
The Birds And The Bees Talk

Upon seeing the three faces, I yelp and quickly hide against Constantine's chest. I grip the front of his shirt in embarrassment. My face must be beet red. This is so embarrassing!

"Well, hello, Constantine. Hello, Genesis. Nice to meet you," says a male voice. His voice full of mirth.

"Hi, Genesis," says Serena.

"Hello," says another male voice. Must be Lazarus.

"Hi," I mumble against Constantine's chest. I'm in hiding.

I hear laughter, so I press my face harder against his chest. There's no way I'm coming out to face them now. I hear the rumble of laughter in his chest and feel his body shakes with laughter.

"Sunshine, are you coming out to meet everyone soon?"

I shake my head and close my eyes. *No.*

I feel his warm hand come up to press gently on my back. They are still laughing.

"What are you guys doing home now anyway? It's not even lunch time yet," he asks his friends.

"Oh, we decided to check in on you and have lunch at home. Where is the cook anyway?" says the first male voice.

"I told her to go home. Order some pizza or Chinese or something," answers Constantine offhandedly as he lifts me up and carries me off. I press my face against his neck. I don't know where he's taking me, but I'm not going to look.

"Nice shirt she's wearing," again the first male voice, sounding wicked.

"Just look away, Caspian," growls Constantine, then in a flash, I'm in his room.

There's no end to my embarrassment today, and it's not even noon yet! I must have inherited the genes from my dad, I decide. My ability to land myself in embarrassing situations.

"I blame my dad," I announce once Constantine places me on my feet and closes the bedroom door.

"What?" he asks, looking puzzled.

"The genes that make me prone to embarrass myself," I explain.

"Okay..." His eyebrows furrow. I can see he's trying very hard to follow my logic.

"I mean, my mom's perfectly normal, you know....most of the time. So it must've come from my dad's side." I conclude. It makes perfect sense to me now.

There's a soft knock on the bedroom door and Serena pokes her head in before Constantine says anything.

She walks in and suddenly I feel inadequate. She's so gorgeous. Definitely one of the most beautiful girls I've ever seen. Her skin is smooth and lightly tanned. Right now her beautiful honey brown eyes are filled with warmth and mischief. Her long shiny golden blond hair falls in soft waves down to her waist.

"I'm borrowing her, and she can wear my clothes," she announces.

Constantine places his arm over my shoulders and tugs me to him. "Or she can just stay in here with me and wear mine," he contradicts her.

Serena rolls her eyes. "The boys and I would like to get to know her too. You've got to learn to share, Constantine." She moves in and grabs my hand.

"No I don't," he mumbles sullenly under his breath, but reluctantly releases my shoulders as Serena pulls me away.

"One hour," he says sourly. Now he looks like a little boy whose favorite toy had just been taken away from him. "Then I'm coming to get you," he informs me.

"Four," counters Serena.

"One," he insists.

"Okay, three," she returns.

"One," he states firmly.

"Oh, come on...give a little. Three," she bargains.

"Alright. Two." He sighs.

"He sounded like he just gave up his Ferrari or Aston Martin instead of just two meager hours without you," she complains as she drags me to her room. "Lycans!"

"You know I can still hear you, right?" says Constantine from his room.

"Good," she mumbles with some satisfaction.

These lycans fight like siblings. You would never have guessed from the way they look when you see them in school.

"How did you end up here? I bet there are more exciting places to live in instead of this little town," I inquire curiously as I glance around hers and Lazarus's bedroom.

"Caspian had this idea about attending and graduating high school. Lazarus and I were supposed to accompany him. I don't know how we ended up here really. Knowing Caspian, he probably threw a dart on the map to decide. Constantine was just supposed to be here for a couple of weeks. Maybe come for a visit once in a while. Well, one day he went to get a sketchbook and some pencils at some art supply store. The next thing we knew, he bought the whole studio and registered into the high school with us," she informs me, smiling cheekily.

Serena lends me a pair of jeans and a pretty white and pink floral top. Good thing we're almost the same size. The jeans and the top fit just perfect.

115

"Thank you for lending these to me. I can't imagine going home in Constantine's shirt," I admit. "I'll return them after I wash them."

She waves her hand in dismissal, then pulls me down to sit on the bed next to her.

"It's time for our birds and the bees talk," she announces.

What??? My cheeks must have turned bright red. I can only stare at her. Horrified.

"Oh, it's not like that!" She laughs. "I mean, now that you're with Constantine, you're going to go through changes soon. You see, I was born a werewolf. Just like you...but I'm a lycan now," she reveals.

I stare at her in surprise. She doesn't look like a she-wolf to me. She's all lycan.

A sudden thought occurs to me. I remember how my eyes, my voice, and my body changed yesterday when I went for a run. Also the changes in my body right now in my human form—my curves, my hair, skin.

"What does that mean?" I ask her carefully.

"You know, werewolves are born with mates that fit them like a puzzle. We are born to fit our mates. But lycans don't have that. So when lycans find their erasthai, the erasthai, whether they're humans, or werewolves or fae would soon change to fit the lycans perfectly after the bond between them started. It's the moon goddess gift to her children since lycans are born without mates.

"The changes happen gradually, but eventually, the mate would look like a lycan. Age as slowly and live as long as the lycan. Be as strong and as deadly as a lycan. Basically, you become a lycan. I guess we need that to balance our mates. Lycans are very strong, a human or even a werewolf wouldn't survive the mating with a lycan," explains Serena.

"Genesis, you're going to go through some changes soon. Your wolf will turn into a lycan. Even your human form will turn. We change to look more attractive, which is funny, because how

116

jealous our mates can get. Lycans are very possessive. It's going to be hard to deal with at first. But you'll find a way around it...we all do," she says.

"Oh how?"

"I think you're already doing it." She laughs.

"Oh, come on, Serena. Tell me! I'm truly lost at how to deal with Constantine sometimes," I plead.

"Why, by using your feminine wiles, of course," she winks at me with a wicked smile on her lips. "You catch more flies with honey, as my aunt used to say."

I burst out laughing. I can just imagine Serena using her feminine wiles on the intimidating Lazarus. Then I imagine me, trying to use feminine wiles on Constantine.

Yikes! My face turns red.

"I can just imagine what's going on in that pretty head of yours." Serena laughs.

I cover my face with my hands. I bet my face is as red as a tomato right now. "Oh, young Genesis, you're adorable." She laughs harder.

"How long did it take for you to change into a lycan? You know, when you phase?" I need to know. And I need to change the subject before I turn into a big red tomato and explode!

"For me, it took almost six months. I could see the changes when I phase, I could feel the power and the bond growing. It was amazing. But every mate is different. Physical changes in human form happened so slowly to me that nobody around me noticed much difference. I noticed that my hair seemed fuller, my features more defined somehow, my body changed within a year or two."

I know I'm changing, but it's very sudden to me. Not like what Serena is saying. My friends certainly noticed the difference in me. I'm already phasing into a lycan, judging by what happened yesterday.

"I'm glad you're Constantine's mate, Genesis. I like you. I think we're going to be great friends." She smiles sincerely.

I think so too... and I think I'm hungry. I could smell pizza. "Oh, what's the deal with the cook?" I ask her as we descend the stairs.

Serena scrunches up her nose in disgust. "Constantine threw her out of his room the other day. She claimed that she's cleaning his room. We have cleaners. She's a damn cook! She's the fifth cook we have this year. Caspian did the hiring. Cooking isn't necessarily the most important qualification for the job," adds Serena.

"Hey, some things are important to whet the appetite," remarks Caspian from the living room.

"You'd better get rid of her. Her cooking isn't too bad, but she's becoming a nuisance," cuts in Lazarus.

"This is my mate Lazarus," says Serena happily as she wraps her hands around his arm.

"It's nice to finally properly meet you," remarks Lazarus. He has the most striking blue eyes I have ever seen. His jet black hair is slightly long and curly. They make an extremely striking, good looking couple.

"Hi, I'm Caspian. It's a pleasure to finally meet you." Caspian takes my hand in his. His bright bottle green eyes sparkle with mischief. Like the rest of them, he is gorgeous. His face is a chiseled perfection and his light blond hair is thick and shiny and perfectly styled in a quiff. He brings my hand up to kiss it, but Constantine snatches it away before it reaches his lips.

"We're going," he snaps.

"She hasn't had any pizza yet...and you've got to learn to share, bruh," says Caspian playfully. His lips curl up in amusement.

Constantine growls in irritation.

"Owww." Caspian yelps. Lazarus had smacked him at the back of his head.

I cover my mouth to stop the laughter from escaping. Constantine isn't looking very amused.

It's nice to meet the rest of the lycans, but I need to talk to Constantine about what's going on and Alpha Carrington's plan. I couldn't talk to him about it this morning when he was trying to hold on to his control. I hope he won't lose his control this time.

*　　　*　　　*

"We never got to eat, you must be hungry," remarks Constantine as he keys in the code. A metal door smoothly slides open to reveal the biggest garage I've ever seen. There must be more than ten cars in there and several motorcycles. Why would they need that many cars? From practical sedans and SUVs to fancy sports cars. There is a BMW, a Jeep, a Buick, a Ferrari, a Porsche, a Bugatti. *Just wow!* There are a few other exotic cars that I have never seen before and have no idea what the make of them, but my mouth waters at the sight of a red 1967 Corvette. *That baby is totally lickable!*

Constantine smiles at the direction where my eyes are drawn to.

"Which one is yours?" I ask him.

"The Ferrari, the Aston Martin, the eco-friendly Tesla we arrived in today, and also the Ducati over there," He points at one of the motorbikes in there.

"The Corvette belongs to Caspian, but I don't think he would mind if we took it for a spin," he adds as he opens a metal cabinet by the wall and produces a set of keys.

"Let's go," He winks as he unlocks the Corvette.

"What do you feel like having, sunshine?" he asks as he accelerates and shifts into 4th gear.

"Anything goes," I whisper in a daze. I stare at the red smooth leather interior of the car. I'm in heaven. I'm in a 1967 Corvette Stingray. I'll eat anything.

Constantine's lips twitch as if he's trying hard not to laugh. His silver gray eyes are full of amusement. I love the way he handles

119

the car. I love watching the way his strong elegant fingers glide on the steering wheel. The way he confidently changes the gear, the way the muscle of his powerful arms contract as he moves and grips the wheel or the gear knob.

I imagine those hands on me—

Fuzzy slippers! Get your mind out of the gutter, woman! Is it hot in here, or is it just me? I need to fan myself, but of course, I'm not going to do that.

His sharp clever eyes rarely miss anything when it comes to me. By the wicked look in his silver gray eyes, he must have an idea what I've been thinking about, which doesn't help my blushing problem.

*   *   *

We end up in an Italian restaurant. I can still remember the smell of that pizza they had in their home and I feel like having pizza now.

The moment we're out of the car, his hand moves to touch the small of my back and stays there. I can feel the warmth of his hand burning through the fabric. My heart starts doing the flip flops again.

Constantine requests a private booth, and we are lead and seated way at the back where nobody can see us. He sits next to me on the bench and places his hand on my thigh underneath the table as soon as we are seated.

The young waiter who comes to take our order stares at me the whole time. I can tell that he's a werewolf. The teenager doesn't take his eyes off me even when he's taking Constantine's order. That earns him a growl and a cold stare from Constantine. He's wise enough to lower his gaze after that.

As soon as the waiter leaves, he pulls me up into his lap and nuzzles my neck, breathing me in. "Genesis," he groans against my neck. "What are you doing to me?"

Shivers run down my spine. "What do you mean?" I ask breathlessly. If he's not careful, I'd jump him right now.

"We lycans are very dangerous. Losing our temper would mean death to those around us. I'm usually very good at controlling my temper. Most lycans do, but with you, I lose control so easily. I could have easily murdered that alpha mutt and other students this morning. Snap that waiter's head just now. With you, I have no control."

"Must you be in control all the time?" I whisper before my lips touch the skin of his throat. My tongue flicks out to taste it. *Mmm.* Yes, totally lickable. With him, my body has a mind of its own.

He groans deep in his throat. "Careful sweetheart." His voice is rough. "You don't know what you're saying." His hand goes into my hair and pulls my head to the side, then his lips attacked my neck. My head rolls back. His lips are magical. Did I say that already?

We are interrupted by the same waiter who is now looking quite uncomfortable, bringing our drinks. His face is bright red as he notes how we're sitting. I try to climb off his lap, but Constantine just tightens his hold on me even more.

"The poor guy looked like he's about to die on the spot," I whisper, as soon as the guy leaves.

"Well, now he knows that you belong to me," he remarks possessively.

He lowers his head and rains soft kisses on my cheeks and along my jaw. "You take over my senses completely, sunshine. When we're in the kitchen, I didn't hear my friends until they entered the house," he whispers in between open mouth kisses. "I'm so addicted to you."

We can't seem to get enough of each other. Now I don't remember why I asked him for some time. I think I'm ready to be fully claimed and marked by him. *Now!*

He only reluctantly lets me off his lap once our food arrives. The waiter cleared our table after we're done. While waiting for our dessert, I fidget with my napkin as I contemplate of how to tell him about Logan's and Alpha Carrington's plan.

"Okay, what is it, sunshine? There's something obviously bothering you. Are you going to tell me about it soon?"

How do I break it to him without him losing his temper? I really have no idea, so I just blurt it out.

"Well...uh, Alpha Carrington wants me to be mated and marked by Logan soon. He wants it done before the party when they're announcing us as Alpha and Luna of the pack."

He doesn't say a word, so I continue, "Constantine, they're planning the party for tomorrow night."

He is so silent. Then he closes his eyes and he clenches his jaw tight. His hands are balled into tight fists. He doesn't utter a word for a good three minutes. It worries me.

"Costa?" I whisper hesitantly. Dangerous vibes radiate off him like tidal waves.

I touch his arm gently and he turns his head and opens his eyes. My breath catches in my throat. Two chasms of black cold pits stare back at me.

I climb up to sit on his lap, straddling him. My hands move up to stroke his cheeks gently before I tangle them in his thick dark silky hair. He closes his eyes and fiercely jerks me into him. His shoves his face into the crook of my neck, nuzzling me there roughly.

I comb my fingers through his silky hair gently and he arches his head back. His eyes closed, his long, sooty eyelashes fan across his cheeks. The expression on his beautiful face is the mixture of torture and ecstasy. My heart flips at the sight. I want to be the cause of more of that look on his face, but certainly not this way.

"Tell me that you're mine," he demands in a thick deep voice that doesn't sound quite like him. My fingers tighten in his hair and he groans as he leans down and presses his face into my neck once again.

"Constantine, I'm yours."

"You're mine. All mine and only mine," he growls against my skin. His powerful sinewy arms holding me tight. "I'll destroy anyone who dares to take you away from me."

CHAPTER XV
Meet The Parents

Constantine thinks that it's time that he should meet my parents. I think so too. People at school already know that I'm with a lycan by now. News like that travels fast; it's better that my parents hear it from us, rather than from someone else.

I ask him to come back later so that I can break it to my parents first before they meet him. They'll be home pretty soon.

"Why can't I come in with you now? I'll be very good," he promises. He constantly needs to be touching me, especially after I told him about Alpha Carrington's plan. It's like he needs to reassure himself that I'm his and nobody's taking me away from him.

"Really? You promise to behave?" I raise an eyebrow at him disbelievingly.

"I didn't say I'll behave. I said I'll be good...very good." His lips curl up into a sexy, naughty smile. His silver gray eyes alight with mischief.

"That's what I'm afraid of," I replied, suppressing a thousand butterflies about to break free in my tummy at the look on his gorgeous face. It's still hard for me to believe that this beautiful, powerful lycan is mine.

"Are you telling me that you didn't enjoy it, sunshine?" He nibbles my ear. I shriek out and laugh. That tickles. I peek out to see if any neighbors are looking at us in the car.

"Bad bad boy." I admonish him, trying to sound stern. I totally ruin it by grinning at the end. "I'll see you in three hours. They'll be home and informed by then." They usually have an employee, Mrs. Adams, or her daughter looking after the store in the evenings.

"30 minutes," he announces, kissing the corner of my lips.

"What???"

"Okay, one hour," he says with a charming grin, flashing his straight white teeth. Blinding me with his dazzling smile. I walk out in a daze. Did I agree to it? I must have, right? I don't remember though.

Gah! I suck! One smile and he get what he wants. I'm such a sucker for his gorgeous face. Time for my self-pep talk.

My mom and dad are surprisingly home when I get in. It's funny how I didn't even notice dad's car parked outside in my Constantine induced stupor.

They are both in the kitchen talking quietly with a pot of coffee between them. Serious expression on their faces. Oooppss. Maybe this is not a good time. I move my feet slowly and silently backward.

"Hi honey," says mom looking up, before I can retreat further. My super ninja skills fail me this time. I slowly trudged my way back into the kitchen, defeated by my mom.

Dad doesn't even raise his head. "We have things to discuss," he states. His brows furrow with apprehension.

There are worry lines between mom's eyes.

I take my seat nervously and wait for them to go on.

"Honey, your Grandpa Quentin is coming over," announces mom.

"Oh, that's great!" I exclaim, smiling in relief.

Phew! For a minute there I thought they were about to tell me that they had accidentally killed a cuddly bunny or threw out my fuzzy old slippers or something.

My Grandpa Quentin is tough, but he loves me and Autumn. He visited us twice, and we visited him and his pack a few times throughout the years.

"Isn't it?" I ask hesitantly, suddenly puzzled by their silence and the serious expression on their faces.

"Why didn't you tell us, sweetie?" asks dad suddenly.

"Uh...tell you what?" I hedge, reminding myself to tread carefully. There are a lot of things I haven't told my parents. I don't want to spill anything I don't need to...ninja skills.

"Why didn't you tell us that Logan was planning to keep you as...as.." Dad's face turns red. "Well...and make Gamma Brown's daughter his luna?"

What? I almost fell off my chair. How did they know?

"Your grandpa and uncle heard about this. That is outrageous, and you know how proud my family is," says dad, shaking his head angrily.

How? How did he know?

"I think they have an inside informant around here." Mom sighs, answering my unvoiced question.

My dad suddenly looks tired. "They have taken offense. To your Grandpa, that is not only rejecting his alpha lineage, but it's also an unforgivable insult to our family and his pack.

"I happen to agree with this. This is not only an insult to you but our family as well."

Oh, no. This is such a mess! Grandpa Quentin always has a strong dislike of Alpha Carrington for placing my dad as an Omega in this pack—and now this.

"Your uncle Ashton has your mating arranged to Alpha Vyacheslav from the Red Convel pack," adds mom. "Your grandpa and Alpha Vyacheslav are coming to take us with them tomorrow since Alpha Carrington refused to release us."

Wait! What?

"No, no, no, no." Constantine is going to flip!

126

"Honey? Are you okay? Breathe sweetheart," says mom urgently as she stroke my back not very gently.

I think I'm hyperventilating. That's good, right? At least I'm not seeing red.

I hear a knock, and I go flying to the door.

"Constantine!"

I fling myself into his arms. His warm strong arms wrap around me tightly. His body shields me protectively, ready for any kind of threat.

"What's the matter, sweetheart?" he asks gently when he didn't sense any danger.

I cling my arms tighter around his neck, breathing in his scent. It calms me down. I'm his, and he's mine. Nobody can take me away from him, right? Or him away from me?

He let me hold on to him like that while his hand moving up and down my back soothingly.

When I'm calmed enough, I realize where we are. I pull back to look at my parents who are standing very still behind me, staring at us both, looking shocked.

"Hello," says Constantine, who seems to be the first to recover.

"You're...you're a lycan," stammers my mom, still in shock.

"Why yes I am, ma'am," answers Constantine smiling innocently. I could've kicked his shin. I can see how amused he is through those beautiful silver-gray eyes of his.

"Mom, dad, this is Constantine. Costa, this is my mom, Lavinia and my dad Aaron Fairchild."

"Good to meet you, Mr. and Mrs. Fairchild," says Constantine, extending his hand to my parents, while his other hand is still resting on my lower back.

My dad finally recovers enough to shake his hand. "Would you have a seat, Constantine?" he says with an awkward gesture.

I'm not sure if my parents ever talked to a lycan before, let alone have one in their home.

127

My parents take their seat on a sofa. Constantine pulls me next to him on a loveseat when I'm about to sit on a chair next to it. He automatically twines our fingers together and places them on his lap.

My parents observe us both with curious eyes. My dad clears his throat. "So..." he says, awkwardly. "What's going on?" he finally asks.

I know he doesn't want to be rude to a lycan, but he's very curious as well.

"Well, Mr. Fairchild. Genesis is my erasthai. She's my mate," states Constantine.

It takes a while for my parents to recover from the shock after Constantine's announcement.

My mom puts her hand on her chest. Then she puts up her hand over her forehead and declares, "You know what, honey? I'm glad we only have two daughters."

"Yeah," says dad. "We should be thankful that we have at least two years to recover from this before Autumn turns eighteen."

The both of them look at each other, then they promptly burst out laughing. Did I tell you that my parents have the most bizarre sense of humor? I'm glad I didn't take after them in that department. I'm glad I'm the normal one in this family.

My face must have turned bright red as I look up at Constantine who stares at my parents as if they'd grown multiple extra heads. Then he looks at me with a raised eyebrow. I smile up at him sheepishly.

"Well, then, I think we have things to discuss," says dad. "I don't know much about lycans and about what being mated to one means, but I know about erasthai. I'm not standing in the way of erasthai. Personally, I'm glad. Genesis has been through a lot. I hope you'll treat her right and make her happy."

"Don't worry, Mr. Fairchild, she's my everything. I'll treasure her and protect her with my life," promises Constantine.

My dad seems to be satisfied with that. Mom has tears in her eyes.

I'm glad we have my parents' blessings. My parents mean the world to me. They've been through a lot these last couple of weeks because of me.

Dad nods his head. "Seeing that you're together, there are things that you should know about."

Remembering Constantine's reaction to the news about Alpha Carrington's plan earlier, I take both of his hands in mine and turn to look at him. "Remember what I told you about Alpha Carrington's plan for tomorrow night?"

His expression turns grim.

"Don't get mad okay?" I grip his hands firmly in mine

"Things just got a little bit more complicated," announces my dad.

Surprisingly Constantine doesn't lose his temper like he did before when my dad informed him of the latest mess. His hands tighten around mine when dad told him about the Alpha of Red Convel Pack coming to claim me.

His silver-gray eyes look thoughtful after that like he's contemplating something.

*   *   *

After that talk with my parents, Constantine took me out for some ice-cream, then we came back to his massive house again.

"So, I heard that you like my Corvette Stingray," says Caspian, looking mischievous. "You know, I can be persuaded to part with it...at a price."

We're now sitting in their living room with the rest of the lycans. Caspian is sitting lazily on one of the plush cozy chairs with his long legs resting on the coffee table.

"You name the price, I'll pay for it," says Constantine.

"No, you don't have to buy the car for me, Costa," I object from my sitting position on his lap.

"No, I don't want your money," states Caspian. "I want my payment from Genesis."

"From me? You pick a wrong person, buddy. I don't have the money to pay for it. I'm dirt poor," I announce proudly.

Serena giggled from where she's lying on the sofa with her head on Lazarus's lap.

"No, I don't want your money, I want a kiss—"

"No!" growls Constantine, tightening his arms around me.

"—On my cheek," finishes Caspian.

"No!" he growls again. "I'll pay for it, just name the price. She's not kissing you anywhere."

Caspian is having too much fun annoying Constantine. This time Caspian gets hit on the head by a flying magazine thrown by Serena.

I like spending time with them, even with Caspian. He's a harmless flirt who likes to banter about everything. He's such a kid.

CHAPTER XVI
I'm a Bunny Cuddler Fuzzy Slipper Wearer

I refused a lift from my friends, and I refused a lift from Constantine this morning. I arrive late to school on purpose and try to hide from everybody by using my mad ninja skills.

Again, my mad ninja skills fail me. Constantine finds me so easily. He wraps his arms around me and buries his face against my neck as soon as he sees me. I'm beginning to suspect that I might not have mad ninja skills after all.

After that, he has his arm around my shoulders and won't let go. Serena, Lazarus and Caspian walk with us. Serena and Lazarus walk hand in hand. They always do. It's kinda weird to be walking with the lycans like I was one of them now.

I get a lot of stares, especially hateful stares from the girls. Strangely, some of the girls get even more brazen. They're giving the lycans even more shameless, flirtatious looks, more top buttons undone and even shorter skirts.

I think it occurs to them now that I'm with a lycan, they might have a chance to be with one too. The problem is, they're not only blatantly flirty with Caspian, but with Lazarus and Constantine as well. It annoys Serena as much as it annoys me.

During lunch, my friends join us at the lycan's usual table. Constantine keeps me on his lap the whole time. His hand around my waist and on my thigh, keeping me in place. Once in a while, his face nuzzles my neck. His lips doing things to my skin that makes my toes curl.

At first, Penny, Reese, and River keep staring at the lycans in awe. The lycans don't talk much around other people. That is so different from the way they were at home.

They are so silent that after a while, I think my friends forget that the lycans are there, and start acting like themselves again. My friends start their pointless bickering like they usually do. Today's important squabble is whether chips are better than fries. Penny loves fries. She has fries almost every day during lunch. River can't survive without chips. The discussion gets so heated after a while that Penny almost threw her fries at River's head. Almost, because "fries are too yummy and precious to be wasted on River's stupid head". Penny's words.

Reese and I can't help but join in their dispute at one point. It is an important topic to discuss after all. Constantine listens attentively, without saying a word. His lips curl up slightly in amusement.

"Your friends are very entertaining to watch," whispers Caspian in my ear later on.

"Entertaining good or bad?" I narrow my eyes at him.

"Ouch, your distrust in me hurts my feelings, Red."

"Red?"

"Yup. You've red hair. Red."

"Don't call me Red, Casper."

"Don't call me Casper, Red."

"Don't call me Red, Caspy."

"Caspy???"

Constantine pulls me away from Caspian, shaking his head in disbelief. This is not going to be the end of our pointless bickering, though. I know it's going to be continued later on.

Logan and all his friends aren't in school today. I think Constantine broke Logan's arm yesterday. Mia and her followers keep giving me dirty looks every time they see me.

Just before the last period, Constantine and the rest of the lycans have to leave school. They say they have 'things to attend to.'

Constantine pulls me outside with him before he leaves.

"I've been wanting to do this the whole day," he mutters before he pulls me flush against him and leans down to place his lips on mine. Fireworks and explosions erupt where our bodies meet. His lips are magical! His lips move against mine, and I forget everything. His tongue slips into my mouth, and I grab a fistful of his hair and tug him closer. He moans deep in his throat, and his kiss gets hungrier and more demanding. His hand moves to wrap my leg around his waist, molding my body closer to his.

Somebody blares the car horn.

"Damn it, Caspian!" He curses, then he leans down for more kisses.

Caspian honks the second time when he finally pulls back. We both breathing raggedly. He nuzzles my neck and breathes me in deeply before he finally let me go. Then he turns around, walks away, and gets into the car without looking back.

I wish he didn't have to leave. I miss him already.

I know I can't go into the classroom looking the way I'm looking right now, so I walk on unsteady legs to the nearest washroom.

I'm so glad that it is empty. Most of the other students must have gone into their classrooms.

I stare at my reflection in the mirror. My hair is all messed up, my lips are red and swollen, my cheeks are flushed, and my clothes are rumpled.

Mia walks in while I'm still fixing myself.

"You must be feeling so good about yourself right now, aren't you?" she says as she locks the door behind her.

Huh?

At my puzzled expression, she snaps,"You must be so proud of having two guys that all the girls in this school want most to be fighting over you."

"No, I don't want anybody to be fighting over me," I reply quickly, watching her warily through the mirror above the sink.

"Oh please, drop the innocent act already," she cries out exasperatedly. "You can stop pretending. I know what a girl like you wants."

"A girl like me?" I narrow my eyes, still looking at her in the mirror.

"Yeah, a nobody. An omega slut of the pack," she spits out venomously. "Always acting so innocent. Must be a dream come true to you to be mated to Logan....quite a jump, from a lowly omega to a mate of an alpha. Unfortunately for you, I was in the way wasn't I? But you're so ambitious. I don't know how you did it, but of all the boys in the school, you managed to snag a lycan. A lycan! You are craftier than I give you credit for. You must be very good in bed. A lycan wants you. Now Logan wants you! How can he choose you over me??? We had a plan and you're ruining it. I'm supposed to be the luna! Me!"

She's now screaming like a crazy bitch. She's getting on my nerves. Really badly. I feel a little heat is starting in my chest.

"You're a nobody! A nobody! I warned you to stay away from him. I'll make sure you'll pay for this, you dirty slut!" She moves in closer and raises her hand to strike my face.

My hand comes up to grip her wrist in reflex. Another hand closes around her throat. She's really really getting on my nerves. I lug her by the throat across the room.

Heavy bitch!

Her feet flailing and dragging across the floor. Her eyes are bulging in her face.

I slam her head against the wall. "I hate it when people yell in my face," I inform her. "I'll stay away from me if I were you. The next time you decide to throw a tantrum like that in my face, I won't be quite as forgiving." I'm throwing her own words back at her.

I squeeze her neck harder before I let go. She falls on the floor wheezing and coughing, clutching at her neck.

I check myself in the mirror, straightening my hair and my shirt. Then I unlock the door and stalk out of there not feeling any better. I wanted to pummel her face in. I walk a little faster because I'm so tempted to go back in there and do just that.

Feeling restless, I decided to go to the library instead of my classroom. Half the lesson is over by now anyway. By the time I reach the library on the third floor, my heart returns to normal. The heat in my chest is gone.

I sit at the very back of the library, wondering how I got so violent. I truly wanted to kill her. Now even the thought of it makes me feel sick. What has gotten into me?

I bang my head against the table loudly several times. "Really Genesis? Really?? Violence is not the answer." I admonish myself. You're a peaceful werewolf. You're a peace lover, tree hugger, bunny cuddler, fuzzy slipper wearer werewolf." I lecture myself as I bang my head on the table a few more times for good measure.

Someone clears her throat. I look up to see Mrs. McBee, our stern librarian, glaring at me suspiciously from over the top of her half-moon-shaped reading glasses.

I must be looking super crazy. I think she's thinks that I'm a very unstable and untrustworthy person to be around her precious books right now.

*   *   *

I stare in disbelief as one black SUV after another pulls up in front of the Pack's house. How many people is Grandpa Quentin bringing with him? The whole army?

I think all the whole pack members are here, staring in amazement like I am right now. Big strong men come out of the vehicles.

Alpha Carrington and Logan are standing at the front with the pack's beta and gamma and delta, along with the elders and some head warriors.

I can see Luna Catherine with the other women there. I recognize some kids from school as well. I spot Mia and her minions in the crowd. She has a scarf around her neck. So I left a mark on her. I feel Ezra's gleeful satisfaction. My wolf somehow worries me a bit these days. I can feel how she's changing.

We just arrived, and I'm standing in the crowd with my parents and Autumn. Penny, Reese, and River are right behind me. Penny said she wants to be near me so that she can be *close to the action*. I should've supplied her with popcorn before we came.

"Ooohh... so many hot men in suits." I hear her giggle behind me. She sounds like a kid in a candy store.

This seems to be a formal occasion. Grandpa's men are in their suits and ties. Alpha Carrington and his top men are also dressed formally. No wonder mom made me and Autumn put our dresses on. I'm wearing a simple dark blue sheath dress with black pumps. Other pack members and my friends are in their casual clothing though.

My dad ushers us to the front of the crowd as soon as Grandpa Quentin steps out of his black Bentley SUV. He's looking strong and sharp as usual. Werewolves age much slower than human. My grandpa is way over a hundred years old, but he looks like someone in his late 40s. Still handsome and distinguished looking. His dark hair has streaks of white at the temples. His light hazel eyes that look so much like mine and Autumn's are sharp with intelligence.

Grandpa Quentin might be in the elder council now, but he's still acting like an alpha of the pack sometimes. I don't think he can help it. I don't think he will stop anytime soon either.

There's another man I've never seen before standing beside him. He's tall, tough and very good looking, probably in his mid-

20s. He has intense black eyes and jet black hair. I'm guessing he's Alpha Vyacheslav of the Red Convel Pack.

Red Convel Pack is known to be very strong and full of the best warriors in the world. I heard that the pack values strength. It's not uncommon for them to mate with the strongest she-wolves if they can't find mates after a certain age, just to breed strong offspring.

The thought gives me the shudders. I can't be mated to *him!* I don't want to be a breeding machine. Besides, I can't even pronounce his name properly!

Grandpa Quentin shakes dad's hand and gives my mom a brief stiff hug. When he reaches me, his eyes soften. I told you he's tough, but he loves me and Autumn.

"My sweet girl, Genesis," he murmurs as he strokes my cheek briefly. There are regret and something else in his eyes.

The alpha standing next to him stares at me the whole time. I raise my eyes to look at him. I can feel his power. He might be tough, but I feel powerful. My caveman Constantine is more intimidating than any other cavemen out there.

Somehow the alpha seems satisfied with the way I refuse to cower in his strong alpha presence. There's approval in his eyes now and my Grandpa Quentin smiles with pride.

Huh? What was that about? I feel like I'm missing something.

*   *   *

So far, the meeting hasn't been going very well. Both sides aren't backing down.

"Your son planned to replace my granddaughter, a pure alpha blood with a gamma," states my grandfather arrogantly. I notice Gamma Brown winces, then his face turns red.

"I had no knowledge of this until recently. For that I am deeply sorry," apologizes Alpha Carrington. "However, that has

137

been rectified, they will be mated and announce alpha and luna soon. I don't see any more issues."

"Oh, there are still issues. The damage has been done. You have deeply insulted us and hurt my granddaughter, then you're forcing them to stay when they wish to move back to our pack. Besides, I have Alpha Vyacheslav of the Red Convel Pack who's willing to accept her as his mate."

"But she's my son's true mate! You have no right to interfere!" yells Alpha Carrington. "This is an internal issue! It should only concern members of my pack!"

"This concerns my granddaughter. Your son has rejected her and disrespected her in the worst way possible and now you won't let her leave. Your pack has not only seriously insulted my family, but you're holding them prisoners!" states my grandfather heatedly. "I'm here just to take my family back."

"You're here to take our future luna away!" interrupts an elder from Shadow Geirolf Pack Council. Then the others from both sides start to join in and yell at the same time.

I think I'm going to have a headache soon.

Penny squeezes my shoulder from behind. River, Reese, and Penny somehow managed to sneak in and grab seats behind us. The huge Pack assembly room is jam-packed. Many pack members are standing and squeezing in at the back.

"Only you can create such a drama, Genesis," Penny whispers in my ear gleefully. "If they have a war over this, you'll be like Helen of Troy or something." She sighs.

What? Who the heck wants to be Helen of Troy? They're not going to have a war over something stupid like this, are they?

"They're not going to have a war over something stupid like this, are they?" I ask my mom worriedly.

"Of course not, dear," says mom, patting my arm. She looks oddly calm. She even has a little smile on her lips. My father is looking very relaxed too.

138

I turn to look at Reese and River. Reese has her head resting on River's shoulder. Both of them give me thumbs up.

Seriously? What's wrong with my family and friends? Why am I the only one who's freaking out about all this?

I lean forward and hide my face in my arms on my lap. If I was a snake, I would slither away and hide under a rock somewhere. Too bad I'm a werewolf. If I was a bird, I'd be a tiny hummingbird and fly quickly away and disappear. Too bad I'm a werewolf. If I was a chameleon....

A sudden silence makes me lift my head up. All attention falls to the back of the room. I turn around to see five figures walking down the aisle between the seats.

Lycans! Five of them. Their formidable power and compelling presence dominate the room.

My eyes quickly seek Constantine. I've never seen him in a suit before, but he's looking imposing and stunning in his dark blue suit. The tailored cut fits him perfectly. The fabric clings to his well muscled, broad shoulders. You could tell how beautifully build he is underneath the formal suit. I can't take my eyes off of him. His expression is solemn and his silver-gray eyes cold. As soon as his eyes fall on me, I can sense other emotion in them, and my lips involuntarily form a smile. I find an answering smile in his eyes even though his lips don't move. His eyes are telling me so many things that words can't say right now. His eyes make me feel safe.

Lazarus and Caspian are looking impressive and are striking in their suits as well. Serena looks breathtakingly gorgeous in a simple black dress. Her shiny blond hair is in a perfect elegant chignon.

The lycan next to Constantine, I recognize as Lord Archer. He's a well known and well respected Ambassador of the Palace. He's an important liaison between the palace and the packs around the world. I've seen his pictures but never seen him in real life before.

All five of them are looking forbidding but perfect and beautiful. Almost out of this world. Untouchable.

Logan bristles, while Alpha Carrington, grandpa Quentin, and the rest of the men look shocked at the appearance of the lycans.

"Your Excellency Lord Archer, it's an honor to have you here, but I don't understand to what do we owe this honor of your presence?" asks Alpha Carrington with awe and respect.

"We are here because you are laying claim to one of us," answers Lord Archer.

"No, she's my mate. She rightfully belongs to me," Logan suddenly protests.

Constantine growls. Lord Archer places a gentle hand on his arm.

"It's funny how you're fighting over a living, intelligent being, yet you never asked her, not even once what she really wants," continues Lord Archer.

"But she's rightfully mine," argues Logan.

"Young, Mr. Carrington, you rejected her. Which is of no consequence. Genesis Fairchild is now one of us," he replies with a touch of arrogance and annoyance.

"With all respect, Lord Archer, Genesis is my granddaughter. She's a werewolf. How is she one of you?" inquires my grandfather, looking puzzled.

Constantine holds his hand out for me. His eyes expectant like that day in the woods near our school. He's standing there waiting for me, looking strong and beautiful, yet only I can see the emotions in his eyes as he stares at me. And suddenly he's all I can see.

I get up from my seat, walk over to him and place my hand in his. His hand is warm and strong. There's a look in his eyes now that I can't look away from. His eyes are always mesmerizing me.

He pulls me to his side. "She is claimed and bonded to Prince Constantine Dimitri Romanov, nephew of King Alexandros Romanov, Lord of the Lycans and Werewolves."

CHAPTER XVII
I Show You Mine, You Show Me Yours

None of the representatives from our pack or Red Convel Pack seems happy with the outcome of the meeting. When the king and the lycans are involved, nobody can do anything but obey. The only person who seems to be very satisfied with the result is my grandfather Quentin. His granddaughter is claimed by a lycan. His pack now has a connection to the royalty. That's quite an honor to our family, he claimed. He walks out of the pack meeting room looking extremely proud and pleased. Alpha Carrington looks visibly upset, and Logan looks furious.

I watch my dad, grandfather Quentin, Alpha Carrington, Lord Archer, Lazarus, Caspian, and Constantine talk outside the pack assembly and party building.

I'm standing under a tree, quite away from everybody else. Serena is standing beside me, looking calm and elegant.

"How did you and Lazarus meet?" I ask her curiously.

A soft smile plays on her lips. "We met during the Great Smog of London in 1952," she says.

That explains the trace of British accent that I can still hear when she talks.

"I was almost 19, I had no family apart from an aunt and my uncle who raised me. I hadn't yet found my mate and was about to be forced to marry a man 20 years my senior. Lazarus just appeared out of nowhere...in the smog. Though there's nothing romantic about the dreadful smog, I thought he was the most beautiful-looking man I'd ever seen. I couldn't take my eyes off of him. I thought if I blinked, he'd disappear." She laughs softly. "We mated and marked each other soon after we met. He took me away from there. Here I am with him now. The only place I want to be. With him."

That got me thinking about me and Constantine. I know I asked for more time...but I'm more than ready to mate and be marked by him now. The Question is, how do I tell him that I'm ready? I can't just bring the subject up. Cuddly bunnies! I'd die of embarrassment.

"You're blushing again. Now what are you thinking?" inquires Serena with an amused, curious look on her exquisite face.

"Uh...Constantine and I, we haven't mated or marked each other yet. I told him I'd like some time."

"But now you're ready," she states, rather than ask. "You know, it's really hard for them to wait. Their instinct is to mark and mate with you right away. I think Constantine is trying to show you how far he's willing to go for you...even if it kills him. He just needs a little signal or a gentle encouragement. That's all."

"How?"

She giggles and whispers wickedly in my ear, "You seduce him."

Seduce him. Okay, seduce him. How?

All the images flitting in my head about how I could go about seducing him are making me hot, bothered, embarrassed, and a little bit dizzy.

After a little while, Constantine disengages himself from the group. His gray eyes zone in on me right away as if he knew where I am at the whole time. He walks over, and my heartbeat accelerates. His dark hair is mussed up sexily, wind-blown. His suit, impeccable except for his tie, being swept aside by the wind.

"See you around, Serena," he says without taking his eyes off of me as he takes hold of my hand.

Serena laughs softly and gives me a wink.

"Where are we going?" I ask him as he ushers me into his Aston Martin DB11.

"I have something to show you," he answers, as he gracefully slides behind the wheel, looking a bit apprehensive.

"What is it?" He's making me a bit nervous.

"No matter what I show you, would you promise not to freak out and run away from me?"

Now he's really making me nervous. "Uh...okay? What is it?"

He doesn't answer me. Instead, he glances at me from the corner of his eyes and takes my hand in his over the center armrest between us. He's holding my hand so tightly like he's never letting it go.

"So, your uncle is the king, huh?" I ask instead, after a few minutes of silence.

"Yeah," he answers as he maneuvers the car out onto the main street. The roar of the engine is enough to set my pulse racing. Everything about him screams power and wealth and beauty. I wonder what he sees in me.

"Why didn't you tell me?"

"Would it make any difference?" he lifts one perfect eyebrow.

I sit silently for a while, thinking. "No," I answer. Well, it really doesn't matter to me.

"Alexandros has been king for five hundred years now. He expressed his desire to step down and hand the reign to his son, Caspian. My idiot cousin, unfortunately, doesn't show enough maturity nor desire to be a king. He is much like my father, free-spirited and footloose. Since I had been carrying most of his royal duties, his father threatened to pass the throne down to me. I doubt that would happen, but still, I'm desperate to get him to grow up soon."

"Caspian? Growing up soon? Might take a few more hundred years," I try hard not to laugh. Oh, poor Constantine. That's a near-impossible task. Constantine looks seriously worried, so I try to look serious, but I think I fail miserably.

He looks at me and grins. "I know, Caspian isn't the most mature person...but laugh now, if I was crowned king, you'll be queen."

Oh uh, I didn't think of that!

Suddenly Constantine laughs. "You should've seen your face, my love. Not so funny now, huh?"

"No. We've got to get Caspian ready to be king...though just the thought of that is scary," I shudder. I don't think I ever want to be a queen. I can't imagine Caspian as a king either. "Either way, we're doomed." I wail. "Let's not think about it yet. It might be a few hundred years in the future, right? Right???"

"Tell me about your family," I ask him instead when he doesn't answer me right away.

"My parents love traveling the world. That's why I was born in Bucharest. My parents traveled even when my mother was heavily pregnant with me. My uncle, King Alexandros is more of a father to me than my own father. Caspian is more like a brother than a cousin to me. Lazarus is also my cousin from my mother's side. He's one of the best warriors and Caspian's personal companion and guardian. We're like brothers."

"You don't have any siblings?"

"No, I'm the only child. Thank goddess. Even though my parents are good lycans, they're not the greatest parents."

"So you, Lazarus, and Caspian grew up together, huh?"

"Yeah, Lazarus, Caspian...and Antonia." He sighs. "She was like a little sister to me." There's heaviness in his voice.

"What happened?"

"She was killed by the rebels."

"I'm sorry." I don't know what else to say to that.

"That was over a hundred years ago." He shrugs.

145

"It still bothers you though." I observe.

"I don't get how they did it. It's not easy to kill a lycan...even Antonia. A bunch of them were arrested and prosecuted.

"Antonia would've loved you and I've no doubt that you would've loved her. She's the sweetest and the gentlest soul...and kind, much like you." He smiles gently.

"You sure you're talking about me?" I smile up at him.

"Yes, my sunshine." He declares confidently, lifting up my hand and kisses it. "You might be silly...and funny...and the weirdest girl I've ever met." he grins adorably. "And I love that about you, but you're also sweet and gentle, and kind."

"Ha! The weirdest girl? I should be offended by that!" I huff and squeeze his hand playfully. "But if she's half as sweet as Serena, I know I would've loved her," I tell him sincerely.

"Come with me," he says, holding out his hand to me as soon as we arrive at his home.

I'm feeling nervous about what he's about to show me, but I place my hand in his and he leads me up to the second floor. He stops before a door next to his bedroom and enters a code on a keypad on the door.

He hesitates and looks thoughtful before he opens the door to a big room with a high ceiling. Three big arched windows are dominating the northern wall, letting plenty of natural light in.

A big wooden easel stands in the center with a stool. Another smaller easel by a wall. A wooden table with paint tubes, jars of brushes and palette knives, and cans of mediums all over them.

It's a studio! His painting studio.

Paintings are all over the walls. There are a few propped up against the walls on the floor. I look closer at them. Are those of me? I look at the various paintings of me around the room, all over the walls. Various poses. Various expressions. There's me staring longingly out the window, probably in a classroom. Me with a

146

mischievous look in my eyes. Me smiling. Me looking thoughtful. Me looking bored. Me looking very young, probably from three years ago. There are pencil sketches and drawings of me too.

Wow, there must be close to a hundred of them. I didn't count them, but there are a lot! This whole studio is like a shrine to me. It doesn't freak me out though. I'm flattered . . . and relieved.

Constantine's eyes never leave my face the whole time I was studying the room.

"Nobody was ever allowed in," he says quietly. "Are you going to run away screaming from me now?"

"Why?"

"Because you can see how obsessed I really am with you."

I giggle. If only he could see my sketchpads and drawing pads I've been keeping secret for the past three years. Admittedly, it's not like this. It's only pads after pads after pads full of pencil, charcoal, and conté drawings of him, but having them made me feel like a crazed psycho stalker or something. Now I don't feel too bad.

"Well, I have a confession to make," I start hesitantly. "I have sketches and drawings of you too...not like this, but..." I grin up sheepishly.

His eyes light up. "I have to see them sometime."

"Maybe."

"Oh, come on, I've shown you mine, now you have to show me yours," he says, with a wicked look in his eyes. He's making it sounds as if he's talking about something else other than just our drawings of each other.

My face reddens, I poke my tongue out at him and he laughs.

I pick up a few drawing books and folders on the floor. A few look so old. The leather covers are worn and tattered. I look at him to see if it's okay for me to look through them. He nods his head.

147

Most of them are drawings of places, people and carriages, and horses. He's very good. I'm fascinated. One sketch pad has various sketches of nude figures.

He runs his fingers through his hair. "Those were mostly humans. I didn't...sleep with any of them... you know..." he stammers.

I just shrug and keep leafing through them. I've done sketches of nudes of both men and women. We have an open studio with live nude models every Thursday evenings at the store.

"I have sketches of nudes," I tell him. "Though I prefer my model to be men," I tease him. He doesn't look too amused.

"No more nude male models for you," he states with a scowl. "If you want a male model, you call me."

"Does that mean I can't model nude for other artists too?" I'm totally kidding. I'm not a prude, but I'll be too self-conscious to be holding poses naked in front of so many people studying and scrutinizing my body.

"No," he growls as he grabs the sketch pads from my hand and unceremoniously drops them back on the floor. "Not ever, but you can model for me anytime."

He grabs me by my waist. His eyes on my face. My hands go up to lie flat against his solid chest.

"You want me to pose nude for you?"

"Only if you want to," he answers seriously. His eyes are smoldering.

"Seduce him," Serena had said. That gives me an idea. "Sure, I'll pose for you." I try to sound nonchalant. His eyebrows rise in surprise.

"You think you can handle it?" I wink at him naughtily.

He smiles roguishly and tugs my hips to his. I yelp in surprise and giggle nervously. The look in his eyes is positively predatory.

CHAPTER XVIII
How to Douse a Fire

"Red, Red, Red, Red..." sings Caspian irritatingly. He's sitting on a bar stool by the kitchen counter, sipping wine from a crystal goblet.

"Hah! You can keep calling me that. Imma calling you Cass or Cass-cass. Yeah! Cass-cass sounds sooo cute!" I exclaim.

"Cass-cass sounds like a girl! You can't call me that! I'm a manly man," he argues.

"I can't believe I'm listening to this," complains Lazarus as he cuts the vegetables. Constantine just shakes his head. Constantine is...well, I'm not really sure what Constantine is doing. So far he has his arms wrapped around me and keeps nuzzling and kissing my neck from behind, making me giggle and my toes curl while I'm trying to stir the creamy mushroom sauce.

Serena finds my exchange with Caspian funny and is giggling hard while trying to flip the meat in the pan.

They've fired Lora, their fifth cook. Now I'm supervising dinner—or trying to. So far, I haven't burned the kitchen down yet.

I think they all know how to cook, they're just too lazy to do so.

We stop bickering as soon as we hear a car pulling into the driveway.

149

"Milan is back," declares Caspian flatly. He then abandons his glass and chugs the expensive Dom Pérignon straight from the bottle.

I feel something changes in the air. I don't know what it is, but I guess I'm about to find out.

The front door opens, and a few minutes later, Milan breezes in. She is stunning. Flawless pale skin. Shiny baby blue eyes and straight jet black hair. Her perfect body is covered in expensive designer clothes and shoes. She looks like a model straight out of the runway.

"Hello. I'm back! Missed me?" she announces, giving Lazarus and Constantine a hug. She doesn't seem to be bothered to do the same with Serena and Caspian.

"Who's this?" Her eyes narrow on me. "Are we keeping company with the werewolves now? Or is she our new cook?"

She says the word werewolf in such a derogatory way; I can sense Serena bristles next to me.

"Milan," says Lazarus warningly.

Constantine frowns. "This is my mate, Genesis," announces Constantine as he pulls me into his arms.

"Your mate???" Her face turns ugly for a second, then she bursts out laughing. "Good one. Stop joking around. I think I saw her around school before. I know she can't be your erasthai. If she was, you'd have claimed her years ago. You would've known she's the one the moment you saw her."

"Yes, she is my erasthai. I did know right away that she's my *one* the moment I set my eyes on her three years ago. She was just too young to be claimed back then," announces Constantine.

"You've got to be kidding me," she scoffs.

"Nope, he's not kidding you. Genesis is Constantine's erasthai and mate," declares Caspian with a smile. I hear smugness in his voice. There's an undercurrent hostility in the way Caspian talks to her.

"Dinner's ready. Let's set the table," suggests Serena abruptly. She wraps her hand over mine and tugs me away. I flash her a look of gratitude. I can't stand the aura of hostility coming from Milan too much longer.

Dinner is uncomfortable for me. The men eat happily enough. Serena cuts her meat and eats delicately, like a proper lady. Milan just sits there sipping her wine moodily. Once in a while, she would glance at me with narrowed eyes over her wine glass. I pretend to eat, but I've actually lost my appetite.

"So you two had been spending all evening in Constantine's bedroom?" asks Caspian. His grin is big and mischievous. His eyes flash to Milan for a second.

"No, we're in his studio," I blurt out, totally mortified. My face turns bright red.

"You let her in your studio?" snarls Milan all of a sudden.

"Yes, I did," answers Constantine calmly.

"But you never let anybody in your studio! How come she gets to go in?" She demands.

"Well, he let her in. Get over it." Caspian snaps, sounding very irritated.

"But you never let me in it," she argues louder.

Constantine frowns. "Genesis is my mate. It's my studio. She can go in whenever she wants."

Milan gives me a hateful glare and walks out. I can hear her stomps her feet all the way up the staircase and slams her door shut.

Constantine sighs and pulls me close against his chest.

"I'm sorry about her," says Constantine.

"It's fine," I answer. "I think it's time for me to go home now."

"Do you really have to go?"

"Yes, we have school tomorrow," I remind him, looking at the time on my phone. It's almost 9.30 pm. As much as I enjoyed spending time with Constantine and the others, I don't feel like

151

staying here right now. I'm feeling very irritated, and that warm feeling is starting in my chest again. I just want to get out of here.

Serena gives me an understanding look.

*   *   *

"Are you sure you're feeling okay, sunshine?" he asks for the third time in the car tonight.

"Yeah, why wouldn't I be?" I reply as he parks his car on the street in front of my parents' house.

He sighs. "I'm sorry Milan is rude to you. She just needs some time to get used to having you around, sweetheart. I'll make sure she apologizes to you tomorrow."

No, I don't want a forced apology from anybody. "Yeah," I answer simply. "I'll see you tomorrow."

He pulls me straight into his lap before my hand could reach the door handle. His arms wrap around me and his lips descend on mine. His touch and his kiss always take my breath away. I wanted the kiss to be brief, but with fireworks and explosions—the kiss deepens. His lips are devouring mine. My tongue exploring his tongue. His warm hands exploring my body. Then his hungry mouth moves to kiss and nip and lick my neck. I bury my fingers in the thickness of his hair. He pulls the neckline of my dress down and his mouth trails down to the rise of my creamy skin above my lacy bra. Pleasurable shivers run down my body.

"Genesis...baby..." He moans against my skin in between kisses. My hands in his hair, tugging him closer to me with a small whimper.

With a groan, he deposits me in the passenger seat. We are both breathing hard. Our hearts are racing. His smoldering eyes move over me and stay to where my black lacy bra is still showing.

"Goddess, you are beyond tempting," he growls, tearing his eyes away, running both hands through his dark tousled hair. When

152

I mark you and take you the first time, it's not going to be in a car," he vows.

He clenches his hands over the steering wheel so hard, his knuckles are turning white. "Every night I come to see you...just to breathe you in. I wish I could stay and hold you all night, but I don't trust myself. I don't have the strength. I want to do more than just to hold you. It's becoming harder and harder to leave you."

I swallow nervously. If he meant to douse the fire in me with his words, he's doing a very poor job at it. In fact, he's doing a very *very* crappy job. Right now, I just want to jump him and yell, "The hell with it. Let's do it in the car, let's do it anywhere..."

Crazy bunnies! Wow! That sounds like green eggs and ham.

"Okay, I'll see you tomorrow then," I hedge closer to the door. He just stares out the window without saying a word. I peer at his beautiful profile while fumbling with the door handle.

Tell him you're ready!

I straighten my dress up and walk out.

Gah! I'm such a coward.

I take off my dress to change into my pajamas. My tummy clench at the sight of red marks all over my neck and my chest. I can almost feel his mouth on my skin.

Just after I step out of my closet, I hear a soft tapping on my window.

Serena! She's holding onto the window frame outside, grinning in through the window. I rush over and open the window for her.

"That's very polite of you. Constantine never knocks, he just barges in whenever he wants," I inform her.

Serena giggles softly. "I'm guessing he does that a lot," she teases me as she steps into my room.

I can feel my face turning red. "It's not that I'm not glad to see you, but what are you doing here?"

"I know how upset you were. I just wanted to see how you're doing," she says as she looks around my room.

"Thanks, Serena, but I'm okay..."

"Genesis, you don't have to pretend with me. I know how you feel. I know what Milan is up to."

"I thought you and Milan were friends," I ask her.

Serena sighs and plonks herself on my bed. "I wouldn't go as far as calling us friends. Milan is not the easiest person to get along with. Milan and I, we tolerate each other."

"It's no fun having someone you *tolerate* around all the time," I say and drop myself next to her.

"No, it can get a bit tiring sometimes. Thankfully, she grows tired of this place very quickly and very often. She rarely stays longer than two weeks at the most. She'll take off to Europe like the last time or somewhere else like she always does soon...hopefully."

"So, why is she here?"

"She's been following Constantine and Lazarus for a while now. Over a hundred years, on and off. She gave me some problem when I first met Lazarus over sixty years ago, even though it's not Lazarus that she's after. She's been hoping that Constantine would take her as his mate."

"But she's not his erasthai," I blurt out. I feel a pang of jealousy in my chest.

"Yeah, but that didn't stop her from trying...but you're here now" She smiles. "Constantine had been waiting for you. He wasn't willing to settle for anything less, just like Lazarus before he met me. The same with Caspian."

"Genesis," she chews on her lips while her perfectly arched eyebrows furrow as if she's contemplating whether or not to tell me something. "Lycans have a massive power that can be felt by werewolves. Much like the dominant power of an alpha...but much more compelling and over-powering. They can control it. They can mask it, by keeping it down so no one can feel it, or draw it out and encompassing the one they love, especially their mates...so you'll feel protected and powerful. They can also cast it out to dominate others, especially werewolves. It can make you feel uneasy and dominated, ready to cower and do their bidding. Might make you feel upset for no reason. If projected too much, it can drive a werewolf or a human into a hysteric...or worse. You'll be able to do that too, in time.

"Milan used to do that to me. She claimed that she couldn't help it, but I don't believe her. I think she did it on purpose. I'm pretty sure she'll do that to you too. The thing is, you can block it, Genesis... if you're strong enough."

"Block it how?" Now I'm pretty sure she did it to me tonight. It didn't make me feel like cowering to her, but I did feel very upset and uneasy the whole time she was there.

"I'm not sure how far your lycan has taken over, but I know you have alpha blood in you. Imagine you project your dominance over some werewolf. Project that power, not to dominate, but wear it like a shield around you. If she can't penetrate that power, she'll have no effect on you."

"Okay." I sigh. "Thank you for telling me this, Serena."

"It's not a problem, young Genesis," she says as she takes my hand in hers. "I like you. It's been a while since I have a girlfriend that I can talk to. I had been waiting for three years for Constantine to claim you. I don't want Milan to draw you away from us. Now I have to get going. I told Lazarus that I just needed to go for a quick run." She giggles. "I think he knew that I was coming here. He knew how excited I am about having you as one of us now."

CHAPTER XIX
Seduction For Dummies

Constantine picks me up for school this morning. The kiss he gives me as soon as I get in the car leaves us both breathless.

Autumn prefers to walk to school with her friends. I suspect that she's actually still feeling shy and intimidated by Constantine.

When I step out of the car with Constantine, there are no wolf whistles or cat calls. They know not to mess up with lycans, the royal ones especially. Constantine wraps his arm around me as soon as we're out of the car. We still get stares and people whispering as we walk by, but I try not to let that bother me.

I'm feeling apprehensive about being around Milan again. She was getting on my nerve last night. I don't know how long I can pretend to be civil around her if she continued to behave like a spoiled brat.

All the lycans are already there when we arrive. It's still early, but the sun is already shining, promising a beautiful warm day. They are all sitting on the picnic bench outside.

Constantine instantly steers me towards where they are gathering.

Milan looks up, watching us from where she is sitting. Her straight, shiny raven black hair is in a stylish, sleek low ponytail. Her makeup is kept to a bare minimum. Well, she is flawlessly gorgeous, she really doesn't need any makeup.

She gets up as soon as we get closer. Her designer ivory lace, midi dress is sexy yet classy. She looks like she's about to walk down the runway rather than go to school.

"Hi." She smiles, approaching us. She comes up to my height in her two inches heels. "Listen, Genesis, I'm sorry about last night. It came as a shock to me, and I reacted badly. I hope you can forgive me," says Milan. Her big baby blue eyes look honest and sincere. "I'd like us to be friends."

"Sure, I'd like that too," I reply, giving her a tentative smile.

"Awesome!" She exclaims, linking her arm through mine.

"Hi," I greet everybody.

"Good morning, Genesis." Serena returns, who looks serene and calm. Her expression giving nothing away. Lazarus beside her, nods his head with a small smile. He has that same intensity in his eyes as Constantine. I notice that his electric blue eyes turn soft whenever he looks at Serena. They are such a contrast, yet so right for each other.

Caspian is lying on his back on the picnic table in front of us with his hands behind his head. His vivid green eyes look cold and his gorgeous face looks bored. He lifts an eyebrow, giving me a certain look that I don't quite understand.

"Now tell me all about yourself," urges Milan.

"There's nothing much to tell, really," I answer, shrugging my shoulders.

"Oh come on. I'd like to get to know you better." She coaxes as she pulls me to sit next to her. "How long have you known that you're Constantine's erasthai? Did you have a mate before? Was he heartbroken?"

"Milan," snaps Constantine who stiffens at the mention of my ex-mate. He seats himself next to Milan as I'm seated at the end of the bench on the other side of her.

"Oh, I'm so sorry. That was insensitive of me," she apologizes quickly. Her expressive eyes look regretful. "Sometimes I don't think before I say something."

157

"There's nothing to be sorry about. It's not a big secret or anything, everybody here knows about it." I shrug my shoulders again. "He's not heartbroken at all. He rejected me. So...no big deal."

"Rejected you? I'm so sorry. Oh, Genesis, it must be awful for you." She covers my hand with hers. Her eyes widen in horror.

"Like I said, it's no big deal."

Caspian shoots me another look from where he's lying down, and this time I lift my eyebrow up in question.

I get the chance to talk to Penny during English Lit. The teacher is late, and Penny is full of stories.

According to Penny, everybody talks about the royal lycans and how my grandfather was the alpha of Cannis Gunnolf Pack, one of the strongest pack in North America. Penny says, there are lots of stories floating around about me and my family and how we're not in Cannis Gunnolf Pack anymore.

One story is that my father left his mate, his pack and he's giving up his title as an alpha to be with my mother. Some people were saying that I was promised to the Alpha of Red Convel Pack to be his mate since I was a baby. My parents broke that promise, that's why we're here. Someone else is saying that I made a pack with the lycans to pretend to be mated to one of them to teach Logan a lesson.

Sheesh. Some people are stupid.

Penny and I giggle over most of the stories.

Logan and Zeke enter the classroom while Penny and I are still giggling over some of the more outrageous stories. The teacher enters right after him and Zeke.

Logan doesn't even look at me. He sits stiffly facing the front of the classroom the whole time. This is almost like the time before we knew we were mates and he wasn't even aware of my existence. Well, except that this time, I know that he's super aware that I'm right here behind him and there's a tension here now.

158

When the class ends, he gathers his stuff and walks out without a single glance my way either. I think I should be thankful about that.

It's frustrating how Constantine and I don't have any classes together. All the lycans have classes together. We just get to meet briefly in the hallway between classes. Every time we see each other in the hallway, he would bury his nose and lips against my neck and breathes in deeply. It's like my scent calms him.

After the fourth period, he grabs me by the waist, throws me over his shoulder, and carries me out. Well, I guess it's okay to skip classes if you're the king's nephew.

"Listen, sunshine," he says as he takes my hand in his across the console of the car. "Caspian, Lazarus and I are leaving for Russia tomorrow morning." He sighs. "I just want to spend today alone with you."

"How long are you going for?" I can't hide the disappointment in my voice.

"Just for two or three days...a week at the most. We've been summoned by King Alexandros just this morning. I knew this day would come. We've been away, abandoning our duties long enough."

"You would have to go back there for good pretty soon, don't you?"

He seems reluctant to answer my question this time. His beautiful gray eyes are looking at me speculatively and apprehensively. "Eventually, yes," he finally answers.

I turn my head to look out the window. There are a lot of things I still don't know about him. I assumed that I'll have to be wherever he'll be. Go wherever he goes. He never asked me to do that. We never really discussed the future.

"Where are we going?" I finally ask. The road we're on is familiar.

"You promised me you would pose for me today...."

159

"You want to do it now?" When I said today, I assumed it would be after school.

"Yeah, but if you changed your mind.."

"No, I'll do it," I quickly cut in. My heart starts hammering in my chest. I'll be posing naked in front of Constantine soon, and I was planning to seduce him!

Cuddly bunnies and crazy slippers!

*   *   *

"So, do you want me to...uh, strip naked for you now?" I ask, restlessly playing with the hem of my shirt.

Constantine looks equally tense. The atmosphere between us changed in the car the moment he suggested that I pose for him now rather than later.

Now, I'm standing in his room, feeling like I'm about to die. I swear, my heart is trying to escape out of my rib cage and the whole zoo just escaped in my tummy.

He blows a few locks of his dark hair that hang over his forehead away.

I suddenly feel like giggling over how nervous we both are. We both look like a couple of little kids about to do something we're not supposed to.

Actually, seeing how nervous he is makes me feel a little bold. Just a little.

"Okay," I say, bringing up my hands and start undoing the buttons of my denim top.

His silver gray eyes suddenly shift to watch my hands work on the buttons. His Adam's apple moves as he swallows hard.

"You know what? If you want, you could put on one of my shirts to start...it's up to you," he suggests hoarsely.

He disappears into his walk-in closet and appears with a white shirt that looks similar to the one I had on after the shower the first time I was here.

160

"I'll be waiting for you in the studio," he says, his hand massaging his neck awkwardly before he walks out the door.

I'm grateful that he's giving me options just to make me feel comfortable, but now I have a decision to make.

"Seduce him," I whisper to myself as I take my bra off. Shirt or no shirt? I'm so nervous! I walk out, then turn around.

Wowza!!! I can't do this! I chicken out.

Nope, you can do this! Okay, the second option just to start. I sigh and put his white shirt on. The feeling of the fabric of his shirt against my bare skin gives me the tingles. I breathe in the wonderful smell of his scent and detergent. "Okay, I can do this. Easy peasy lemon squeezy."

I happen to glance at myself in the mirror. Funny bunnies! The white shirt doesn't hide much. When did the shirt become so thin and transparent?

Genesis, you are a grown confident woman. You so can do this! Yeah! With that, I march into his studio.

Well...okay, I don't exactly march in there. I sorta shuffle my feet there. I told you I was such a coward. I still am.

I am so doing this!!! Seduce him...

When I walk into the studio, he's hunching over a table, arranging his paint, pencil jars, conté, erasers, and tortillons around. The flexing muscles of his broad shoulders and arms draw my eyes. He doesn't even look up from what he's doing.

There's something about a big strong man totally focused on doing something simple and delicate that makes me feel hot all over. Okay, don't jump him yet. Seduce him, seduce him.

There's a deep red velvet antique French Chaise lounge, that wasn't here before, placed by the window.

"Do you want me to sit down on the sofa? Or do you want me to do several quick gesture poses first?"

"You can just lie down on the sofa." He gestures offhandedly towards the sofa without even looking directly at me.

161

I'm getting a bit irritated that he's not looking at me when I'm feeling like I'm about to burst from being so nervous. Okay, lie down on the sofa.

Slowly, I lower myself on the red sofa into lying position. "Like this?" I ask.

"Yeah, that's good." He's still ignoring me.

I get up again and stack several pillows behind my back. I undo several top buttons all the way down past my cleavage as well. Then, I lie back down, arching my back to push my chest and my hips out. I relax my arms above my head. Well, this is my seductive position. If this doesn't work, I don't know what else I'd do. Now, I wish I had read a book Seduction For Dummies or something like that before I came.

"How about this?" I ask again.

"That's great," comes his reply, still not looking up.

Oh goddess, I give up! Maybe I should just take everything off. I bite my bottom lip and contemplate taking the shirt off when he finally straightens up.

When he finally looks at me, the expression on his face is unreadable.

He moves in closer and I try to calm my heartbeat. I stare at him, mesmerized. His intense silver gray eyes look so focused. His sensual pink lips look stiff. He moves my hair to one side and his fingers brush my neck. The sparks ignite and spread over me at the touch of his hand on my skin, I almost moaned aloud. His warm breath tickles my skin. He looks so unaffected. Maybe I should just jump him.

Next, he moves to my feet. His eyes skimming over my body. His warm hands take one of my legs and bend it to his liking. Goddess, shivers run down my spine at his touch and closeness. I think his hands stay on my leg longer than necessary. I think his fingers brush my skin in a soft burning caress before he lets go. Or maybe it's just my heated imagination.

It's been five minutes since I'm lying here on a deep red velvet antique French Chaise lounge. I play the Jeopardy music in my head. This shirt is a bad idea. Maybe I should just really jump him.

I watch Constantine in fascination. How gorgeous he is. My fingers itch to smooth back a few locks of dark hair that fall over his thick eyebrows.

His smoldering eyes moving up and down my body. I can feel the heat of his gaze burning my skin, and then he shifts his eyes back onto the sketchpad in front of him. His hand is moving fast. The pencil snaps between his fingers. He quickly snatches another pencil from the jar of pencils beside him and returns his gaze to me.

I start imagining things I could do to seduce him as I stare at his muscled arms, and shoulders, and back; my cheeks get redder with every image that I have in my head, my breath gets uneven. Then, I notice that for a while now, his hand isn't moving, and his eyes haven't shifted back to the sketchpad in front of him. My heart almost stops at the look of hunger in his eyes. My body feels like it's on fire from his intense gaze. I take a deep breath and involuntarily lick my dry lips. His nostrils flare and his eyes darken.

He lets out a groan that sounds tortured. He pushes the jars of pencils and brushes onto the floor. Pencils and brushes rolling everywhere.

I look up to see Constantine standing stiffly by the window. He's facing away from me, his head is bowed and both his hands are deep in his hair.

Oh, no. Did I push him too far?

"If you're not ready for me to take you yet, you'd better get out of here, Genesis. Go. Now," he growls.

"What if I don't want to go? Constantine—"

And before I can even finish, Constantine is already on top of me.

"Don't tease me, sweetheart," he growls between clenched teeth, breathing hard. His hands on either side of me are gripping

163

the sofa tightly as if trying to stop himself from touching me. His eyes are intense, dark and hungry.

"Constantine..." I breathe. My heart is racing. I reach my hand up to touch his cheek, he closes his eyes and his jaw clenches. The expression on his face is like a man tortured, and I hear the wood cracks loudly in his grip. I think the sofa is broken.

Suddenly, his hands are on me. His mouth slams onto mine. Oh, the explosions! The crackling fire, breaking all over my skin. His tongue already finds entry into my mouth. This kiss is all tongue, dueling with each other; hungry and desperate. I barely notice when he lifts me up, with my legs around his waist, and carries me back to his room.

I'm being lowered onto the bed. When he straightens up, his eyes are half concealed by long, thick, sooty eyelashes. His face is intense and unreadable as he stares at me from head to toe. His eyes are raking my body.

He pulls off his white t-shirt and my eyes are drawn to his muscled arms, his glorious shoulders and chest, down to his perfect abs that lead down to the deep v and a little trail of hair that disappears down his low hanging jeans. He is gorgeous. Perfection.

"You are perfect," he breathes just before he climbs onto the bed over me and fervently crushes my lips with his. Shudders run through my body.

I marvel at the feeling of his bare skin. My hands move up to his back and shoulders, feeling his rippling muscles.

I wrap my legs around his waist and pull him closer still. His mouth is devouring mine like a starving man. Fuzzy whatever...I'm drunk on his taste.

I roll my hips against his.

"Oh, sweetheart..." he moans against my mouth.

My tongue is sliding against his. His mouth moves to the side of my neck, giving me wet open mouth kisses. One hand is on my side, supporting the weight of his upper body, while his lower body is grinding against mine. His other hand moves up underneath my shirt. His exploring hand is trailing fire over my already heated skin.

I feel him stiffen above me and my passion clouded brain registers the persistence knocking at the door.

He groans. "Ignore it," he murmurs and trails his mouth fervently down my throat and across my collarbone.

The knocking gets louder.

Arrgghhh!!! No, no, no no. This is not happening!

I lay back and sigh, running my fingers through my hair in frustration.

Constantine buries his face on my chest, groaning loudly. The knocking gets even louder and a few seconds later he raises his head, scowling at the door as if it's his enemy. A muscle ticking at his jaw.

"I swear it, if it's Caspian playing tricks on us, I'm going to murder him," he growls fiercely.

I'd happily help bury the body.

"Who is it?" he growls at the door.

No answer, but the knocking continues.

He swears and moodily pushes himself off me. He pulls the sheet over me before he walks over, unlocks the door and yanks it open.

Milan is standing on the other side, staring at him, wide eyed. Then her eyes move to look at me still lying on the bed.

"I'm sorry. I didn't interrupt anything did I?" She sounds apologetic, but there's a gleam in her eyes that doesn't make it sound believable to my ears. Or maybe that's just my sex crazed brain thinking.

"Yes, you did. We're busy. Now go away," says Constantine gruffly.

"Oh come on you, Mr. Grumpy. I just can't wait to bond with Genesis." She forcefully pushes the door open wider just as Constantine is about to close it on her face.

165

"Come shopping with me. Then we'll go to the spa. We'll be so much fun together!" she invites me enthusiastically. There's a note of desperation in her voice.

What? Is she kidding me? NO! I don't want to go shopping. I don't want to go to the spa. Right now, I just want to kill somebody while howling out my frustration.

Constantine is looking livid. His eyes are turning black.

"What's going on?" asks Caspian at the door just as I was about to go and calm Constantine down.

I lay back down and pull the sheets tighter around me since I remember I'm not wearing much.

I hear Constantine growls before he disappears. Billowing curtains is the only indication of where he's gone off to.

CHAPTER XX
Flip, Sip or Strip

I don't feel like seeing anybody today. Thank goodness it's Saturday. I even turned my phone off since last night.

Lazarus and Serena drove me home last night. We didn't talk much during the drive. Even Serena was awfully quiet.

I stare at the ceiling of my bedroom moodily. I didn't sleep well, and now it's almost morning and I'm already wide awake. The scene from last night keeps replaying in my mind. I wonder if they've already left for Russia.

Argghh. I feel like kicking something.

Cold air blows in as my window slides open. Constantine! I jump out of bed and straight into his arms.

His strong arms gather me close into him. "I have to see you before I go," he mutters against my neck.

"I'm sorry about yesterday evening. I shouldn't have gone off like that," he apologizes. "I just can't stay without hurting any of my friends."

"That's okay. I understand." I do understand, actually. I felt like hurting Milan last night. Well, not like I can really hurt her. She's a full-blooded lycan, I'm just a werewolf. "So you went for a run?"

"Yeah." He sighs. "I think I went as far as Inuvik, Canada."

I gasp. "No, you didn't!"

"No I didn't," he agrees, laughing softly.

He nuzzles my cheek, my jawline, then buries his face in my neck, breathing in deeply. Oh goodness, he feels so good and smells so good. He has that delicious smell of him, and pine needles, and fresh air, and early morning dew.

"You haven't been home all night, have you?" I suddenly ask him. Actually, I shouldn't be surprised if he made it all the way to the Northwest Territories, Canada last night.

"No. I went for a run all night and then I came here. I have to see you before we have to take off just after dawn."

I tighten my arms around him. I really don't want him to go.

"Sunshine, I want so much to mark you." He breathes against my neck. His teeth nipping my skin. I can feel his canine. Shivers run through me. My eyelids flutter shut.

"Then mark me," I whisper breathlessly.

"I'd love to...but you don't want to wake your family up to hear something they don't need to hear, do you, sweetheart?"

My eyes widen.

"I thought not." He laughs. "Soon," he whispers before he swoops down and gently kisses my lips.

"I have to go now," he murmurs against my lips. "I'll see you soon." He gives me another soft lingering kiss, then he's gone.

I feel like a part of me is being ripped away. "I'm going to miss you," I whisper into thin air. I'm already missing him.

I have late breakfast with my family this morning. I sit around the house feeling miserable, doing nothing later on. It seems like everybody else is busy doing something and NOT being miserable like I am right now. I suspect my family is just trying to make themselves scarce just to stay out of my way.

Gosh, I miss Constantine.

Ezra's unhappy and it's making it worse for me. I wonder where he is right now and what he's doing. I think I'm going through a withdrawal.

168

Nope, I can't keep doing this. I'm going to get up and do something! Yeah! Let's do something fun that totally doesn't suck, like homework.

I'm trying to do some homework when Penny texts me about going to a party at her cousin's house this evening. Penny's cousin, Olivia, just turned 18 and we are all invited to the party.

Queen Penny: Come with us, please?

Me: No thanks.

Queen Penny: You can't mope around the house every time Constantine's not there!

Me: Not moping. I'm busy.

Queen Penny: Doing what???

Me: Homework.

Queen Penny: □□ We're coming over.

Penny and Reese are very persistent, might as well put my party dress on now.

I find myself standing in the driveway of a big white ranch style-house, wearing a light blue crop top with dark blue ripped skinny jeans and a pair of nude wedge sandals. So yeah, they managed to drag me out of the house, kicking and screaming. Well okay, not quite, but close. That's why we arrived kinda late.

"Those jeans look hot on you," compliments Reese, adjusting a few strands of long necklaces that she dropped around my neck earlier on.

Yeah, they're super tight, especially on my derriére. I don't know if Constantine would be happy with me wearing these to a party without him.

Reese is looking pretty too in her pink short tiered dress and pink strappy sandals.

"Wow, the party's going crazy already," observes Penny. She has a pair of dark denim shorts on with a black tank top and a pair of black vans. The words Hot Geek are written across the front of her top in glittery letters.

"Come on, girls. I think we're fashionably late enough," urges River as he wraps an arm around Reese's shoulders and another around mine.

I see some kids I know from school loitering the front lawn. They huddle closer and start whispering when they saw us. I hear the music from out here. I can tell right away that I'm not going to enjoy this party.

The party is in full swing when we get inside. The music is deafening with kids dancing, twerking, and grinding up against each other.

River whispers something into Reese's ear before they disappear into the crowd.

"Let's go find the birthday girl," yells Penny over the music as she pulls me in further inside the house.

We find Olivia, Penny's cousin, in the kitchen in the middle of a drinking game Flip, Sip or Strip. By the look of it, she's already buzzed and lost half her clothing already.

Flip, sip or strip is a game where you flip a coin and call head or tail before it lands. If you guess wrong, you must drink or strip an article of clothing. If you guess right, you can pass the coin to your left or choose to go again. If you go again and guess right the second time, you can choose anybody to drink or strip. You can't choose to do the same thing twice in a row.

I look around at several people in various states of undress. A couple of girls are already only in their bras and panties. I immediately notice Logan in the middle of the crowd. His shirt is already missing. His ocean blue eyes are staring at me broodingly and sulkily. He's still looking attractive to me. I think he always will.

"Really cousin? Already drunk at your own party?" says Penny to Olivia as a form of greeting.

"Oh my gosh, Penny...you've gotta join this game. We need more people or we'll all be naked... like soon!!!" giggles Olivia.

We werewolves do get drunk, but we sober up quicker than humans due to our high metabolism, I think.

"Happy Birthday, Olivia," I chime in.

"Genesis! Thank you!" She flings her arms around me. "I'm glad you're here. Come, join our game," she pleads, pulling my arm.

Olivia is pretty wild, and we don't hang out with the same crowd, but she's always nice to me.

"Yeah, Genesis. Why don't you join in the game?" taunts a familiar voice suddenly.

Logan.

His tone and eyes are full of challenge. His golden hair is slightly wild, and his toned chest is glistening with sweat and whatever drinks they're having.

All eyes are focused on me now.

Logan smirks, daring me to say no and daring me to say yes; daring me to join the game and daring me to run off.

"In fact, why don't we make it more interesting? Why don't we make it just between you and me? What do you think, Genesis?" He moves in closer.

I try to step back, but my back hits several people behind me. The room suddenly feels too crowded and too suffocating for me.

"Logan..." comes a familiar voice, full of warning.

"Shut up, Hunter!" growls Logan fiercely. His eyes are staring fixedly at me. My eyes shift quickly to Hunter who is standing by the wall, then back to Logan.

"Come on, sweetheart. You're not scared, are you?" He's too close now. I feel his breath on my skin. I can smell the alcohol. He runs the back of his fingers slowly down my cheek and my neck, down to my collarbone and lower. I feel sparks breaking out on my skin where he touches, and shivers run down my back.

"Logan, please," I plead. Damn the mate bond.

"Please what, mate?" he whispers in my ear. His hand is going lower.

No! He's not my mate!

171

"Stop it, Logan!" I hiss, grabbing his hand that's already on my chest.

"Why? Why, stop?" he snarls. "I want to touch what's mine. I want to see what's mine. Why does he get to do it and not me?"

"You're drunk!" I snap at him, pushing him off me with an extra force. He staggers backward.

"You're mine, Genesis! Don't think I'm just going to give up!" he yells at me as I fight my way through all those people to get out of there.

I stumble out through the back door. There is a bonfire in the backyard. A group of ten people or so are sitting around with beer bottles in their hands.

"Genesis! Genesis!!!" Logan calls out.

Oh no! I dart quickly to the side of the house.

I lean against the siding of the house. My heart is thudding fast in my chest. The full moon is shining its pale silvery light everywhere. There are plenty of shadows of trees and shrubs for me to hide behind.

"Genesis! Stop running. I can smell you," he sings out. He's drunker than I thought.

I peek around the house, preparing to run if I had to.

"Logan, come on, man. Lets' go," says one of his friends, holding him back.

"No! Let me go. I need to mark her."

"Logan, remember what you promised your dad. You've got to go," says Hunter.

"But she's mine! Mine!" he growls.

"I know," allows Hunter. "Zeke, Caleb, Jordan, take him home. Alpha is going to be upset if you let him get anywhere near her."

I lean back against the wall, trying to calm my heartbeat as they drag him away, cursing them for manhandling him.

Screw, Logan. Screw mate attraction that I still have for him. Screw the drama and free entertainment we just provided those people in there. No doubt there will be plenty of stuff for everybody to talk about. By Monday, it will be all over the school.

Scrunching earth and snapping twigs make me jump. That draws my attention to an approaching figure. The familiar smell reassures me enough to let my guard down a little.

"Hey," greets a familiar voice in the dark. Hunter.

"Are you following me?" I ask him, smiling a little in relief. I don't feel like talking to anybody right now, but I always like Hunter. Did I tell you that already? Well, yeah. I think he's a nice guy. He also managed to get Logan away just now.

"Maybe," he answers, smiling back. "I just want to make sure that you're okay...and I thought, uh... maybe you might need someone to talk to...or just to make sure you're safe. Lots of drunken mutts out here..." He grabs the back of his neck awkwardly. "Sorry, I'm blabbering..."

I can't help but laugh softly. He's funny.

"Thanks," I reply. "That's very nice of you, Hunter."

"I'm sorry about Logan," he says as he leans against the wall next to me.

I shrug my shoulders and look around us. We're pretty well-hidden. "It's not your fault. You shouldn't have to apologize for it. Thank you for taking him away."

"Well, he had his orders to stay away from you. I knew he wouldn't listen to it for too long. Being drunk tonight wasn't helping either," he explains. I assume the order came from Alpha Carrington.

I turn to look at him to find his eyes already on me. "Logan's just being a jerk," I sigh. What else is new?

"He messed things up with you big time. I can't imagine living without your mate, knowing that it's your fault that you're not with her," he answers. "If you were mine, I wouldn't have given you up for the world."

173

"You're a good person, Hunter. Whoever turns out to be your mate is a very lucky girl." I say softly.

"Well, I wish I'd meet her already," he mumbles. He pushes his hands inside the pockets of his jeans and stares broodingly out into the woods.

He looks troubled. I straighten up and touch his shoulder lightly. "You will, Hunter. She's somewhere out there waiting for you," I tell him. He stares at me, looking amazed. "When you meet her, it'll be awesome!" I smile brightly, thinking of Constantine and how he makes me feel.

He's about to say something when my phone beeps. "Oops... sorry, must be my friends looking for me."

Sure enough, it's a text from Penny asking me where I am. She's been looking all over the place for me. I've missed a couple of messages from Reese and River as well—and a phone call from Constantine. My heart skips a beat when I see his name.

"Tell them I'm sending you home...unless you still want to stay," says Hunter.

"Nope, I've had enough. Are you sure you want to leave the party though?"

"Yeah, I'm not much of a party animal. I'll be happy to be out of here," he answers with a small smile.

I text my friends that Hunter is sending me home.

As we're walking across the lawn, a couple of guys are streaking pass us. A group of five or so people behind us egging them on. One of the naked boys sees me and yells, "Hey, Genesis!!!" Then he howls. The rest of them join in the howling, then laugh hysterically.

I glance at Hunter who's scowling at them. Well, he's not amused. At other times, I might find it funny, but after what happened with Logan tonight, my patience is stretched thin. Stupid drunk boys.

Hunter is very quiet on the drive home. He seems to be deep in thought. I wonder if he's worried about not meeting his mate yet. He really shouldn't be worried; he's still very young. He's just a few months older than I am. I know this because I was invited to his birthday party a few months back. He's a nice guy. I hope he'll meet his mate soon.

"Thank you, Hunter, for driving me home," I tell him when we arrive in front of my driveway. "And don't worry, you'll meet her soon enough."

"Yeah," he smiles sheepishly. Awww... he's so cute like that. I impulsively lean in and kiss him lightly on his cheek before I let myself out of the car.

"Oh, you're home already," greets mom smiling cheekily when I walk in through the door. "Your dad is getting himself ready to wait for his daughters and drag you two home if you're not back by midnight." She laughs.

I just remember that Autumn was invited to another birthday party tonight as well. I'm glad she's not at Olivia's. Otherwise, I would have dragged her home myself. Olivia's parties tend to get very wild.

"Well, I won't be dragging you home, honey. Maybe Autumn," assures dad as he carries two steaming mugs of coffee for mom and himself.

"Yeah, of course, you won't, seeing that I'm already home," I tease him.

My dad grins as he sneakily grabs the remote control from mom. She swats his hand away and regains her control over the remote.

"Now, we know who's wearing the pants in this house," I can't resist saying as I climb up the stairs.

"Oh, shush with you!" scolds mom, but with a big mischievous smile on her face.

"Hey!" protests dad.

It's only ten thirty now. I know my parents never really worried about me partying or anything. I love dancing like some silly wacko and have fun with my friends at parties, but I'm not much into drinking or doing anything too crazy. My body is my temple, I'm big on self-preservation, and all that.

Who needs crazy stunts when you have a big enough mouth to land you into crazy and embarrassing situations already? Not me.

CHAPTER XXI
Best Way To Wake up Ever

It's 11 pm. Saturday night, and I'm lying in my bed thinking about what had happened tonight. Logan is still a jerk, I decided. I hope when he said that he's not giving up, that's just him being drunk talking.

Poor Hunter, he's such a nice guy, I hope he'll find his mate soon.

I wonder what Constantine is doing.

I'm so going to kill my friends the next time I see them.

My phone goes off and starts playing Back at One by Brian McKnight. My heart starts racing, and butterflies do the crazy dance in my tummy. Constantine! I know it's a very classic cheesy song, but that's how he makes me feel. Gosh, I'm the sappiest girl ever.

I try to grab my phone on the nightstand as fast as I can, but my legs got tangled in the sheets, and I fall into an unsightly heap on the floor.

Owww... I think I broke my butt...again.

By the time I manage to break free from the vicious bed sheet, I'm out of breath.

"Hello?" I manage to say breathlessly into the phone, finally. My voice sounds more like I'm in the throes of passionate lovemaking instead of just having lost a fight with the ferocious, violent, and vicious bed sheet.

There's a noticeable silence from the other end for a few seconds before he says something, "Hi, what have you been up to, sunshine?"

Oh, my goddess! That voice. That deep, beautiful voice that makes my knees go all weak. It makes me even more breathless.

"N—Nothing…" I answer. Way to go, Genesis.

"Really? Nothing?" There's laughter in his voice now. "Should I be worried?"

"Uh...No?" Why does my brain stop functioning now, of all time to stop functioning? I must've broken more than just my butt from the tumble just now.

"Did I wake you up?" His voice is deep and smooth. I could get pregnant just listening to his voice.

Fuzzy slippers!

"No," is all I manage to choke up.

"I didn't know you were this shy on the phone, sweetheart." Oh, he's definitely laughing at me now! I can hear it in his beautiful voice.

"So... wanna have phone sex?" comes his sinfully naughty, sexy voice.

"What???"

He's openly laughing at me now. His delicious laughter echoes through the line.

Oh, my ovaries!

"Listen, I have to get going soon, my love. I know there's an eight-hour difference between us. It's morning here, and it's after eleven there. I just want to hear your voice and say goodnight. I miss you, sunshine," he whispers. "Goodnight and sweet dreams, love." A few seconds of silence in the line, then he's gone.

"I miss you too," I whisper into a disconnected line.

Arghhh! Idiot! Idiot! Idiot!

I pound my pillow several times. Why oh why can't I be like other normal girls?

I fall asleep with Constantine on my mind. I wake up Sunday morning with Constantine on my mind.

I'm missing him so badly that I don't feel like going out or watching any movies on Netflix. I finish doing all my homework though. Well, that's new. If this keeps happening, I'll be valedictorian this year.

Reese and River arrive later in the day and apologize for dragging me to the party. I shrug it off. I decided to forgive them after that phone call from Constantine last night. How would they know that it would end up like that? I know my friends meant well.

Penny arrives not long after and we talk about what happened. We decided that it's best if I avoid Logan as much as possible.

Penny thinks that Hunter is bae and confesses to having a crush on him. So, like good friends that we are, we tease her mercilessly after that. I didn't know that Penny actually has a crush on Hunter. I must have been very clueless about things around me all this time. Huh, who would have thought that? I think it would be great if Hunter turned out to be Penny's mate.

Monday morning, I don't feel like going to school, but I drag myself out of bed. I walk to school with my sister.

The staring and the whispering start as soon as I enter the school ground. I ignore them as best as I can.

I really miss Constantine. Something is seriously wrong with my world since he's not around. The thought that I rely so much on him to make me feel whole and happy scares me a little. Well, maybe a lot. But, oh goddess, how could I not? I didn't stand a chance the moment I laid my eyes on him and after he claimed me.

I meet Penny, Reese, and River by our lockers as usual. Today, I decided to use my mad ninja skills again to avoid certain people around school, especially Logan.

That mad ninja skill is totally crushed by first period. English literature, the *Bane* of my existence. I have Logan in that class with me.

For the first time ever, Logan is already sitting in his chair when I walk in with Penny. His ocean blue eyes follow me as I make my way to my seat.

Penny nudges me so hard, I seriously consider getting a new best friend. "Owww... thanks, Penny!" I scowl at her, furiously rubbing my side. One day, she's really going to break my rib cage.

Logan doesn't do anything else other than making me uncomfortable the whole period with his stares. As soon as the class ends, though, he grabs my wrist.

"You feel that?" he whispers in my ear, while his thumb strokes the inside of my wrist. Sparks flares where our skin touch. "I know you still want me as much as I want you."

"Stay away from me, Logan," I hiss, pulling my hand out of his grip.

"Would be easier if you just come back to me," he retorts. Easier for who? I choose not to answer him.

"What an asshole," mumbles Penny crossly, linking her arm through mine as we walk out of the classroom together.

It seems like the golden couple, Mia and Logan aren't together anymore. They're even sitting at different tables during lunch now.

Logan, however, has another girl sitting on his lap while he openly stares at me during lunch. So much for wanting me. He kisses her down her neck, then her lips, all the while keeping his eyes trained on me.

What is his problem?

Mia, who is sitting at another table glares at them, then turns to give me a death glare as well.

What did I do?

"This is fascinating and sick at the same time, you know," remarks River, happily munching on his pizza.

"It's disgusting," announces Penny, glaring at him.

"Just ignore them, GenGen," advises Reese, squeezing my arm comfortingly.

Hunter flashes me a rueful smile, and I nudge Penny's side. She accuses me of trying to break her rib cage. My friend is such a drama queen!

School is uneventful apart from that. Well, by now I'd take uneventful over eventful any day.

I'm hoping that Constantine would call again tonight. I have a whole script memorized and a list of questions ready, just in case my brain decides to freeze again. Yeah, I'm that pathetic.

I miss Constantine. I wonder if he misses me just as much.

Maybe it's just all me because he never called. I fall asleep with the phone in my hand just so that I don't have to fight with the bed sheet again.

Early the next morning, I have a dream with mainly Constantine in it.

"Sunshine," he whispers, as he lifts the covers up and climbs into bed with me. His strong warm arms gather me close and he buries his face into my neck.

"Constantine," I sigh blissfully, burying my fingers in his thick silky hair.

Shudders run through me as I feel the length of his body covering mine. I wrap my legs around him, pulling him closer. He groans against my skin before he starts kissing, sucking and licking my neck, like a man dying of thirst, and I'm his first sip of water.

I start moaning aloud before he quickly covers my lips with his. This feels so good. My tongue finds its way into his mouth. The taste of him, I can never get enough of. I could stay in this dream forever.

"Sweetie, are you up? Don't be late for school," calls mom, knocking loudly on the door.

Nooooo! I don't want to wake up yet. Not ever.

I open my eyes to stare up directly into a pair of gorgeous silver-gray eyes.

"Constantine?" I ask hesitantly, touching his cheek.

His eyebrows shoot up in surprise. "Do you have another lover waking you up like this every morning?" His voice is deep and sexy.

Oh, my goddess!

"You're here!" I wrap my arms and legs around him, and we both nearly fall off my tiny bed when I flip us onto our sides.

His chest rumbles with silent laughter as he shifts our positions so that we won't fall off my tiny bed.

"We arrived this morning. I came straight here. To be away from you for three days is killing me, sunshine," he murmurs, nuzzling my cheek. "Are you happy to see me?" he demands to know. His mouth now travels to my neck.

"Umm...yes," I reply breathily. So happy, he has no idea. His lips are doing things to me. My heart thumps crazily in my chest, and my eyelids flutter shut. "I should get ready for school," I manage to slur.

"Uumm..yeah," he mumbles between kisses. "Five more minutes." He breathes, kissing and sucking on my neck. "I missed you so much." His mouth travels down lower. "Tell me you missed me too."

"I missed you too...so much," I mumble back.

Oh, my brain isn't working when his lips are doing things to me. "Missed you...mmm...love you..."my hands are in his hair tugging him to me.

He pulls back all of a sudden. His passion clouded eyes are now looking alert and shining brightly. *What?*

"Sweetheart, you said you love me."

Did I?

"I...I meant to say that I li-like you. That's what I meant to say."

Urghh!!! I'm an idiot!

"No, no take back, darling." He slams his lips to mine and proceeds to kiss me till we're both breathless. He pulls back and gazes down at me with such look of passion, tenderness, and love that I could cry.

"I love you too, sunshine," he whispers, looking deep into my eyes. I think I just died. "No take back," he reminds me.

He looks down at me, grinning wide. The kind of grin that makes him look so adorable while manage to make me weak in the knees.

"I'll see you soon," he says before he plants another kiss on my lips. Gentle and sweet, yet passionate. Then he disappears through the window.

I feel lightheaded like I was about to faint. I giggle softly to myself. I cover my mouth with a pillow as my giggle gets louder. I think I'm going bonkers and I don't care.

Best. Way. To. Wake up. Ever.

He's back! He's back!

He said he loves me. He loves me! I feel like singing that over and over again this morning.

"Looks like our moping girl is gone," announces mom slyly when I get down for breakfast.

Is it that obvious? I feel my cheeks flood with color.

"Good morning," I greet everybody as I pour myself a mug of steaming hot coffee. I can't stop smiling and I feel like my feet aren't even touching the ground.

"So, Constantine is back, huh?" asks dad. He seems to be very interested to know about the lycans now, especially Constantine's royal commitment and involvement with the palace.

"Yeah," I answer, grinning wide.

Autumn rolls her eyes then flicks her Coco Pops cereal at my forehead. I catch it before it reaches my face and pop it in my mouth with a big smile. Her aim is good, but I'm better at catching.

Her mouth drops open. "Shut up!" she mumbles sourly.

"Glad somebody's happy," declares mom, with a teasing smile.

I smile sheepishly and quickly sip my coffee to escape as soon as I can. I should make like a banana and split before mom starts asking questions or before I start spilling even without being asked because I feel like telling somebody. I feel like doing some crazy chicken dance too. I should get going before I start doing any of those things.

Oh my gosh, did I just drink my coffee black?

Constantine is already waiting for me when I step out of the house. He's leaning against the side of the car, looking hot in his dark blue jeans, a gray t-shirt and a pair of black high top sneakers. His arms are crossed at the chest, showing off his muscled arms. I just noticed that his hair is a little shorter than before he left but still as messy.

His eyes zoom in on me, as soon as I step out of the house. He straightens up slowly, looking alert. My tummy clenches and my heart goes crazy.

At least I paid attention to my looks this morning, more than I did the last couple of days. I have my black skinny jeans on, paired with a white sleeveless chiffon top and a pair of black ankle boots. I let my hair loose in its natural wave.

His gorgeous gray eyes are intense yet playful as he scans me from head to toe. His sensual lips slowly curl up into a sexy little smile as he watches me make my way towards him. It's a miracle that I didn't trip over my own feet.

"Good morning, stranger," he murmurs when I'm standing in front of him.

I give him a big smile and he cups my face in his hands, leans in and places his lips on mine. The kiss is brief and sweet and gives me tingles all over.

"I love you," he whispers against my lips.

"Mhmm..." I answer. I'm still not used to hearing him say that. My cheeks are flushing beet red, my heart is beating a thousand times per minute, and my vocal cord is lodged somewhere—probably at the bottom of my boots.

He silently and patiently waits for a few seconds before he finally says, "Sweetheart, you're supposed to say you love me too."

I take a deep breath and says, "Yeah...what you said."

He pulls back, looking appalled. He stares down at my face for a second before he bites his bottom lip like he's trying not to laugh, then sticks it out into a pout. How in the world can a pout looks so hot and manly on a man?

"Oh, I'm hurt," he announces.

Oh, for the love of fuzzy slippers!

"I love you too! I love you, okay?" I say out loud...maybe too loud.

I hear snickers behind me, followed by giggles.

Autumn is giving me a disgusted look, while her friends are giggling behind her. I'd probably just announced it to the whole neighborhood!

Oh, goddess! I dive forward and press my face to his chest. I'm in hiding. My cheeks are flaming hot. I can feel the rumble of laughter in his chest. Kill me now.

He's driving the eco-friendly Tesla again today. I actually prefer this, rather than his two other flashier cars. He takes my hand in his and places our entwined hands on his lap while he's driving.

"I'm happy to be back here with you again, sunshine," he lifts my hand up to his lips and kisses every finger. His lips feel soft and warm. My stomach clenches and my toes curl.

He keeps the back of my fingers against his lips, and I can feel his lips move as he suddenly smiles wickedly.

"Sunshine, about Friday... we never got to finish it. Would you pose for me again sometime soon?" I almost choke on the double meaning.

"Maybe," I answer, looking away. My cheeks are flaming red, I'm sure of it.

He throws back his head and laughs that delicious laugh. His hand tightens around mine and his thumb stroked the back of my hand.

"You are adorable when you blush," he finally says. Yeah, sometimes I suspect he purposely says things just to make me blush.

"Milan apologized about what happened on Friday. She didn't mean to interrupt us. She's just excited about having a girlfriend, you know. She never really had one," he explains.

"Serena's great. Why aren't they friends?" I ask.

"I don't know, for some reason, they never get along that well. So, I'm glad that she's taken a liking to you," he explains.

Truth is, I was pretty pissed after she interrupted us on Friday, but I'm not the one to hold grudges for too long. Depending on the crime, I sometimes need a couple of days to cool down. Most of the time, though, I forgive my friends easily after they apologize.

I find myself being pulled into a big tight hug by Milan when we get to school.

"I'm so sorry about the other day, Genesis. I didn't mean to bother you or anything," she apologizes. "I guess I was just getting too excited. It won't happen again."

"Yeah, okay," I reply before Caspian pulls me away and gives me a big bear hug of his own.

"Glad that you're back too, Caspian," I manage to say before Constantine pulls me away with a growl. Caspian shoots him a wicked grin.

I smile at Serena when she gives my hand a gentle squeeze. Lazarus just pats my shoulder affectionately.

Yup, I'm glad that they're all back. Even Caspian.

CHAPTER XXII
Of Time And Space

During lunch, River, Reese, and Penny join me at the lycans' table like before. This is the first time they join the table when Milan is around. She just raises an eyebrow when my werewolf friends take their seat at the table.

Constantine takes my hand in his as soon as we're seated. He leans down and burrows his face against my neck, breathing in deeply. I lift my head up above Constantine's just in time to see Milan watching us with narrowed eyes before she looks away.

The table is awfully quiet. All the lycans seem okay, but my werewolf friends seem tense. I feel a sense of dread hitting the pit of my stomach not long after. Ezra is very uneasy and restless. Nobody seems to be interested in talking.

The feeling of sickness increases and I glance over at Milan. She looks innocent, but I sense the source of angst coming from her.

I remember what Serena told me the other night, so I concentrate on trying to project my Alpha and lycan dominance. Instead of dominating, I project it as a protection for my friends and myself.

I've never done this before. This better work, otherwise I'll wreck my friends even more! After a while, a sense of relief fills me. My were friends seem more relaxed. Wow, I can't believe it's working! I observe Milan's eyes widen. Now, I'm sure she's doing this on purpose.

Milan isn't even sparing me a glance, but I see a gleeful glint in her eyes and I can feel her projecting an even stronger wave of dominance. It's taking more and more out of me to keep my guard up. I can feel Ezra's struggle to keep me protected. This is the first time I've ever done anything like this. Before long, I can feel my energy slipping.

That sickening feeling in my stomach is back. Ezra is defiant, but she's weakening and it's getting worse every second. I glance at Serena in panic. She looks back at me with that unreadable serene expression, but I suddenly feel her protective, calming presence wrapping around me. I know Ezra has long bonded with her lycan, Ambrosia.

I think only the three of us, Milan, Serena, and myself are aware of the power play that's going on at this table right now.

My three werewolf friends are looking sick and pale. Penny excuses herself early. She throws most of her lunch away. River and Reese follow soon after. They hadn't eaten much. My friends never threw away good food. This is not okay with me. I feel like screaming at her, but I grit my teeth, trying to calm myself.

Right after Penny, Reese, and River left the table, Milan looks up and watches me speculatively for a while.

"We had fun in Russia, too bad you didn't come with us," she says to me finally, her beautifully manicured fingers touching Constantine's arm.

That's news to me. I didn't know she went with them. "Well, good for you. I'm glad you had fun." Something twisted in my chest.

"So, Genesis, let's hang out after school today," she suggests suddenly. "We can watch a movie, or go shopping or something. Yeah, shopping sounds like fun, don't you think? I could use a new pair of shoes, or two."

"Uh, no thanks," I answer. As if I'd go anywhere with her after what she did just now. I'd rather have lunch with a boa constrictor.

"Look, I know you don't have much money. Don't worry, I'll pay for everything!" She sounds enthusiastic and innocent. I can see the steely glint and challenge in her eyes and hear the insult.

"No, thanks. I have tons of homework today."

"Okay, what about tomorrow? We can do our homework together," she asks hopefully.

I glance casually at Serena. I can see some emotions in her eyes, but her face is still a blank mask of serenity.

Caspian, Lazarus, and Constantine are staring at us, listening to our exchange.

"No, that's okay," I reply. I can see what she's doing, but there is nothing I can do about it.

"Well...what about any other day then?" she asks uncertainly. Well, hell and damnation! She's a very good actress, and persistent.

"No...I have things to do," I answer. That makes me sound like a heartless bitch.

"Oh, okay...." She manages to sound sad. Her beautiful eyes downcast, and her shoulders slump forward, looking hurt and disappointed. Then she looks up into Constantine's eyes with those big sad eyes. If I didn't know any better, I'd feel very sorry for her.

I've been feeling pissed off the whole day at school today. The anger is just simmering underneath the surface. It's bad enough that Milan pulled that stunt on me, but that she had to go and involved my unsuspecting friends too, that's just low in my book. Nobody messes with my friends.

Constantine seems to be aware of my mood today. We are both very quiet on the drive back. When we arrive in front of my driveway, he kills the engine.

"Sunshine," he sighs. "What's the matter?"

"Nothing," I answer. "All is good."

189

"No, don't give me that. Talk to me." He takes my hand in his.

"You really want to know what's wrong?" I ask him. "I'll tell you what's wrong. It's wrong when Milan used her dominance over me and my friends. That's uncalled for."

"Sunshine, I'm sorry about that..."

"And why do you have to say sorry for everything that she did? Like ALL the time?" I'm on a roll now and can't seem to stop talking. "What have we done to her to deserve that?"

"Listen, Genesis...she can't help it. She didn't mean to make you or your friends uncomfortable. She explained to us how she can't control it." For some reason, him defending Milan rubs me the wrong way.

"And you believe her?"

"Of course, why shouldn't I believe her? We've been friends for a long time."

Yeah, and I only know him for less than a month. Why would he believe me over her?

"Genesis, she's really making an effort to be friends with you. She never made an effort like that with anyone before. You hurt her feelings today."

What? Now I'm bristling. "Yeah, I'm sure she's very hurt," I scoff.

"It's not easy for her. She's used to having things a certain way, it's hard for her to adjust to something new....but I can tell that she really wants to be your friend."

"Have you ever slept with her?" I shouldn't have asked, but some stupid part of me needs to know. Maybe I'm secretly a glutton for punishment.

My question is met with silence. That answers enough for me. I try to open the door, but he clicks the lock on.

"It happened before I met you," he explains. "Long before I met you."

"Yeah, okay." And that makes it all better. I know I shouldn't be mad at something that happened before we even met, but I am. It hurts just to imagine him ever being with Milan that way. I'm aware that Ezra is more lycan than wolf by now and I can feel her hatred for Milan since lunchtime, and it's affecting me. She's possessive too, and this is not helping.

"Genesis, I'm sorry. I don't know how else to apologize for something that happened before I met you. I'm not a player, but I never claimed to be a monk either." He sighs, running his fingers through his hair, making it messier than it already was. "Look, she was there for me when I needed somebody. She's been a good friend to me...and that's all we are now. Good friends. That's why I want you two to be friends. I just want us all to get along. Just give her another chance, sweetheart. She can be really nice."

"Yeah, she's awesome," I say flatly. One big happy family. Sure. I hate, *hate, hate* the way he's always defending her. I hate that she's important to him. I hate that they used to be more than friends.

"Look, I need to go now. I think I'm just tired, that's all." I think I've heard enough.

"Okay then," he says carefully. "Can I come in and just...hold you?"

"No!" I answer quickly. "I just need some space, you know?"

There's a look of hurt flashed in his eyes before he blinks once and it's gone. His face now is a blank mask of indifference.

Something in my heart twisted painfully. Why do I feel like crying now? I unlock the door, grip the handle and push it open.

"I'm coming to pick you up for school tomorrow," he informs me stiffly.

Don't bother, I want to say, but I nod and walk out without looking back. If I look back, I know for sure I'm going to burst into tears right in front of him.

I'm so pissed and hurt right now. Heat starts to spread in my chest just from thinking about Milan. I'm pissed off that he's taking her side. It feels like he's choosing her over me. I'm pissed off that they used to be lovers. I'm actually pissed off that she went with them to Russia and he didn't tell me about it. I'm also pissed off that I'm pissed off about it.

Arrgghh.

I'm so pissed off that I'm pissed off that I'm not making any sense anymore.

I burst into tears as soon as I reach my room. How did this happen? I started off today with a feeling like I can fly, now I'm feeling like I'm dying inside. That warmth in my chest is growing. I know that when a lycan is feeling angry, the outcome is never good. I just want to sit here and feel sorry for myself. So I keep myself from phasing and cry till I fall asleep.

I wake up an hour later still feeling sad. At least I'm not angry anymore, just sad. I reach for Ezra and phase into my lycan. I stand in front of the mirror and watch in fascination as I begin changing. My eyes turn all black. I notice that my vision doesn't turn red while changing when I'm not consumed by anger. Certain colors disappear or pale away, while some other colors become sharper. Red in color disappears, but red in temperature is very vivid as I detect heat. I can see my own heart pumping crimson in my chest.

Dark blue veins appear around my eyes. They snake out all over my face, then spread down all over my body. My limbs elongated. I begin to grow bigger and taller...and feel more powerful. I can feel Ezra taking over most of my feelings.

While I'm still changing, I jump out of the window with one swift kick.

I don't know how far I went, but I feel better when I arrive back home. I take a long hot shower and I fall asleep as soon as my head hit the pillow. It doesn't last too long though, I wake up before dawn feeling restless again.

192

I miss Constantine. I don't think he stopped by like he always did last night. I know I asked for space, but I'm feeling pissed off about that and that makes me feel mad all over again about other stuff too. I think I'm going crazy. He's driving me crazy.

*   *   *

Constantine picks me up again this morning. He's looking gorgeous as usual, but something is different about him today. I can feel waves of controlled anger coming off him the moment I get in the car. His wonderful scent engulfs me and I feel a sense relief, but I'm still hurt. I still don't feel like talking to him. I stare out the window the whole way. I can feel his eyes on me from time to time, all the five minutes' drive to school.

"So, how long are you going to keep this up?" he finally asks. His voice sounds measured. "Or have you decided not to talk to me ever again?"

"I just need some space. I need some time." If he's going to keep defending his precious Milan, then I need more time. A lot more time.

"I thought I'm already giving you time?" he asks through gritted teeth.

"Well, maybe I need more time," I announce, pushing the door open, but his hand snatches my wrist in a firm grip before I can jump out and run off.

He leans over me and closes the door. "I'm usually not a very patient man, Genesis," he whispers in my ear. His chest is pinning me back against the leather seat of the car. There is something dark and feral in his voice, lurking underneath that calm surface. I am suddenly reminded of what he really is. A powerful, deadly, and dangerous lycan. "So far I have been very patient with you." He grazes his nose and lips against my cheek and down my neck. Goosebumps and sparks breaking across my skin. Though I'm trying to push him away, my body wants him.

"I heard about you partying while I was away." Anger and jealousy are evident in his voice. "Just how much fun did you have that night, sweetheart?"

"Let me guess, Milan told you this," I snap.

"She just overheard some kids talking about it," he replies. "Tread carefully, my love," he warns. His voice sounds menacing. Suddenly he pushes the shirt off my shoulder. He places his mouth on my bare skin and runs his tongue from my neck, all the way to my shoulder. Ripples of pleasure run through me. Just as my eyelids flutter shut, his mouth clamps on my shoulder, making me take a sharp breath, and my eyelids fly open. I feel his canine pressing on the skin of my shoulder hard, but not enough to break the skin.

"I might decide to collect what's mine very soon, whether you're ready or not."

*   *   *

I still have faith in my mad ninja skills. Yeah, I'm the glass half full kinda person. The whole day I've been busy avoiding everybody. I've been busy trying to look busy, which, by the way, isn't as easy as it sounds.

Avoiding and hiding from Constantine is the hardest. Even when I don't see him, I can feel his eyes on me, especially in hallways between classes. Sometimes I wish I could still pretend that he's looking at something behind me.

During lunch, I can feel his gaze burning holes through the side of my head.

"He hasn't taken his eyes off of you yet," reports Penny. "Don't look now, but that bitch Milan is clinging onto him like a leech..."

"Penny," utters Reese warningly. After yesterday's incident, my friends decided to sit at our usual table. I decided to join them.

Oh, and that warning from Penny not to look? It makes me look. It's hard enough to keep my eyes away from him most of the time today. He is like a magnet to my eyes.

Sure enough, Milan is clinging onto his arm like a vine. She's even resting her chin on his shoulder, her face so close to his. I feel like scratching her perfect face.

Constantine's eyes are fixed on me, intense and challenging. He's daring me with his eyes to look away. Our eyes locked for a minute or two before I manage to tear my gaze away.

I glance back a few minutes later to see them whispering to each other. Heads close together. It hurts. Why does it hurt so much?

"You should go sit with them, GenGen," says Reese softly.

"But I'm not leaving you guys here. You are my best friends." And I don't want to sit anywhere near that bitch.

"Yeah, we're her best friends. She's not going to abandon us to sit with the lycans," hisses Penny, glaring at Reese.

"But she is one of them now," argues Reese.

"No, I'm not. I'm one of you," I argue back.

"Genesis, I don't know if you realize this, but you are one of them now. You look like them. You feel like one of them. You are as intimidating as they are."

"I intimidate you?" I squeak, appalled.

"No...that's not what I meant. What I meant to say is, you have that presence that only a lycan has. All of us werewolves can feel it now."

"Well, I'm not leaving you guys," I announce stubbornly.

"Yeah, she's not leaving us. We've been friends since we're in diapers, the lycans just knew her," says Penny as she links her arm around mine. Her bottom lip juts out into a determined pout.

"But he's her mate," insists Reese.

"Let it go, baby. It's her choice to make," says River, rubbing her shoulder soothingly.

"Okay, but all I'm saying is, if it's River sitting over there with some other girl hanging over his arm like she belonged there, I'd scratched her eyes out and claimed my place. I won't be sitting here and cower away," states Reese fiercely.

"I'm not cowering away. I just need some time to think," I say and pout.

I can feel eyes on me. I can see fingers pointing and hear their whispering. I know people are talking and speculating about why I'm not with Constantine or sitting with the lycans anymore.

I see Logan staring. I see so many people staring, it's suffocating.

CHAPTER XXIII
Stupid Royal Brat

I stomp up to my bedroom as soon as I get home. The whole house is quiet, nobody's home yet it seems. I ran out of school as soon as the last bell rang. I ran all the way home so that I won't have to see anybody, especially Constantine. I'm such a coward, I know.

Urghh. I feel like breaking something. Something like Constantine's gorgeous face. Stupid lycan.

"You would think, after living for hundreds of years they'd understand women better," I mumble to myself. "Fine is not FINE. When I said I needed space, I meant—"

"Do you always talk to yourself, Red?"

I jump in fright, holding both my hands up to my chest. "Caspian!!!"

"Is this a normal habit of yours? Is it harmless...or should I be worried?" He drawls playfully. Caspian is sitting comfortably on my bed, casually flipping through my sketchpad.

"Oh shut up, Caspian!" I snatch the pad out of his hands. "Are you trying to kill me? You almost gave me a heart attack!"

He laughs. "Oh, Genesis, even when you're mad, you're entertaining. If Constantine hadn't claimed you, I would've claimed you myself."

"How did you get in here?" I demand to know. My hands on my hips.

He grins charmingly, displaying his straight white teeth, then he glances at the wide open window.

I should've known. I really should teach these lycans how to use the front door.

"Not that it's not an honor and all that crap, but why are you here, Your Royal Highness?"

"Ha! You're in a foul mood...almost as bad as Constantine." He observes. My heart flips just from hearing his name. I'm hopeless.

"How very observant of you. Now, why are you here, Caspian?" I really just want to be alone and wallow in self-pity—and make a doll of Milan with straws and poke pins and needles on it. Then I'll gouge its eyes out, cut it into tiny pieces and burn it. Preferably doing it all while having a tub of Ben and Jerry's.

"Why, I missed you, Red," he replies with an injured expression. "I hardly get any chance to talk to you since we got back from Russia...and others are no fun."

I almost laugh at his glum expression. He's such a kid. Set the two of us lose together somewhere, and we're talking about the beginning of a major disaster.

"Did he ever tell you about Antonia?" he asks suddenly. "We don't talk about her much, but I expect Constantine to tell you about her." He pats a spot on the bed beside him.

"Yeah, he did," I sigh and plonk myself down. I really have no way of getting rid of Caspian, until he's good and ready to go. Maybe it's a good thing to have somebody to talk to. Even if that somebody is Caspian.

"She was like a little sister to us all. When Antonia died, it affected us deeply. Constantine especially. Though no bloodbath, he destroyed a part of the palace. As for Milan, I know her game. She was never very nice to Antonia either...nor to Serena. We knew she won't like having you around. I guess that's why we never mentioned you in front of her. Lazarus and Constantine are always blind when it comes to her. Sometimes, I think Constantine and

Lazarus see her as a replacement for Antonia. To me, she'll never be that. She's completely the opposite of Antonia. Antonia was sweet, sincere, and loyal. Milan is deceitful, manipulative, and self-serving.

"She wants Constantine, but she wants the crown more. When father expressed his desire to pass the throne down to me, she came to me hoping that I'll make her my mate and my queen. Now that my father threatened to hand the crown to Constantine, she's determined to dig her claws back into him."

"Oh..." is all I manage to say. I only want Constantine, I never wanted the crown. "Will you though?"

"Huh?"

"Will you ever make her your queen if you become king?"

He throws his head back and laughs. "Make that scheming, conniving bitch queen? Never. I was just having my fun with her. In case you haven't noticed, there are not many lycans around and we can only have our fun with our erasthai or another lycan," he says wickedly. "Genesis, I'm waiting for my erasthai. I want what Lazarus has with Serena. I want what Constantine has with you. I'll wait forever for my erasthai if I have to."

"So you've slept with her too," I sigh, shaking my head. "Well, I hope you find your erasthai soon...though I pity whoever that turns out to be." I jab him in the rib with my elbow.

"No, you should envy her. I mean, come on. She's getting all this," he says cockily, indicating his body with his hands.

"Oh please." I pretend to gag. He is amazingly gorgeous, but his ego is just as amazing. I don't need to inflate it further. He might explode.

"Seriously though, being a mate to a lycan is not a bad thing. I think a lycan's mate is even more powerful than the born lycan. There's a strict law against harming a mate of a lycan. Harming a lycan's mate is punishable by death, no hearing required."

199

"Oh...why is that? We were born as mere werewolves or humans after all, not as great and mighty as you born lycans."

He just grins at my jab. "A lycan who lost his mate is deadly. The carnage, destruction, and havoc they can wreak is unimaginable. The only way to stop them from the killing spree is by killing the lycan...which is not easy to do."

I wonder if Constantine even cares if anybody killed me now. "And you're telling me this because you think I regret being Constantine's mate?"

"Are you?" he asks seriously.

"Why does it matter?"

"Because you're one of us," he answers simply. "Even though you don't act like one now."

"What does—" I stop talking when I hear mom's car pulling into our driveway.

"My mom's home. You've gotta leave," I tell him.

Caspian grins mischievously and lifts his long legs up onto my bed and lies down, looking very comfortable. What the—? He's making himself right at home.

"Caspian!!!" I whisper fiercely as I listen to my mom's footsteps coming in the front door. Sometimes I feel like crashing something on top of his gorgeous, obnoxious head. This is one of those times.

"Caspian! Out!!!" I grab his hands and start pulling and tugging him up, but he's so heavy...and strong. He's not budging an inch.

I climb up the bed and put my knee on each side of him, gripping his muscled shoulders, tugging very hard. Still nothing.

All the while, he's just lying there looking very relaxed with his lips clamped together like he's trying very hard not to burst out laughing. His bright vivid green eyes are openly laughing at me. He is so laughing at me, I can see it!

That makes me even more determined to get him out of my bed. I put one hand on the back of his neck and another one underneath his arm and keep pulling.

"Caspian!" I groan in frustration.

"Genesis? Are you okay?" asks mom, knocking once, then my door swings open.

Oh no!

My mom gasps, staring at us with wide eyes. She seems frozen shock. Then I realize the position I'm in with Caspian.

I'm basically straddling him on my bed with my hands around him and now the evil knucklehead has his both hands on my waist. We are both staring at her like she just caught us in the act of a steamy make out session or something. *Arghhh!*

"I'm sorry, sweetheart. I think I'd better go now," he says smoothly. I see the wicked gleam in his eyes as he sits up and kisses my cheek before he disappears out the window.

That royal brat! Arrrghh.

He did this on purpose! I will KILL him! I will slay him and feed him to hungry ducks all around the world! I will.

"Genesis," says mom sternly. "I did not raise you to be like this. Are you cheating on Constantine? With Prince Casper?"

Ha! Prince Casper. Take that Caspian! I hope he's listening. I almost laugh, but then I remember how much trouble I am in right now.

"I know they're both extremely good looking, but..." Mom sighs. "Come downstairs. I know, you're technically an adult now, but I think it's time we should have a proper mother daughter talk."

Oh Noooo! I. WILL. SLAY. HIM.

I think I hear his laughter from somewhere outside my window. Stupid royal brat.

CHAPTER XXIV
The Heart Wants What it Wants

I slept badly again last night. All I can think about is Constantine. What is he doing to me? I miss him so much, I've lost my appetite. That never ever happened before. I'm a fervent lover of food!

I miss him so much it hurts to breathe at times. This is even worse than when he left for Russia. It's actually even worse because I can see him at school, but I'm not with him. It's pure torture.

I blame him for the reason I woke up late this morning. I refused a lift from Reese because I'm still upset about yesterday, and now I'm super duper late! Sometimes pride and a stubborn head is a very bad combination if you want to make it to school on time.

I run all the way to school. I rush in through the door and almost collide with a figure standing in front of the school's office door.

"Whoa!" says a voice, while two hands grip my arms, stopping me from falling head first.

I look up into a pair of hazel eyes. A human. I've never seen him around before.

"Sorry," I apologize. "Silly me always run into things...and people," I grin up at him.

He's tall and good looking, and a human. He's probably around 6' 3" or so. He just stands there staring down at me wide eyed, not even blinking.

"Uh...hello?" I tap his shoulder lightly, he's still not moving. "I didn't hurt you, did I?" Now I'm a bit worried. What if I banged his head real hard just now, but my head is too dense to feel it? If he went into a comatose state, would I be held accountable?

Oh, cuddly bunny and fuzzy slippers!

I'm so not cut for the life in the slammers. I'd also ruin this boy's life! Oh, the poor unsuspecting victim of my clumsiness!

"I'm so sorry...I didn't mean to hurt you. I promise," I start to blabber.

"Uh...hi.." He finally comes to life.

I sigh and my shoulders sag in relief. "Thank goodness you're okay!"

"Yeah..." He smiles sheepishly. He runs his fingers through his reddish brown hair and his cheeks turn pink. *Awww.* He's shy. How sweet. But I'm sooo late!

"Glad you're okay. See you around. Bye!" I start moving away, but his hand comes up to grip my arm.

"Wait!" he says, then he quickly retracts his hand as if my skin burns.

"Yes?" I raise an eyebrow, waiting for him to say something. I really should get going.

"I'm...I'm Evan. I'm new here."

"Oookay..." I say, still waiting for him to explain why he's keeping me here.

"I think I need help to figure out where I'm going," he explains.

I sigh. That's it, between Constantine and doing a good deed like helping this guy out, the school might call my parents up anytime now about me missing so many classes.

"Okay, let me see your schedule."

He hands me all the papers he stuffed into his backpack.

Boys! I snort to myself. They're like preschoolers sometimes, I swear. I sort them out and find his locker numbers and schedule.

"Let me show you to your locker first. My name is Genesis, by the way," I offer him my hand.

"Glad to meet you, Genesis," he says as he takes my hand. His cheeks turn red again.

Oh my gosh! He's a blusher just like me! How adorable! That makes me smile up at him again. His step falters and he seems to freeze up again.

Now I'm really starting to worry about him. I'm not sure if I should ask him if he has a condition or something.

"Uh...you're okay?" I ask him hesitantly.

"You are the most beautiful girl I'd ever seen," he blurts, then blushed deeply.

Huh? *Awww*. How sweet! I burst out laughing. Wait till he sees Serena, and Milan, and Reese, and Penny or even Mia and all the other girls in this school. He's going to faint!

He blushes even more. Now even his ears turn red.

"Thanks, but you should see all the other girls in this school first before you say something like that," I smile up at him.

His eyebrows shoot up, but he doesn't say anything more.

"Here's your classroom, Evan. The teacher, Mr. Ryan's pretty nice and fun, you're lucky to have him. See you around. Bye!"

"Genesis, wait!" he calls out before I can run off. "Do we have any class together?"

"I don't know...I didn't check, but I know we have lunch break together." I smile. "See ya! Bye!"

I am so late!

Everybody is staring at me when I slip into the classroom almost 20 minutes late. Penny's rounded eyes are full of questions. The teacher doesn't say a word about me being late. I wonder if it has anything to do with me being Constantine's mate. Maybe I could run around naked and sing Frozen song, Let it go and get away with it.

Genesis, don't think crazy thoughts, I warn myself. I have the tendency to act out my thoughts.

During lunch time I sit with my friends again. I can feel Constantine's eyes burning through my skull as he stares at me. That's not helping my non-existent appetite at all.

"Hi, Genesis!"

I look up to see Evan with his tray of food standing beside me with that look in his eyes.

"Hey, Evan. What's up?" I smile up at him.

"Uh, can I sit with you?" he asks sheepishly.

"Uh...yeah..." I answer feeling very uneasy suddenly.

He quickly slides next to me and I look around to see my friends, River, Reese and Penny staring at me and Evan with wide eyes. In fact, I feel like the whole cafeteria is staring at us.

My eyes dart automatically to Constantine. The whole table of lycans are staring, and I'm pretty sure they're not staring at something behind me. Constantine is furious. I can tell. Well, maybe it's time for me to scram. I don't feel like eating anyway. Yeah, time to run.

I'm such a coward, I know.

"Evan, these are my friends River, Reese, and Penny. Guys, this is Evan. Be nice to him. He's new," I introduce him to my friends quickly. "Oh wow! I just remember I haven't finished my English literature assignment. Gotta go! See ya!" I exclaim as I pick up my tray.

"Wait! What assignment? We have English Lit together. Is there an assignment I don't know about?" asks Penny looking worried.

"Yeah!" I answer as I take off.

Cuddly bunny and fuzzy slippers! Why did I say English lit? Idiot!

Actually, I run from the cafeteria all the way home. Now, I'm feeling guilty for missing so many classes that I'm trying to do my homework. Yeah, trying because I can't seem to concentrate. How can I concentrate when he's in my head all the time? I lie down on my bed in frustration. I should probably talk to Constantine soon. I can't go on like this.

I take out my drawing pad from underneath my bed and stare at his silver gray eyes that I worked so hard to capture sometime ago. Those eyes. I should let go of my pride and forgive him. I'll try to get along with Milan if that's what it takes to be with him. I'm that desperate now, not to mention, tired and hungry.

I hear knocking on the front door downstairs. It takes me a while to figure out that nobody else is home. I should get the door. I really don't feel like socializing right now. I know none of the lycans would even think of using, let alone knocking on the front door.

I drag my feet to the top of the stairs but stop short when I smell a familiar scent. It seems that this one does use the front door after all.

I open the front door and my eyebrows raise instinctively. Milan is standing there looking impatient.

"I want to talk to you," she declares.

Oh really? Well, I don't! I hate it when people say that they want to talk to me. Of course, I didn't say those things out loud. I did promise myself to play nice. I just nod and open the door wider.

"No, I'd rather talk outside," she says airily. I thought I saw her wrinkle her nose at the sight of my living room. Maybe it's just my imagination.

We walk to the side of my house where a swing set is sitting underneath an old maple tree. We both opt to stand, though.

"Let me get straight to the point, Genesis." She turns to look at me. "I want Constantine."

Oh wow, my jaw almost drops at her directness. Ezra is clawing at my chest to get out. I clench my teeth and ball my hands into fists to control myself.

"I know you two haven't fully mated and marked each other yet," announces Milan. "So you're not really mates. He can still mate and mark somebody else. I'll make sure that it is me. Do you know that we're lovers once? We're about to be together again just before you came into the picture. It's no problem though. Now that I know what the problem is, I know what to do. We're going to be together again. He's going to be my mate in the end, Genesis. You might as well give up now."

"You're not even his erasthai. I am," I growl through clenched teeth.

"Maybe not, but that's not a big deal. We're both lycans, we're a better match for each other. Besides, I was there for him when he needed somebody. You just met him. You don't know him as well as I do."

She then looks at me sympathetically. "Oh, Genesis, you should realize it by now, he loves me. That's why he took me to Russia with him and left you here...so that the two of us can have some time together. Alone. If you know what I mean." She ends it with a smug smile. That hurts. "Don't worry, I can make him forget all about you. I can make him happy. He'll believe me over you...every time. He'll pick me over you anytime. You'll never win."

With those parting words, she struts out. Loose gravel scrunching under her expensive shoes. A minute later I hear her car driving away.

I feel my clenched hands shaking as I fall on my knees. Trying to hold Ezra in while feeling like my world is tilting sideways, tearing me apart.

*   *   *

207

There's an assembly at the gym this morning. I try to slip in and blend in with the crowd, but Penny grabs my arm from behind and drags me to sit next to her on the bleachers. Reese and River join us soon after.

My eyes zero in on the lycans standing near the door by the end of the bleachers. Constantine is standing there with the rest of them, looking extremely bored. He is so gorgeous though. Those eyes, the sculptured cheekbones, and nose, and chin, and those lips, hot messy hair. I'm seriously hopeless.

Milan is standing right next to him. She looks at me with a small smile playing on her lips and a triumphant look in her eyes. She wraps her arms around one of his and rests her head on his broad shoulder. I grit my teeth and look away.

I wish I could stop loving him. I wish I could hate him. I wish I weren't this pathetic.

My eyes fall on Hunter who is looking at me with a sympathetic look. I like Hunter. I think he's very nice, but I don't want any sympathy from anybody. I take a deep breath and give him a big smile. He smiles back, looking somehow sort of relieved.

I feel the heat of *his* stare burning through my skull, as if commanding me to look, and my eyes are drawn back towards where the lycans are standing. Constantine is staring fiercely back. His eyes move to Hunter then back to me. I can feel his anger from here. He turns to look away first. His jaw tight. Milan leans in close to his ear and whispers something. I have to admit, they are both stunningly beautiful. They look good together. That thought is like a dagger to my heart.

"Genesis!" Evan is smiling up at me, as he makes his way over. "Can I sit here?"

"Uh, yeah...sure." What else can I say?

Evan lowers himself right next to me. He's too close for my liking. His thigh is pressed up against mine. Ezra's seriously not liking this. There's not much I can do though. There's not much room for me to wiggle away. His arm goes around my back.

208

I look up to people staring at me again. My eyes automatically flash to Constantine who's staring at me with steely cold eyes. He's not even hiding his jealousy. His jaw is clenched tight and his nostrils are flaring. I could almost feel the scorching heat of his fury. Well, he has Milan hanging onto his arm, so...whatever. I stare defiantly back even when I feel like cowering from his intense anger.

Mr. Bennet, our principal, takes the mic and starts talking about the upcoming sports events. I'm so tense, I'm not paying attention to a single word he says.

It feels like more eyes are staring at me than at our principal. I feel like everybody's waiting in anticipation for something to happen. They're hungry for blood. My blood. Or maybe that's just my food deprived stomach and sleep deprived brain thinking.

All the lycans are definitely looking at me. Caspian is staring at me broodingly as well. What is his problem?

I tear my eyes away from Constantine and all the other lycans to have my eyes fall on Hunter who's also scowling. Then on pissed off Logan and his friends and other people around. None of them are looking too happy. What is everybody's problem? If looks could kill, I'd be minced meat.

I feel Penny's hand tightens around mine.

"Uh, why is everybody staring at us?" whispers Evan close to my ear.

"I have no idea," I whisper back.

"They're not all your boyfriends, are they?" He jokes, chuckling a little.

"No, not all of them. No," At least that one is not a lie.

I gulp nervously, and my gaze is drawn back towards the lycans. Caspian is saying something heatedly to Constantine who is looking livid. A few seconds later, Constantine takes off. Milan runs off after him immediately.

I feel sick. I feel sick and furious.

"They're all beautiful, huh?" utters Evan.

"Huh? What?" I blink back tears.

"Those kids. They're hard to miss. I mean this school is full of hot looking people. I wonder what's going on when I first got here," explains Evan. "But those five. They definitely stand out even among these good-looking people."

Then he pauses for a little while and turns to look at me. "And then there's you...you're still the most beautiful girl I've ever seen. You seem to belong to that group more than anywhere else." He sounds thoughtful like he's trying to solve a puzzle.

I suddenly feel like bawling my eyes out. I can't take any more of this. I feel my heart breaking into tiny pieces. I find the stares suffocating. I feel the crowd closing in on me. I feel my world tearing apart.

"I have to go. Excuse me," I mumble, getting up.

"Where are you going? Are you okay?" asks Penny sounding worried.

"I just need to use the washroom," I reply as I try to find my way down the bleachers through the crowd. My progress down is agonizingly slow. I feel eyes following me. They're following me everywhere. I hate attention!

I lock the door of the washroom and really bawl my eyes out. Gosh, I feel so pathetic.

After a while, I wash my face and stare at my red-rimmed eyes. I'm such a wreck. Just thinking about Constantine makes my heart twist in pain. Why is it that with him I feel either euphorically happy or intensely in pain? Why does it have to be one extreme to another? I splash cold water on my face again, then pat it dry and straighten myself before I finally walk out of the washroom.

Hunter is waiting for me outside the door. Oh great, a witness to my pathetic miserable tear fest. But then again, I guess that's why nobody was knocking on the door of the washroom while I was in there. Hunter was guarding the door. I should be thankful for that, I suppose.

The hallway is deserted. Everybody seems to have gone back to their classrooms.

"Are you okay?" There's concern in his voice and eyes.

I just nod my head. I try to smile, but I think I fail miserably when he pulls me into his arms and walks me out of there.

"Where are we going?" I ask him.

"Out of here. Away from prying eyes," he answers.

We end up sitting at the end of the bleachers next to each other by the football field. The second time I'm on the bleachers today.

"I'm not going to ask if you're okay again. Clearly, you're not okay," he says, glancing sideways at me.

"I don't know how life can get so complicated, Hunter. All I wanted before was a mate, finish high school together, maybe go to college...or not. Have babies, clean poopy diapers, pay bills together, then have teenage kids who mouth off to you...you know, all that fun stuff," I explain, my voice comes out sounding wobbly and pathetic.

"All that fun stuff," he repeats after me, smiling a little. "See? That's what I love about you. You manage to stay upbeat and funny...no matter what life throws at you."

"Upbeat? Did you not notice how awful I'm looking right now, Hunter?"

He turns to look at me. His eyes roaming my face before staring into my eyes. "You're not looking awful, Genesis," he mumbles. "You never look awful."

Why do I suddenly feel awkward? "I'm sorry you have to rescue me all the time, Hunter. You've been great. Thank you." I turn to look away.

"I don't mind. I want you to come to me if you need rescuing," he says. "I wish..."

I turn to look at him, quizzically. "You wish?"

He sighs heavily. "I wish I was your mate, Genesis. I told you that already. I would've made you so happy."

Oh gosh! I stare up at him in silence for a few seconds. His chocolate brown eyes are staring at me earnestly. His feelings are clearly on display as clear as daylight. Why didn't I see it before?

He's really an attractive guy. He's a wonderful person. I know any girl would be so lucky to have him as her mate...but he's not for me. He's not the one who makes my heart race with his presence. He's not the one who haunts my mind day and night. His touch isn't the one that I crave for. He's not the one causing my skin to tingle with a simple touch. He's not the one who makes me feel whole and complete. The heart wants what it wants.

"I'm so sorry, Hunter."

"Yeah," he whispers regretfully. "I just needed to tell you...I'll never hurt you if..." he trails off, staring down at his shoes.

"Yeah," I whisper back, but deep down I know I can't do that. Even if Constantine decided to mark Milan as his mate, I'm not going to take someone else's mate away just because I don't want to be alone. His mate is out there somewhere. I can't take that away from him.

CHAPTER XXV
Too Much Thinking Hurts My Brain

As soon as I get back into the building after my talk with Hunter, I decided to look for the lycans. I know I'm such a coward, but it's high time that I stop running...for now.

It's in between classes, Caspian, Lazarus, and Serena are standing by the end of the hallway, talking to each other quietly. Constantine and Milan are still missing.

As soon as I get near them, they stop talking. The three of them turn to look at me. Caspian especially looks furious. He closes the distance between us with a couple of steps. He grabs my shoulders, then he leans in and places his nose close to my neck.

Wait! What the... Is he sniffing me?

"So now you decide to come back to us?" growls Caspian accusingly, close to my ear. Then he pushes me away. "Why don't you just go back to that human boy or that beta mutt that I smell on you?" he adds before stalking away angrily, sounding almost like he's jealous.

I stare at his retreating figure in shock...and hurt. Caspian may be mischievous, a troublemaker, and a serial flirt but it's always in a playful, fun and harmless way. Sometimes, he's even affectionate. He's never mean or unkind. It hurts to have him talk to me that way.

"What is his problem? " I scowl at his retreating figure.

I turn to look at Lazarus who isn't looking very friendly either.

Fine! Be that way. I walk away, almost stomping my feet like a five-year-old. What's everyone's problem?

"Genesis!" Serena comes running after me. She takes my arm and leads me out the front exit, straight to the parking lot.

"Wait! School is not over yet," I protest as she unlocks her shiny red Mercedes Cabriolet and shoves me inside.

"It is over for us," she answers me firmly as she starts the engine.

She drives down the main street in silence for a couple of miles. Then she makes a swift turn into a dirt road and keeps driving until we finally reach a small bridge. There, she pulls to the side and turns off the engine. It's quite a nice place. It's isolated and surrounded by trees. I can hear the peaceful sound of water running underneath the bridge.

Wait! What if she's mad at me too, and now she's decided to kill me here?

She gets out of the car, and I follow suit. Oh well, if a lycan decided to kill you, there's no way you can avoid it. Might as well die in the hands of sweet and beautiful Serena rather anyone else's. By anyone else I mean Milan. I bet she'll make it very painful for me.

Sheesh...thinking about my own death is making me hungry. Did I have anything for dinner last night? Or lunch yesterday? Why am I thinking about my own death and food right now? I don't know. I think lack of food and sleep is making me bonkers. I'm losing it. I'm blaming it all on Constantine.

"We're almost in another pack's territory." Serena points out, breaking my crazy inner monologue. We find a spot to sit on, on the river bank.

We sit quietly listening to the sound of the running river, and the rustling of the leaves and branches, the chirping of birds and the crows in the distance.

214

"Werewolves are gregarious beings. They like to travel and stay in packs," she states casually after a while. "Lycans are like that too. It might not seem that way sometimes, but we are. Though we can travel alone, we prefer to be in a pack or at least as a couple. That's one of the reasons mates are important to us," she explains. "Genesis, whether you realize it or not, we are a pack. A small pack, but a pack nonetheless. You are one of us. You have been for the last three years."

Wait! I've been a member of a lycans pack for the last three years and I wasn't even aware of it? They're like the elite group in our school that even the populars can't touch. I had been walking around school looking at them all in awe like everyone else, and I was one of them? Oh, my head hurts. Too much thinking in one day.

I comb my fingers through my hair and sit staring at the slow moving water of the river, trying to make sense of everything.

"Wow, we're a very small pack," I finally comment.

"We are lycans. We don't need numbers. We are strong enough as we are," replies Serena.

I sigh. "Okay, but what is up with Caspian now? Why is he so mad at me?"

"Remember when I told you that lycans are very possessive?" asks Serena. "Well, we're not only possessive of our own mate, we're possessive of our pack members too. You might be Constantine's mate, but Caspian sees you as ours. He and Lazarus aren't happy that you're close to that human and the other mutts and not being with us."

"Wait. Are you telling me that instead of having to deal with one, I have three possessive lycans to deal with?"

"Four, actually," she confesses.

"Serena! Not you too!"

"You're one of us. You're like a sister to me. Any threat of you being taken away from us, we don't like," she argues defensively.

215

"But I'm not joining another pack."

"Yes, but you going with another male is a threat that you're being taken away from the pack, especially since Constantine hasn't fully marked you yet."

"But he's going to mark Milan...even if I'm not with another man."

"What? Says who?" She looks aghast.

"Milan.."

"Genesis, Milan says a lot of things. Mostly lies."

"But there is a lot of truth in there too!"

"Okay...like what?" She challenges me.

"Don't tell me she and Constantine weren't lovers...and didn't they have fun in Russia? Don't tell me she didn't go. What's up with him always defending her?"

"Genesis, listen to me. Yes, they might have a history, but I wouldn't call them lovers. It was over a hundred years ago. I know they haven't been together since I became a part of this pack. Constantine is not interested in her that way. I suspect he never was.

I went with them to Russia too. Those three were there to do their duties, not for pleasure. They need to tie some loose ends so that they're free to come back here again. Constantine, Lazarus, and Caspian were busy the whole time we were there. I barely saw Lazarus," explains Serena. "Genesis, Constantine thought of no one else but you in Russia. He was busy getting things done so that he can be back here as soon as he can to be with you. Believe me, there's no room for anyone else in his head and his heart."

"But Milan said.."

"No, don't listen to that bitch. You should talk to Constantine," she says vehemently. "Genesis, I know you're young, but always talk to your mate first. Constantine and Lazarus are the same in the way that they don't explain things that need explaining. They've been alone for too long to understand that we need explanation sometimes. Ask the right question, and they will talk. They will tell you the truth, but you have to make them explain.

"As for him taking her side, my guess is, it's because he's so used to doing that. Both him and Lazarus are loyal, and are used to defending Milan."

"He's driving me crazy, though." I wail, in frustration.

"I know, men. Lazarus does that to me sometimes," she agrees. "But Genesis, you're driving him crazy too. Constantine and Lazarus are the most cultured, and controlled lycans I know. They're royalty and they're very powerful. They can't afford to lose control easily. Lives could be lost, properties destroyed. I've never seen Constantine lost control more often than these last couple of weeks because of you," she tells me seriously. Then her lips curl up into an amused smile.

"You really did a number on him. Being around him had been unbearable these last couple of days since the two of you started fighting. Milan had been trying to give him a shoulder to lean on. I don't think that got her anywhere." She smirks.

"So...you think he's with Milan now?" Jealousy is still searing through me.

Serena laughs. "Oh, I don't think so...he's very pissed when he took off. He'll take anybody's head off if anyone dared to get close to him when he's like that. Even Milan isn't stupid enough to know that.

"If I were you, I wouldn't worry about Milan, Genesis. She's been trying for over a hundred years. If he wanted her, he would have made her his mate a long time ago. Constantine is crazy about you. He's crazy loyal too," she assures me.

Oh goddess, that's a lot for me to take in. So he didn't spend time alone and having fun with Milan in Russia? Should I believe Serena? She's one of them after all. If I didn't believe her, then it's like me believing Milan over Serena and Constantine. Oh, my head hurts, too much thinking.

217

Serena drives me back right after our talk. I take a shower to get rid of the smells on me that seem to offend so many people today. I fiddle about for a bit trying to figure out what to do next. It's still quite early, the school isn't out yet. Oh, Constantine...what a mess.

I think I should go for a run. I'm tired of thinking for today. My brain keeps going around and around. It needs some rest, I decided.

I quickly phase and jump out...feeling free. Just me and Ezra. It's exhilarating.

I return a couple of hours later, climbing in through the window, feeling better than I did this morning.

"Where have you been?" asks Constantine, standing in my bedroom.

I almost fell out of the window.

I put a foot in cautiously while keeping a watchful eye on Constantine. Just one of my feet is in, while the rest of my body is still hanging out the window.

Constantine's whole body is tense. His eyes narrow as he watches my every movement as if expecting me to make a run for it at any second. Well now, that doesn't seem like a bad idea.

"Don't even think about it, sweetheart," he warns. "I'll just catch you, and you won't like what I might do to you once I do."

Oh uh, this is not good.

"Why don't you come in, my love?" He coaxes me. I don't like the way he's saying that. It sounds too much like a trap. The way he's looking at me is too much like a predator eyeing its prey.

"Uh, I think I'll just stay out here, thank you," I answer. "I quite like the fresh air," I add, holding onto the window frame. This is such an awkward position.

"Do you now?" His voice is smooth.

"Uh huh," I nod my head enthusiastically and gulp audibly. My eyes must be huge on my face as I stare at him warily.

"Maybe I should join you there. I quite like the fresh air myself," He takes a slow step towards me.

I've never seen him quite like this before, and it's putting me on edge. A loud sound of warning bells starts to go off in my head. There's something about him that seems very dangerous right now. It's there, in the glitter of his watchful silver-gray eyes, in his measured, calculating movement, in the mesmerizing tone of his voice.

Before he gets any closer, I take off.

Ninja!!!

I fling myself as far as I can from the house. As soon as my feet touch the ground, I sprint to the nearest tree and grab a branch to haul myself up.

I'm still in my human form, but I've learned in the last couple of days that I'm getting faster and stronger even without phasing. Maybe not as fast and deadly as in my lycan form, but I'm still very fast.

I can hear the whooshing sound of the wind in my ears as I propel myself forward faster and faster. I push my feet against a tree when my hands barely touch it, to grab another sturdy looking branch.

I sense movement behind me. I try to phase, but I can't seem to concentrate hard enough to do so. My heart is hammering, and my blood is pumping in my ears. Pure adrenaline is rushing through me. I kick harder and swing faster onto further hanging branches and trees. I think I'm losing him.

Suddenly, I feel his presence very close behind me. I fling myself quickly upwards, with my hands outstretch to grab the next tree. I yelp as an arm snatches me in mid-air around my waist. He presses me close to his body and lowers us both to the ground, but he keeps going. His arm is like a steel band around me. There's nothing I can do but to wrap my arms around his neck and my legs around his waist.

Oh, he smells heavenly. How I miss his amazing scent. Wait! What am I thinking? Suddenly, I remember his threat. My stomach clench at the thought of what he might do to me.

He's moving very fast. Everything seems to be a blur around me. What was I thinking trying to outrun him?

He keeps going further and further, and I have no idea where we are when he finally stops. He releases his hold on me, and I quickly jump a few feet away from him.

"Now my sunshine, we're all alone," he utters with some satisfaction. His hair is mussed up sexily. His skin is a bit flushed from all the running he just did. Oh goddess, he's still the sexiest man I've ever laid my eyes on.

"What are you planning to do to me?" I ask him warily.

His eyes rake up and down my body as if he can see through my clothing. "What do you think I would do to you, sunshine?" He sounds amused, almost indulgent. His lips curl up into a feral smile. His silver-gray eyes flashed with anger, hunger, and desperation. It sets my pulse racing.

He's not really amused. I can tell. "Maybe I'm tired of waiting. Maybe I'm tired of chasing after you. Maybe it's time for me to catch you, Genesis."

Cuddly bunny and fuzzy slippers!

I don't know about this. Do I want to get caught? I'm not waiting around to find out. I look around, trying to think of a way to escape. We're in a grassy clearing, up on top of a mountain, from what I can see. There's only one tree right in the middle of the clearing as if it was planted there. There are trees and mountains for miles around us. Miles and miles of them.

He's very still, standing there silently watching my every movement like a big cat or rather a lycan, waiting for its prey's next move.

He takes one step closer, and I skittishly jump back. He stops as if he's assessing the situation, then deciding to change the tactics.

I have to admit, it confuses me when he casually leans back against the lone tree. "So...what did you do while I was away? Were you busy forming your own reverse harem?" he asks conversationally, linking his hands behind his head. He looks and sounds totally relaxed, but the intensity in his eyes is anything but relaxed.

I gulp nervously, but I figure it's safer to move as far away from him as possible by slowly taking a couple of steps back. "No, I don't know what you're talking about."

"You never answered me, did you have fun with that alpha mutt at the party you went to? Or was it with the Beta that you disappeared with?" His eyes flash with hurt, anger, and jealousy. I sense that his body is like a tightly coiled spring even when he is leaning passively against the tree.

"Didn't Milan tell you all about it already?"

"Don't you think you're the one who should be telling me all about that? Tell me, did you enjoy your time with those two?"

Talking about Milan makes my blood boil.

"What if I did? What's it to you?" I blurt out angrily.

In a blink of an eye, he's on me. His nose flares and his eyes flash dangerously. His hand goes to my back to pin my body up against his. The other hand grabs the back of my neck while his thumb pushes my chin up so that I'm looking up into his face.

"Don't you dare to say that again. You are mine! Every single inch of you is mine," he growls possessively. His eyes are darkening around the edges. Me and my big mouth.

"Tell me, sweetheart, did any of them touch these lips?" His index finger traces my lips, not very gently, pulling them apart. My lips tingle with pleasure from his touch. "These lips belong to me."

He pushes his finger into my mouth. My tongue involuntarily comes up to lick his finger. "Did he taste this mouth? This tongue?" His breath teases my skin. "This mouth is mine. This tongue belongs only to me."

He leans in close. His own lips graze my cheek, delicious explosions of heat spread like wildfire across my skin.

Suddenly, he rips my shirt open. His eyes roam over my exposed body hungrily. "Mine," he growls as I try to cover myself. He only pulls my ripped shirt all the way off and tosses it aside. "Only I'm allowed to see this. Touch this. I'm never letting you go. I've warned you. It's time for you to remember that." His voice sounds even deeper now. I can see his canine very clearly. He leans down and licks my neck, and my shoulder, while his canine grazes my skin.

CHAPTER XXVI
Tell Me Where it Hurts

He leans down and licks my neck, and my shoulder, while his canine grazes my skin. I shudder as chills of pleasure run up and down my body. My eyelids flutter shut. The feel of his warm, hard body covering mine, his heated, wet, and wicked mouth, and tongue on my skin.

Oh goddess, yes. Noo...

I want him to mark me, but at the same time, I don't. My brain is saying no, but my body has a mind of its own. I want to push him off me, but instead, my fingers disappear into his thick dark silky hair and tug him closer. Breathless moaning comes out of my mouth.

No, no, no. I push him off my neck, but then my hands move to stroke his cheeks.

His long, thick, sooty eyelashes fan his cheeks as he closes his eyes and leans into my touch. His nose flares. I stroke his cheeks gently and he's almost purring, losing himself in the pleasure of the simple touch. I'm mesmerized. I can't take my eyes off of his beautiful face. His passion-filled yet tortured expression so lost in ecstasy. This is my doing. I can't believe I have such a lethal, powerful creature purring under the touch of my hands.

"It's been so long since the last time you touched me," he murmurs, his voice so low like he's drowning in pleasure. "Tell me that you're mine," he demands hoarsely with his eyes still closed.

He brings his face down to mine again. His nose nuzzles my ear, then my jaw, then his sensual lips seek that spot behind my ear. My eyes roll to the back of my head. It's not fair; he knows my body so well. His hands are trailing fire, roaming over my exposed stomach, then cupping me over my lacy bra. My body comes alive under his touch. The pleasure is too much, it numbs my mind.

"Say it," he growls into my ear. "Say that you're mine."

Think! Think! Yes. No.

"My body's yours," I gasp. "Are you happy now?" I add rebelliously.

"Not yet....not until you can't stay away from me. Not until you need me so bad, you can't think, you can't sleep, you can't breathe until you're in my arms," he says harshly. "Not until you feel like you're going out of your mind like you're only half of a being without me around. Not until you feel what I feel."

Goddess, is that not how I had been feeling for the last couple of days? I felt like I wasn't going to survive without him.

"Now tell me that you need me," he demands.

"I..I.." Oh gosh, I can't even form a simple sentence when he's holding me like this.

"Say it, Genesis. Tell me you need me. Tell me you want me. Tell me you want this. Say it."

I need him, yes. I want him. Oh, so much! I want him so badly NOW. But, I'd rather die than be second to anyone in his life. It will kill me eventually if I had to watch him with Milan or anyone else. Milan will always be in his life. Milan.

"NO!" I yell, pushing him away. I must have taken him by surprise because he loses his grip on me and staggers back. We stand, wide-eyed, staring at each other intensely with a few feet between us, breathing hard. Emotions flit across his face. First is shock, then hurt, disbelieve, then hurt again...and anger.

"No?" His silver-gray eyes flash dangerously. He moves in closer again, and his hands come up to grip my upper arms possessively. "It's one of those boys, isn't it? Who is it? Is it that

224

useless alpha mutt? Are you going back to him? Or that beta? No? The stupid human boy then?" he demands through clenched teeth. His eyes are darkening around the edges again. It's bleeding slowly into the whites.

"Why does it matter?"

"Why does it matter??? It matters because you're mine! You love only me! Whoever it is, I'll destroy him," he vows. His voice is changing. His still changing eyes burn into mine as if he's reaching inside my brain, reading into my deepest secrets.

He's still furious, and I should be calming him if I was smart, but I'm not smart. Especially when I am seething myself. He has no right to be jealous when he had Milan hanging onto his arm. The image of them together in my head is enough to make me simmer inside.

"Screw you!" I yell, trying to pull my arms out of his grip.

"Yeah, let me show you how good it is to screw me," he growls before his mouth slams onto mine. His hand moves up into my hair to hold my head in place for his punishing kiss. His other hand is firmly on my ass, holding me up, molding my body to his. My feet are off the ground. I struggle to be free, but he's much too strong. He grinds his mouth against mine, but I keep my mouth clamp shut. He bites my lower lip with enough pressure for him to be able to pry my mouth open for his invasion. His tongue slips inside, and my brain goes hazy. The taste of him—his tongue exploring my mouth and tangling with mine. Fireworks and explosions are breaking out through my entire body. This kiss is rough and meant to show dominance and possession. Why am I enjoying this?

Mmm. Screw this!

I return his punishing kiss with my own. We're all lips and tongues and teeth, clashing, dueling and punishing. This kiss is frantic and furious and hungry. Pain and pleasure. Torture and passion. My hand moves up to grab a fistful of his luscious hair and tug roughly. My other hand sinks into his back. He moans into my mouth, and I sink my teeth into his lower lip...and taste blood.

"Bastard," I growl before I attack his lips again and grip his hair harder.

He responds by grinding his lips roughly against mine. His mouth then moves to trail my jaw and lower. His hand pulls at my hair to angle my head to the side so that his hungry mouth has better access to my neck.

"Douche," I moan as he licks and sucks and nibbles.

Gosh! His mouth is still magic.

"You're a scumbag... ohhh... asshole… pig... mmm... jerk." I tug at his hair harder. "Jackass." I manage before his mouth covers mine again.

"Oh, the mouth you have on you..." he whispers against my lips. "And you kiss me with this mouth.." he says and kisses me again.

"I'm going to mark you...I need to mark you," he says. "You're all I can think about. Whenever I see any of those guys near you, I want to go on a rampage. You need me as much as I need you. Tell me you want me too."

Yes, I do want him to mark me, but then again my brain keeps taking me back to Milan.

"No! No, I don't," I reply, pushing him off. My voice is almost breaking. "If you mark me now, I'll hate you forever."

"No!" He stares at me as if he's seeing me for the first time. "Why are you doing this? You need me as much as I need you. You love me," he declares vehemently and desperately.

"No, I don't. I don't need you," I lie. "Why do you think I keep asking for more space and time? I love someone else," I feel my heart breaking as I say those words.

He reels back as if I just hit him. "No," he mumbles, shaking his head in denial. "I don't believe you. No. You need me. You love me. You told me so...you do."

"No, I lied. I don't need you. I never loved you." Oh Gosh, it's hard to breathe. My chest is hurting.

Constantine is clutching his chest too, still shaking his head. "No...you're lying."

Tears are pooling in my eyes, and I turn away from him. I'm feeling very sick, and cold, and weak, as if all blood just drained from my body. My chest is hurting even more. My feet can barely hold my body up. I almost fall when he kneels in front of me.

"Tell me that's not true," he says. "Tell me..." He suddenly wraps his arms around me tightly and presses his face against my stomach. He's holding me like he's hanging for dear life. My tears start to fall in heavy downpours.

I'm in so much pain, I can't manage to choke a single word out. Ezra is in pain.

"Tell me what I can do to make you love me," he begs against my stomach. "Just tell me...anything, and I'll do it."

I try to move, but he won't let go of me. "I won't let you go," he vows, but his voice sounds tortured. "You love me...please."

"No." I try so hard to stop crying, but my tears soon turn into silent sobs.

He looks up when big fat tears start falling onto his arms, and my body starts shaking uncontrollably.

Why can't I lie without feeling such pain? Why can't I stop crying? His eyes turn from confusion to a dawning of understanding as he stares up at me.

"You do love me," he declares with sudden clarity as he gets to his feet.

"No, I don't," I choke out, shaking my head.

"Yes, you do. Why are you lying to me?" he demands to know, cupping my face firmly in his hands. He tilts my face up, and I closed my eyes tightly.

"Look at me!"

I stubbornly keep my eyes closed, willing the tears to stop falling. They keep coming. My sobs turn louder.

"Sunshine..." he groans before his mouth takes mine in a soft, gentle kiss. He kisses me like I was made of glass. He holds and kisses me like I was the most precious thing he ever held and touched. That only makes me cry harder.

"Sweetheart, what can I do?" he asks, leaning his forehead against mine. "Tell me.."

"Let...let me g go," I gasp between sobs.

"No!" he growls, pulling away. "Anything but that," he announces, gripping my shoulders tightly. "I told you, I'll never let you go. You don't seem to get it, sunshine. I might sound like a selfish bastard, but I've waited all my life for you. Over three hundred lonely years. You're my erasthai. Mine! I'm never letting you go."

"What about Milan?" I suddenly spit out. I can't keep it in any longer. He will not have us both. I did not escape from almost being Logan's side mate to become Constantine's second choice. It was painful to hear it from Logan. It would kill me if I had to go through the same thing with Constantine.

His eyebrows rise in surprise. Then he frowns in confusion. It's like that was the last thing he expected me to say. "What about her?"

"Aren't you in love with her? Aren't you going to keep her too?"

"What???" he says, looking appalled. "What gave you that idea?"

"Milan! You wanted to have fun with her in Russia. That's why you left me here!" I snap. My sadness has turned into rage. "Well, I won't be anyone's woman on the side. Next time you want to spend time alone with her, don't even bother to lie...because...because... I won't be here for you to lie to. You two can spend all the time alone together. Forever!!!" I yell the last part as loud as I can, with all the fury I feel in me. Then I turn around,

228

intent to make my grand getaway. Gosh! I sounded like a jealous housewife! If I had something in front of me now, I would totally bang my head against it—several times!

His powerful arm snakes around my waist faster than I can move. Totally ruined my dramatic escape. Gah! This man! Can't I at least keep some of whatever dignity I have left?

"You're jealous." He states in surprise, turning me around to face him. "That's it? All this? All this is because you're jealous?" He sounds almost amazed, and disbelieving... and happy. "There's no other man is there? You're just jealous."

Oh, he'd better not be laughing at me now!

Jerk! I grit my teeth and glare up at him with my most vicious scowl. Ever.

"You're jealous? Of Milan?" he states again, sounding incredulous.

If he repeated those words again, I'll knee him in his baby maker. I swear it!

"But sunshine, I have no interest in Milan at all. She's just a friend. You're my erasthai. You're my mate. Don't you understand how important you are to me? There's no one else for me but you!" His silver-gray eyes gaze into mine with such intensity as if willing me to understand.

"You took her side when I told you she was hurting me and my friends. You chose to believe her over me. You chose her over me." I cry. I feel the hurt all over again.

"Oh, sweetheart..." he groans, cradling the back of my head with his hands. His thumbs are wiping my tears. "I'm so sorry..." He pulls me close and rests his forehead against mine. "I didn't realize I was doing that. The last thing I want to do is hurt you. I would never intentionally hurt you. I certainly never, ever, choose anyone over you. Will you forgive me?"

"What about Russia? Milan told me herself how you two had fun in Russia. She said you went there to be alone with her. Away from me." I pull away from him.

He clenches his jaw. "I see... sounds like she's been very busy telling you things. When did she tell you all this? What else had she been telling you?"

"She came to my house yesterday. She told me to back off. She said that you love her and that you two are getting back together again. She said you'd believe her over me, that you'd choose her over me anytime."

"I see." His eyes narrow and seem thoughtful.

"She said that you two were lovers and that you two were going to be mates," I can't keep the hurt from my voice. "She said she would make you happy and forget all about me."

I'm throwing her under the bus by telling him all about this, but I don't care. Serena told me to talk to my mate, and that's what I'm doing right now.

"Forget all about you?" He scoffs. Constantine suddenly laughs. It doesn't sound like his usual amused laughter though. It was brief and harsh. It sounds like he finds the idea absurd. In fact, his laughter sounds like he's furious.

"Sweetheart, it happened only one time, a week after Antonia died. That was over a hundred years ago. I wasn't in the right mind. She was there for me when Antonia died. Maybe it's grief. I don't know why I did it. I thought it would make me feel better, but it didn't, and I regretted it right away. It's empty, and it means nothing. It's nothing like what we share, Genesis. Believe me, one touch, one glance from you means a lot more to me than that one time.

"I actually felt worse after it happened and I saw that she wanted more. Right away, I knew that it was a mistake. I apologized to her. I told her that it'll never happen again and that nothing will come out of it because I was waiting for my erasthai. She seemed okay with it. She said she's waiting for hers too."

"Well, she's not okay with it," I mumble. "She hates me."

"Sweetheart, I've been alive for over three hundred years. It was a lonely existence, but I had no intention of ever making anyone else my mate. I was waiting for you. The moment I saw you, I knew you're worth every second of the wait. My, fiery sunshine, I'll wait another thousand years for you if I have to," he says, looking earnestly into my eyes. His hand tugging a lock of my hair around his fingers. He always seems to have a thing for my hair.

"As for Russia, I didn't take her with me. She decided to come with us. Besides, I didn't talk to her at all back then because I was still very mad at how she interrupted our... err... painting session." His eyes flash briefly with the remembered session, and my cheeks flushed red. "I didn't see her in Russia at all until we boarded the plane to come home.

"I didn't bring you along because I had no intention of staying there longer than two days. I thought I'd be okay without you for that short amount of time. I thought you might be a distraction to me because we're there to work.

"We went there to set borders among a few Southern Packs to create peace. They've been at war for years. We started the peace deal a few years back, but it fell through when one of the packs broke the temporary truce agreement. We needed to start the negotiations right away while all the pack leaders are in the agreement.

"Also, we needed to convince King Alexandros to let us stay here a bit longer. I know you're not ready to leave yet. I drove Lazarus and Caspian crazy by cracking the whip on them to finish everything in less than two days. We left while some of them were still negotiating. Sunshine, I can't be away from you ever again. I'm never leaving you behind. I might have to work day and night, but at least I know you're there, not thousands of miles away. Not worrying if you're safe or if any other males are trying to get close to you, feeling jealous, and thinking of the worst ...driving myself crazy, wanting to get back here even before our plane touched the ground in Moscow.

"I think I drove everyone crazy these last couple of days. I wanted to take you, mark you as mine, but I didn't want you to hate me for doing it forcefully. I wanted you to want it as much as I did. Sweetheart, these last couple of days were pure torture...now will you forgive me?"

"You always have Milan hanging on your shoulder. I thought you chose her over me. I thought you're getting back together again."

"Sweetheart, we were never together, to begin with. It's always been you for me."

"But you're always whispering together."

"Yeah, all we did was talking about you. She's always giving me advice about getting you back."

"How very helpful of her," I respond cattily.

"Might not be the best person for me to listen to, but I was pretty desperate to get you back. You have no idea how crazy you're driving me," he says, pressing his forehead to mine. "Please forgive me for making you feel like you're second to somebody else. That was never my intention. You must know, you'll always come first. Always, sweetheart," he vows. "Forgive me?"

"You never came to see me at night like you always did either." I pout.

"Sunshine, you asked for some space and time. I thought that was because you're not sure about us, but I wasn't ever going to let you go. I stayed away because I was hoping you'd figure out that you couldn't live without me...only it backfired. It was pure torture. I couldn't stand it. I saw all the boys around you like vultures, ready to pounce on my girl as soon as they thought I was out of the picture. It drove me crazy. I was ready to snap all the men's head who even dared to look at you. Now will you forgive me?" he asks again.

"For the record, I'd never apologized to anyone as much as I'm apologizing to you right now," he adds suddenly.

"Yeah, you're pretty desperate to get into my pants," I return flippantly. I blushed beet red as soon as the words escaped my lips. Me and my big mouth.

His eyes widen in surprise for a second, then he grins wickedly. "Is it working? Do I get to be in you... I mean, in your pants soon?"

I puff my cheeks, trying to ignore the buzzing excitement in my tummy and my racing heartbeat at his naughty looks and words.

"Nothing happened between me and Logan at the party," I say instead. "Nor with Hunter, the beta. I ran out of there....Hunter drove me home. That's all."

"You're very good at running, my love...though I'm glad you did," he remarks. "I trust none of those guys, though. I'm thankful that the beta sent you home...but he wants you. I can see it in his eyes every time he looks at you. The same with that human boy. He's smitten with you. Can't take his eyes off you. I could happily snap his head off every time he's staring at you with that sickening lovestruck look on his face."

"Constantine, I don't care about any of them. I only want you. There's no one else for me but you."

CHAPTER XXVII
The One Who Catches Her

He gathers me into his arms. The look in his eyes takes my breath away. Those beautiful intense silver-gray eyes that I missed so much are now staring into mine with so many emotions. How could anyone think they're so cold?

"And there's no one else for me but you," he vows, his fingers gently tracing the curve of my cheek. "Be mine? Will you spend eternity with me?"

"Yes," I whisper back.

His eyes flash as we stare at each other. Telling each other with our eyes what mere words can't deliver. Never have I bared my soul so completely to one person.

"Yes," I whisper again, and his thick sooty eyelashes sweep down as his attention is drawn to my lips.

He leans down and plants a soft kiss on my lips. Jolts of electricity pass between us and shoot straight to my core. He deepens the kiss and soon the two of us pull back breathless.

"Constantine, we're out in the open," I pull back as he leans in again.

"Sweetheart, we're hundreds of miles away from civilization. We're up on the mountain. Can you smell any humans or werewolves or lycans around?"

"No," I answer against his lips.

"Good. Be mine..." he groans just before his mouth captures mine desperately and hungrily. "Be mine," he breathes against my mouth again.

His hands travel down my bare skin, pulling me to him. His tongue invades my mouth and I lose all thoughts. We're all tongues and lips and limbs tangled, attached to each other, straining and fighting to get closer.

Oh, the taste of him on my tongue...the feel of his warm hands on my bare skin. My heart thunders wildly in my chest and the heat spread all over me.

I slip my hands underneath his shirt and spread my fingers over the hard planes of his back and abs. I just want to feel his warm skin beneath my hands.

He reaches behind his back, and in one swift motion, he tugs his shirt off. I gaze up at his glorious chest, then down to the ridges of his abs, to the deep v and the little trail of hair that disappear beneath the waistband of his jeans. He's watching me with half-lidded eyes.

He reaches back and releases the clasp of my white lacy bra. My cheeks burn from the intensity of his gaze. He's devouring me with his eyes. "Mine," he utters as his hand comes up to touch my heated bare skin.

His mouth closes over me, licking and sucking hungrily.

Oh, goddess. Little sounds escapes my lips. I arch my back up. My hands grab a handful of his hair and tug him closer to my body. I can't think.

"Constantine..." I moan that out loud. He's devouring me with his mouth, and his hands are spreading pleasurable bursts of flames all over me. The heat burns in my chest all the way down to my core. I feel like I'm losing control. My eyes are turning black.

My hands sweep over the solid muscles of his back and broad shoulders. I feel him shuddering above me.

"I don't want to hurt you.." he groans against my throat. His voice is changing. His hands clenched, crushing the stones and earth on either side of me.

Well, screw slow. I want him so badly and I want him now! I feel my lycan taking over. My long nails clawing at his back. I wrap my legs around his waist and flip us over so that I'm on top of him. I grind myself fiercely against him. My hands roam freely, mapping the hollow and the ridges of his body. My mouth goes to attack his chest, all the way up to his neck, kissing, sucking and nipping and licking.

Oh, he taste so...delectable.

All of a sudden I'm being flipped back down. He's breathing hard. His coal black eyes are staring fiercely into mine. His nostrils flare. His fingers slip inside the waistband of my jeans and pull it down my legs with urgency. Then the rest of his own clothing come off.

He's on top of me again, trailing fire over my skin with his touch. The feeling of skin on skin. Our hands, tongues, and mouths move fervently and frantically against each other.

He takes my hand in his and holds it on the ground over our heads. His mouth finds mine in a feverish kiss and I feel our lycans are in control when we become one.

I feel his warm wet tongue licking my shoulder before his mouth latches onto it and his canines break through my skin. I scream out in pain and pleasure. Torture and ecstasy. Before I know it, my own mouth closes over his shoulder and bites hard, letting my canines pierce through his skin. He roars as I taste his blood on my tongue.

"Constantine..." I scream out his name as I ride waves after waves of pleasure that erupt like explosions through my entire body. His body turns rigid. Powerful shudders go through him and he groans out loud above me. His cheeks are flushed. The look of pure ecstasy on his face.

My body feels boneless as I gaze into his eyes. We're both lying on our back, breathless and his dark hair is wet with sweat. Dark shiny eyes staring into mine until they turn back into beautiful silver gray.

We've marked each other and it's more than just skin deep. I can feel it right in my very soul. He's right there.

He reaches out and stroke my cheek gently with the back of his fingers. "I love you," he murmurs.

"I love you too," I mumble back sleepily.

"I'm sorry I wasn't able to take it slow for our first time," he whispers.

"It was perfect," I whisper back, smiling softly. I don't have anything to compare it with, but to me that was amazing. More than amazing. Now I'm totally his and he's truly mine, that's all I ever wanted and more...and that's perfect.

My eyes are already drooping. He pulls me into his arms and lifts half of my body onto his. I rest my head on his chest and feels his lips place a soft kiss on my forehead.

"Did I do okay?" I ask faintly.

"You did perfect," I hear him answer.

I fall asleep listening to the steady rhythm of his heartbeat and his hand playing with my hair.

*   *   *

I open my eyes to the sight of soft fluffy white clouds floating across the azure blue sky. To the sounds of the chirping birds, and the rustling of the grass and leaves in the wind. To the heat of the sun cooled by the gentle breeze kissing my skin. To the weight of Constantine's arm across my body, holding me close to him. To the wonderful scent of my mate. I start to smile as I remember what happened.

I didn't expect to feel any difference after being mated and marked by Constantine, but I do. I feel our connection that wasn't there before. I can sense his feelings like I can feel Ezra. He's truly mine as I am truly his. Constantine used to cast his power, not only to stake his claim but also as a protection around me from time to time before. Now it's there all the time, even more powerful, secure, and permanent. It makes me feel powerful and strong.

I can also feel the connection to the lycans. I can feel my bond with Caspian, Serena, and Lazarus. I could feel it before, but not quite as strongly. Now I can understand the possessiveness that they feel for me. I truly am part of their pack.

"Good morning, sweetheart...or rather good afternoon," he drawls lazily. His voice deep and playful and sexy. He's looking down at me with a smile on his lips.

Suddenly, I realize that I'm not wearing anything, and I'm pressed up to his equally naked body. My cheeks start turning red and I raise my hand to cover myself.

He takes a hold of my hands and rolls slightly on top of me. "Sunshine, I've been watching you sleeping like that for a while now." He chuckles deeply.

He lets go of my hands and I quickly covers my face with both hands.

Fuzzy slippers! I'm in hiding.

"How long had I been sleeping?" I ask through my fingers.

"Just over half an hour," he answers.

"And you've been watching me?" I shriek in horror.

"Sunshine—" he pries my hands off my face. "—you are beautiful...I could look at you for days and not do anything else....well, maybe I could think of a few things." He amends wickedly, which makes me blush harder.

"Pervert," I mutter.

He laughs. "Sweetheart, You're mine, you don't need to hide from me," he murmurs. "You're mine..." he whispers again and I look up into his face. The expression on his face takes my breath away. "Truly and totally mine." His thumb strokes his mark

238

on my shoulder. The look in his eyes when he gazes down at me—with reverence, tenderness, love, and possessiveness.

Our bite marks don't turn into tattoos or anything like that. They stay as bite marks forever. A bite mark from each werewolf or lycan is as unique as a fingerprint. Not one is the same.

Marks from werewolves are different from that of lycans. I turn to look at mine on my left shoulder. Yup, I am marked by a lycan. A deep big bite mark that is shaped like a crescent moon. His two incisors are deeper than the rest. The mark is already darkening. It's going to turn black in a few more days. A mark by a werewolf is smaller and a bit more longish and dark purplish red on the skin.

"Yours," I smile up at him. "And you're mine," I growl playfully, fiercely tugging him closer. My finger traces my mark on his shoulder. I am amazed that my mark on him also looks like that of a lycan's.

"Mine," I whisper, and I'm totally serious. This powerful, dangerous, gorgeous creature truly is mine.

He throws his head back and laughs that amazing toe curling laugh. "My mate is possessive," he states, sounding oddly proud about it. We have to get back soon," he announces, observing the sky. It is getting late.

I kiss his naked chest lightly as I slide out from underneath him. Now, if only I can find my clothing.

Constantine just lies back, with his hands underneath his head, observing me as I try to find my clothes. His eyes full of amusement and hunger. I can feel his hunger for me growing as his eyes rake my body. I've been averting my own eyes from his glorious hard muscled, beautiful body. Why does he have to be so gorgeous?

"Aren't you going to help me look for my clothes?" I ask in exasperation as my cheeks turn a deeper red.

"Nope, I'm enjoying the view," he replies helpfully.

"Way too much," I mumble to myself, but I think he can hear me as he chuckles and hauls his impressive body gracefully up.

"I thought you're going to help me look for my clothes," I complain half-heartedly when he playfully tugs me to him.

"Yes, I am. What do you think I was trying to do?" he says as he hands me my clothing. His eyes twinkled mischievously and his lips curl up into that hot amused smile.

My cheeks burn. Gah! This man. He thinks he's so funny. "Not funny! I'm very hungry." I pout. I haven't been eating much these last few days, and now I'm hungry.

"No, it's not. I'm sorry, sweetheart," he agrees, but his smile is growing. "How I missed you." He leans in and crushes his lips on mine in a quick, passionate kiss. I make a small sound of protest when he pulls back.

He flashes me a big grin. His gray eyes shining brightly. That's what I had been missing these last couple of days.

"First order of things, feed you," he announces.

Suddenly I remember something. "You just took off during assembly. Where did you go off to today?"

"I just went for a run," he answers vaguely. Pulling his pants on.

"Why? You looked like you're about ready to rip Caspian's head off...or my head off."

He sighs and says, "I would never hurt you, sunshine, no matter what happens, or how mad I was with you. I wouldn't mind hurting Caspian badly, though." He pulls his shirt on and seems reluctant to go on.

"What made you mad enough to storm off like that?" I ask again, very curious.

"Caspian said he'll mark you himself if I didn't do it soon," he finally answers gruffly. A frown marring his forehead. "I said I'll snap his head off if he as much as looks at you the wrong way...then I just took off before I really started ripping his head off and that human boy's arm that's holding you off its socket." He's

240

scowling moodily at the ground as he's remembering the event from this morning.

"Constantine...there's really no need for you to be mad or hurt anybody. I only love you, I don't care about any other boys," I state firmly, touching his arm. "By the way, you owe me a brand new top. You shredded one of my favorite tops to pieces." I only have my jeans and bra on. I hold my ripped shirt up. The torn up fabric pieces waving in the wind.

He's so wild sometimes, and I love it!

He smiles and peels his own shirt back off and slips it over my head. "I'll buy you a thousand more tops and dresses...anything you want, my love."

Everything I want. *Him*. I have everything that I want.

Running with Constantine is amazing. I love jumping and swinging from one tree branch to another, flying through the air. Constantine prefers running, though once in a while, he would be up on a tree right next to me. I suspect he's slowing his own run to keep pace with me.

Twenty minutes into our run, he snatches me in my mid-flight by the waist and drapes my body around his without missing a step. I wind my arms around his neck, and my legs around his waist.

"Should I be calling you my Chunky Monkey?" he teases me.

"Call me chunky, and I'll strangle you right now, my love," I warn him with the sweetest smile. His delicious laughter echoes through the woods.

Everything goes by in a blur. I can't keep my eyes from staring at the chiseled perfection of his jaw, his neck...his honey, golden-tan skin. How does he keep his skin that perfect golden-tan? My mouth itches to have a taste of that addictive deliciousness again. Without thinking, I lean in and place my lips on the golden column of his neck. I kiss it slowly, then I flick my tongue to taste it.

241

Mmmm.... Then I start sucking.

Vaguely I hear him curse before we both tumble down the forest floor. He curves his body around me so that I'm protected and don't get much impact from the fall. We hit a few trees and a couple of sharp boulder rocks.

"Sweetheart," comes a groan from underneath me. "You're a hazard," he announces as I try to untangle myself and get myself up.

I find myself being lifted up and set on my feet. He then starts checking my body for injuries. His own shoulder and arm have a few little scrapes and scratches from the fall.

"I'm sorry, Costa." I apologize regretfully as I gingerly place a soft kiss on his scraped shoulder. They're already healing.

"Well, I'm not," he announces. "I wasn't really complaining. I was enjoying that way too much to concentrate on my footing," he adds, grinning adorably before he pushes me up against a tree. His mouth swoops down on mine.

At this rate, it's going to be morning before we can make it home.

We arrive at the school's parking lot where his shiny red Ferrari is parked; the only car left. It's already seven in the evening.

"I should go home and take a shower and have a change of clothes," I suggest as he opens the trunk of his car and retrieves a white t-shirt for himself.

"What's wrong with what you're wearing now?" he asks as he pulls the shirt over his impressive torso, which is a shame, in my opinion. Such a delectable perfection should not be covered. But then again, I don't want anyone else to be enjoying the view that's supposed to be mine alone.

"Well...Costa, sweetheart," I begin, and his lips curl up into a smile.

"I like you calling me that, but with much less sarcasm," he comments. "And with a little more love," he suggests with amusement in his voice.

"Costa, my love," I try again. My tone still dripping with sarcasm.

"I take it how I can get it." He sighs with exaggerated heaviness, but with a wicked glint in his eyes.

"First off, I'm wearing your shirt. Secondly, I smell like...ummm.."

"Like what, sweetheart?" he asks wickedly. His silver-gray eyes shine with amusement and mischief.

"Like...uh, you know." My cheeks are flushed beet red.

"No, I don't know," he inquires. "Tell me." His voice lowers a few octaves. He moves dangerously closer. "You smell like you've just been thoroughly mated and marked? You smell like me?" He whispers into my ear. My stomach clenches at the intimacy. Delicious chills run up and down my body at his closeness and the sound of his seductive voice.

His hands grip my waist possessively, and his nose nuzzles my neck. "I happen to think it's a wonderful thing. I smell like you, and you smell like me. It tells other men that you belong to me."

I can feel his hunger for me building, but he quickly deposits me into the passenger side of the car.

He takes a deep breath as if calming himself before he gets into the car himself.

"Gotta feed you first before I get to eat myself," he remarks as he slides into the car. It sounds innocent enough. I would've believed it to be innocent too if I didn't catch the tiny naughty twist of his lips and the wicked glimmer in his eyes before his eyelids sweep down to cover it.

It's actually not helping when his feelings can get mixed up with mine. His feelings heighten mine.

I feel warm all over again, and my stomach clenches deliciously as I watch him drive. I watch the flex of the muscles of his arms as he handles the car. I watch the graceful way his elegant fingers move as if caressing the steering wheel, and I imagine what those fingers could do. I watch the concentration he gives to the traffic around him...or not...as he groans.

"What?" I jump, coming out of my Constantine filled haze.

"I can feel your desire for me, sweetheart," he groans, his hands gripping the steering wheel harder than necessary.

"Did NOT!" I gasp, turning bright tomato red. I totally forgot about that. He can totally feel me.

"I think I'm going to lock you up in my room for a month..or two...right after I feed you," he mutters almost to himself. Yes, please!

Oh, Cuddly bunny and fuzzy slippers! So not helping! Hussy! I scold myself.

CHAPTER XXVIII
This I Pledge to You

"Costa, I'm not dressed for this," I protest as we turn into Pacifica Drive. This is the area where the rich go to. It's the place for fancy restaurants, swanky nightclubs, glitzy boutiques, and luxurious hotels.

"You look gorgeous, sunshine," he counters, lifting my hand up to his lips.

I remember when River used to drive Reese, Penny, and I around the area just to look at the people and the bright lights. I came dining around here a few times when grandpa Quentin came to visit. Mom made us dressed up very nicely. I look down at myself: black jeans, Constantine's expensive white shirt, but a couple of sizes too big for me, and a pair of white converse. I wonder if there are twigs and dry leaves in my hair.

Constantine pulls in front of The Monarchy, the fanciest hotel and restaurant in the city.

Oh, I am so not dressed for this!

In a flash, he's out of the car, pushing aside the man who's about to take my hand to help me out of the car. He hands the key to his Ferrari to the valet and almost has to drag-carry the very reluctant me up the shiny black marble steps and into the grand foyer.

A man, together with a very well-groomed woman in her early thirties hurries over even before we step inside the opulent restaurant. The maître d' is hot on her heels.

"Your Highness Prince Constantine," greets the woman with a dip of her well-coiffed head.

"Your Highness," says the man. "It's so good to see you again."

They acknowledge me with a respectful little bow of their heads, not even batting an eyelid over my scruffy appearance.

"Marisol, Jefferson," Constantine acknowledges them with a curt, but polite nod.

"They're already waiting, Your Highness," informs the woman.

"Right this way," says the man, extending his hand towards the restaurant.

"You come here often?" I ask Constantine.

"Sometimes..." he answers. "My family from my mother's side owns this place."

The restaurant is posh and stylish with luminous natural stone walls, and floor to ceiling glass paneling overlooking the well-lit gardens. The interior gleams with polished wine glasses and moody lighting from the chandeliers and well-placed ambiance lights. Another thing I notice besides the elegant setting is the delicious smell of food.

Ahhh... food.

The opulent room is full of guests. Men in their expensive suits, and women in beautiful designer dresses. I want to disappear into the walls.

Some of them are humans, but I sense many of them are werewolves. Conversations hushed and the well-dressed patrons look up as soon as we step in. I can't blame them. Constantine looks gorgeous even in just his t-shirt and jeans. His hair is carelessly and sexily mussed up as usual. He reeks the air of importance and power. There's also a combination of danger and reckless sex appeal that is hard to ignore. I probably look like something that a cat or rather a lycan drags in.

Constantine pulls me closer to him as we walk past the tables. His hand on the small of my back moves to grip my hip possessively.

"I can't stand it when the men stare at you like that," he growls lowly in my ear.

Like what? All I can see is the women eyeing him with interest, even those dining with their partners. I notice their lustful gaze following his every footstep.

We walk through the restaurant to the side door that leads to a magnificent courtyard. Beautiful miniature trees and flower bushes, a fish pond with a water fountain right in the center, filled with koi. Lights illuminate every tree and bush and from inside the pond. I don't have the time to appreciate the beauty as we walk briskly through it into another building.

A very good-looking group of two men and three women come up to meet us. Lycans.

"Constantine," says a gorgeous man who looks like he's in his mid-twenties. He approaches us with an outstretched hand.

"Sullivan," replies Constantine, casually taking the man's hand in his. The man fondly and playfully slaps his back with familiarity.

"We are all the King's loyal and humble subjects, eager to meet his nephew's beautiful mate," he turns his attention to me. "I've known Constantine since he was just a little troublemaker." He grins.

"Still is," I mumble and the man lets out a hearty laugh.

"We consider them close family friends. They've been working for us for centuries," remarks Constantine to me after he made the introduction.

"King Alexandros and your grandmother must be eager to meet your lovely mate soon," suggests one of the ladies.

I never thought about meeting his family!

247

We are then lead into a beautiful private room where Caspian, Lazarus, and Serena are already waiting.

As soon as they left, Serena leaps up and quickly engulfs me in a big hug. "You are truly and totally one of us now," she exclaims. "You're a Romanov!"

"Finally!" Caspian jumps in while Lazarus pounds Constantine's back enthusiastically.

I can feel my cheeks burning up. Oh, for the love of everything fuzzy! How did everyone know? I could dig a hole, crawl in and hide inside it forever!

As soon as Serena releases me, Caspian wraps his massive arms around me and twirls me around happily. I guess his ire for me this morning is all forgotten now.

Constantine growls warningly and Caspian put me down on my feet right away, grinning widely.

Constantine's big strong arms pull me against his muscled chest as soon as my feet touch the ground.

"Now the celebration," announces Lazarus.

I guess this is like marriage to humans. Only markings hold more meaning to us. Once we've marked each other, we are forever connected. We leave a mark forever, not only on each other's skin but also on each other's soul. Entwining our souls together. One cannot survive with only half a soul. One cannot live without the other for too long. We sometimes hold a wedding ceremony just for the formality or for the celebration, and as an announcement of our union. The true vow of our union is in our mating and marking, which is just between the two of us.

"How'd you know?" I manage to ask.

"We felt the connection as soon as you were marked," answers Serena.

"Nothing is private around here." I sigh. Oh, well, so much for going into the mountains, far away from civilization for privacy.

"Oh, be thankful, love. Hundreds of years ago, they used to have the mating and the marking ceremony out in the open field, beside big bonfires with pack members in attendance," remarks Caspian, gleefully ruffling my hair.

"Ewww..." I wrinkle my nose in disgust, swatting his hand away.

"Prude," mutters Caspian, with a smirk.

"Shut up!" I reply.

"We'd better separate these two before they start a food fight or something," suggests Lazarus. "I don't know what everybody wants, so I ordered us a small buffet."

Ahhh... food!

Now I notice a table covered in a pristine white damask table cloth, laden with delectable food at the far end of the room. That's where the smell comes from. A lavish buffet just for the five of us. I think I'm so hungry, I suddenly developed a tunnel vision. I can see nothing else but food. *Oh food, how I missed you.*

There is an antipasto section with a selection of cheeses, fresh fruits, nuts, cured meats, and vegetables; a section of delicious spread of international cuisine, from Continental to Asian; succulent chicken, beef, and seafood dishes; and mouthwatering desserts. This is not a small buffet, but I'm not complaining. Everything looks good. I pile everything I can fit onto my plate. I stuff myself until I'm...well, stuffed.

"Now time for your pledge," announces Lazarus after dinner before Caspian and I can get deeper into another round of bickering. I actually missed bickering with Caspian. Unbelievable!

"Pledge? What pledge?"

"You're my mate. You're a member of our pack, as you have been for the last three years," explains Constantine, unfolding his long legs from under the chair next to me to stand in the middle of the room.

"This has been our tradition for generations, this is our way," adds Lazarus, standing up next to him.

"We did ours when we're very young, we would like it to continue," continues Caspian, taking his place next to Lazarus.

"Each of us here had to go through it, now it's your turn," says Serena, taking my hand in hers. She leads me to Constantine and places my hand in his.

"This is just a formality of tradition, sweetheart. You're already my mate," explains Constantine. "Would you agree to take a pledge as my mate, and do you agree to do this willingly?"

"Yes," I answer unequivocally.

"Then follow my lead and repeat after me," he says.

Lazarus picks up an old copper goblet with carvings of a crown guarded by a lycan and a wolf, surrounded by strange symbols. There is something that looks like a little piece of cloth inside the goblet. He drops in a lighted match and sets the cloth on fire. Then he hands Constantine a very old looking dagger that has carvings of strange symbols along the blade. The handle is embedded with a brilliant red ruby surrounded by gleaming emeralds.

"This blood symbolizes our lives, our vows, and my bond to you and yours to me," Constantine clarifies, cutting a small line in the middle of his palm with the blade without taking his eyes off mine. A few drops spilled into the goblet and suddenly the flame burns bright. It pops and fizzles, then goes down again.

"I swear my life to you, my mate. Our souls are one. You are privy to my feelings and senses, the keeper of my secrets. I pledge you my protection, my honor, and my companionship. My loyalty shall be yours. My strength shall quell your weakness, my courage shall absolve your fear. This is my pledge to you," he vows looking deep into my eyes, right into my very soul. I feel my breath caught and my heartbeat picks up.

He hands me the dagger. It's heavier than I thought. I wrap my fingers around it and make a little cut in the middle of my palm. I tilt my hand so that a drop falls into the goblet. As soon as my blood drops in, the fire glows brilliantly before it crackles and pops and goes down again.

The cut on my hand is already healing.

250

Constantine recites the pledge again so that I can repeat after him. I recite the vow without taking my eyes off him.

After I finished reciting the pledge, he nods solemnly and pulls me into a quick and deep kiss. Then he releases me and hands the dagger to Lazarus.

"Do you agree to be a member of this pack and do you agree to take this oath willingly?" asks Lazarus.

"Yes, I do," I answer him.

He slashes his palm the way Constantine did then recites, "I swear my allegiance to you, as a member of my pack. Our souls are linked. You are privy to my feelings and senses, the keeper of my secrets. I pledge you my protection, in my honor. My loyalty shall be yours. My strength shall quell your weakness, my courage shall absolve your fear. This is my pledge to you."

I repeat the pledge after him. Then he leans in and kisses my cheek.

This, I repeat with Caspian, then finally with Serena.

I didn't realize that I have tears running down my face until Serena wipes my wet cheeks with her fingertips. Her own cheeks are also wet with tears. She laughs softly and pulls me into her arms. I feel the men wrap their arms around the both of us as well.

When I recited those oaths, I meant every word. Now I truly feel like I belong with these lycans. I am one of them.

CHAPTER XXIX
Some Things Money Can't Buy

"Why is Milan not here?" I ask. No, I don't really want to deal with her now. This evening has been great and I don't want to ruin it. But I have to ask.

"That's because she's not part of the pack," answers Constantine.

"Oh?" I raise an eyebrow.

"To be part of the pack, you have to be approved, not just by the majority, but by all members of the pack," answers Serena at my questioning look.

"Serena and I didn't want her to be a part of this pack," informs Caspian with a smirk.

"Besides, she's not always with us. She comes and goes as she pleases. She would stay with us for a few months or so, then she's off to Europe or somewhere. She'll disappear for months or sometimes years before she shows her face around here again," comments Serena, shrugging her shoulders.

"This is the longest she's ever stayed with us. Almost a year now," explains Lazarus.

"Where is she, anyway?" asks Constantine. From the tone of his voice, I sense a confrontation coming.

"We don't know," answers Serena looking at Lazarus.

"We haven't seen her since this morning after you left," says Lazarus.

"Come home with me tonight?" Constantine has been trying to persuade me to spend the night at his place, while I feel that I should go home. I feel kinda awkward about telling my parents that I'm spending the night at his place. Besides, I left everything at home when I went for the run this afternoon. I don't even have my phone with me.

"Maybe some other time?" I'm blushing beet red. Oh, goddess, why am I so weird, and awkward....and weird? Why, oh, why can't I be normal?

"What about me spending some time at yours?" He smiles roguishly. His silver-gray eyes glinting mischievously. I get the feeling that he's enjoying making me blush way too much. He also knows how much I want to spend the whole night with him. He's so hot and—blast him and this mate bond feeling, sharing thingy!

"This thing....about sensing each other's feeling, it's great and all...but is there any way I can keep my feelings to myself?" I finally ask him.

"What, you don't want to share your feelings with me, sweetheart?" He flashes his straight white teeth.

"I do, but...not all the time." Especially not now.

"I know. There's no off button anywhere, but you can hide it a bit...sort of like turning the volume of a radio down. You can't totally turn it off, especially if you're experiencing some strong feelings like extreme sadness or fear, or anger....or passion," he whispers the last word in my ear. The warmth of his breath teasing my skin.

Fuzzy bunnies! I grab the back of his neck and slam my lips against his. I kiss him long, hard and good until we're both panting.

"Meet me up in my room later tonight," I inform him breathlessly.

He grins like he just won a round of battle. Well, he just did. That was an easy win for him.

Gah! I'm such a sucker for this hot, delicious, irresistible...

"Sweetheart," he groans, reaching for me again. Oops... I forgot that he can totally feel me.

It's fifteen minutes later that I finally walk on unsteady legs across our driveway. Sheesh, I need a shower. A cold one. Wait! I didn't even get to know how to tune my feelings down from him.

Genesis! One little whisper and you forgot everything. I suck!

The TV in our living room is on. I know mom and dad are watching their favorite show. I sneak around to the back of the house and climb up through the window into my room. I'm amazed at my own agility now. I doubt that my parents or Autumn heard me.

I quickly gather my pajamas and head for the shower. The warm water feels good on my skin. I wish I had Constantine's amazing shower. Constantine—just the thought of him makes me smile like a crazy woman.

I stop in front of the bathroom mirror on my way out. My skin seems to glow. The mark on my shoulder seems darker. I put on a pair of yoga pants and a tank top and run a comb through my hair.

I can hear my parents talking and laughing downstairs. I haven't seen them since this morning. I should go downstairs and talk to them.

"Hey, sweetie!" greets mom as I enter the living room.

They are watching The Golden Girls. My parents love that old tv show. Autumn is on another chair munching on chips. It's Friday night, she gets to stay up late. I'm surprised she's not out with her friends.

"I didn't even know you were home until I heard the shower going," says dad.

I grin, walk over and squeeze myself in between the two of them on the sofa. I used to do that a lot when I was a little girl. I still like to do it from time to time even though I'm all grown up now.

"My baby girl," mom squeezes my cheeks. I giggle when dad kisses my other cheek. Ahhh... just like old times.

"Genesis sandwich." Dad laughs.

"Hey! What about me?!!" yells Autumn just before she launches herself right on top of me.

Oommpphh!!! Cuddly bunnies!!!

"Flattened out Genesis," I groan from under her. "Autumn, you heavy cow," I manage to muffle out as she squishes her back against my poor mushed up face.

"Genesis mashed!" she yells as she jumps up and down on top of me. I have a heavy cow for a sister. A crazy one at that.

It's funny how my life has turned out to be. If Logan had accepted me, I'd probably be living in the pack house as the luna of the pack now. Instead, here I am, mated to a lycan and still acting like a kid. I know sooner or later I would have to grow up and leave my family to live with my new pack, wherever they decide to move to. Right now, I'm just going to enjoy my time with my family.

Thankfully mom rescues me by digging me out from underneath my demented sister.

"Oh, my goddess!" exclaims mom suddenly, pulling on my shoulder. "You're marked!"

My cheeks heat up as mom pulls me into a hug, then she turns me around to study the mark on my shoulder again.

"Lycan's mark," she marvels.

"Well, finally," mutters dad. "For a lycan, he showed a lot of restraint. Even a werewolf would have marked her a long time ago."

What? I almost choke on my embarrassment.

"Yeah, well...your dad marked me a couple of days after we met, and that's very considerate of him."

I so don't want to hear this! Autumn and I start covering our ears.

255

Mom laughs and pulls our hands down.

"We should celebrate," she suggests enthusiastically.

Suddenly, my chest burns. Something is wrong.

Constantine.

"Something's not right," I blurt out, pressing a hand to my chest. My phone starts to buzz and I jump up to answer it.

"Genesis, you should come right away," Serena's voice comes through the line as soon as I swipe right to answer.

"Why? What's wrong?" My heartbeat picks up with burning anger and fury that's not mine.

"It's Constantine. Caspian is on his way over to pick you up," she says before she ends the call.

"That was Serena. I have to go," I inform my parents.

"What's going on? What's wrong?" asks dad.

"I don't know, but I have to go. Caspian's on the way over to pick me up."

"Do you want us to come with you?" Mom looks worried.

"No, I don't think so. I'll let you know when I know for sure what's happening," I assure them. I'm feeling so much fury, my eyes keep changing. Constantine. I have to get to him fast.

The roar of a car engine just outside our house alerts us to Caspian's arrival. He must have been speeding to get here so fast. I sprint to his car. He guns the engine as soon as I close the door to his sleek silver Porsche.

"Okay, I'm freaking out. Tell me what's going on Caspian?"

We're flying along the highway. I don't think a regular police patrol car would be able to catch us.

"Well..." he says, checking the traffic beside us before he switches the lane, then he speeds up even more. "When we got home this evening, we found the door to Constantine's studio wide open. Apparently, that crazy bitch Milan broke in and went into a fit of frenzy. She pretty much destroyed the studio...and the paintings."

Oh, My Gosh! All those beautiful paintings. They're not just paintings to him. There was so much passion and emotions poured into those magnificent artworks. To him, part of them represented me. All the years he was waiting for me. Each and every one of them held a special meaning and were very precious— it's something that money can't replace.

Constantine—I feel his rage and now it's mingled with my own. This is not helping.

"How is he doing?" I ask Caspian, trying to calm myself down.

"Not great. He was tearing her room apart the last time I saw him before I came to get you."

"Where is Milan?"

"I don't know. She wasn't there when we got back, but we can smell her scent everywhere in that studio. You can sniff the crazy, you know..."

I can now sense Caspian's anger as well. He's gritting his teeth when he's explaining this to me. His knuckles are white on the steering wheel.

We arrive in front of the mansion in record time.

"Come on, Red," urges Caspian, touching my arm gently after he kills the engine.

Serena is waiting for me by the front door. She is looking outwardly calm, but I can sense her inner turmoil. Together, we walk in through the massive heavy double doors. I can hear the commotion even before we fully step inside the grand entryway.

Lazarus meets us at the foot of the stairs. The sound of banging and things breaking get louder as we climb up the grand staircase.

"None of us dare to go in there. We're just waiting for you," explains Lazarus. The four of us are standing in front of a closed door, listening to the sound of destruction inside.

"You better get in there and calm him down before he tears the whole place apart," says Caspian.

"Sure, feed me to the lion, why don't you?" I mumble and manage to get some smiles from the three lycans.

I gingerly pull the door open. I feel somebody pushes me inside and closes the door behind me. Darn, it Caspian! So much for pack loyalty and love.

Cuddly bunny and fuzzy slippers!

This is what I call destruction. I think my mouth is opening and closing several times without any sound coming out as I gape at the sight before me. The only thing that is still intact in the whole room is the ceiling. Torn fabrics, splinters of broken wood and glass are everywhere. The windows are all smashed and broken. Gaping holes in the walls.

My mate is standing in the middle of it. His shirt is torn. His glistening chest rising and falling. He raises his black vacant eyes to stare at me as soon as I step in the room. I'm not afraid, but the hair at the back of my neck stands up from the chill of his stare and the anger that I feel still brewing inside of him.

At least he hasn't phase into a full lycan yet.

There's a big difference between phasing intentionally and phasing when we lose control due to anger or pain. When we deliberately change, we are one with our lycans. Our thinking will work together with our lycan instinct and our judgment will still largely govern our actions. If we lost control, the lycans take over completely, acting on instinct in retaliation to pain or anger.

"Costa...Constantine?" I whisper. I think he can hear me because he tilts his head to the side, listening to my voice. I gingerly take a few steps towards him. Waves of red hot fury coming off him hitting me right where I am standing.

In less than a blink of an eye, he is standing right before me. His eyes, two black shiny soulless marbles stare into mine. So cold and so void of any other feelings but rage.

He looks like my Constantine, but different. His beautiful face is etched with dark blue veins starting from his eye sockets, spreading all over his features down to his neck. A few lines even reach his broad chest. His white teeth are sharp and his canines are longer and more visible. I'm not even sure if he recognized me, but I know with deep certainty that he would never hurt me.

His hands suddenly come up to grip my shoulders. His long sharp fingernails are digging into my flesh.

"Constantine, please...?" I whimper and he flinches. His grip loosens up a little bit.

I bring my hands up to touch his cheek gently. I try to calm my own feelings and mind, hoping that he can feel it too.

He pulls back, while his hands are now very gentle on my arms, holding me like he's afraid he's going to break me. Pitch black eyes still regarding me coldly. It's like two persons fighting over control.

"Costa, I'm here. It's me. I'm here for you." I reach out to him again. His eyebrows furrow when I put my both hands on his cheeks.

His long sooty eyelashes fan across his cheeks as he closes his eyes as I gently stroke his face.

"Help me." He leans in closer and wraps his powerful arms around me. His voice is unnaturally deep and guttural. His lycan is still in control.

One hand moves up to grip the back of my head, while his face nuzzling my neck, feverishly breathing in my scent. "Help me before I hurt or kill..."

I can feel the pent up fury that's still raging inside of him, like a trapped wild beast fighting to get out.

"I'm here now. You have me," I murmur softly.

"She destroyed everything. Everything!" He snarls. "Those paintings of you—"

"Shhh... listen to me. You have me. You have all of me. We can make new paintings together. We have the rest of our lives to make new paintings together. I'll model for you anytime you want me to."

He closes his eyes as he listens to my voice. I lean my cheek against his. One of my hands plays with the silky dark curls at the nape of his neck, while another keeps stroking the other side of his face.

"I love you and I'll stay with you forever. I'll follow you to the end of the world," I vow as I trace the dark blue veins along his cheek with my fingers. So wild, so strong, and so dangerous, my mate... mine.

"Promise?"

"Huh?"

"Promise me you'll stay with me forever."

"Yes, of course, for as long as you want me."

"Forever. I love you. I need you." He breathes against my cheek. "Nothing will take you away from me. I'll destroy her if she takes you away from me. I'll destroy anyone—"

"Shhh..." I grab his face with both hands and press my lips against his before he gives in to his anger again. He returns the kiss instantly, crushing my lips with his. His tongue finds its way into my mouth and his hands lift me up and move to wrap my legs around his waist.

I wind my arms around his neck, losing myself in his kiss and the taste of him. I barely register anything around us as he presses me against the wall. His kiss grows more urgent and demanding.

"Owww..." Something is digging into my back.

"Oh, sweetheart, did I hurt you?" He instantly pulls back and set me back on my feet to see if I was hurt.

I giggle as I reach behind me and pull a piece of wood that was sticking out from the wall of what I think used to be a walk-in closet.

"No, I'm fine, but the room isn't." I grin as I toss the wood across the room.

He sighs and pushes his back against the wall beside me. I turn my head to look at him to find him already staring at me. His eyes are still all black, but the dark veins on his face are slowly fading.

We stand like that, with our backs against the wall, watching each other. I watch him until all the visible veins disappear. I watch his eyes slowly turning back to silver gray. Those beautiful eyes that always hold me entranced. He studies my features as if he's memorizing it. He lifts his hand and traces a finger slowly down my face.

"I know your every feature. I know your eyes, the tilt of your nose, the dips of your lips, the slope of your chin... I drew them and I painted them hundreds of times," he says.

"And you will do it again," I whisper, taking his hand in mine.

"When I saw those paintings all torn to pieces, I felt as if she destroyed you. A part of you that I get to hold on to all these years. I wanted to end her. I wanted to do to her what she did to you. I lost control. I'm sorry," he says regretfully.

"I don't blame you for losing it. That was an awful thing for her to do. All those amazing artworks, they can never be replaced," I reply. "But Costa, I don't want you to feel like you've lost any part of me because of that. I'm right here. I'm yours forever."

CHAPTER XXX
All's Fair in Love and War

He pulls me close and we stand there in each other's arms. I try to share the feeling of calmness with him. We stand there until I feel a feeling of completeness engulfing me, and I know that feeling comes from him.

"I really appreciate you calming me. Only you can do that, sunshine. But uh...but really? Jeopardy music?"

What? "What? You heard that???"

Yeah, so okay, I play Jeopardy music in my head when I try to calm myself down sometimes. He's not supposed to know that! He couldn't have heard that! He can't hear *my* thoughts as well, can he?

"Yeah, of course, I can hear it...since you hummed it like that."

I hummed it? NO!

"It's not my favorite music, but it did help distract me from my anger. It reminded me how lucky I am." His lips twitch as he says this. "That I have a very strange and uh...funny mate."

I wasn't trying to be funny! It was supposed to calm me. Sheeshh!

"Don't diss Jeopardy music! It's an awesome classic piece," I defend my *happy* music. "And...Hey!!! I'm strange and funny???"

"Okay, sorry. Actually, you are unique...and uh...witty."

I stare at him warily as I watch him biting his lower lip like he's trying hard not to laugh.

Then he just bursts out laughing. Unbelievable!

"I heard some laughing. Is it safe to come in now?" asks Caspian warily poking his head through the doorway.

"Go away," I snap at him.

Caspian takes that as an invitation to come in. He steps inside and gazes around the wreckage, looking oddly excited. "Nice," he observes with a grin. One of these days I really am going to drop something over his golden head.

"We'll get the cleaning and fixing crew in first thing tomorrow morning," says Lazarus from behind him. Serena just raises an eyebrow in amusement as she surveys the destroyed bedroom.

"The last time we had a room looking like this was four years ago," remarks Lazarus.

"It wasn't this bad," Caspian quickly points out, suddenly looking glum.

"Not this bad," agrees Lazarus. "But you did a pretty good job with your bed chamber. They had to replace all the furniture."

"Caspian and his mother, Queen Sophia don't get along," Serena mock-whispers conspiratorially to me, even though everybody in the room can hear her.

"It's no big secret, unfortunately." Constantine sighs against the side of my forehead. His hand is idly rubbing my shoulder. "We thought it's a good idea to put an ocean between them after that last big fight."

"Hey, this is not about me," protests Caspian. "Besides, it got us here. Constantine gets to meet Genesis."

I think there's more to the story, but I would rather get out of the destroyed bedroom. I think the others got the same idea as we make our way out of there, walking over broken furniture and pieces of drywall.

Caspian pours everybody a drink, while we take our seats in front of a big fireplace in the great room. Constantine pulls me up onto his lap. The roaring fire cast a warm orange glow over everyone.

"We've got to find out where she's gone off to," says Constantine, grimly. We immediately know who he's talking about and the atmosphere in the room instantly becomes tense.

"Already on it," replies Lazarus. "Our men tracked her to the airport. She took a commercial flight out to Belarus this evening."

"She'll be back," announces Caspian, staring into his glass solemnly.

"Find her. Get our men to find her exact whereabouts and keep us posted," says Constantine tugging me to him. "I don't want her anywhere near my mate."

I ended up spending the night at their place anyway. I texted my mom, telling her that everything's fine now and that I was spending the night here.

He holds me close to him all night. It's like he needs to reassure himself that I'm safe with him.

I wake up lying half on top of him with my cheek pressed against his solid chest. His arms wrapped around me and our limbs tangled together. I had the best night sleep I've had in a while despite everything that happened last night.

His bed is the most comfortable bed I've ever slept in. Well, I've been lying on top of him as well...so, he can be a very comfortable pillow substitute. I don't know if I should tell him that.

Anyway, what was I talking about? Oh yeah, his bed. It is the most comfortable bed ever. It's like sleeping on a soft warm cloud. Not that I know what sleeping on a cloud feels like, but if I were to imagine it, this is what it would have felt like.

"What are you smiling about?" His voice is deep, husky and sexy. Oh, who am I kidding? Everything about this lycan prince is sexy.

264

"I think I'm in love with your bed," I sigh.

I feel, rather than hear the deep rumble of laughter in his chest.

He suddenly flips us, so that I'm lying underneath him instead of on top of him.

"Sunshine, you're in love with my shower, now you're in love with my bed...and I'm pretty sure that you're in love with me."

"Pretty sure?" I gasp as he playfully nips my earlobe with his teeth.

"Ummm... yea, quite sure," he mumbles as he rains tiny kisses along my jaw down to the side of my neck. "There's only one logical thing you need to do..."

"What's that?" I gulp as tingles of heat and fireworks erupt all over my body.

"Move in with me."

"Is this how you....plan to...convince me to...ummm... gosh... move in?" I manage to choke out as his mouth manages to find that spot behind my ear.

"Ummm... Is it working?"

Oh yes, it's working, but he doesn't need to know that yet. At least not until he feeds me breakfast.

*   *   *

Constantine wasn't kidding when he told me that he sleeps au naturel.

I avert my eyes when he gets up from the bed. He laughs and saunters unhurriedly to the bathroom as I cover my face with a pillow. Don't look! Don't look!!! Well, maybe a little peek.

Last night he reluctantly taught me how to hide some of my feelings from him. It involves conditioning my lycan, Ezra, to keep my *emotional volume* down. I did it after a little practice. Of course, I can't keep everything from him. He would still be able to feel strong emotions coming off of me.

265

The thing is, when I hide my feelings from him, I can barely feel his emotions as well. I understand why he doesn't like this. I don't plan on hiding my feelings from him all the time. Only some of the time...like right now...when I'm thinking of his naked body...

I wonder what time it is, but I'm too lazy to even try to reach out for my phone. I just lie back and listen to the sound of the shower going in the en-suite, then I realize that he didn't even close the bathroom door! Steam rolling in from the open door.

Gah! That man! I think teasing me is his favorite past time.

It doesn't help that he has the most glorious body I'd ever seen.

How can I go back to sleep when there's a completely hot, naked Greek God with water running down his body in the next room, showering with the door wide open. You slept just fine draped all over his glorious naked body last night, I remind myself. Why am I so weird?

"What are you muttering about, sunshine?" Of course, now he's walking around in a little towel tied low around his waist.

"Nothing," I mumble against the blanket I just pulled over my eyes.

"Come on, get up, sleepy head!" He chuckles as he yanks the blanket down. "I can smell breakfast from here."

I sit up on the bed at the mention of food. Yes, I can smell food!

I yelp and cover my eyes when he casually drops the towel as he strolls into his walk-in closet. I can hear his laughter from behind the closet door.

*　　　*　　　*

Lazarus and Serena are already sitting at the breakfast table when we get into the kitchen.

They both look up and smile. Serena gives me a wink as she shoves a mouthful of fruit into her mouth. A huge serving of fresh fruits topped with yogurt and a generous drizzle of strawberry sauce sitting in front of her.

There is a man in his late twenties standing by the stove.

"Good morning," greets Lazarus with a smile. His dark curls are tied back this morning. "Genesis, meet our new cook, Duncan."

"I decided to hire a real cook, rather than let Caspian employ one of those blow-up doll airheads again," explains Serena.

"Hi!" I smile at the man. A human, by the smell of him.

"Hello, Genesis," he returns my greeting. He's a bit shorter than I am. Average looking man, but he has a pair of kind blue eyes. I decided that I like him right away.

"What would you like me to make you this morning?" Yup! I definitely like him.

"Anything you're making, Duncan. Whatever it is you're cooking, it smells good."

"I'm making Benedict Trevino, it's my family's all-time favorite," he says with an easy smile. "I'm betting on my first born son that you will like it."

"Oh, you have a son?"

"Nope, not married either, that's why I'm betting on a son. I'm not betting on anything that you can really take away from me!"

That leaves Serena and me giggling. I find it very easy to talk to and joke with Duncan.

Serena and I are laughing and bantering back and forth with Duncan when Caspian decided to make an appearance in nothing but a pair of boxer shorts. He's yawning and stretching. His golden hair is sticking all over the place. I guess if I agree to move in with them, I would have to get used to seeing naked or half-naked gorgeous men parading around the place.

Caspian takes his seat at the table, rubbing his eyes sleepily. He almost looks like an adorable five-year-old like this, except for his muscular body and chiseled appearance. His heavy-lidded eyes survey the room once and he grins mischievously.

Duncan serves us his creation of poached eggs topped with Hollandaise sauce, smoked cheese, and some other stuff that look like chopped sausages or something and tomatoes over English Toast.

"This is amazing!" mumbles Serena after taking the first bite. "You're amazing!"

"Oh, Duncan... Uummm...." I close my eyes and moan over a mouthful. Ohhh, yes. I'm having a foodgasm.

I sigh with contentment and am about to compliment Duncan again when my eyes fall on scowling Constantine and Lazarus. Caspian is sitting back in his chair, watching Constantine and Lazarus with a wicked smirk on his face. He looks like he's thoroughly enjoying himself.

Surly looking Lazarus loudly scrapes his chair back to leave the table. I think I heard him mumble under his breath, "I think I'd let Caspian do the hiring next time."

Constantine who isn't looking much happier brusquely wipes his mouth, tosses the napkin onto the plate then leaves the table right after Lazarus, mumbling about having some work to do.

Serena looks at me with a raised eyebrow.

"So, can I have what they're having and some coffee too now?" asks Caspian, turning to Duncan with a big grin.

*   *   *

"Hey?" I push open the office door and cautiously peek inside where Constantine has been working all morning. The house had been bustling with workers cleaning and fixing what used to be Milan's bedroom.

He's sitting behind a big dark mahogany table glowering at the computer screen.

268

"Hey," he answers sullenly, not even taking his eyes off the screen. He scrawls some words onto a writing pad in front of him. I think he's using more force than necessary, I'm surprised that he hasn't broken that very expensive looking pen yet.

"Can I come in?"

He shrugs his broad shoulders nonchalantly, but sulkily says, "I thought you'd rather be flirting with the new cook than talking to me."

"I wasn't flirting with him," I protest.

"Oh, really?" He stops writing to finally look at me.

"Yeah, really."

"Then what about, "Oh, Duncan... Oohhh... Ummmm... Ahh.." He badly mimics my voice followed by a high pitch moaning. "You're practically moaning like... Well, you can go back to talking to him and ignore me. I have things to do anyway," he adds, sounding like a five-year-old boy about to throw a tantrum. Oh boy, he looks so hot when he's jealous.

I bite my lip and hide my smile behind my hand. "I can?"

"No!" he growls. "You're my mate, you're supposed to want to spend time with me! Only I'm allowed to make you moan like that."

"Oh, honey, you look so hot when you're jealous like that," I sigh breathlessly. Ooppss! I didn't mean to say that out loud. For a few seconds, the both of us stare at each other speechless. Neither of us could believe I just said what I just said. Goddamit!

The corners of his mouth suddenly twitch like he's about to burst out laughing. He shakes his head disbelievingly while biting his lower lip. "Oh, that is not fair," he mutters.

Hah! I think I could use this to my advantage. So I step behind the big heavy desk and climb to straddle him.

"I'm still mad at you," he says, but without any conviction at all, since his lips sexily curl up at the corners like that.

"Are you really?" I ask him as I drop a kiss at a corner of his lips.

"Yes. This is not fair...Genesis," he protests, but I can see that smile.

I rain tiny kisses along his perfect jawline. "Are you still mad at me now?"

"Yes," he mutters, closing his eyes.

"Now?"

"Yes, very much," he says, settling back comfortably in his chair as I move lower, kissing down his neck.

"What about now?" I lick and suck the lower part of his neck just underneath his Adam's apple. Umm...love his taste. I let my fingers trail down and start unbuttoning his shirt.

"Oh, yes...still." His voice grows husky.

"Ummm... now?" I push his shirt wide open, slipping my hands inside it while I slide down his body, kissing, nipping, licking, sucking his magnificent hard chest down to his cut abs.

He groans while his hands come up to grip my upper arms and pull me back up onto his lap. His mouth swoops down to take mine in a searing demanding kiss. I wind my arms around his neck, returning his kiss.

I could kiss him forever. I'm so lost in his kiss that I barely register the soft knocking at the door.

"I'm sorry to interrupt, but I need to talk to you, Constantine," says Lazarus from the doorway. The door is just slightly open.

"This better be important," warns Constantine. He closes his eyes and rests his forehead against mine while trying to get his ragged breathing under control.

"Yes, it's important. You would want to know about this," confirms Lazarus.

I get off him and lean against the big office table. Constantine unfolds himself off the chair. He buttons up his shirt without taking his eyes off me. His silver-gray eyes are warning me that this isn't over.

270

Ooohhh... I'm shaking in my boots or rather converse. Not! I roll my eyes. His lips curl up into a sensual little smile like he knows exactly what I'm thinking about.

Then he walks out the door, disappearing with Lazarus into another office.

I look around the room for the first time. This is a very manly man's office. All heavy dark wood furniture, dark wood wainscoting walls, and dark hardwood floor. Floor to ceiling bookcases dominating half the walls. The heavy drapes over the windows are light cream and gold. The only bright colors in this room are from three big, semi-abstract paintings on the wall behind the office table. I take it this is Constantine's office, while the one across the hall they just went into is Lazarus's.

Then I feel a sudden anger. Constantine. Something is making him furious.

Serena is sitting, almost lying down on the sofa in the living room by herself. Her feet are resting on the ottoman in front of her. A drink in her hand.

She looks up and places her drink on the side table next to her when she hears me coming. Her beautiful heart-shaped face looks serene as usual, but I can sense her inner turmoil. Probably it has something to do with the anger I feel coming off Constantine, and the sound of voices coming from Lazarus's office. These rooms are soundproof, but I can still hear their muffled voices.

"What's going on?" I ask as I sit right next to her. She rests her head on my shoulder and sighs heavily.

"Genesis, we're not ever going to let anything bad happen to you," she whispers.

"O-kay... well, that doesn't sound weird or anything at all." I speculate, trying to make sense of what she's saying. I feel, rather than see her smile when I feel her cheek moves against my shoulder.

The door to the office opens suddenly and grim-faced Constantine, Caspian, and Lazarus step out. Serena suddenly looks alert and sits up to face the three men.

Constantine lifts me off my seat and buries his face in my neck. All sorts of feelings coming off of him. Anger is predominant. My scent and my touch calm him.

"We lost her. Milan. We lost track of her," says Caspian, running his hand through his golden locks.

"Our men tracked her down and found her in Minsk. She took a train to Ukraine, but our men never saw her coming out of the train in Kiev," informs Lazarus.

"So we lost her between Belarus and Ukraine?" asks Serena. "She could be anywhere by now!"

"Tell us something we don't already know," mutters Caspian.

"But how?" questions Serena, sounding both, perplexed and troubled.

"Apparently she knows how to mask her scent," sighs Lazarus, dropping himself onto the sofa next to her. "We've assigned more men to look for her now."

"I'm sorry, sunshine. I've failed you. It should have been easy. We sent our best trackers and still, we failed," says Constantine. His arms are still tightly wrapped around me.

"Hey, we'll find her. You didn't fail me, Costa. Besides, she's somewhere in Europe, and I'm right here with you."

CHAPTER XXXI
Ring With The Heart and Crown

"So let me get this straight, you want me for my body and Duncan for food?" Constantine raises an eyebrow.

"No, I didn't say that...exactly. I mean, Duncan is good for his skills in the kitchen," I argue. "But I want you more than just for your body...and you know that." I purr with what I hope is a seductive voice. Actually, I think that sounds more like a cat choking on its hairball.

The corners of his lips curl up while his eyes alight with humor. "No, I don't know that." He keeps arguing, but now I know he finds it amusing.

"The point is, I'm not at all interested in Duncan or any other men."

"I know that...but I'm still jealous when there are other males around you."

"Why? Don't you trust me?"

We're sitting at the edge of the cliff watching the city below us. Our fingers intertwined. This is the cliff we came to that first time he told me that I was his erasthai. Constantine thought it's a good idea for us to be out of the house for the evening.

It is the beginning of dusk and the sky is beautiful even though we're not directly facing the sunset. It is painted with different shades and hues of orange, pink, blue and purple. It's the

273

end of spring and the sky is darkening slowly. The streetlights are on, and soon so are the lights in houses and other buildings.

Not too long ago, I thought my world was ending because of my mate, the one who was supposed to be with me forever, rejected me. The pain was unbearable, but now I wouldn't have it any other way. Because of it, I end up with Constantine. Now I can't imagine my life without him in it.

I glance at my mate beside me. His dark brown hair tousled and gently blown by the evening breeze, a few silky locks fallen over one eyebrow. The glow of the setting sun falls on one side of his face, emphasizing the sharp planes of his perfectly chiseled features. His long eyelashes create shadows across the bridge of his nose and his cheek. His pale silver-gray eyes look almost golden in this light. I still can't believe that he's mine.

"I can feel your love for me." He smiles gently. "Yes, I do trust you. I have to apologize in advance because I would still be jealous, no matter what. I can't help it. I'm a possessive beast."

"Well, as long as you know that I want only you. Besides, you're a hot beast when you're jealous."

He throws his head back and laughs then says, "I knew you want me for my body."

"Yeah, yeah, yeah...that's why I'm moving in with you. Well, your body, your shower heads, your—" I don't get to finish the sentence. His mouth comes down to land on mine in a brief but heated kiss that leaves me breathless.

"Good," he says with a smug grin. "I thought I was going to have to tie you to my bedpost to keep you with me at all times."

"Neanderthal," I mutter to myself, but I can't help smiling. We're mated, that's equivalent to being married for humans. It shouldn't even be a question about me moving in with him, it's expected. I'm just so weird. I guess I puzzled my own family when I was still home and never mentioned about moving in with my mate the other night...well, maybe not. My family is just as weird as

I am. I'm glad that he had asked instead of ordering me or forcing me to move in. My mate is awesome!

"Genesis," he suddenly grabs my other hand and his expression turns serious. "This is the place where I told you that you're my erasthai, my one and only. The place where I first told you that I intend to make you my mate...for life."

He suddenly looks nervous. "I have something that I want you to have. I had been waiting for it to arrive."

He reaches into his leather jacket pocket and produces a small blue velvet box. "It belonged to my grandmother."

He opens the box and nestled inside is a ring. A gold ring with a brilliant violet-blue, oval cut sapphire, surrounded by a circle of diamonds. It's beautiful! It glitters even in the fading sunlight.

"I know it's old-fashioned. It is very old. I mean, you don't have to wear it if you don't like it."

"Costa, I love it!"

"Or we can have it redesigned. If you don't like the sapphire, we can have it changed."

"No, Costa. It's beautiful! I love it the way it is. I wouldn't change a single thing," I interrupt him.

"Are you sure?" he asks, but there is a relief in his eyes and in him that I feel.

"Yes, it's gorgeous and it's special because it was your grandmother's. I'm honored to wear it."

I almost cry at the love that I feel coming from him and that I can see in his eyes. He lifts my left hand and slips the ring on my finger. It fits! He kissed my hand before letting it go.

I think I grin so wide as I admire the ring on my finger. Wow! I am mated. I really am mated! He put a ring on it. I don't know why, but Beyoncé's song starts playing in my head.

"Well, now you have to meet my grandmother," he interrupts my thoughts.

Bunnies!!! Way to kill my buzz.

He laughs. "you don't need to look as if I was about to deliver you to the gallows, my love."

"But what if your grandmother doesn't like me?"

"Oh, she'll love you. She knows all about you and now she can't wait to meet her new granddaughter," he reassures me.

"So we have to go to Russia?"

"No, my grandmother lives mostly in Chevalier Caye, her island in Belize. She's my maternal grandmother. She's not a royalty, but she owns The Monarchy, the restaurant that we went to last night. She's also the major shareholder of chains of restaurants and hotels throughout Europe and North America," he says. "I'm sorry if I sounded like I was boasting, but I'm very proud of my grandmother. She's a strong lady. She worked hard to get to where she's at, but she's still a kind grandmother to me. As a matter of fact, in some ways, she's like you."

Oh uh. "What do you mean, *in some ways,* she's like me?"

"Oh, you'll see." He grins mischievously. "On second thought, maybe it's not such a good idea to have both of you together. Goddess knows what harm you could do to the unsuspecting people around you if you're together."

Now I'm curious. If she's a bit like me, then it couldn't be that bad, right? Right?

"The school is going to be over in less than a month. I think we should go visit her then. You'll love Chevalier Caye."

Constantine sounds like he's very fond of his grandmother. Well, if he loves her, then I should meet her and make an effort to get to know her.

"Tell me more about your grandmother," I urge him softly.

"My grandmother isn't the type to bake cookies, knit sweaters or one who smells of lemon and honey. She disapproved of my parents going off leaving me to the governess and the nannies. I am the sole heir to her business empire, so she wanted to raise me herself. My uncle, King Alexandros, however, decided that I was to be brought up in the palace, learning the Palace's ways and the royal duties. I ended up growing up in the palace but I visit her once or twice a year, a month or two each time," he explains.

"I was ten when she told me about erasthais and mates. She showed me this ring and promised me that one day this ring will be on the finger of my mate. She was worried that my mating would not be to my erasthai, but arranged due to royal duties, like King Alexandros and Queen Sophia," he informs me. "That's why she's so happy to hear that I've found you."

I smile up at him. The thought of meeting his family still makes me nervous. "So, the king and the queen's mating was arranged?" I ask instead.

"Yes, it's not uncommon among the royalties and lycan nobilities. It's more for convenience, mergers of territories, peace treaties, forming or strengthening alliances."

"I feel sorry for them." That sounds so cold to me.

"Yes, they'll never have what we have, sunshine. I wouldn't trade us for the world." He wraps his arm around my shoulders and kisses my forehead.

A sudden thought occurs to me. "Have they ever tried to...arrange yours?"

"Arrange my mating? Yes, Queen Sophia did try to match me to a daughter of one of the noblemen," he replies. I feel my anger rising at that. He squeezes my shoulder and continues. "But she wasn't as serious about it as she is about matching Caspian to Lady Celeste. The daughter of one of her best friends. She wants him to mate her and be ready to take over the throne. Caspian wants to wait for his erasthai. It caused a lot of friction, to call it mildly, between the two. It's been going on for years, it's no longer a secret in the castle.

"Their last big argument was over three years ago. That caused Caspian to destroy his suite in the palace. King Alexandros decided that it's best if he left Russia for a while. That's why we're here. Queen Sophia can be relentless, though. She can wear you down. I don't know, Caspian might give in at some point. Eventually."

Poor Caspian. I always saw him as a carefree, devil-may-care, spoiled royal brat. Now I see him in a different light...a bit. Well, okay, he's still a childish, spoiled royal brat, but he was born into privilege and with that, a huge responsibility and expectations. I can't imagine having to mate for life with someone you're not in love with to just to fulfill an obligation thrust upon you since birth.

"I feel bad for Caspian." I sigh.

"Yeah...but enough about him. I'm happy you're wearing the ring, finally. I've waited a long time for this," he whispers against my mouth before his lips cover mine. My hands find their way into his thick luscious hair as his tongue finds its way inside my mouth.

Our tongues slide against each other. It's his taste that I can't get enough of. His hand at the back of my neck pulls me closer. His mouth grows more heated and more demanding.

I think I made a small sound of protest when he pulls back. He chuckles softly. Oh gosh! I swear my brain turns to mush whenever this man touches me.

"We better get home, sweetheart. This place is not as private and as secluded as the mountains," he says as he helps me up.

"This is not over," he whispers in my ear before he flashes me a wolfish grin. There's a wicked glint in his eyes that makes my heart skips a few beats and delicious chills run up and down my body.

I'm conscious of how close we are in the confines of the car. His eyes keep sliding towards me as if he can't keep his eyes off me. His hand on my thigh. I think we're way over the speed limit. I love watching his elegant, strong hands moving on the steering wheel.

Constantine groans and I turn to see my parents SUV parked in front of the huge mansion.

"Don't get me wrong, sunshine, I like your parents, but couldn't they pick another time to pay us a visit?"

I giggle. So much for wanting privacy.

"We're here to bring some of your things that you might need, sweetie," explains mom cheerfully when we meet them inside the house. Autumn is also here with them. "I know you would be moving in here soon, but we thought you might need these for tonight and tomorrow."

Yeah, right! Knowing my dad, it's probably his idea to come and check out the place. I know he's still very curious about the lycans.

"Thanks! How long have you been here?"

"Not that long. Maybe about fifteen minutes or so," answers my dad.

Serena, Lazarus, and Caspian had been entertaining my family before we arrived back. I found out that they had invited my parents to stay for dinner. Duncan is cooking up a storm in the kitchen.

"Oh goodness, it's beautiful, sweetie!" exclaims Mom when I showed her the ring.

"So he finally gave you the *ring*!" exclaims Serena.

Serena, mom, and even Autumn gush over the ring, while the men disappear down the basement where I believe they have a man cave, also known as the weapon, sparring and training room. Constantine was telling me last night that I would have to start training and learn how to use the weapons soon. I think I'd rather sit on the couch with a bowl of popcorn, watching a good movie instead. That's enough exercise for my hand, my mouth, and my brain.

The men come back upstairs when dinner is ready. I try to be nicer to Caspian tonight since I feel sorry for him. It doesn't last too long, though. Soon he's irritating me without even trying or having to say a word to me.

Autumn has stars in her eyes as she gazes up at Caspian. I can understand why. Caspian is stunning, just like the rest of them, and he is extra charming tonight, so different than when she saw him at school. He flashes his straight pearly white teeth often tonight when you barely see them at school. He even winked at her once, and that makes me feel like smacking him upside the head. My dad keeps calling him Prince Caspian or Your Highness. That makes me feel like correcting my dad. I felt like saying, "Just call him Casper, dad."

Play nice. Play nice! For the love of everything fuzzy, just play nice!!! So I just grit my teeth and smile.

Duncan served cucumber avocado Caprese salad as an appetizer; the main dish is Pesto chicken Florentine, and mango-lime sorbet with chunks of fresh mango for dessert.

Constantine is sitting next to me during dinner. Between cucumber avocado salad and Pesto chicken Florentine, I feel his warm thigh pressing up against mine. The warmth sizzles even through the thin fabrics between our skin. Not long after I feel his hand on my knee. Then his hand slowly creeps down the inner side of my thigh. The whole room falls away as the heat spreads all over my body. I bite my lip and clench my hands into tight fists to stop from moaning.

"Don't you think so, Genesis?" says mom, looking at me expectantly.

"Huh?"

Constantine's mouth curls up at the corners in a smirk before he turns to look at me with an innocent expression on his beautiful face. His hand continues to move up my thigh.

"Yeah, sure mom," I answer, even though I have no clue what she was asking me about.

Looking at Constantine's angelic looking face, I decide that two can play the game.

I lay my hand gently on the inner side of his upper thigh and even before I start moving it upward, he moans.

Ooppsss...

His moan is loud enough to cause everybody to pause from talking and eating. Everybody looks up and stares. Yikes!

"Uuummm...this is very good." He tries to cover up. "I mean, this is a very good...uhh...chicken," he continues then clears his throat awkwardly. His smooth golden cheeks are suddenly stained pink.

Serena covers her mouth with a napkin, stifling her laugh. Caspian drops his fork on the plate then sits back in his chair, smirking. Lazarus just resumes eating, though his mouth is curled up at the corners and his eyes glint with amusement.

My parents just look a bit puzzled but quickly agree with Constantine. "Yes, this is a very excellent meal. Your cook is exceptionally good," says dad.

I'm happy that my family gets along very well with my lycan family. It's after ten when my mom, my dad, and my sister Autumn take off.

"You," growls Constantine in my ear from behind as I try to help clear the table.

"Me?"

"Yes, you! Payback time for what you did to me during dinner." He nuzzles my neck. His mouth teasing, nipping and licking me behind my ear.

Ooohhh... goosebumps.

In a quick swift motion, he turns me around, then grabs me by my waist and throws me over his shoulder.

"Hey! Where are you going?" yells Caspian as Constantine carries me up the stairs.

"Painting session," answers Constantine off-handedly.

"What???" I yelp.

"But I thought your studio isn't quite ready yet?" Caspian sounds amused. I can hear Serena laughing behind him.

CHAPTER XXXII
Mature Eyes Immature Hearts

He kicks the door to his bedroom close and throws me onto the bed. I bounce up and down on the huge bed, staring up at him.

"What are you going to do to me?"

"Wouldn't you like to know?" he drawls playfully. "The real question is, what wouldn't I do to you, my love?"

He pounces, and I yelp and bound onto the other side of the bed. He looks up and predatory look enters his eyes, and his smile turns wicked.

"I thought we're doing a painting session?" I squeak, scanning the room for any possible area to escape.

Taking my eyes off him proves to be a mistake as he leaps gracefully out of the bed. I manage to jump to the other side of the bed in time...just barely.

"Well, then...take off all your clothes and model for me," he suggests, his voice sounds amused.

"What??? Uh...now?"

"Or maybe we're skipping the painting part and doing what comes right after," he adds with a widening smile.

Yikes! I walk slowly around the bed to the furthest side away from him. His eyes follow my movement with a watchful but playful and amused look. It reminds me of a big cat playing with its meal before the kill.

I think me running away from him just provokes his predatory nature, and him stalking me just triggers my flight instinct. I'm set on winning....I think.

I grin at him, showing my full set of pearly whites as we observe each other, trying to read each other's next move. I can feel his excitement growing at this cat and mouse game...as well as his hunger for me. That makes my stomach clenched in excitement.

"Wait till I get my hands on you," he warns me, grinning wickedly.

"IF you ever get your hands on me," I challenge him with a smirk.

"I take that as a challenge. You know how much challenges excite me, my love."

"You know how good I am at running, my darling," I return haughtily.

"Is that so?"

"Yes!"

I spring right over the bed as he leaps to my side and makes a grab for my waist. I manage to elude him again this time. I think he's just playing with me, though. We both know how fast he can be when he's really serious about it.

He smiles roguishly as he observes the distance between us. I tip my chin up and raise an eyebrow daringly at him. Ha!!! I know I'm losing, but I'd rather go down with style and spunk.

He looks like he's trying hard not to laugh at my audacity. He winks just before he dives to the right, and I run. At the last moment he turns the other way, and in a blink of an eye, he has me pinned to the wall with both my hands trapped in one of his above my head. Darn it!!!

"Gotcha!" he grins wolfishly down at me.

His silver-gray eyes darken in excitement. His warm breath is teasing my skin. My chest rises up and down as my heart beats fast and my breathing labored from the excitement of the chase.

His thick sooty eyelashes fan downward as he stares down at my lips, then they go lower still to my rising and falling chest.

Men! They get distracted by breasts so easily. I try to take advantage of the situation by trying to jerk my hands out of his grip. No such luck! He's so strong. He just grins but keeps his eyes trained on my chest.

He leans in closer, his lips lightly graze my cheek and the shell of my ear. "You know how good I am at catching you, my darling...and you're not getting away from me," he whispers. My heart beats faster and my stomach clenches deliciously with excitement and anticipation.

His hand comes up and starts to undo the button of my top slowly, one by one. His eyes watch the fabric part with every button he loosens with fascination. After he released the last button, his smoldering silver-gray eyes move up to meet mine. The hunger in his eyes is stark and unmistakable.

He never takes his eyes off me as he leans down between my breasts and slowly places his mouth there. He kisses my heated skin, then his tongue comes up to lick me softly. Oh, my good goddess. Explosions of pleasure burst from the touch of his mouth and tongue spread all over me. I arch my back and closed my eyes. Small sighs and moans escape my lips.

"Beautiful..." he whispers reverently against my skin as he moves his mouth upwards. I open my eyes to find his heavy-lidded gray eyes still watching me with fascination and passion. When his warm firm lips touch my neck, I'm lost again.

"Constantine..." I sigh breathlessly, and that seems to snap his control.

His mouth devours mine. His tongue tangles wildly with mine. Oh, the taste of him. I strain to get closer. He finally let go of my hand, and I run my fingers through his hair. My other hand slips underneath his shirt to roam the contours of his back and broad shoulders. I feel him shudders.

My top falls away and I vaguely aware of the feel of the soft fabric against my back as he lays me down on the bed. His hands are touching and kneading my body, making me lose all coherent thoughts. My whole body is engulfed in flames. His mouth on me does things that make me moan so loud.

He pushes himself up, kneeling on the bed with my body between his legs. He never takes his smoldering silver-gray eyes off me as he reaches behind his back, and in one swift motion, he tugs his shirt off. I gaze up at his glorious chest, then down to the ridges of his abs and lower. He unbuttons his jeans, and my eyes travel back all the way up to his half-lidded eyes.

He pulls both our jeans off, then he grins wickedly before pushes my legs open and kneels down.

"What are you...?" I start to ask. "Ohhh..." His magical mouth is devouring me. I think I'm phasing. My eyes are turning black. I think the Earth shakes.

Then he comes up, and his shiny black eyes are looking back into mine. His lips parted to show his sharp canines just before his lips cover mine. I moan and grip his back when he enters me. "You are mine. All of you belong to me."

*　　　*　　　*

"No, mom I didn't do it," I mumble, pulling the blanket back over my head.

I hear a chuckle. "Do what, exactly?" Someone is pulling the blanket back down.

Oh Gosh! It's too early for this. My brain doesn't work properly in the morning.

"Whatever it is...not my fault.... I swear, I didn't do it," I mumble out again, trying to pull the blanket right over my head again.

My pillow shakes with laughter. I groan and lift my head up to look into Constantine's beautiful icy gray eyes that are lit up with amusement.

My first thought is: nope, definitely not my mom. Not unless my mom turned into a hot god-like Adonis with sexy morning stubble and messy hair and hard body overnight.

Yikes! My brain is broken.

Second thought is: oh no, I can't be mated to one of those annoying morning people, or lycans.

"I'm sorry, I will have to let you go," I mutter sleepily as I lie my head back down on a real pillow this time. I try to turn my body away from him, but he just tightens his grip on my waist.

"Oh no, you don't," he says. "Sweetheart, I didn't realize how hard it is to wake you up in the morning."

"Uummm..hmmm...mmm," I mumble. What I meant to say was, "Go away. Let me lie in peace, or else I might have to kill you." Yeah, I'm grumpy in the morning.

Everything was quiet and peaceful for a while until I feel his hand spreading over my stomach. Then his lips are peppering tiny kisses along my shoulder and neck.

Ummm....well, hello.

∗   ∗   ∗

"So....how did your painting session go last night?" asks Caspian with a mischievous smile. In front of him is a plateful of pancakes, sausages, hash browns, and scrambled eggs. He's only in his cotton pajama pants that hang low on his hips today. It's already after ten, Sunday morning.

Lazarus walks in behind me. "Very well, by the sound of it," Lazarus deadpans.

Caspian's hand quickly comes up to cover his mouth, but not before a choke of laughter escaped.

286

"Shut up, guys!" I poke my tongue out as my face is flooded with color.

Lazarus is followed by Serena who slaps his behind playfully, though her eyes twinkle with mirth. Both of them are already showered and dressed. Looks like Caspian and I are the only two who are not morning people or rather lycans in this house.

I'm also still in my pajamas, except that I had put Constantine's big bathrobe on before I came out of the room. Constantine was still in the shower when I followed my nose down to the kitchen where I smelled food.

Duncan is behind the stove with his earphone on, listening to his iPod. I can actually hear the song that he's listening to. It's Starboy by The Weeknd. He's cheerfully singing and dancing to the song while pouring the batter of pancakes onto the skillet.

Oh Gosh! He really can't sing, and he's a terrible dancer. The man makes good pancakes, though. Yes, very good pancakes, I decide as I steal another forkful from Caspian's plate.

"Good morning," greets Constantine as he wraps his arms around me and nuzzles his face into the crook of my neck from behind. He's shaven off his stubble. I really don't mind it, I think Constantine with stubble looks hot.

"Good morning...though you sounded like you had a great night too," quips Caspian.

I can feel Constantine smile against my neck. So I drag Caspian's whole plate in front of me and start to feed Constantine his breakfast too.

"Oh, great! Now you took my whole plate," complains Caspian, raising his hands up in defeat. That's what he gets for teasing me non-stop this morning.

Duncan keeps his out of tune singing and peculiar dancing while serving everybody breakfast.

"You did good," I squeeze Serena's hand. "You hired a good cook and provide us free entertainment too."

Serena bursts out laughing while the three men groan in unison.

*   *   *

We decided that I should move in today. Lazarus, Serena, and Caspian decided to help as well.

Constantine drives Lazarus's Range Rover with me in the passenger seat so that we have enough space to put my worldly possession in. Caspian is forced to drive his Audi when he lost an argument with Serena who refused to crouch in the back seat of his flashier Porsche.

We managed to pack all my things in luggage and boxes in no time...well, right after Serena and I kicked Caspian out of my room. He seemed too happy and too distracted by my underwear drawer, even Constantine started to get irritated with him. Gosh, he's such a kid! Sometimes I'm worried about him.

The lycans are all so strong, they carried everything as if they weighed nothing, and we finished in no time at all.

It's kinda sad to see my room bare of all my belongings. I suppose it has to happen at some point.

"My baby is all grown up," says mom as we get downstairs with the last box of my things.

"Aww, mom..."

"You're not too far away. You come back often, you hear?" She squeezes me in a big bear hug.

I don't have a lot of stuff. We only brought my clothing, toiletries, books, painting equipment, and shoes. I still left a few things in my old bedroom. I can visit my parents anytime I want.

*   *   *

"Just leave everything there, sunshine. The staff will be here tomorrow to put everything away," says Constantine as I look around his walk-in closet. It's bigger than the size of my old bedroom and very well organized. I can see that he cleared more than half the space for me.

"I'll just do what I can, for now, then I'll let them put everything else away. Besides, I need to know where everything is to get ready for school tomorrow."

"Okay then." He kisses my cheek. "Come downstairs when you're done. I think Caspian is killing everybody with his version of Karaoke, and Duncan seems very eager to join in once he's done cooking dinner."

"Oh, good Lord," I groan. May goddess help us all.

"We might need your help to put an end to this madness," he grins.

As soon as he leaves, I open a small box that I had been keeping in my underwear drawer in my old room. Inside, is some money. One hundred and twenty-three dollars and fifty cents. That's what's left from the sale of my painting. I have another one hundred and fifty dollars that I saved from my allowances. Two hundred and seventy-three dollars and fifty cents. That's the amount that I have to my name in this world. I slip the money into my school bag. I have a plan for this money.

CHAPTER XXXIII
Ring With Hearts and Flowers

"Time for school, sweetheart." I feel a hand stroking my cheek.

"Five more minutes," I mumble, snuggling deeper into the warmth of his arms. "Tired."

It's all Constantine's fault. Our.....uh..painting sessions lasted a while last night, and we had several throughout the night, and again this morning at dawn. Now I'm still tired. How can he be so cheerful and energetic in the morning?

"Did I wear you out, sunshine?" He chuckles.

"Never," I answer with my eyes closed.

"Oh really? Hmmm..." He burrows his face into the crook of my shoulder, then starts kissing and nibbling on the skin just above my collarbone. He moves lower. Oh, my....

I open my eyes just in time to see his silky dark head disappearing underneath the blanket.

*   *   *

"Are we going to start going to school late every day now?" asks Caspian, grinning mischievously. He's sitting on the hood of Lazarus's shiny black Escalade with his long legs casually dangling down the front of the SUV.

290

"You could just have left without us, you know," remarks Constantine.

"Nope, we're driving together today," Caspian says as he gracefully hops off the car.

Yes, we're running a bit late this morning. We have ten more minutes before the first bell rings. It's a good ten minutes drive from here to get to the school if you observed the speed limit and followed all the traffic rules but with the way these lycans drive, I'm sure we'll make it there with a plenty of time to spare.

Lazarus and Serena are already waiting in the car. Lazarus is in the driver's seat and Serena is riding shotgun. Constantine opens the door for me and I climb in to sit in the third row. He climbs in to sit next to me, while Caspian takes his seat in front of us.

Lazarus pulls out of the long, winding driveway then speeds down the road. I lace my fingers through Constantine's and he plants a kiss on the back of my hand.

"I heard from our men this morning," remarks Lazarus suddenly. So that's why they were waiting for us this morning. They need to talk. "They had reasons to believe that Milan was in Krasnoïarsk."

"Was in Krasnoïarsk?" interrupts Constantine. He sounds aggravated. "Her family's in Krasnoïarsk. She has comrades in Krasnoïarsk. I specifically told them that's among the first places they should be looking for her."

"They weren't able to find her there...until someone spotted her at Yemelyanovo International Airport last night."

"Tell me they're on her tail now," asks Constantine. When Lazarus doesn't answer right away, he spits out several foreign words. I have no clue what he's saying, but it sounds so much like a string of expletives to me. Lazarus then starts talking in the same language, followed by Caspian barking out what sounds like curses as well. Pretty soon the three of them start conversing rapidly in a foreign language. I'm guessing Russian.

Serena turns around in her seat to look at me with a raised eyebrow. "They do this quite often," she says to me over their voices. That seems to make them pause for a second, then they continue to exchange a few more words.

A minute later, the car is unusually quiet until Caspian snaps, "*чертовы идиоты*," (damn idiots) followed by grunts of agreement from the other two.

Constantine sighs, sitting back in his seat while at the same time wrapping an arm around my shoulders, pulling me down with him. I place my head on the headrest next to his.

"They saw her in Yemelyanovo International Airport in Russia. They followed her all the way to Heathrow Airport, England, only to find out that it wasn't her. The woman was dressed to look like her and smelled like her," he explains. His voice is monotonous with frustration and heavy with the Russian accent. His eyes are trained on the headliner of the car. "They detained the woman and are questioning her right now. They also brought in a couple of her comrades in Krasnoïarsk for questioning."

I wait for him to continue, but when he remains quiet, I have to ask, "that's good though, right?"

"What do you mean that's good, sunshine? We lost her, we're back to square one."

"Not really. You have a lead now. You have that woman and those other two."

"Still, the men are incompetent. They're supposed to be very good trackers and they let her slip through their fingers like that." Is it bad that I find his heavily accented voice terribly hot?

The other day I overheard him on the phone speaking in French. Right after that, his English was thick with the French accent. I found that incredibly hot. It took everything in me not to jump his bone and I bet he knew it too.

Fuzzy slippers! This is not the time to think of his hot accent. Focus Genesis! I can still feel the anger raging inside him.

I comb my fingers through his hair gently, trying to calm him down. He sighs and buries his face in my neck, breathing in deeply. I continue playing with his hair while trying to share my sense of peacefulness with him.

Caspian and Lazarus aren't in much better mood themselves. I wonder if there's something they're not telling Serena and me.

Caspian is clenching and unclenching his jaw while looking out the window absently. That's not normal for Caspian. When he's not out to get me, something is not right. It actually bothers me when he's not bugging me. I think I should get my head checked.

Serena is talking softly to Lazarus, no doubt trying to cheer him up as well.

Constantine seems a lot calmer by the time we arrive in school. However, the weird apprehensive mood seems to follow us like a dense thunderstorm cloud over our heads. Maybe I'm just picking up on the collective feelings of our pack members this morning.

Serena and Lazarus have their arms loosely around each other's waist. Constantine wraps his arm around my shoulders as soon as we step out of the car, while Caspian walks in front of us with his usual arrogant swagger. These three men can really walk as if they owned the place, no matter where they are.

I feel eyes following us as we walk down the hallways of the school. If I pay attention, I can hear what they're whispering about with my lycan hearing too, but I chose to ignore it.

*   *   *

I see Penny in English Lit first. Her eyes zero in on the ring before I can say funny bunnies. She squeals and jumps up and down like a crazy woman and the whole class stare at her like she just lost her mind. Good thing the teacher isn't here yet.

Logan and Zeke are also nowhere to be seen. I'm feeling kinda relief about that. I don't feel like facing Logan, even though he's been ignoring me most of the time now.

"You're going to help me with my birthday party, right?" asks Penny suddenly. I almost forgot that Penny's birthday is coming soon. She's planning to have a big party next weekend.

"Wouldn't it be great if I found my mate right that night at my own birthday party?" She sighs dreamily.

"Really? What happens if it turns out to be someone you don't like? What if he happens to be one of those man-whores like Zeke or Caleb or Jordan?"

"Don't you dare kill my buzz, Genesis," she warns me. "Besides, I might or might not have made a list of all the available, eligible, good-looking boys that I might or might not have a crush on to be invited to my party." She grins mischievously.

"Just how many boys are you currently crushing on Penny?"

"Wouldn't you like to know?" She giggles and sticks her tongue out at me just before she turns around when the teacher enters the classroom.

*   *   *

It sucks that I don't have a class with any of the lycans at all. Well, at least Constantine is always waiting by the door of my classroom after my every class.

At lunchtime, I meet up with Constantine and Serena just outside the cafeteria. Lazarus and Caspian already have their food. We decided to eat outside since the weather is so beautiful today. Quite a few other students have the same idea.

The sun is shining warm and bright when I step outside with Serena and Constantine.

Caspian and Lazarus are already sitting at their regular spot, which is a picnic table underneath a maple tree with benches on either side. It's way near the end, just by the fence. No other students sit there usually. It's always known that the lycans sit there when they're outside.

"Genesis!!!" Penny and Reese are waving their arms about from another picnic table.

We head over, and I hold out my ring finger up immediately. Reese and Penny jump up excitedly. Trust Penny to act as if she just saw it for the first time...again.

"Oh my Gosh! Oh my gosh!" squeals Reese, jumping up and down, holding my hand. River just laughs and shakes his head, watching us.

Constantine chuckles quietly against my shoulder before he let go of me. He kisses me lightly on the cheek before he heads towards Caspian and Lazarus, leaving me with the girls and River.

"It's gorgeous!" breathes Reese.

"It's very big, isn't it?" says Penny.

"It's also very old. It's believed that it used to belong to Empress Milica of Serbia," chimes in Serena.

"Oh, my goddess..." whispers Reese, staring at it in awe.

Wait. What? He didn't tell me that! "Wait a minute!" I choke out. "This thing must be expensive."

"Priceless," says Serena simply, smiling at my flabbergasted expression. It's priceless, and he let me wear it? My mate is out of his mind! OUT OF HIS FREAKING MIND. And I'm freaking out.

Serena shakes her head and laughs. "Oh, sweetie, why are you suddenly looking at it like it's a poisonous snake or something?"

"You don't understand, Serena. What if I lost it? What if somebody stole it or robbed it off me? I am NOT the type of person who should be wearing something this valuable."

"You're a lycan, Genesis. Who would dare to rob it off your finger? And as for losing it, I'm sure it's insured. Besides,

Constantine doesn't care for the ring as much as he cares about you."

I let the girls know about my plan to get Constantine a ring. Now I really feel bad about it. He gave me a priceless ring. A ring that used to grace the finger of an empress and I'm about to get him a ring at the mall. Not to mention it can't go over my budget of two hundred and seventy-five dollars and fifty cents.

"I think it's only fair that he should be wearing a ring to show other bitches that he's taken when you're wearing his ring. So what if the ring you get him is cheaper than the one he gave you? At least you're giving him a brand new ring. He gave you a used ring," announces Penny. *Penny logic.*

Serena looks like she's having a hard time not to burst out laughing. Reese just shakes her head at what she calls "Penny's illogical logic" as usual.

"Don't fret about it, Genesis. You could give him a coke can ring tab to wear, and he would still love it," assures Serena.

"True! Everyone can see that the man is crazy about you, GenGen. Price doesn't matter. No matter what you give him, he'll love it," agrees Reese. "What do you think, River?"

"Yup, as a guy, I know he'll love it...as long as you don't make him wear a girly ring with hearts and flowers." River grins.

"A ring with hearts and flowers, where d'you get that?" scoffs Penny.

"So we can go out shopping today or tomorrow after school. We have a perfect excuse to go shopping for dresses for Penny's birthday party," suggests Serena.

"Yes!" agrees Penny excitedly.

I'm glad that Serena gets along well with Reese and Penny.

"Genesis, can I talk to you for a moment?" Logan is standing right next to me. Reese, Penny, and River don't look happy at all to see Logan.

I turn to look at Constantine's direction. He's already staring at us. His eyes narrow speculatively.

"Please?"

I turn to look at Logan again. He looks awful. He's unshaven. Fuzzy, light-brown hair covers half his face. His golden hair isn't as shiny and nicely combed and styled as usual. The light in his sea blue eyes are gone. They are dulled, troubled, and red-rimmed.

I'm suddenly feeling conflicted. I really don't want to, but I feel like I need to talk to Logan at some point. There's always a sense of an unfinished business between us. At the same time, I know my mate wouldn't like me to be talking to him. I know I wouldn't like it too if it was Constantine who's going off to talk to his ex-lover or some other girl.

I do need to talk to Logan though. I can't have this unfinished business hanging over my head forever. I stand up hesitantly and Serena put a hand on my arm. She has a blank look on her face, but I can feel her unease. I feel the pack disapproval. I feel Constantine's warning anger growing.

CHAPTER XXXIV
One With the Ninja Power

"I have to do this," I whisper to Serena, Reese, Penny, and River.

Serena eases her hold on my arm. Reese, Penny, and River are giving Logan death glares.

I turn to face Constantine once again. The heat of his anger is there. I plead with my eyes for him to understand just before I follow Logan to the other side of the building.

Logan's minions are standing at the corner, watching us. He nods at them and they move a bit further away, giving us a bit more privacy.

His eyes scan me from top to bottom then up again before they linger on my face. I fidget with the edge of my top for a while, waiting for him to say something.

"You're looking good, Genesis," he starts finally. "Hell, you're looking better than good. I bet you already knew that," he adds almost bitterly.

And you're not looking so good. Well, I'm just thinking that. I don't think it's wise to say that out loud. Oh, he's still attractive, but I think he could do with a shower and a shave. I don't think he looks too hot with a five o'clock shadow. Unlike Constantine.

"Uh...thank you, I think. Is that all you need to talk to me about?" I didn't mean to sound so snotty, it just comes out that way.

"No," he scowls. "He's marked you." It's more of a statement rather than a question. His gaze travels to my neck. His eyes show his confusion for a while at the lack of a mark on it.

My mark is on my shoulder, rather than on the neck like werewolves. I was told that only other lycans can sense another marked lycans. Most werewolves can't sense this.

"But I felt it." He looks puzzled.

"Huh?"

"I felt it when he marked you...he must have...I mean, the pain was intense. And last night..." his voice trails away and his eyebrows furrow.

"Yes, he did. He's marked me," I reply. He must have felt our... uh... painting sessions last night too. Yikes! I don't know how to feel about that. I wanted to get back at him for making me suffer from his sleeping around before, but I'm not so sure now. I mean, I've moved on. I'm happy with Constantine. I don't care about revenge anymore and I certainly don't want him to "feel" anything every time I'm "with" Constantine.

"So that was it. That's what I felt last night. The pain. I felt it every damn time he's fucking you," he spits. He grits his teeth and he runs his fingers through his unruly hair in agitation.

"No more than I felt you when you're sleeping around with anything that moves," I snap back. I suffered through those pain, I refuse to feel guilty for what he's feeling now.

"Okay, so we hurt each other...."

"Yeah, so now we should just move on," I intercept him. I'm about done with this discussion.

"So, we hurt each other..." He repeats louder through a clenched jaw. "We're even now. We should put this behind us and get back together."

For a moment, I all could do is just stand there and gape at him. What is he? Daft?

"That's the way it should be, Genesis. You're my mate, you're born to be with me...look at me. I need you. You have to come back to me."

"We were never together, to begin with, Logan," I remind him. "You should've thought of that before you rejected me."

"Okay, look...I'm sorry. I was a jerk. It was stupid and I regretted it the moment I did it, but I was too proud and I can't show my weakness to others."

"You were too proud? Your pride caused me a lot of pain. Well, congratulations to you and your pride. May you live a long and happy life together."

"NO! Genesis, you need to come back to me...you're my mate." Now he sounds like he's begging.

"I'm not your mate, Logan. I already have a mate."

He winces at that.

"You could reject him, and come back to me."

"Why would I do that, Logan? I love him."

"I could mark you and we could be mates again." He's acting as if I haven't said anything.

What? Seriously? He's losing his mind.

"NO. You don't want to do that, Logan. I'm a lycan now...and I am marked by a lycan. My blood will only poison you and if you're not killed by my blood, my mate will."

Suddenly, his eyes turn icy and his hands clenched into tight fists at his side. "Look at you, all high and mighty now. You're such a tease. You could've been my mistress." He jeers, moving closer. "I could've had you."

"Stop it, Logan! You haven't changed!" I take a step back.

He's behaving like a madman. One minute he's apologetic and begging me to go back to him, the next moment he's all mad and condescending—and crazy. I can't deal with his multiple personalities.

300

"I wish you happiness. I truly do. I hope you'll find yourself a good mate and a suitable luna for this pack," I continue while I take a few steps away from him.

"You're not walking away from me, Genesis! You are mine! You'll always be mine. You know how you like my touch. Let me remind you..."

I take another step back and utter the words that I should have uttered a long time ago. "I Genesis Fairchild accept your—"

"NO! STOP!" he yells and his hand suddenly grabs my wrist, but something flashed by me in a blur of a movement and then my wrist is free.

Constantine.

One of Constantine's hand is pinning Logan against the wall by the throat, while another is gripping Logan's hand that was holding my wrist a moment ago. Oh gosh, this is almost a replay of what happened in the hallways of the school not too long ago.

I'm glad to see that at least his eyes are still very human, even though they darken considerably by his anger. At least he's still in control of his lycan. He snarls viciously at Logan, showing his sharp teeth and elongated canines. I can feel that he's seriously contemplating killing Logan.

"No, Constantine...stop! Costa...please," I plead, closing my hand around his solid arm.

Logan's friends move in a little closer in alarm, but none of them dares do anything. A few other students are standing around, watching us. At least they have enough sense to do that at a good distance.

The lycans are here too. I sense and see that they have no intention of interfering. They're just observing coolly. Serena looks calm as usual, Lazarus is unreadable, and Caspian is leaning against the wall of the school building, looking bored.

Constantine is a good few inches taller. He's towering over Logan, staring down at him contemplatively. Right now, he's

301

looking like he's deciding whether to rip Logan's heart right out of his chest or snap his head right off his body.

"Sweetheart, please..." I plead again urgently. I touch his cheek to gain his attention, my other hand is holding on tightly onto his arm. His eyes never waver from Logan's face.

I notice Logan grits his teeth at the way I'm talking to Constantine and touching him.

"I want nothing more than to crush your skull right now," he informs Logan quietly with a dangerous cruel smile playing on his lips. "Talk to my mate again, or go anywhere near her, and I swear I will end you."

Then he turns to look at me and smiles. A wide smile that shows off his straight white teeth and his sharp canines. I'm not fooled by that smile though. I know he's not happy. Just as I thought he's about to let Logan go, I hear a crunch of a broken bone and Logan screaming out in agony.

He walks off while Logan is still screaming, holding on to his broken right arm.

Just as I'm about to take off after Constantine, Logan crouches low then growls and springs up from his crouch, snapping his teeth, swiping his long sharp nails at Constantine's back.

I instinctively leap in front of Logan, pinning him to the wall behind us with his good arm in my grip.

I wring his arm till I feel and hear a sickening crunch of a bone breaking. He's howling loudly in my ear. That one was me saving his life. Constantine could have ended him with a flick of a wrist. I move my hands to his upper arm and press hard until I feel it snaps and hears that cracking sound again, and this one is for trying to harm my mate, even though I know there is no way he could've hurt a lycan.

"I accept your rejection, Logan Carrington," I whisper in his ear before I walk away, leaving him howling, screaming, and crumpled on the ground.

Strangely I feel lighter. No, it doesn't feel good to hurt somebody, even when that somebody is my jerk ex-mate who hurt me more than anybody ever did in my life. I think I feel lighter because that connection is totally severed now. I do wish him well, but I don't want anything to do with him anymore.

Constantine is standing not too far away, looking at me with pride, and something else in his eyes. The rest of the lycans are standing around him. I take Constantine's outstretched hand, and we walk away from there, followed by the rest of the lycans.

"Costa...I'm sorry," I whisper urgently, staring at his beautiful stern profile as we cross the small field. "Costa...?" I tug at his hand.

I can feel his anger. I don't like it when he's angry with me.

He suddenly changes direction with my hand still firmly in his. We're now walking away from the school building. The rest of the lycans keep walking into the school without us.

When we reach the first tree at the end of the field, he stops. He turns his blazing gray eyes to look at me for the first time since he brought me here.

"I'm not angry with you. I understand what you needed to do... I'm not happy that you went off with him like that, but I understand," he says. "I'm still mad at him though. The only reason he's still alive is because you didn't want me to kill him, and I know for sure that there's no way in hell he can have you. If I believe otherwise, he'd be dead by now."

"Okay," I smile. "So you're not angry with me."

"Sweetheart, I'm not. Even if I was, you know I can't stay angry with you for too long." He sighs. "What am I going to do with you?" He shakes his head.

"Oh, I can think of a few things..." I move in closer.

"You look so hot when you saved me from his attack just now." His eyes darken with something else now instead of anger. "I know you're trying to save him...but you look so dangerous and sexy as hell. I could've taken you then...right after you broke his arm, the second time."

He leans in and takes my mouth in a hot searing kiss. I press my body up against his and grab a hold of the back of his neck and tangle my fingers in his thick silky hair. His tongue delves into my mouth, and he presses me up against the tree behind me. Our tongues glide together. Oh, the taste of him. He moans against my lips.

He picks me up and wraps my legs around his waist. Heat surges through my whole body from everywhere that we're touching.

"We have to get to class," he murmurs. His voice is deliciously husky. His mouth is now kissing, sucking and nibbling me behind my ear and slowly moving down my neck.

"Yes." I moan as he grabs my hair and moves my head to the side to give him better access to my neck.

He pushes me harder against the tree, grinding his body against mine. His mouth covers mine as a moan escapes my lips. Constantine...

"Goddess....I'm addicted to you," he groans, tearing his mouth off mine. We're both panting hard.

*   *   *

Constantine walks me to my classroom, which is art. Good thing it's the class that I like. It's good that my art teacher, Mrs. Winters, likes me too. I have learned to ignore the stares and the whispers around us. Today, more than any other day, I have to pretend not to notice any of it. I just broke the future alpha's arm. It's easy to ignore them when I'm with Constantine and with my lycan pack. When I'm in the confines of a classroom though, it's harder to ignore. My lycan hearing can hear every word they're saying about me.

Well, at least none of them has the courage to come up and say it to my face. They know not to mess up with a lycan...especially after what I just did to Logan's arm.

Ha!!! Ninja power!

Mia Brown enters my classroom about thirty minutes later. She usually gives me death glares from afar whenever she sees me now, and I can see so much hatred in her eyes.

She talks to the teacher and hands her a note. A few minutes later, Mrs. Winters looks at me and says, "Genesis, you're expected in the principal's office right now, dear."

I was half expecting that. I mean I just broke my ex-mate, the golden boy, the future alpha's arm in two places. Besides, I haven't visited the principal's office for quite a while. The principal must have missed me.

The last time I was in trouble was late last year when Penny and I placed a few fake cockroaches and fake dead rats at the most inspired, well-chosen places around the cafeteria. River dared us. So, it was partly his fault. I don't know how they figured out it was us though. Well, okay, maybe because we got into trouble for something like that a few times before.

It was a beautiful sight though, girls and even guys were screaming, some jump onto the tables and chairs, and food flying everywhere. *Ahhh... good times.*

I grab all my brushes and place the painting I've been working on at the back of the classroom. I can feel eyes following my every movement. After I finished cleaning up, I gather up all my stuff and look up to see Mia still waiting by the door.

I'm not feeling too eager to face our principal though. No, I don't miss him all that much.

Mia walks with a spring in her steps. She doesn't say a word until we reach the front of the office.

"Alpha Carrington would like to see you," she says with a smug look on her face and a gleeful glint in her eyes.

305

CHAPTER XXXV
I Can Smell Your Fear

"There's law against harming your own mate," declares Alpha Carrington. "You broke both his arms!"

Well, I just broke his one arm. In two places, admittedly, but technically still just one arm. Constantine broke his other arm. Another thing, important one, Logan is not my mate! *Sheesh!*

I saved his life too. Three times now. But, hey, who's counting?

I'm very sure Logan's arms are healing and repairing themselves as we're speaking. Werewolves heal quite fast.

Right now, I'm sitting in the principal's office, listening to Alpha Carrington's rant, while having a monologue in my own head. What? He yaks so much that I can't get a word in edgeways. So I talk to myself, in my own head. Well, okay, I am weird.

Alpha Carrington has his two big warriors standing guard at the door in the reception area. He goes everywhere with his guards. I know he's an alpha and all, but really? I guess there's no cure for delusions of grandeur. I have an urge to roll my eyes, but under current circumstances, I don't think that's a great idea.

Our school principal, Mr. Bennet, is sitting behind his desk, staring at his folded hands in front of him. Now, here's the man who is stuck between a rock and a hard place. He can't go against his own alpha, but I can't imagine him punishing the mate of a king's nephew either. Oh, poor principal Bennet.

Mr. Bennet isn't that bad actually. I gave the man such headaches countless times. I'm surprised he still keeps his job. Pretty soon I'm sure he's going to press his fingers against the bridge of his nose like he always did when Penny and I put our innocent faces on and answered his questions with our own vague questions.

"My boy Logan has suffered enough. Soon he's going to be an alpha. He needs a luna by his side." Alpha Carrington keeps on ranting. Oh gosh, it's not over yet. Is this torture ever going to end? I would fast forward it if I could. Okay, back to monologue.

Principal Bennet has that little bald spot on his head. That always bothers me. I bet if he uses a dark eyeliner....

"Genesis?" principal Bennet is asking me.

Huh? "What?" *Oh, fuzzy slippers.* I was too deep in the monologue.

He sighs. "I said, you should tell us your side of the story. What happened, Genesis?"

"What did Logan tell you?" Gosh, I didn't even realize that I was doing it again. Answering his question with another question.

Like I predicted, Principal Bennet is now squeezing the bridge of his nose. I'm psychic!

"She broke his arms! What else is there to know? My son just wanted to discuss rationally if there's a possibility she would consider coming back to him, but she broke his arms!" Alpha Carrington explodes. See what I mean? He wouldn't even let me tell my side of the story.

Anyway, that's about correct except that he went crazy while discussing it. Logan is insane to ever think I'd consider leaving Constantine to be with him even for a minute.

Principal Bennet then rubs his forehead and closes his eyes. "Okay then, Genesis. This is serious, but you only have just over a week before your exams start. So, I'll give you a week of suspension." He sighs.

"A week of suspension???" Alpha Carrington springs out of his chair. His voice reverberates throughout the whole office. "She broke the future alpha's arms. She injured her own mate! She would have to stand in council's trial. She would have to be held in the pack's cell while awaiting trial."

Wait! What? "What?" Pack's cell is only for murderers and rogues! I can't be in the pack's cell. It's nasty down there.

Principal Bennet's eyes about bulged in their sockets. He then says timidly, "Now, Alpha Carrington, if I may..."

Alpha Carrington seems to be just warming up to this idea and his quest to find justice for his wronged son. "If found guilty, she could face the opprobrium punishment. She would be leashed and shackled to a tree in the pack's house backyard for all to see until her mate forgives her. After that, she would be by his side, making up for what she did to him. She would give him strong offspring and a successor and serve him loyally until her last breath."

Oh, for the love of everything fuzzy! The hell I would!

"I am not your son's mate!" I screech, jumping out of my own chair. "I will not be leashed to a tree, and I will certainly NOT bear his offspring and serve him till my last breath!"

His face turns an ugly shade of red. I guess he's not used to having anybody defying him or yelling back at him.

"Remember to whom you are speaking to, girl!" he roars using his alpha's voice and dominance. Principal Bennet shrinks back and lowers his head in submission. I'm starting to feel the heat in my chest. Now my eyesight is tinged with red. My Ezra is now a lycan, and she does not like to be talked to like that by a mere alpha. I will not cower to this man. He is not my alpha. Not anymore.

I know he's taller than I am and right now I'm standing up on my tippy toes, staring defiantly up at his face while he's looking down at me.

"And you! You should remember to whom you're speaking to!" I thunder back with my lycan force.

He retreats a few steps behind the table, and for a second, Alpha Carrington lowers his head, but he quickly and shakily forces his head back up. His hands are gripping the edge of the table so hard that his knuckles are turning white. That table is going to break. His jaw is clenched tight, and his eyes are now red around the edges. He's fighting the urge to submit.

Principal Bennet is nowhere to be seen. I can only conclude that he's somewhere underneath the table If he hasn't crawled out of his office already.

"You are no longer my alpha. You have no control over me," I talk through my gritted teeth.

"I might no longer be your alpha, but your family and friends are still under my authority. Accidents can sometimes happen," he answers. His voice is quivering.

"Are you threatening me?" I narrow my eyes. Destroy him before he destroys the people I love. I don't know if that's me or if it's Ezra influencing my thinking, but I agree. Ezra's anger and my anger is red hot iron burning in my chest. I'm starting to see only red. He's threatening my family and friends! He's going to hurt them. I swear I'm going on a rampage. I will kill everything that moves. Starting from HIM!

"You dare to threaten me???" I hiss out through my sharp elongated teeth and canines. My voice is changing. I feel the dark veins bulging and snaking out from around my eye sockets.

I can see his eyes widening as if it just dawned on him what he had just done and what he's facing with. He stares at me for a second before he suddenly drags the big table he's been holding onto in front of me. I hear things falling and breaking on the floor.

Ha! As if that table is going to stop me.

"I will destroy everything you hold dear...first I will tear you piece by piece." I move in slowly, eyeing him and the table between us. He takes a few hasty steps back until his back is pressed up against the corner of the office. "I will start with your healthy beating heart," I continue to stalk him. He presses his back harder against the wall like he wants to melt into it. I can hear his heart thumping crazily in the cavity of his chest. "I can smell your fear, Alpha Carrington." I smile and lick my lips as I stare at his chest where his red-hot pulsing heart is.

I jump onto the table, and he starts yelling, "BOYS!!! BOYS!!!" Beads of sweat are forming on his forehead and above his upper lip.

The door bursts open then I hear footsteps. They stop at the door. I know nobody dares to get any closer. He stares at his men then he crouches low on the floor. His bones are cracking, his face is changing shape. Thick black hair is covering his body. He snarls, showing off his sharp teeth and deadly looking canines. That's good. I will cover my body with a wolf pelt today.

I crawl slowly across the table. I hear footsteps again, then I sniff the air and almost close my eyes. Something smells good. So very good, but the wolf in front of me growls and snaps its jaw. I need to get rid of it. I can smell his blood and his fear.

"Genesis...sunshine…"

I pause for a bit, then continue crawling across the table. I have my prey cornered. So close. I lick my lips hungrily.

"Sweetheart, look at me. Right here, I'm right here, sweetheart." I snarl when a hand touches my arm. That touch feels so good. Ripples of pleasure spread through my body from that touch. That smell, that voice, and that touch.

"Genesis, my love, look at me." A warm, gentle hand is stroking my cheek, turning my face away from my prey. Beautiful mesmerizing gray eyes are staring down at me. I can't help leaning into the touch. Everything about him is calling to me. I nuzzle my nose and lips into the palm of his hand, taking in his scent.

A sudden growl from the wolf makes me turn my head towards my prey again. My prey.

I spring off the table and land right on the wolf, pinning it on the floor with my legs and my hand. Its paw with long sharp nails tries to take a swipe at me, its jaws snapping close to my face. I gleefully bury my fingers in its chest. It howls in pain, and I stare at its exposed throat. Before I could sink my teeth into it and dig my fingers deeper into his chest, a hand firmly turns my head to the side. I growl in fury, but before I could snap that hand off, my eyes fall on the most fascinating eyes and face.

"Enough, sweetheart," he strokes my cheeks gently. "Come with me." I'm being lifted off the howling wolf and into his arms. I bury my face into the crook of his neck and inhale. The best smell ever.

* * *

I remember being carried to the car by Constantine, surrounded by my lycan pack mates and their protective and calming presence.

When we get home, Constantine starts the bath and undresses me gently all the while talking softly to me. He lowers me into the warm water before he strips himself and gets into the bath with me. He washes my blood-stained fingers, my body, and my hair.

By the time he dries me up with a big fluffy towel, I'm feeling like myself again. He lays me in bed and pulls the blanket comfortably over me. After he dried himself, he crawls into bed with me. I lay my head on his chest, and he wraps his arms securely around me.

"Costa?"

"Yes, my love?"

"I'm sorry."

"Don't be. It's his own fault. The alpha called you in the office knowing full well that I or any of our pack members wouldn't be there with you. He wanted you alone because he

311

thought he can manipulate you. That was very sneaky of him. Only it backfired on him."

I trace a finger absently over the ridges of his abs, thinking back about what happened today at school.

"Costa?"

"Yes, love?

"Today, Logan said he felt it when you marked me and when we're *together*. How could he still feel it when I didn't feel him anymore?"

"Probably because of a couple of things. You didn't accept his rejection to sever the ties totally then. You're also a lycan. So you're much stronger. Apart from that, our bond is protecting you from feeling any more pain. Our bond was there since that first time we saw each other when you're fifteen, but you were still a werewolf then and our bond wasn't as strong as it is now. Still, it protected your wolf from leaving or worse, dying. I'm glad we bonded earlier. I just wish that you didn't have to go through all that pain. I wish I had protected you better."

I really don't need him to protect me twenty-four seven. I'm a grown woman, not a baby who needs to be looked after every minute of the day, but I'm not going to argue with him on that right now.

"Would you really have left me alone if I was happy with my mate?"

"I honestly don't know. I don't know if I could really ever leave you alone. When you almost turned eighteen, I had the worst time. I wanted to do the honorable thing and let you be happy with your mate, but the thought of you being with another man is driving me insane. The morning of your birthday, I was walking down the school hallway with Caspian and Lazarus. You were at your locker with your friend Penny. I knew there was a possibility of you finding your mate that day. I was so tempted to snatch you up, mark you, and claim you to be mine, but you were excited about finding your mate.

"I didn't expect him to reject you. I mean, I saw the way boys were looking at you, even at fifteen. You're so beautiful and amazing and perfect, what man would do that? But that stupid alpha mutt did, and there's nothing I could do to stop you from feeling the pain of the rejection once it started."

His fingers play with my hair at the back of my head.

"I planned to court you slowly and seduce you once you got over the rejection," he admits. I glance up to see his cheeks tinged pink. He's actually blushing! "But then you approached me that day, and..."

"And...?"

"You asked to be friends, and all my plans went out the window. I thought, friends? Hell no. I wanted more than that. A lot more. Caspian had a good laugh at me after that. I'd been patient for three years, yet you talked to me once, and suddenly I can't wait anymore. You went out with that human boy afterward, and I tried to stay away because I knew he was no competition."

"Oh, how would you know? I might be interested in him. I mean, I could be." I pull myself up on my elbow.

"Sunshine, I heard you say no to his face so many times! I think the whole school must have heard you say no to him at least once. But then I learned that alpha mutt went and ruined your date, and claimed you for himself, and I couldn't wait any longer. I was awake almost the whole night thinking, and the very next morning I just had to see you."

Yeah, he had to wake me up at six thirty on a Sunday morning. He also had the subtlety of a bulldozer. Oh, well, I love him anyway. I lay my head back down on his muscled chest.

"Constantine?"

"Yes, sweetheart?"

"Today in the office, you could've stopped me. You could've stopped me from harming a hair on Alpha Carrington's body. Why didn't you?"

313

"So you caught on to that huh?" He chuckles quietly. "Well, he must have said or done something to make you mad enough to lose control. The least I could do is to let you have a little bit of fun. He must have deserved it."

Huh, my mate is as weird as I am. I'm glad he gave me that chance. I am not sorry at all for what I did. I'm glad I did it. I wish I had done more damage to him....like scratch his eyeballs out.

"He threatened my family and friends," I whisper fiercely. Good thing Constantine's presence is calming me, otherwise I might phase again as I remember his threat, and go after him again tonight.

"Constantine?"

"Yes?"

"I don't trust him."

"You are wise not to trust him, my love."

"Constantine?"

"Mmmmm?"

"I think I'm in love with your bed."

"Okay."

"I think I want to marry it and have little plushy comfy babies with it."

Suddenly he's on top of me, pinning my hands over my head. "Now say that you love only Constantine and you want to have babies only with him."

"You love only Constantine..." I repeat. "NO. NO. NO!!!!" I start giggling helplessly as he tickles me.

"Now tell me you love only me." He presses. "And what do plushy comfy babies even mean?"

CHAPTER XXXVI
One With The Pack

I open my eyes to a dimly lit room. A tiny sliver of sunlight seeps in through a gap between two heavy curtains. It's still very early and I'm already awake, so I'm feeling very proud of myself. I lift Constantine's arm that's resting possessively over my hips carefully and slink out quietly.

After a shower, I put on a pair of ripped black skinny jeans and a white tank top and stand at the foot of the bed brushing my hair while watching him sleep. I'm such a creeper, I know. But hey, when you have a mate with a body of a Greek god, who is now lying naked on his stomach in bed with the sheet barely covering his tight sexy behind, who could blame me? His head is lying sideways on the pillow, so I can see his sharp angular profile with high cheekbone, a strong nose, and chin, and sensual lips. His hair is tousled, and his thick dark eyelashes lay across his cheek.

He moves and his breathing changes as he's waking up and the bed sheet slips even lower. Instantly his hand is searching for me over the bed, his eyes still closed. When his hand can't find me, he frowns. Suddenly, he opens his eyes and raises his head up, looking alert. His eyes quickly search the bed then the room until they land on me. He sighs and lay his head back down while his lips slowly curl up into a lazy, heart-stopping smile.

"What are you doing over there? You should be in here." His voice is still husky from sleep.

"Nu-uh, I'm early today. I shall not be persuaded by you and your wicked ways to remain in bed till...uh, we're late again."

He turns over, throws his head back and chuckles deliciously. "You enjoy it though. Come on, admit that you enjoy my wicked ways, way more than standing there."

I stubbornly shake my head while brushing my hair, trying to look away from his hard muscled body. He's hard everywhere! I mean *everywhere*!

"Get over here," he commands, patting the comfortable looking space on the bed, beside him. "You know you want to." His silver-gray eyes are smoldering.

Crazy cow and funny slippers or whatever! My heart does a little pitter patter. His smile is growing. I bet he can feel that I'm weakening.

Just as I'm about to give in and jump into bed with him, he gets up. "Very well, have it your way." He sighs deeply. There's a wicked smile playing on his lips that I don't quite trust. He's up to something. I don't know what it is yet, but I know he is up to something. I can feel it.

He slowly saunters across the room in all his naked glory. His body is magnificent and he knows it. He takes his time picking up yesterday's items of clothing off the floor and chucks them into the hamper. His muscles flex as he moves. Just before he steps into the bathroom he turns to me and says, "Too bad you've already showered. I could have my wicked ways with you in the shower too."

"You're still welcome to join me and my wicked ways, though," he announces through the open bathroom door as he starts the shower. The water in this house warms up very quickly as soon as you turn on the tap. I can see him clearly through the shower clear glass enclosure. Streams of water running down his face, his naked chest, and flat stomach, and— Gah! Run! Run! No, stay! I'm so weak.

I manage to tear my eyes away and walk out of our bedroom on unsteady legs. Darn that lycan mate of mine!

I'm surprised to see Caspian standing on the landing of the grand staircase as if he's waiting for me as I walk down the stairs.

"Hey, Red?" he calls. His unusual green eyes look serious, though, there is a tiny smile playing on his lips. "No matter what people say or what happens after this, remember that the alpha and his mutt deserved it. I think you totally rock yesterday."

He holds his hand up, and I slap it with mine in a high five. We grin at each other and proceed to walk down the stairs together. Caspian can be obnoxious at times, but he's fiercely loyal. Oh, he's charming this morning, and that makes me want to go and squish those adorable cheeks of his and give him a big hug.

Then he goes and ruins it by adding, "You totally look hot as a lycan. I'd totally do you if you're not Constantine's mate."

I whack the back of his head with my planner file. Boy, that was satisfying. I had been wanting to whack his head for a very long time.

"Owww... you're a violent woman! I bet my mate isn't going to be this violent," he complains while rubbing the back of his head.

I hope she's even more violent! I bite my lips to stifle my laugh. Oh, I love him like a brother. I know what he meant to say though. There would be consequences to what I did to Alpha Carrington yesterday, but my pack is behind me, no matter what.

Lazarus and Serena are already at the breakfast table, quietly sipping their coffee. Serena stands up and wraps her arms around me as soon as I walk into the kitchen. I return her warm hug and take my seat. Lazarus squeezes my hand and flashes me his rare smile. I'm glad that my pack has my back.

"Thanks, Duncan." I smile up at Duncan as he places a plate of warm waffles and a mug of coffee in front of me. A little sip and I'm in heaven.

Ahhh. Just the way I like it— strong, with a dash of French vanilla cream and sugar. I look around the table, feeling baffled. Everybody doesn't seem to be in a hurry to finish their meal to get to school.

An arm slips around my waist. "Sweetheart, we're not going to school today," says Constantine as he kisses the back of my neck.

He settles on a seat next to me and his hand slides onto my thigh. His eyes shine with a wicked glint. "You're suspended, remember? *That* and the Pack Elder Council wants to see you."

I sigh. I attacked an alpha yesterday. I knew something like this would happen.

"Okay...that would explain why I won't be going to school, but why aren't you guys going?"

"We're here because we're a pack," answers Serena. "We're going to face the council with you."

"I know the alpha can't hurt you, but you told me that the alpha threatened your family and friends. That is very serious," says Constantine.

"Not to mention dangerous," adds Caspian. "What happened yesterday was nothing compared to what would happen if he really hurt any of your family or your friends."

"Yesterday, Constantine was able to coax you back very easily. Some human part of you was still in control. You and your lycan wanted to kill the alpha, but you were mainly just playing with him. If he truly hurt any of your loved ones, you would have killed him in a matter of seconds before you blindly move on to your next target and kill without remorse. You will be controlled by your lycan and driven by your fury. It'll be a bloodbath before Constantine would be able to stop you," explains Lazarus.

Whoaa. That thought scares me. I don't want to go on a killing spree. So many innocent people would get killed. "Is that what happens to the lycans whose mates got killed?"

"No, sweetheart, it'll be much worse. There would be no mates to console them and to stop them. The king's enforcer troop would have to be sent in. The lycan would have to be killed." Constantine takes my hand and laces his fingers through mine as he explains this.

I know it's not easy to kill a lycan. You have to sever the spine from his or her body. To do that, you have to manage to get close enough without getting killed brutally and without mercy. A lycan on a killing rampage is almost undefeatable. I guess that is why a troop of enforcers would have to be called in if anything like that were to happen. Silver doesn't have any effect on lycans as it does on werewolves either.

"If the lycan belongs to a pack, the whole pack members would likely have to be eliminated as well," states Lazarus, as matter-of-factly.

"But why???"

"Because honey, we won't stand idly aside if any one of us is going to get killed. Our lycans won't stand for it. We'll protect each other, even from the king's enforcers," answers Serena.

"They would have to go through all of us," Caspian remarks in agreement when I look at him. His eyes look serious for once.

I don't know what that would mean if anything were to happen to any one of us, but I know it wouldn't be pretty, especially with Caspian and Constantine being the royal princes. The first and second in line to the throne. I don't think the king would be keen to slaughter his own son and nephew. On the other hand, innocent lives would still have to be saved.

"So what's going to happen at the meeting with the Pack Council?" I ask them. I have absolutely no idea what is going to happen today. I have never even been to a council meeting except for that one time when my Grandfather and the Alpha of Red Convel Pack came to claim me.

"To tell you the truth, we have no idea what's going to happen either. It would all depend on what they're planning to do, but I don't imagine they want the Palace's involvement in this matter," answers Constantine.

"It could happen if they insisted on a punishment for you," adds Lazarus.

"Palace involvement or a fight with a few lycans," mutters Caspian with a grin. His eyes bright with excitement and anticipation. Did I tell you that sometimes I'm worried about him?

I understand now that what would happen to me would affect all of my pack members. I know that none of the werewolves would stand a chance against a lycan, let alone a pack of us. I still don't like the idea of any of my lycan pack members getting involved in something like this. Or the werewolves died because of me. I can't imagine life without Constantine. I love Serena, Lazarus, and Caspian, and I would give up my life for them in a heartbeat, but I grew up with these werewolves.

*   *   *

The meeting with the Pack Elder Council is at ten in the morning. By quarter after nine, I'm ready.

I know I should dress formally, but some rebellious part of me decided to wear something more free-spirited and casual. I opt for a black boho tunic dress that ends mid-thigh. I have black spandex biker shorts that peek out underneath the dress and a pair of knee-length black boots on. The black biker shorts is for just in case I need to kick some asses. I leave my red hair to cascade freely down my back.

Serena looks stunning and elegant yet badass at the same time. She has a simple yet classy short black, sheath dress. I think she has the same idea about ass-kicking because she has lace trim black stretchable shorts underneath and a pair of black ankle boots. Her blond hair is in a sleek high ponytail.

"Looking good there, sister!" I smile at her.

"You're not looking too shabby yourself there, honey." She drawls playfully and holds my arm as we walk down the stairs together.

The men are already waiting for us in the foyer. They're all looking spectacular in their button-up shirts with dark dress pants and dress shoes, but my eyes seek Constantine right away.

His intense silver-gray eyes are already on me. It's cute that he tries to tame his hair by pushing it back like that. A few locks still fall across his forehead and eyebrows. *Oh, so hot!*

We all decide to go in Lazarus's black Escalade. Lazarus is driving with Serena sitting beside him, Caspian sitting behind them, and Constantine and I sit in the third row. Just like yesterday.

Constantine wraps his arm around me, and I rest my head against his shoulder. His scent and his touch calm me.

"Do you have any idea what happens to Logan and Alpha Carrington and how they're doing?" I ask reluctantly. I'd really rather not know.

"Well, last time I heard, Logan had two broken arms. One arm is broken in two places," Caspian informs me with a gleeful look in his eyes. "The Alpha was still in the Pack's hospital with injuries in the chest, a few broken ribs, a dislocated elbow, a sprained ankle and some cuts and bruises."

Oh, Gosh. I feel like hiding my face in shame. I had never physically injured anybody in my life, and now I've injured the alpha and the future alpha—all in one day!

Great going there, Genesis.

Constantine squeezes my shoulder and lifts my face up with a finger under my chin. "You know they deserved it, sweetheart."

My lycan Ezra is rejoicing. In fact, I think it's doing a happy dance in my head. Unfortunately, the human part of me still feels some shame.

"The bad news is, they're recovering fast. Both of them are probably out of the hospital by now," says Caspian, thumping me on my shoulder. I appreciate that he's trying to make me feel better, but did he really need to thump on my shoulder that hard? Was that a payback for smacking him upside the head on the landing this morning? I don't know. I eye him suspiciously, and he grins charmingly and innocently back.

We arrive at the pack's house twenty minutes later, and I'm stunned to see so many pack's best fighters lining up the driveway all the way from the guard post. Strong, tall, big muscled, intimidating looking werewolf warriors in full warrior uniforms. A lot more are standing in formation in front of the pack's house.

I hear Caspian snickers in front of us. Beside me, Constantine smiles, baring his straight white teeth and canines.

CHAPTER XXXVII
The Art of Love and War

The guard post is about fifty meters away from the main pack house. The driveway is wide and lined with pine trees on both sides. About halfway through, a clearing appears, and you have a nice view of the huge impressive pack house. The main pack house itself is five-story high. It's a Federal Colonial style gray brick house with white trims. Tall columns stand on each side of grand curved steps that lead up to the main entrance. The garden is very well-tended.

One of the men signals us to stop in front of the main building. I don't see any kids running around in the front yard as usual. I don't see women tending to the kids and the garden or talking among themselves today. Today, the ground of the pack house is crawling with pack warriors.

If they're planning to intimidate us with their display of army, they're sadly failing. This is just fueling the hunger for battle in our lycans' basic instinct.

Our car is surrounded by big Shadow Geirolf Pack's fighters. Most are male, but I see a few female fighters as well.

Both Serena and Lazarus turn to look at us in the back seat. There's a look in Serena's beautiful face that I've never seen before. Her golden brown eyes are bright and threatening. She looks feral and dangerous.

I can feel our combined energy sizzles in the confine of the car.

Whatever is waiting for us outside of this car, we're ready for it. In fact, I think Caspian, Lazarus, and Constantine are excited to unleash their power and strength on these werewolf warriors. I can feel their excitement building. They are all looking deadly.

"Okay, before we go out. Promise me nobody has to die if they don't need to?" I look at them with hopeful eyes.

"If they don't need to," agrees Constantine. His smile looks lethal with his canines already showing. He suddenly grabs the back of my head and slams his lips on mine in a quick, fierce, hungry kiss that leaves me panting for more.

Beta Stevens is standing at the bottom of the steps, flanked by a few pack warriors. Delta Walker and Gamma Brown are standing further behind him. Wise men. They must know that their army could do nothing to stop us if we decided to fight. They'd better be fast runners if the battle breaks out.

The car doors are opened for us, and as soon as I step outside, one of the warriors seizes my shoulders. I instinctively hiss and whip my head around growling at him only to find Constantine's hand already gripping his throat. Fierce growls can be heard around me, not only from my pack members but also from the pack warriors around us.

Beta Stevens come running ahead of his guards. "STOP!!!" he yells, with both hands extended in front of him. "Back off, boys!" he commands his men. He gives them a fierce glare when nobody moves immediately.

The men slowly take a few steps back. I can sense their collective feelings in my heightened sense state. Most of these warriors can feel the power that we radiate, and are secretly relieved to be out of our vicinity. There are still a few fools who would love to take us on though.

I touch Constantine's arm, and he releases his hold on the man with a warning growl.

"Ahhh.. .Beta Stevens." Caspian smiles charmingly, stepping forward. He has that boyish charm and deceptively innocent smile. I can tell that, behind that smile, he's pissed and ready for a good fight.

"Your Highness," acknowledges Beta Stevens with a little bow.

"I thought we're here to discuss things. Not for a battle?" his smile never falters, though his eyes narrow as he glances around pointedly.

"No, we invited Ms. Fairchild, and of course all of you, to talk, not to fight," agrees Beta Stevens quickly.

I know Constantine isn't very pleased that he addressed me as Ms. Fairchild. I squeezed his hand gently to calm him down.

"Doesn't seem like that from where I'm standing," remarks Constantine. "I've seen fewer warriors in a battle than this."

"I'm sorry, Your Highness. Alpha's orders. He wanted to make sure that we're... uh, safe."

"Safe?" scoffs Lazarus, eyeing the men around us. "Do you realize that you're not safe from us if we decide to battle, even with the size of army you've got right now?"

"Yes, I am aware of that," answers Beta Stevens with a sigh. The man seems to have aged ten years from the last time I saw him, and that was just a few weeks ago during dinner with Alpha Carrington. "I'm also very sorry that one of our men lay a hand on Ms. Fairchild. That won't happen again."

He turns to me and offers a small, tentative smile. "I'm very sorry for that, Genesis. He was acting out of order."

I give him a little nod. Beta Stevens is Hunter's dad, and he looks so much like Hunter. He has the same brown eyes and dark hair. His face is a bit wider than Hunter's, and his hair is cut very short. Even their voices sound almost the same.

"This way, if you please," he says. "The Council is waiting inside."

We let Beta Stevens lead us. Constantine is holding my hand firmly in his. Caspian takes his position on my other side while Serena and Lazarus walk behind us.

I give our surrounding a cursory glance and make a mental note of the position of the warriors.

I see curtains move discreetly on a few windows upstairs and smile at how foolish this is.

We will kill anybody who tries to harm us. However, we are not complete beasts when we choose to phase to protect ourselves. Those kids and innocent people will be spared. Those warriors? They don't stand a chance.

We are led through a foyer and into a room on our immediate right. There are more pack warriors stationed inside. Why am I not surprised?

It's a good-sized meeting room with a big, long table in the middle and chairs all around it. Tall windows on one side of the walls are now covered with heavy damask curtains, no doubt to muffle any sounds from being heard by sharp werewolves ears outside of this room.

Six men are sitting at a big long table. They immediately stand up as soon as we enter the room. I recognize them as the pack elders. Most of them I really don't know much about, except for one. Elder Faulkner, unfortunately. Younger werewolves don't like him. He's always loud and opinionated. My mom once called him an old fool. I always had a suspicion that Elder Faulkner had something to do with my dad being relegated to an omega.

Beta Stevens makes an introduction around the room and invites us to have our seats.

Alpha Carrington enters the meeting room in a wheelchair with Logan behind him before we begin. Two big strong guards are flanking them both. They're different guards from the last time, I note.

326

Logan's arms are already healing, it seems. I wonder if Alpha Carrington really needed that wheelchair. I wouldn't be surprised if he's using that to garner sympathy and gain support.

Alpha Carrington eyes me warily as he is being wheeled in. It really isn't me he should be worried about. Constantine isn't his biggest fan right now. I can feel his anger. I quietly slip my hand in his underneath the table, twining our fingers together.

"Since everybody is here. Let's get straight to the point," he starts. "I don't want to drag things much further, except that I want a just punishment for what was done to me and my son. Just because she's mated to a royalty doesn't mean she can do all she wants to us werewolves," he states. "I can't imagine the king would want to tarnish the palace's name like that."

"So you would like the palace's involvement in this matter? Is that what you're saying?" Caspian raises his eyebrows and tips his chin up haughtily. He looks very much like a royalty right now.

"We can work out a settlement without the king's involvement if you'd prefer," answers Alpha Carrington, smiling slyly. I can almost see greedy gears turning in his head.

"Alpha Carrington, are you blackmailing us?" Constantine asks playfully with a feral looking smile.

"Oh, certainly not, Your Highness. Merely negotiating our... conditions," he denies.

"You are not in the position to negotiate anything with us. You know we have the upper hand," states Constantine carelessly. "You are free to invite the palace's involvement in this matter if you so wished."

"Or we can make use of all your warriors you've assembled today. We can wipe them all out then we can discuss what we can do with you if you're still breathing," adds Caspian, clearly looking bored. I can sense that he's done with the whole conversation by now.

"How is it that you have the upper hand when you injured our alpha and future alpha?" asks Elder Faulkner looking alarmed at Caspian's threat.

It's obvious that these werewolves are not aware of so many things regarding the lycans. They must have been fooled by their youthful appearances to know that these three are older and much more cunning than they are.

I know Constantine is pissed off by the way Logan keeps glancing at me like a lovesick puppy the entire time since the moment he entered the room. I know our mate connection is severed, so that can't be blamed on mate connection anymore. I wonder if it has something to do with wanting something that you can't have.

I know that Constantine, Caspian, and Lazarus wouldn't mind a good fight. My lycan Ezra wants a good fight, but my human side is against it. Werewolves and lycans world is filled with violence despite our civilized appearance. I must have more of my parents' hippy peace-loving heart than I know.

I squeeze Constantine's hand and put my hand on Caspian's shoulder gently while giving Serena a look. I know she would be calming Lazarus.

I should make this quick if I don't want any bloodbath. My lycan friends are getting impatient. We should be out of here very soon or else there would be a brutal fight.

"Gentlemen," I look around the room, then bring my eyes back to Alpha Carrington. "You are free to bring this up to the palace. However, I wonder what case are you going to bring up to them. Are you going to tell them that you are trying to force a mated lycan, one who's mated to the king's nephew, to abandon her mate and take your future alpha instead? Are you going to tell them that your alpha threatened my family's safety in order bend me to his will?"

"I-I did not," stutters Alpha Carrington, while his men are staring at him wide-eyed. "I wouldn't threaten my own pack members."

"It will be your word against mine, Alpha Carrington." I smile at him challengingly. "As for your son, I saved his life when I broke his arm. He was about to attack my mate, a lycan. If I didn't stop him, he would be dead by now. And finally, do you really want me as your daughter-in-law?" I smile at him, baring my teeth. "Not to mention my blood is now poisonous to your son. I am a lycan. He will die if he as much as tried to mark me."

I stand up, and the rest of the lycans follow suit.

"How can you know that? I am an alpha. I have an alpha blood in me," announces Logan arrogantly.

Constantine growls, and I squeeze his hand.

Looking at Logan now, I realize something. I realize how spoiled he is. He goes to school driving expensive cars, does whatever he pleases. He is used to getting what he wants. Partly it's his father's fault that he is the way he is.

"Alpha Carrington," I take a few steps towards him but stop when he cringes away. Who could blame him, yesterday I was on top of him, hell-bent on ripping his heart right out of his chest.

"Bring this up to the palace, we don't care," I finally say. I'm done talking.

He tips his chin up without saying a word; his eyes are hostile. His hand is gripping the armrest of the wheelchair very hard; the metal part is twisting. I can see how much he wishes to get off that chair and give me a good beating. I tip my head up and whirl around. We both know that's not possible.

"Where is your loyalty to your pack?" yells Elder Faulkner on our retreating backs.

Oh, I'm very loyal to my pack. My lycan pack.

"I don't trust that alpha. Not one bit," murmurs Serena as we make our way across the lobby. This is the first time I heard her say anything since we got here.

329

None of the werewolf warriors make any attempt to stop us as we make our way to the car.

Everybody is quiet, but I can sense so much pent-up energy in the car on our drive back home. Our natural hunger for a fight and bloodshed was fueled by the sight of so many warriors and hostile energy back at the pack house. I can almost hear my own blood pumping in my veins. So much aggression that needs a release.

"We're going for a run," says Serena as soon as we arrive home. Her hand is firmly clasped in Lazarus's.

"Great. I'm going for some training," Caspian announces. His eyes flash dangerously. "Where are you guys going?"

"Painting session," answers Constantine as he grabs my waist and throws me over his shoulder.

Crazy bunnies!

As soon as we reach our room, he kicks the door closed. He sets me on my feet, and his intense, smoldering gray eyes zero in on me. He moves in closer and pushes me up against the door and instantly his ravenous mouth is on me. Devouring me like I'm his favorite dessert. An explosion of electricity and heat spread like wildfire from the points where our bodies meet throughout my whole body. I return his kiss with all the pent-up aggression and energy. Our tongues are clashing and dueling with each other. I bite his lower lip and taste blood. His mouth moves to my neck and starts kissing and licking and sucking. I tug at his silky dark hair.

Oh, goddess... I want more.

I push him up roughly against the wall beside us. When he tries to move, I shove and pin his shoulders harder against it. I smile menacingly up at him and, in a swift movement, ripped his expensive shirt off. He laughs darkly. His silver-gray eyes are watchful and intent on me. I place my mouth on his neck and start kissing and licking and sucking and nibbling. My hands are tracing the ridges of his hard body. For a minute, he let me do what I want, moving from his neck down to his chest and abdomen. His moans

330

and groans under my hands and my mouth only fuel my hunger. The expression on his beautiful face is full of ecstasy and torment.

Then he takes over again, pinning me with his hard body against the wall, attacking me with passion with his hands and mouth. We battle for dominance. We make love like we're fighting. Gnashing teeth and warring tongues. We touch, push and tug each other with wild abandon. I vaguely hear things falling, breaking and cracking around us. I don't hold back on my moaning and screaming. It's rough, raw, and wild and I love it.

*   *   *

My brain takes a while to start working in the morning. I thought being a lycan could fix that. I guess I was wrong. There's no cure for that. There's no hope for me. It's a disease I will have to carry to my grave.

Constantine's arm is lying across my hips. I sit up quietly and look around the room uncomprehendingly.

Furniture lying broken on the floor. Our big mirror is broken. The bathroom door is no more. Floor lamp, picture frames, night stands, table lamps—all in pieces all over the floor. Why is our room destroyed?

Cuddly bunny and fuzzy slippers! Did somebody come and destroy our room while we're sleeping? Then the event from yesterday flashes across my mind. Well, at least the bed is still standing. Thank goddess!

"Thank goddess! You're alive!!! You're still alive!!!! I love you, bed." I kiss my pillow and the bed over and over again. "I love you!"

I guess you learn to appreciate things more when you come close to losing them.

The mattress around me starts shaking. Constantine grabs a pillow beside him and covers his face with it. I can hear muffled laughter coming from underneath the pillow.

331

CHAPTER XXXVIII
Anything Worse Than PennyZilla

I was so relieved that the bed is still standing that I forgot myself and started kissing the bed. I mean who does that? Me! A crazy person! That's who. Now my mate is laughing at me.

He removes the pillow from his face after a while and sits up leaning on his elbow staring at me with bright eyes and biting his twitching lips.

"I'm sorry I didn't mean to laugh at you, sweetheart,"

"That's okay." I guess.

"Then why are you looking so sad?"

"Haven't you notice? Our room is destroyed," I almost wail.

"That's okay, sunshine, we'll replace everything." He tugs at a lock of my hair playfully.

"And I kissed the bed," I add sadly. "You've got a crazy mate."

His eyes shine with laughter again. "I don't mind you kissing the bed. You can kiss it anytime you want. As long as you're not kissing anyone else, I'm good," he answers with a smug smile.

"And for destroying the room." He looks around then turns to look at me with pride in his eyes. "You're a wild woman. I couldn't ask for a better mate. You're a match for me in every way."

He crawls up on top of me and starts kissing and nibbling on my shoulder and collarbone. Chills of pleasure are running up and down my body.

"You can use this chance...to umm—" he mumbles between kisses "—decorate." His lips trail up to my neck. His hand runs down the side of my body, arranging my body into the position he wants. "..the way you want."

Yeah! The room was much too masculine. I can re-decorate! Yes!

"I can go pick the furniture and everything!" I exclaimed, sitting up, starting to get excited about the possibility of making the room feel more feminine and more mine...uh, I mean ours.

"What? You want to do that now?" he asks, looking a bit dazed. Then he looks adorable with his messy hair and his strong eyebrows come down in a scowl that makes him look like a three-year-old being denied his favorite treat.

"Later," he pushes me back down and pins my body with his.

Oh yes. Where were we?

*   *   *

Duncan is making lunch and a few humans are going back and forth, up and down the stairs. Some are fixing the walls and installing the door in our bedroom. Some are carrying boxes, replacing our destroyed furniture. I'd chosen and ordered them online. Constantine called in and asked them to be delivered today before lunch. They come right on time. Apparently, we are important clients since the furniture in this house needs to be replaced so many times. Having tons of money helps too.

"Just what did you guys do while we're away?" asks Lazarus, his eyebrows furrowing. His eyes fixed on the busy workers struggling to lift a heavy antique armoire that I ordered. It's one of those crazy things you do when you're shopping, like ordering an expensive armoire that you don't need, but you know would look good in your room that you just got to have it.

"Don't ask me. I wasn't invited," says Caspian, biting his twitching lip. His eyes light up mischievously.

Lazarus and Serena just got in an hour ago. One has to wonder where they were and what they were up to the whole night last night and this morning.

*   *   *

During lunch, we discuss having my parents and my friends over for dinner sometime. Rumors are flying around and they must be very concerned. We all agreed that this also concerns them and they should be informed about what's going on.

"We'll find out when is the most convenient time for everyone and I'll let Duncan know of the dinner arrangements when the time comes," agrees Serena. "Genesis and I are going to the mall this afternoon. We'll be back in a few hours."

"What do you need at the mall? Why can't we come with you?" asks Lazarus. I guess they never had Serena going shopping with another girl before.

"We need girl stuff, you know..like new underwear, shoes, a new lipstick or something," answers Serena, glancing at me.

Serena and I discussed going to the mall sometime today. We have to get rid of the boys for a couple of hours so that we can get a ring for Constantine and spend some girl time together.

"Yeah, boring girly stuff," I add.

"Well, I won't call lingerie and underwear as boring girly stuff...you could model them for me. I won't mind," says Constantine. He whispers the last part in my ear, but I doubt if the others can't hear him with their lycan super hearing.

Suddenly an inspiration struck me. "Yeah, it'll be fun having Caspian ogling us in underwear and lingerie. Let alone let him loose in a lingerie store. You saw what happened when he saw my underwear drawer right?"

Everybody groans and Lazarus extends his hands far back enough to smack Caspian who is staring at me with disbelieving eyes upside the head.

"Owww... what did I do?" he complains, rubbing the back of his head. "I got smacked for something I haven't done yet! How's that fair? Red, I swear you are one evil woman."

In the end, the men agree to let us go off shopping on our own. I think they're planning on working out and doing weapon training and sparring. In other words, they're babysitting Caspian.

"Now behave yourselves. Don't do anything I wouldn't do and try not to miss me too much." I grin at them.

"Anything she wouldn't do? That means we can do just about everything, but anything that makes sense," I heard Caspian mutters under his breath. He's obviously still smarting over my underwear remark. Sorry, pretty boy! Not!

Constantine pulls me to him with a growl, and his mouth swoops down on mine for a soft yet demanding kiss. Pleasure coursed through me and I open my mouth for the invasion of his tongue. Ummm. It should be illegal for a man to taste and feel this good.

*   *   *

"Great! Now I feel like a kept woman." I stare at the credit card with my name on it that Constantine slipped in my hand just after he kissed me.

"Oh, stop complaining, you! Admit it, you enjoy being Constantine's kept woman," teases Serena.

Well, yeah, fine. Being Constantine's mate isn't the worst thing in the world. Okay, who am I kidding? It's freaking amazing! I grin as I look at Serena and she laughs.

We enter the jewelry store first where Serena helps me look for a ring for Constantine. I secretly took the measurement to his ring finger a couple of night before with a piece of string while he's asleep. I felt like such a creeper. Well, okay, so I am when it comes to my hot-as-hell mate.

The lady behind the counter shows us selection after selection of men's wedding ring. I just want a simple gold wedding band that wouldn't go over my budget of two hundred and seventy-three dollars and fifty cents. Serena suggests using the credit card and even offers her own money so I can get something that I really like, but I want to buy the ring with my own money. We finally found something that seems perfect for the budget that I have and Serena assures me that Constantine is going to love it.

"The guy is crazy about you, he'll love anything you give him," she assures me.

We also manage to get something for Penny for her birthday. This time I have to use the credit card. We got her a matching set of a pretty white gold filigree bracelet, a necklace, and a filigree pendant with a single diamond in the middle from all of us.

*   *   *

I plan to give the ring to Constantine this weekend. I'm going to take us back to the cliff where he first told me that he intended to make me his and where he gave his ring to me. I'm going to ask Duncan to prepare some food for a nice picnic for us.

I feel excited and nervous at the same time. What if he doesn't like it? Arrgghh. I think I'm just torturing myself.

We also promised Penny that we would help with her birthday party preparations. The promise that I'm very much regretting at this very moment.

It's her 18th birthday party, so everything has to be perfect, according to Penny. Tonight might be the night she would finally meet her mate, she said. It's Friday just after school, and we have a few hours before her party tonight.

Right now she's standing in the middle of her living room with her hands on her hips, yelling at River just because he hung the banner a bit crooked. Then she's off to yell at somebody else. She's like a drill sergeant! May goddess help us all.

Earlier on, she glared at me for horsing around with her adorable five-year-old cousin, Danica. What? I just finished spreading the tablecloth like she asked me to, and Danica is seriously adorable! She has short straight dark hair like Penny's, chubby pink cheeks, and two missing front teeth. She has the cutest giggle ever!

Penny had also asked Constantine and Lazarus to help pick another long dining table at her uncle's because she didn't think that the table she already has at the moment is big enough. The guys jumped at the request. I'm guessing they're just eager to get away from her. Caspian practically begged to go along with them. Only Penny has the power to scare even the mighty lycans off like that.

I start calling her *Pennyzilla* in my head. You know, my ship name for Penny and Godzilla? I love that girl to death, but now I'm convinced there's nothing worse than a Pennyzilla.

"Genesis, Penny needs your help!" the little five-year-old Danica runs in yelling. I knew it! Penny's worse than a bride on her wedding day. Somebody has to put an end to this madness.

"Okay, sweet pea, where is she?"

She points her index finger to the kitchen and flashes me her adorable toothless smile.

"Thanks, doll." She giggles when I tickle her belly as I walk past her.

"Penny?" I call out. Obviously, she's not in the kitchen. Where's that *birthdayzilla* now? I open the back door that leads into the backyard. A familiar scent assaults my nose the same time a sharp sting hit me at the back of my neck.

Ouch! I swivel around to come face to face with Mia.

"What did you do?" I touch the back of my neck. It still stings.

"Say bye bye princess." She holds an empty syringe up with a smug smile.

"Bitch!" I grab her throat, and the smile disappears from her face. I squeeze hard even as my vision grows hazy and I lose the feeling of my limbs.

*   *   *

This is not my bed. My bed isn't cold and hard. The voice is too loud. Someone should go and take that yelling elsewhere. Owww. I can't move. I can't even feel my legs.

Wait a minute, where am I? My eyelids are heavy too, but I force them open.

I'm in some sort of a tiny room. There's no window. Sunlight is pouring in through a big gaping hole in the roof.

There's absolutely nothing in this room from what I can see. The bare, cold cement floor that I'm lying on is coated in thick dust as if it hasn't been used in a long time. I'm lying on my side, and my cheek is pressed onto the floor.

The voice is too loud, though. I know that voice! Logan?

He's yelling at someone. Suddenly, the door bursts open and Mia steps in.

"Oh, look! She's awake!" she says. Her voice comes out in an odd, croaky-whisper-yell sort of way. Her eyes are bloodshot, and there are red fingerprints around her neck.

"Look at what you did to me, bitch!" She spits. Ha! her voice sounds funny. I did that.

Suddenly her foot connects with my stomach. Over and over again. My fingers twitch, but that's it. I can't even move to stop the blow. The pain! Bitch!! I think she broke a couple of my ribs.

339

"Mia! Stop that!" Logan wraps his arm around her waist from behind and hurls her hard against the wall.

"Get out!" he yells.

"What are you going to do? Are you going to mark her, Logan? Huh? Are you going to mate with her now?" cries Mia in that funny croaky voice. Her bloodshot eyes are now welling with tears. "What? Are you in love with her now?"

"I said get out!" He shoves her roughly out the door and slams the door behind her. "And stay out!"

He walks over and kneels beside me. "I'm sorry, princess. Are you okay?"

Huh? Princess? I can't even open my mouth to answer.

He leans in, and I can see his eyes looking down at me with concern. He gently put his hands on my shoulders and pushes me to lie on my back. The pain in my stomach and my rib is killing me.

"I'm sorry it has to be this way, baby, but soon we'll be together."

What the hell?

He's clean shaven, and his blond hair is perfectly styled today. His eyes that I used to find mesmerizing before are now staring down at me with tenderness and adoration. What I wouldn't give to have him look at me like this when I first found out that we're mates. Now I just want Constantine.

His fingers are gently rubbing the side of my dirty cheek. "You are so beautiful. I don't know how I didn't see it before. I was so stupid to reject my own mate. You were made for me. Mine! Don't worry, things are going to change. We'll be so happy together soon. The way we're supposed to be."

You are crazy! Get your hands off me! Gah! I can only move my eyelids. Where's my big mouth when I need it?

He leans in further, close to my neck and breathes in deeply. "Goddess, you still smell so good, Genesis."

I try to move away from him, but my body refuses to obey.

The door bursts open again, and Mia is standing there looking pissed.

"What do you want, Mia? I told you to stay out there."

"She's here," she answers with a lift to her chin. Her eyes are looking at Logan defiantly. I see the longing in there too. When her eyes shift to me, all I can see is hatred in them. "She wants to see you," she adds before she leaves.

She? Who's she?

"She's going to turn you back into a werewolf, just the way you were before. Then I'll be able to mark you, and you'll be my mate again. Mine." He leans in and kisses my forehead softly. "That lycan, Constantine, is going to kill you if he ever tries to mark you or mate with you again. He's going to have to leave you alone. He'll never have you again, princess," he says. "He can't have you. He'll have no choice but to leave you alone." He repeats determinedly, and with that he leaves the room, closing the door gently behind him.

No! No, no, no. Constantine! Tears start falling down the side of my face.

CHAPTER XXXIX
The Devil Wears Prada

This can't be happening. My heart is calling out for him so desperately.

This is a nightmare. I will wake up anytime now, and I will be in our room, in our comfy bed, with his arms around me. He will gaze at me with those beautiful, unusual silver-gray eyes of his from under his long, dark, sooty eyelashes. His hair will be all mussed with a few locks falling over his forehead. He will smile at me with those sensual, firm yet soft lips of his. He will laugh that deep laugh that always leaves me weak at the knees once I tell him about this nightmare. He will sooth away my fears with his warm hug and amazing kisses.

None of this is real. *None of this is real.* Yet the cold, hard cement floor underneath me feels so real. How long have I been here? Can't be too long since I can see light filtering in from the gaping roof.

The thought of not being with Constantine again makes my heart feels like it's shattering into tiny million pieces. I know I wouldn't survive it.

Then another thought comes to my mind. What if I didn't survive this? What would happen to my mate? Constantine would lose it. They would have to kill him. They would have to kill all of my pack— Caspian, Lazarus, Serena. NO! My heart weeps for them all.

With all my might, I try to move my hands and my feet. Move! Damn it! My toes move a little bit, and my fingers twitch, but nothing else. That's not going to help me. I feel so weak and pathetic lying here not able to move a muscle.

I try to phase, reaching out to my Ezra, but I can't feel her. It feels empty like she's not even there.

I hear footsteps approaching before the door swings open.

"Well, look at what we have here," says a familiar voice.

Standing on the threshold, all decked up in a designer dress and shoes, is Milan. She looks out of place here in her printed silk dress that hugs the curve of her body perfectly, a dark leather, purse hanging from her arm, and her black, expensive high heels. Her shiny, raven black hair is swept back in an elegant chignon.

She steps inside and her nose wrinkled in distaste as she looks around the tiny room. She stops a couple of feet away from me and looks down at me with her head tilted to the side.

"Awww... look at you. Lying there in the dirt." Her mouth puckers up, and her eyebrows turn up in a mock-pity expression. Her eyes glitter with malice and glee. "Pathetic looks pretty on you."

Something catches her eyes, and she squats down next to me. "What is that?" She leans in and picks my left hand up. "Is that what I think it is? Did he give this to you?" She looks closer at the ring Constantine gave me. "It is, isn't it? This is the ring. Oh, he waited so long to give it to someone. It's so beautiful!"

Her beautifully manicured fingers touch the ring softly as if caressing it. Then they close around it, trying to pull the ring off my finger.

NO! I close my fingers into a fist, determine not to let her have something that symbolizes our love and our bond. My fingers are still very weak though. She pries my fingers open very easily. She laughs as she wrenches the ring off my finger very roughly, leaving a long red mark of her fingernail on the back of my hand and my ring finger.

She slips it on her ring finger and holds it up to the light with a sigh. "Absolutely gorgeous!" She breathes. "You don't need it anymore. It's such a waste on you anyway. It should've been mine right from the very beginning."

Constantine. My heart is breaking. I hope he could feel how much I long for him and love him. My eyes are blurred by tears.

"Awww... honey, are you crying? Tsk tsk. You should never cry over a man. Didn't your mother teach you that?

"Oh, don't you worry about him, I'll take good care of him for you. It might take a bit of time, but he'll forget about you. You won't expect him to remember you forever, would you? Of course, not. You would want him to be happy and I'll make him a very happy man. I'll make sure he becomes a king too."

"Bitch!" I manage to slur out. I shocked myself that I was able to say that out loud.

"Oh, you're able to speak now. The effect of the helenalin toxin is wearing off very quickly, I see. We would have to do something about that soon. Too bad you're a lycan now. If you're still a werewolf, the toxin would've killed you the moment it entered your system. You should be proud, toxins from any regular wolfsbanes wouldn't work on us lycans. It's Aconitum Lycoctonum. I traveled all the way to Belarus and Ukraine to find it."

"Milan!" says Logan at the door. Mia is standing beside him with a sour expression on her face. "We've done what you've asked."

"Good!" says Milan, straightening up. She glances at a slim gold watch on her wrist. I notice she's been looking at it as if she's waiting for someone.

"You sure that thing that we sprayed will mask our scents?" asks Mia. Her voice is loaded with skepticism and mistrust.

"I told you to do something and you do it, mutt. I'm a lycan. Don't you dare question me," snaps Milan. She glares at Mia who glares right back for a second before she lowers her head in submission. Lycan's dominance is even stronger than that of an alpha.

It's strange that I can only smell a very faint scent of Milan, though I can smell Logan and Mia just fine.

"Well, we've done all you've asked of us," says Logan, breaking the silence. "Now, are you going to turn her back into a werewolf as she was before?"

"Wait a minute!" yells Mia, suddenly raising her head back up. Her eyes move from Logan to Milan. "You said you were going to kill her. You didn't say anything about turning her back into a werewolf."

Milan starts laughing. "Oh, you stupid mutt. Of course, I'm going to get rid of her."

"But that wasn't our agreement! You said you were going to turn her. You said you weren't going to hurt her," yells Logan. His posture changed like he's about to charge.

Milan laughs harder. "I lied! There's no way anybody can turn her back into a werewolf. She's a lycan now and she's going to die a lycan."

Beside him, Mia is smiling wide.

"No, you promised you won't hurt her! I won't let you touch her," he growls.

"Oh, you won't let me?" Milan raises an eyebrow, looking at Logan with her eyes narrow warningly. "You're forgetting your place, werewolf."

"You're all gonna die," I mutter. It came out in a slur, but I'm sure they all can understand me.

"Shut up, bitch! You're the one who's going to die!" snaps Mia.

"My mate will kill all of you and your family. The whole pack will die." I force out. It sounds clearer this time.

"I said shut up!" yells Mia, taking a step towards where I'm lying on the floor. Logan pushes her back roughly.

345

Milan laughs. "She's right. Constantine will wipe the whole city," she agrees. Her eyes shine with pride.

"The stuff that I asked you to spray, they masked my scent. Your scent though would be all over the place. I will be gone by the time Constantine exacts his revenge and brings his wrath down on everything in his path. Good thing a raging lycan won't be asking questions. He'll just follow your scent and kill. There's nowhere for you to run."

Mia's face blanched. Did she really think that she was going to get away with this?

Milan once again glances at her watch then she looks at Mia who seems frozen on the spot. Logan is still glaring at her in anger.

"If I were you, I'd start running now." She mock-whisper to Mia and Logan. "Not that it would do you any good. You'd be the first he would go after and shred to pieces. This whole place reeks of you two."

Her eyes shine with excitement and glee. "I suggest you start running to the pack house. The whole place would be in a rubble. It will be bathed in blood before midnight tonight."

That seems to bring Mia out of whatever shocked trance she was under when she finally realized what she had done. She leaps out through the open door and just takes off.

"I'm sorry, Genesis. I didn't mean for you to get hurt." Logan suddenly turns to me. His blue eyes are pleading me to forgive him.

Logan suddenly jumps on Milan, grabbing her around the neck with both hands. She grabs his hand and I can hear crunching sounds. She's broken his fingers to disentangle his hands from around her slender neck. She swipes him back with one arm. The little room shakes when Logan hit the wall hard. His body falls and crumples on the floor at an odd angle. I wonder if he's still breathing.

Her impeccable chignon came undone in the little scuffle. She flicks her hair back in annoyance.

"You won't get away with this." My speech sounds almost normal. I can move my hands now, though I try not to let her notice this.

Milan looks at me and smiles proudly. "I have and I will. I had gotten away with it before and I will again," she announces.

"What do you mean?"

"Oh, you're so stupid." She sighs in exasperation. "Antonia, remember? Who do you think got rid of her? It was messy. Messier than I thought it would be. Oh, it's so hard to kill a lycan!" she complains. "Do you know a lycan can only be killed by severing the spine from the body? Do you have any idea how hard it is to do that? That trusting bitch put up a good fight, had blood and guts and bones all over my dress and shoes. My beautiful dress and shoes! Ruined! " She scowls at the inconvenience.

Goddess! This bitch is crazier than I thought!

"Don't you worry, I've since learned my lesson. This time I won't get my fingers dirty." She smiles as she gazes lovingly at my ring on her finger again.

Stupid bitch! I hope my mate will see that ring on her finger after I'm gone and finish her off...in the most painful way.

This woman is so set on my mate and the crown, she can't even see straight.

She killed Antonia. My heart weeps for the girl I'll never get to meet.

"What happens when you find your erasthai? Don't you want to wait for him?" I want to keep her talking. I want her to still be here when my mate finds us. I want him to kill her even if I wasn't alive anymore to see it.

"My erasthai?" She laughs bitterly. "I've found my erasthai! I found him over a century ago. A French peasant boy. A human! No matter how beautiful he was. I can't have a human for a mate! I am a born lycan! I am destined for greatness. I should be the queen!"

I narrow my eyes, looking at her with contempt when a sudden thought occurs to me." What did you do to him?"

"I didn't do anything to him. A bunch of rogue werewolves was there, at the edge of the forest, just waiting to maul him. Those big beautiful, brown eyes pleaded with me to save him, but I left him there and let them kill him. They killed him. I watched them from afar. I watched them rip him apart."

How could she do that? How could she? I'd die if anything like that happened to Constantine. That or I'd go insane! Was that what had driven her to be the mad woman in front of me now?

My sensitive hearing is back. I can hear footsteps approaching. My hope for rescue goes up until the cold wind blows in through the open doorway. Unfamiliar and unpleasant smell assault my nose.

Milan sniffs the air and smiles. "Now then. I have to get going. Before I go, I'm going to have to pump in more toxin into you." She produces a beautiful leather case from inside her Louis Vuitton purse. "You didn't think that it escaped my notice that you can almost stand up by now, do you?"

From inside the case, she takes out a syringe.

No! I will not be helpless again. I try to move. There's no point of pretending that I still can't move a muscle now.

"You realize they're going to kill him once he's out of control and goes on a rampage, don't you?" I push myself up into a sitting position. My legs are still weak, but at least I can move them now.

"They can't kill him, he's the future king. Besides, I'll be there for him. I'll bring him back. I'll get him back in control." She advances towards me.

"Only I can bring him back in control. He's going to kill you when he sees you."

"No, he won't kill me. He won't hurt me. He loves me. You see, we have a connection. Constantine and I." Her voice sounds confident, but there's a look of desperation and obsession in her eyes.

I shuffle back, dragging my behind across the floor until my back hits the wall behind me. I push myself up with the aid of the wall.

"Don't be such a baby, this won't hurt a bit," Milan says as she advances closer. My eyes are fixed on the needle in her hand.

My limbs feel heavy still. I have no illusions. There is no way I can win this fight with Milan now.

She grabs my arm in a tight grip, and I pull back, trying to get away from the needle.

A figure jumps over and knocks Milan sideways.

"Stupid mutt!" she yells as she gets back on her feet, dusting off her dress.

Logan is kneeling on the floor with both hands supporting his weight.

"Stay away from her," he growls. He looks like he's about to phase.

"I've had enough of your interference," she growls back. She pounces on him and tears into him before I can blink. It is savage and brutal and quick. Then she tosses his lifeless body into the corner of the room.

She straightens up, and blood is dripping from her mouth and her hands.

"Damn it! Now look at what he made me do," she complains, trying to wipe the blood off the front of her dress. That only makes it worse as her fingers are covered in blood. "My new Prada, ruined!"

Logan is a crumpled, bloody mess on the floor. The pool of blood underneath him is growing bigger. His golden blond hair is wet and red with blood underneath him. His sea blue eyes are open, staring vacantly at me. The shine is gone from his eyes.

CHAPTER XL
My Other Half

CONSTANTINE

"I can't believe we're on an errand to pick up a table on a Friday evening," mutters Caspian. He is now sitting in between Lazarus and me in Penny's father's pick-up truck. Lazarus is driving.

"Stop whining, Your Royal Highness. You know you would do anything for Genesis," comments Lazarus drily.

"Well...maybe, but we're not getting the darn table *for* Genesis. This is for her friend, Penny," Caspian keeps complaining.

I'm proud and happy that my pack has grown to accept my beautiful sunshine so readily and love her so deeply. In fact, I think they've already started to love her three years ago when I first broke the news that I've finally found my erasthai. Who wouldn't? My mate is lovable. A bit quirky maybe, but that's what makes her absolutely adorable.

"Penny is Genesis's best friend, ergo we're doing this for Genesis. Besides, we could've left you there at Penny's if we knew you're going to whine like a three-year-old," I return.

"Oh goddess, have mercy." He shudders. "She's crazy scary isn't she?"

"Batshit crazy." Lazarus nods.

All of us start grinning at each other. Finally, something all of us could agree on. That girl is scary. I don't know how or why Genesis likes her so much. I just can't see it, but hey, if my girl loves her, who am I to judge? I'd do anything to make my mate happy. Just the thought of my mate leaves me smiling like a fool.

"You're sooo...pussywhipped" Caspian coughs the last word into his hand.

I smack the back of his head playfully.

I remember her kissing the bed the other morning. I bit my lip as I feel laughter rising up. I remember what we did before that, that led to the bed kissing and feel myself harden.

"Okay, let's get this table quick!" I urge the guys. I wish Lazarus would drive faster. We're over the speed limit as it is, but I need to get back to my flaming red-haired minx of a mate real quick.

*   *   *

I can see that they were expecting us when we get there. Somebody must have called ahead and warned them about us coming. Penny's uncle, Robert bows respectfully and leads us into the backyard where the table is.

"This is my wife, Helen," he says, pointing to a lady who curtsies awkwardly, then she just stands there staring at us with an expression of awe on her face.

"Then, there is my daughter, Olivia and her two friends." He indicates three girls who are sunbathing in the backyard in their skimpy bikinis.

Huh, who knew somebody would be sunbathing in this weather. The sun is out once in a while, but most of the time it's a bit overcast. It's too windy and chilly to be in something so skimpy outside.

Lazarus and I both stare at the table. The table is big and quite long, but I know one of us could've carried it without any problem.

Caspian nudges Lazarus and me with his shoulders. Apparently, one of the girls has taken her top off. Nothing I haven't seen before.

We both bring our attention back to the table. It's not the weight that we're concerned about, it's the length. It might be too long to fit at the back of the truck.

"What do you think?" I ask Lazarus.

"Might be too long," he answers.

"Might be doable if one side goes over the top of the roof," I suggest. "Somebody would have to hold it up there just so it won't slide off."

"Or we could tie it up there," suggests Lazarus.

"You want to carry that, man?" Caspian asks Lazarus and me.

"You can sit out at the back and hold it in place, you begged to come after all," I say to Caspian before I grab the middle of the table and place it over my shoulder. Let's get this over with.

"That looks very heavy, do you guys need any help?" yells one of the girls from where she's lying on the grass.

"No, we're good," answers Lazarus quickly, grabbing the front of the table.

"Oh, no...we'd love to help," says another girl.

"No, we don't need any help," I answer, and signal for Lazarus to start moving.

Apparently, the word no is hard to be understood by some people. They come running to help us carry the table anyway.

Caspian grins at us as all the three girls start crowding around. His smile drops when a girl steps in too close to him.

"You're Prince Caspian, right?" says the girl, batting her eyelashes up at him. He gives her a cold, hard stare as an answer and the girl totters backward real quick.

353

"Hi, my name's Olivia," says the topless girl, moving in way too close to me. I find her scent very irritating. Her hand reaches over and touches my chest. I drop the table, step back and look around. Aren't the parents going to put a stop to this? They are nowhere to be seen. How convenient. Being a royalty means you have to put up with crap like this sometimes.

"Let's get moving now," says Lazarus. Usually, they leave us alone when they sense our lethal dominance and cold indifference. We have problems like this with human girls because they don't understand our power even when they sense it. Most female werewolves, however, don't dare approach us, but this girl is persistent.

"Genesis was at my 18th birthday party a few weeks ago...I think she had fun," she says, smiling suggestively up to me. Her hands are once again reaching up to touch my pecks. I feel my jaw clenching. She must have seen something in my eyes because she suddenly paled and steps back. Yeah, keep moving, mutt.

Lazarus is scowling, holding the table up awkwardly. He's the only one holding the table up right now and one girl is standing very close to him. Lazarus is too gentlemanly to say anything rude to a woman. He's one of our toughest warriors, but a situation like this makes him uneasy. He has Serena to fight battles like this for him usually.

I know my sunshine is very possessive. I wonder what she would do if she was here.

I'm about to grab the table when I feel a sudden pain in my chest. Like a heartbreak. That's the only way to describe it. The only time I felt something close to this was when Genesis told me she didn't love me. The pain is intense.

Lazarus and Caspian must have felt too because Lazarus dropped the table and Caspian is staring at me with an alarmed look on his face. Something that could be felt by the whole pack is something that shouldn't be ignored. My chest tightens. Genesis!

I rush to the truck, followed by Caspian and Lazarus.

"Your Highness! The table! You forgot the table," yells Penny's uncle.

We ignore the man and jump into the truck.

I'm very sure it's not Serena. I can feel it deep down in my guts that it's Genesis.

"I'm sure it's fine, man," says Lazarus trying to calm me down, but I can see that he's worrying as well. Caspian is sitting back quietly. The three of us become broodingly quiet.

"She's a lycan. What could go wrong? It's going to be fine," mutters Caspian finally, as if trying to convince himself as much as trying to convince us.

The speedometer on the truck is close to 100 mph, yet this is the slowest car ride in the history of mankind and lycans. We'd be much faster if we're in one of our sports cars.

A thousand worst-case scenarios cross my mind. The tightness in my chest is getting worse by the second. Once in a while, my vision turns red, urging me to jump out of the car and run, but I keep it down. I need to be in control for this.

Genesis. Sunshine. My beautiful mate. I'm never letting her out of my sight again.

I refuse to entertain any thoughts that I won't see my mate alive, safe, and happy again. I refuse to believe that my world is crumbling.

CHAPTER XLI
Red

I can't seem to take my eyes off of Logan. No! I feel like I was going to puke my guts out. The smell of blood and death is overwhelming.

Logan. I had been trying to keep him alive. Despite what he did to me, it shouldn't have ended this way.

"Now where is that toxin?" she mumbles, searching the floor of the tiny room.

I shuffle my feet slowly while leaning against the wall. My chance of getting out of here is pretty slim, but I'm going to keep trying.

"Ahhhh... there it is," she exclaims, standing over Logan's still figure. She picks up his bloody arm and I can see Logan's hand still tightly gripping the syringe. She pries the needle off his stiff, broken fingers.

I almost weep when I see that it's empty. Logan must have squirted it all out before Milan attacked him.

"Damn it!" She hurls the syringe across the room. She's about to kick his unmoving body but changed her mind when she notices the pool of blood gathering around it. Probably thinking about her precious Louboutins.

I hear footsteps approaching closer and the putrid smell is almost overwhelming. It overpowers even the smell of blood and death in this room.

2, 3, 5....I count the footsteps, trying to determine how many men are there. 10, 15...about 15 or 16 men.

"It really doesn't matter anymore. You're not going anywhere now." She smirks at me.

"He's going to be here soon. Constantine is going to get here before you go anywhere and he's going to kill you. All my pack mates are coming after you," I growl.

She seems unconcerned. "Oh, they're not going to be here for a while. The sun might already set by the time they get here. You'll be long dead, and I'll be long gone.

"You see, I planned everything perfectly. They're following your scent, and right now they're on their way to Lake Michigan. Totally the opposite direction, darling." she says proudly. "We have plenty of time."

We hear footsteps approaching, and Milan scrunches her nose prettily and glances at the open doorway.

Right on cue, a half-naked, big burly man appears in the doorway. He looks scruffy with a long tangled mass of blond hair. A long scar runs from the top of his eyebrow, barely missing his eye, all the way down his cheek and disappears behind his mustache and beard. His dark blue eyes are wild and cold. He is shirtless, and his black pants are dirty and torn. He is big muscled, and his skin is heavily tanned. So heavily tanned that it's darker than his hair. Scars decorated his torso as well.

He is a werewolf, of that I'm sure. Is he a rogue? I've never seen one before. I had been living a very sheltered life as a werewolf, I realize.

"You're very late!" snaps Milan.

"Look at what we found," he gruffly says instead and steps in.

Another half-dressed man fills out the doorway, holding Mia in front of him. She tries to fight him, but the man easily shoves her into the room with one hand holding both her arms back and another gripping her hair in a very tight hold. He is almost as big as the first one and as equally dirty. His greasy, long, jet black hair almost reaches his waist, and dark mustache and beard are covering half his face.

"You bitch!" Mia spits. "You crazy, double-crossing bitch!!!!"

She yelps when the man yanks her hair back.

Milan just ignores her outburst, but a cold, calculating smile is playing on her lips.

I almost gag at the smell when both men entered the tiny windowless room. Their wild eyes survey the room and quickly zero in on me. Mia gasps when she notices Logan's body at the corner, then she breaks down into loud sobs. Both men stare at me with interest. I fight down another urge to puke.

"Is that part of our payment too?" asks the dark-haired man above the sound of Mia's howling. The blond guy looks like he's close to licking his lips.

"No. She is your job. I want her dealt with immediately," Milan instructs them.

"You need all my men here just to deal with one little girl?" asks the blonde.

"She's not just one little girl, you fool! I told you she's a lycan. She'll tear you to pieces once she regains her strength."

"A pity, " he says, stepping in closer, eyeing me up and down.

"What about you? Aren't you going to stay for a bit of fun, beautiful?" The dark haired one sneers as he turns to Milan. His eyes are raking her figure hungrily.

She narrows her eyes menacingly, and I can feel that she's projecting her dominance to intimidate them. "Watch your mouth. Remember who you're talking to. I'm paying you, and I'm a lycan. I could end you and all your friends out there in a matter of minutes."

Both men bowed their heads grudgingly, growling like feral animals.

358

"Well, I'd better be off now. You know what to do," she says to the men. She then turns to me and says, "Try not to worry too much about Constantine, darling. I'll take good care of him." With that, she walks out.

"What do you want us to do with this one?" asks the second man who is still holding the sobbing Mia just before Milan disappears around the corner.

"Do what you want with the mutt. Have fun with her. Kill her. I don't care," she answers offhandedly without even looking back. "Just remember, I want the other one dead right away." Then she's gone.

"This is great! Two girls to entertain ourselves and our men," says the dark-haired man. Mia's wailing gets louder.

"Control your bitch! Fuck! Her howling is seriously pissing me off!" yells the blonde.

"Shut up, bitch!" The dark haired man yells at Mia. He yanks her hair back. When she shows no sign of stopping, he slaps her face. Hard. Blood and spits fly out of her mouth. That doesn't stop her wailing.

"Fuck it! I'm taking her outside. See if any of them men are willing to have fun with a howling bitch." The man smiles, showing his sharp teeth and canines. "Are you gonna share that one?" He points at me.

"No," answers the other man gruffly.

"Come on, at least let me have a turn."

"I said, NO!" The blondie roars. The other man recoils and Mia stops wailing for a second. Well, now we know who's in charge.

As soon as they left, the big blond guy looks at me and smiles menacingly. I lean back against the wall and observe him from underneath my eyelashes. If I didn't have the damn toxin in my body, I could've ended him and all his friends out there so easily.

He bends down and pulls out a big bowie knife that's tied to the side of his leg. That's a really big knife. A very big shiny knife.

"Sterling silver," he murmurs half to himself, eyeing the knife, looking very smug. Silver wouldn't kill a lycan the way it would a werewolf, but it would still hurt. Besides, a knife is a knife. He's going to butcher me. Separate my spine from my body, along with it, my head. Oh, goddess, that's not a good look for me, I decided.

"My mate is going to kill you," I inform him.

He doesn't answer me. The eyes that meet mine are remote and cold.

"I bet you never had a lycan before," I try again.

"No, but you're going to kill me if you get the chance, aren't you, princess?" he asks with a sneer.

"Are you going to use the knife? Why don't you phase and kill me as a werewolf that you are?" I taunt him.

His face changed, and suddenly he pushes forward, pressing his nose up against mine. Oh, the smell! His hand grips my face hard. His long dirty fingernails are pressing into my cheeks.

"Because I'm not stupid. I know your blood is poison to me," he answers through gritted teeth. His foul breath fans over my face and I hold my breath, but only after I had a good whiff of it. I'm so close to puking. I should puke my guts out all over his face. That would probably be his first shower in years!

He must have noticed the look of disgust on my face because he suddenly grins. It doesn't soften the looks in his eyes at all. It looks more like a menacing grimace.

He licks his lips, then places his revolting wet tongue on my chin and drags it along my cheek all the way up to my hairline. I feel his thick slobber running slowly down my cheek, dripping down my chin. I close my eyes and shudder in disgust.

Oh, dear goddess. There has got to be a better way to die than this. I try to reach for Ezra again.

For the love of everything fuzzy, Ezra! I need you!
She's there. I can feel her. She's very weak.

"You find me disgusting, little lady?" He sneers. "Good. That's just the beginning. Now time for the real fun." That's when he rams his knife right into my stomach.

I open my eyes to find myself staring into his cold yet oddly gleeful eyes. He's deriving sick pleasure from this, I realize. He smiles as he pushes the knife deeper into me. I don't want his to be the last pair of eyes I see before I die. I want Constantine.

Strangely, I'm not feeling any pain, just some pressure and the coldness of steel inside me. I look down in puzzle at the knife buried to the hilt in my stomach. I watch when he pulls the long blade out of me. I can even feel the blade being pulled out. I watch in fascination as blood gushes out. So red. Like my hair. Constantine loves my red hair.

The smell of blood—and death.

Then it starts to burn.

Arghhh!!!!! How it burns!!!

The whole inside of my stomach burns.

Vaguely I hear a bloodcurdling scream. When it gets louder, I realize that it's my own.

My knees give out from under me, but he's gripping my shoulder in a tight vice to keep me upright while he plunges the knife in again. The pain is so unbearable that I stop breathing. I see red. Red. Red everywhere.

He holds the knife up to my chest, and he grins wide as he pushes the blade in. I can feel the blade lodged in my chest. He pulls the knife out and laughs. Blood splashes his face. Red blood running down his tangled beard. He's bathed in my blood.

"Time to carve out your spine, princess." He spits as he holds my shoulders with his blood-soaked hands and turns me around.

He pins me to the wall and tears my shirt with the knife before I feel the knife slicing my back. Oh goddess, the damn rogue is carving out my spine. Excruciating pain and throbbing agony spread through my veins until I feel like my whole body is engulfed in flames and I scream as I've never screamed before. The more he digs, the louder I scream.

My voice sounds different. His eyes widened when I turn to look at him. I see red. Ezra has awakened.

I grab the hand that's holding the knife and bite into the wrist as another wave of pain sears through me. I hear a god awful scream that's not my own. I barely register his other hand clawing at me. My teeth and canine pierce through the skin, muscle, and tendons. I feel the bones crunching under the pressure of my jaw and teeth. Salty, metallic taste hits my tongue. My mouth is flooded with blood. Blood is running down my chin.

I twist his mangled hand and ram the knife right through his stomach the way he did to me. I find his scream very irritating. So I bite through his neck and pull out his vocal cords. There, all quiet now.

His blood sprays out like fountains, and I'm bathed in it. I pull the knife out of his stomach and discard the unmoving body aside. The fury that is Ezra wants more kill, but I'm very weak. Ezra retreats, and the pain somewhat subsides except for the pain in my spine, which is very excruciating. I don't know how bad it is.

My top is in shreds, and the back is gone. The only thing that's holding it to my body is the blood. It's soaking wet with blood, so are my jeans. Blood is dripping out of my mouth and from my spine, and my wounds. The pain is now throbbing and burning. The remnant of the toxin is still in my system. It's stopping my wounds from healing the way they should. If it's not for the poison, I would have stopped bleeding by now.

I lean against the wall, gripping the knife in my hand as I stagger out. I'm smearing blood on the light brown wall and dripping blood on the dusty gray floor along the way. The rest of the building is really just another tiny room with only one exit door.

I'm standing in the doorway, looking around me. I deduct that this building is in a little clearing of a forest. There are probably around fifteen or so men out there. Some of them are already in their wolves form. They are all standing still like statues. All staring in alarm at the doorway where I'm currently standing. Every one of them is in an aggressive stance. They probably heard the wailing of their leader, the blondie in there.

I spot Mia lying on the ground. Her clothes in shreds. I don't know if she's still breathing. Frankly, I can't bring myself to care right now.

I know in my current state, I won't be able to take on fifteen big wild rogue werewolves. The pain is excruciating, and I can barely stand on my own. I'm done for, but I will not go down without a fight. They will try to separate my spine out of my body, and they will all die after tasting my blood.

Constantine, I love you, I send out to the wind.

I hear their fierce growling. They are all ready to attack. All at once, all of them start moving. Cautiously, one step at a time they're circling me. Almost like a ritualistic dance. Their crazed wild eyes vigilantly fixed on me.

One figure steps out to the front of the group, his eyes blazing. That black haired man. I figure he must be the second in command. He crouches low, and his body and features start to change. His face elongated and his fangs lengthened. Thick black hair grows, covering his whole body. Soon, a big black wolf is crouching in front of me, ready to pounce.

I try to stay upright. The throbbing pain in my spine is dulling my senses and I'm so tired. The blood-soaked knife feels slippery in my hand.

I know he's going to aim his sharp claws for my neck and my face. So I wait. I grip the knife tightly, and when he springs up, I duck and ram the knife into him. The knife didn't go too far in but he roars in pain from the silver. They are all snarling and moving in. They're closing in on me, hungry for my blood now.

Ha! I'm going to die, but I'm bringing them with me.

A big gray wolf jumps on me, and I raise my hands up to push him off. His jaw locked on my shoulder. Another one jumps on my back. His canine sink deep right to my bone. I'm sinking fast.

Suddenly I sense that something is different.

He's here!

They're all here. I can sleep now.

I hear roars all around me. My eyes are closing, when I hear a fierce growling. One minute I'm surrounded by rogues hell-bent on ripping me to shreds, the next I see my mate snapping off the head of the wolf whose jaw was clamped on my back.

All around me I see my pack mates fiercely ripping the bodies and the heads off our enemies.

*   *   *

Constantine. My beautiful mate. He's cradling my head gently in his arms. I look up and smile. Those eyes. I never thought I'd see them again.

He turns me all of a sudden to inspect my back. "No... no, no, no..." he murmurs, breathing hard. "Sunshine," he whispers. He looks pained and confused. "Why isn't she healing? Why isn't she healing???"

He keeps yelling this over and over again. I want to say something, but the blood keeps surging out of my mouth. I want to keep looking into his eyes, but my eyelids are so heavy now.

CHAPTER XLII
Tracking Bad Blood

"Sweetheart, open your eyes, talk to me. Sweetheart." He sounds anguished. His hands cupping my cheek.

My eyes feel so heavy. I'm so tired, even my heartbeat is slowing down.

"No! No, no, no, no. Open your eyes, Genesis!!! Look at me!!! I said look at me!!!! No, you don't get to leave me. Come on, sweetheart. Please, open your eyes."

Crashing anguish, sadness, and desperation. I feel it. I do. I struggle to open my eyes.

"Please. I'm begging you...if you love me, you won't leave me. You promised me. Genesis!"

I love you. I want to say. I'm just so tired. That's all. Just let me sleep. Just one minute. Just one minute.

"Why isn't she healing???" he's desperately asking somebody.

I know why. "Hel… nalin...toxin," I mumble heavily. I manage to open my eyes just a little bit.

Tears. My mate has tears in his eyes. Why? His beautiful silver-gray eyes turn black, then back again, then back to black.

So tired now. I'm drifting off.

"Helenalin Toxin?" Serena's voice. Too far away. "Phase into your lycan. Honey, phase into your lycan.." urges Serena

365

desperately, gripping my hand tightly. She's getting further. "Tell her to phase! Constantine! Tell her to phase!"

"Sunshine, phase into your lycan. Please. Open your eyes. Look at me! Look at me!"

I'm so tired. They should let me sleep.

Intense misery, fear, grief, despair, and anger suddenly consume me like a floodgate of feelings being opened and I gasp. My eyes fly open. My mate.

My mate is bending over me. His eyes are black pools of rage, fear, and devastation.

"PHASE!" he orders.

Automatically, Ezra comes to the surface, and the pain starts to throb fiercely and burns more intensely than ever.

I'm screaming loudly as waves after waves of throbbing agony assault my whole body. My pack members are holding me down as I thrash about.

I want to get up and destroy and kill everything in my path. I want to rip apart everything and everyone who caused me this pain.

"That's it, sweetheart, stay in this shape. It will burn the poison faster," Constantine whispers into my ear. His big hands are cradling my head.

"Let me go!!! Let me kill!" I scream until I blacked out.

*   *   *

It's dark. There's still a little tinge of orange glow on the horizon. There's a big roaring fire about fifty feet away from where I'm lying on the ground. I'm in a clearing in the middle of a forest with trees all around me. The smell of burning hair and flesh is strong and nauseating.

Two strong yet graceful figures are moving back and forth, laboriously and aggressively throwing broken bloody limbs into the fire. Caspian and Lazarus. My pack mates.

Everything comes back to me now. The nightmare. The anger. The pain.

The vicious pain I felt before is now a dull throbbing in my back, chest, stomach, and shoulder. The anger is now a raging inferno that keeps turning my vision red.

My eyes scan the area, searching for my mate.

On the other side of the clearing, I see him pacing the ground like a caged tiger. He is shirtless and his whole body is stiff with restrained fury. He is beautiful and dangerous. I realize suddenly that the rage I'm feeling now is mostly his.

"You're awake!" says Serena softly. She rushes over to envelope me in a vicious hug.

"What is he doing?" I cling to her arm to sit up. I find his shirt on the ground underneath my head.

We both look at Constantine.

"He's been doing that for a while now. He wants to kill whoever did this to you, yet he's unwilling to leave you."

"Constantine," I whisper. All of a sudden he stops pacing. He tilts his head to the side as if he's listening to the wind. He then turns his face towards me. All of a sudden, I feel the wind blows, and in a heartbeat, I'm in his warm, powerful arms. His face is buried in the crook of my shoulder.

I raise my arms to wind them around his neck and catch the sight of my hands. I'm covered in mostly dried blood. Goddess knows how I smell.

I weave my fingers through his dark, silky hair and tug at it, pulling his face away from my neck. Black shiny orbs are staring back at me. He's half lycan. He's holding on to his human form by a thread.

"Oh, Constantine, I love you," I whisper to him. Those words I thought I'd never get the chance to say to him again.

His eyes change back to their silver-gray color.

"I love you. So much. I thought my life was over when ..." he doesn't finish the sentence. Black bleeds back into his eyes.

367

Swallowing all whites and silver-gray. They look like shiny black onyx. He's powerful and dangerous and so full of rage.

I feel the changes in the wind and sense their presence behind me. Lazarus, Caspian, and Serena.

I'm still very weak, but this has got to be done. My lycan demands it. With one hand, I grip the back of Constantine's neck and held him tightly to me, while I stroke his cheek softly with the other.

"We have to find Milan. Now," I state.

My mate growls viciously, and I tighten my hold on him.

"We suspected she was behind this," snarls Caspian. His voice is different than normal.

I turn to look at my other pack mates, and they move in closer. They're in an aggressive stance. Three more pairs of shiny black eyes are staring back at me, and I realize my pack mates are still hungry for battle, especially after I confirmed their suspicion about Milan. None of them is looking much like a human now. Even Serena.

I can feel their fury. Sitting here in the middle of them in my human form feels like I'm sitting in the middle of a raging tornado. A maelstrom of dangerous and lethal power and rage.

I don't want them to unleash their wrath on just anybody. I need them to focus their anger and senses on getting Milan.

"But you're still weak," Serena hisses. Her voice sounds cold and sinister, so different from her normal soft, caring, and melodious voice.

"She left no scent at all. Hard to track her down," growls Lazarus. His frustration and rage are almost tangible.

"That's why we have to track her now. She leaves no scent of her own, but she had Logan's blood all over her. If we can follow that scent before it fades or she cleans up and gets far away, we'll have a better chance at finding her," I explain.

"Then let's go find her," says Lazarus.

Constantine slides an arm under my knee and another around my back and effortlessly lifts me up.

"You can leave me here. I'm slowing you down," I tell him. I won't be able to run with them. I'm very weak. My body aches and the wounds throb still.

"You're never leaving my sight," he growls, tightening his hold on me.

They then phase fully into their lycan form. Their bodies are so much bulkier and taller. Their eyes are jet black. The veins forming from their eyes sockets are now completely snaking around their whole bodies. Their eyebrows are thicker and more prominent. Their bigger and more powerful jaws are filled with sharp teeth and two very extended and deadly looking canines.

Unlike werewolves, even when fully phased, lycans walk on two feet. Our bodies, even though hairier than normal, are not fully covered with hair like werewolves. Our senses are heightened in our lycan form.

"The scent is faint, but it's still there," hisses Lazarus, sniffing the air.

Constantine easily transfers me onto his back. I wrap my arms and legs around him and bury my face in the thick silkiness of his dark hair at the back of his head.

Lazarus leads the way. Once in a while, he stops to decide which way the wind blows and which way the scent really comes from.

We don't have to travel very far in the forest. The scent leads us to a small road, and it ends there. We conclude that she must have driven a car from that point on.

Knowing Milan, they decided to follow the road to the North since that would lead to the nearest civilization, instead of the hills and endless highways. They're careful to stay close to the trees, and they're very fast. I close my eyes and listen to the whooshing sound of the wind in my ears.

They run till we reach a small town. We are now out of the Shadow Geirolf Pack's territory. There's nothing much in this small town that I can see except for a small gas station, a convenience store, and an auto repair shop.

There are so many possibilities from that point onwards of where she would have gone to. Lazarus tells everybody to split up and sniff around.

I'm still on Constantine's back, and he's careful to stay in the shadows so that no humans can see us. Not many people are out and about. We're on one of the side streets, lined with small brick houses. Warm lights are coming from the windows of the houses.

"You can put me down. I think I can walk on my own now," I whisper in his ear.

"I'm not letting you down. You're not going anywhere without me," comes his gruff gravelly reply. Oh, for the love of everything fuzzy! Constantine in his lycan form is even more possessive than ever. I might end up being a monkey on his back forever. I'd be a *chunky monkey* from lack of exercises.

"Caspian found something," he says suddenly, and we're off again.

We all meet Caspian near a diner. That reminds me of how hungry I am. He's standing in the shadows of the trees.

"I smell other lycans in this area," explains Caspian.

"At least two others," agrees Constantine.

"It could be her accomplices," suggests Lazarus. It's probably not very normal for lycans to be in a place like this.

We follow the scent of the lycans. It leads us to a small run-down motel not too far from the town. I wouldn't believe that Milan would even step her foot in a place like this if it's not for the smell of Logan's blood. It is stronger here.

The motel is a single story building. The vacancy sign is in a tacky bright pink neon light at the front of the building. The sign above it simply says "Motel".

We go through the back, trying not to be seen lurking around in our lycan form. We follow the scent to a room at the very end of the block.

The room is dark. We can't hear any sound of any movement or any voices coming from it either. Lazarus grabs the window by its frame and just tugs it off its hinges. Good thing this place isn't equipped with an alarm system.

Lazarus climbs quietly in through the window. He disappears inside for less than a minute before we get a signal to go in.

I'm disappointed to find the place to be empty. We turn on the light to find the place to be cleared of any belongings.

I glance around, caught the sight of myself in the mirror and almost fainted. I look like a character in a horror movie. My top is in tatters, and I'm covered in blood from head to toe.

We found Milan's Prada silk dress with blood in the big garbage bin just outside the door, but they're gone. They're gone.

"What now?" I sit on the bed, feeling dejected and very, *very* tired.

"Right now, I'm taking you home to get you something to eat and give you a hot bath," answers Constantine.

I can feel their disappointment as well as my own. They are all back in their human forms now.

"But we can't let her get away," I protest, close to tears. I remember what she said about making Constantine the next king and look at Caspian. It's not just me that I'm worried about.

Constantine sits right next to me and wraps his sinewy arms around my shoulders. His closeness is comforting. I thought I'd never feel this again.

"We'll find her, sweetheart. You know we won't rest until we find her, but right now you need to get some rest. You nearly..." His voice breaks and he doesn't finish the sentence. Instead, he kisses the top of my head and draws me closer to him. I glance up once again at Caspian then look down at my hands clasped firmly together on my lap.

"You don't understand! If we didn't find her on time, she's going to do something much worse," I murmur. I blink my eyes rapidly to stop the tears.

"What's worse than killing you, sweetheart?" asks Constantine, scowling.

"I'm getting my men over here. They're on their way right now as we speak. We got their scent and we're going to track them right from here on. We're not stopping until we find her. The king has also been alerted about what's going on. He's sending his own men out as a reinforcement to get the job done," explains Lazarus, trying to calm me down.

Caspian sits on the floor in front of me and takes my tightly clasped hands in his. "Tell me what is it that got you this upset, Red? I know attempts on your life wouldn't get you all ruffled up like this."

Oh, I hate it when he calls me Red. I don't know whether to kick him in the nuts or hug him and tell him to be safe. Right now, I settle for just giving him a big scowl.

"You don't understand! She's coming after you next!" I exclaim, looking at Caspian. "She's planning something worse. She's not going to stop until she gets the throne. She let her erasthai get killed because he was a human and she wanted to be queen. She wants to be queen next to Constantine. She's not going to stop." My tears flow down my cheeks. I'm so very tired. Everything hurts.

I hear Constantine and Lazarus let out a few strings of curse words.

"So, you're worried that she's going to kill me??" exclaims Caspian. "Oh, Red." He sighs, then he looks thoughtful for a second. "I knew you love me." He suddenly grins, wiping a tear from my cheek with his thumb.

"Do you know that you look like you've just got dunked into a tankful of blood?" he asks, showing me his thumb that is

372

now wet and red with my tears mixed with blood caking my cheek. "Or like in that movie. What was that called?" he adds, snapping his fingers. "Oh yes, Carrie!"

"Shut up, Caspian!"

How can he make a joke when I just told him his life might be in danger? Oh, he's beyond irritating!

*   *   *

"I think it's time for you to have a good bath," suggests Serena, touching my hair. Yeah, I know my hair is stiff from dried blood. "I'm going to make you something to eat."

I think it's almost midnight now and Duncan, our cook, has gone home. Serena, Constantine and I came home, while Lazarus and Caspian stay at the motel with their men to discuss their next move.

I wanted to go hunting with them, but I kept falling asleep in Constantine's arms even while waiting for the men to arrive. I felt kinda embarrassed to raise too much objection after that. Besides, their men who arrived, ten good-looking lycans, looked at me as if they just saw a living dead or a zombie or something. *Sheesh!* Try being poisoned, stabbed a few times, bitten, then kill a couple of rogues and almost died and still look like a runaway model. Ha!

I told Constantine that I'd rather take a warm shower rather than a bath. I don't want to sit in a tub of bloody water.

He starts the shower, rips my clothes off and sits me down on the granite bench in the shower. He washes me from head to toe. The water that swirls around before it goes into the drain is deep red.

I think I had fallen asleep while I was still in the shower. Next thing I know I'm being wrapped up in a thick, fluffy towel. I keep drifting in and out of consciousness.

373

Serena made me some soup. I think I had the soup. Somebody fed me the soup...maybe? Too sleepy to remember.

Then, I find myself lying in our warm, comfortable bed in Constantine's arms. This is my heaven.

"Sunshine, my sunshine... you're never leaving my side again." He breathes. "I'll tie you to me if I have to."

"I love you," I whisper to him. My eyelids are already closing.

"I love you. You're my life. I've nothing to live for if you're..." He buries his face against my neck and inhales deeply. "I love you."

*   *   *

"Sweetheart, hey...time to get up." What? Is it morning already?

"Too tired. Don't wanna go to school," I mumble sleepily. Gosh! I hate school. Why does it have to start so early?

I hear a deep chuckle. "Time to go hunting, my love."

My eyelids flutter wide open.

CHAPTER XLIII
To Russia With Love

Apparently, Milan and her friends caught a red-eye flight to Russia last night. I think she starts to feel comfortable and too cocky that she managed to escape so far. Lazarus has their men waiting at Domodedovo International Airport, Russia. He also has some men stationed in Krasnoïarsk, where her family and most of her accomplices live.

It's only 5 am. and I only had a few hours of sleep, but we don't want to lose ground on our lead or let the trail go cold. Constantine knows that I'm still tired and a bit sore, but he said I could sleep on the plane. The intense pain I felt yesterday is now just a little twinge and only hurt when I move too much. I'll be back to normal by tonight.

Constantine keeps my passport with his. I don't know how he managed to obtain a visa for me to travel to Russia so quickly. I guess that's one of the perks of being a Lycan Prince. It suddenly dawns on me how powerful he really is. It just occurred to me that if I changed my mind about being his, there's no place for me to run to where he can't get me back. Lycan have their people in so many high places in governments across the world. Good thing I *want* to be his.

The thought should scare me, but it only excites me. My eyes slide to where he's slipping a white t-shirt over his glorious body. The shirt stretched tight over his broad chest and shoulders.

He's about to shrug a black leather jacket on when he returns my gaze as he feels my eyes on him. He raises an eyebrow in question. His sensual lips curl up at the corners into a sexy smirk as he continues putting his jacket on without taking his eyes off me. I could jump him right now!

"Stop looking at me like that if you want to make it to Russia anytime today...or this year," he growls into my ear as his hands grip my hips and yank me to him. He moves so fast! My back is against his warm muscled chest. His teeth nip my earlobe playfully. Delicious bursts of heat erupt through my body. I can feel how hard he is through his jeans pressing up against my behind.

Flying cows and crazy bunnies! Nope. Not going anywhere. I'm keeping this lycan for life.

My hand grips the tiny black velvet box that I had been keeping in my underwear drawer. I've been planning to give this ring to him later during a picnic, but if I learned anything from yesterday's event, "later" might not come. I might not be here for later to happen...or worse—he might not be. Now that I don't even have the ring that he gave me, I want more than ever for him to at least have something from me. I want him to wear something as a symbol of our connection and love apart from my mark.

I turn around to look at him and watch him from underneath my eyelashes. What if he doesn't like it? Now I'm chewing my bottom lip and gripping the box harder.

He's filling up his traveling bag with some shirts, but his eyes are regarding me with amusement. Finally, he smiles and sighs. "Okay, what is it, sweetheart?"

"What makes you say that?" I ask, shuffling my feet nervously, gripping the box behind my back now.

He just raises his eyebrows as if to say "Really?"

Suddenly, I have an idea. I step to where he's standing by the bed and go down on my knees while trying to keep a straight face.

He turns to look at me with curiosity and amusement.

376

I open the box, hold it up and says, "Constantine Dimitri Romanov, would you do me the honor of wearing this ring as a symbol of our bond and love? And also to show other women that you belong to me. So help me, goddess, whoever messes with my man will be bitchslapped so hard her ugly face will forever be facing her ass?" Then I smile innocently and angelically up to him.

There's a surprised look on his face for a few seconds before it is replaced with a look of tenderness and love, then amusement and mirth. He then throws his head back and laughs. That deep beautiful laugh that never fails to make me weak in the knees.

He puts his hands over his heart and in a funny slightly high pitch voice dramatically says, "Yes! Yes! A thousand times yes!"

I giggle, and he grabs my shoulders and pulls me up to my feet.

"I'd be more than happy to wear it, sunshine," he says in a serious voice.

I slip the ring on his finger, and we both grin at each other goofily.

"Together, forever," I say it like a vow and nod my head.

"Together, forever," he agrees. "Thank you, sweetheart."

He places his lips on mine. The kiss is gentle and sweet, yet I feel tingles running up and down my body. I know he feels it too because the kiss quickly becomes heated. He pulls away first this time, and I'm thankful for that because I totally wouldn't be able to do that.

"I love it," he spreads his fingers to look at it.

He has such nice, strong, long, elegant fingers. I think the ring looks good on his finger.

Mine.

*   *   *

We all pack very lightly. I unzip my duffel bag, throw in a few changes of underwear, a few pairs of jeans, tops, toiletries, and I'm done. He has already done packing as well. He zips up my bag, hoists it over one shoulder while carrying his own leather duffel bag in his other hand and we make our way down the stairs.

Caspian is sitting alone at the breakfast table, munching on his bowl of colorful Froot Loops. His hair is nicely styled but still damp from the shower. I eye the Domenico Vacca duffel bag at his feet. This prince really likes his luxury.

"Did you just get in?" I ask him.

"Yeah, about less than an hour ago," he answers. "I'll catch some shut-eye on the plane."

It sounds like everyone has the same idea.

I'm still feeling very tired. Constantine pulls me to him, and I curl up in his lap and yawn. It's too early for me to have breakfast.

Lazarus and Serena walk in not long after. Lazarus is carrying a duffel bag and a small suitcase. I assume the bright yellow suitcase must belong to Serena.

A limo is waiting for us at the front. Constantine waits for me to get in, then he climbs in after. He picks me up and settles me on his lap.

Lazarus, Constantine, and Caspian start to discuss their findings on Milan and her associates and also the latest development in tracking her. It seems that she's been involved in more than just my kidnapping. She's involved in building up the rebel army. The rebels have been attacking our ally packs in the Southern Region for many years now, contributing greatly to the state of unrest in that region. So many deaths of the innocence and destruction of properties caused by them. From what I gather, the rebels are getting bigger in number and strength.

They got the information that she's on the way to meet another important leader of the group. If the lead is correct, she will be leading us straight to the man. The Palace has been looking for him for a long time. So this is a great breakthrough for the Palace as well.

I try to listen in to their conversation, but I can't keep my eyes open. I snuggle up closer to Constantine, wrapping my arms tightly around him and burrowing my face in his neck, getting more comfortable. He wraps his arms protectively around me. His long elegant fingers at the base of my neck gently massaging my scalp. Ummm...very comfortable. Like I'm home in our bed. Maybe it's not the bed I'm in love with after all. We fit perfectly together. Nice. I listen to the deep, beautiful, and soothing timbre of his voice talking as I let my eyelids flutter shut.

I wake up in Constantine's arms just as our car pulls up on the tarmac beside the plane.

"Wait, we're flying on a private jet?" My eyes grow big.

"Yes. Our princess over there is allergic to commercial airlines," answers Serena, laughing while tipping her head towards Caspian.

"Say what you want, but five minutes in a crowded airport, going through the customs and security checkpoints, you'll be begging to come with me," replies Caspian with a smirk. "You'll say, you are right, Prince Caspian. You are always right. Oh, Prince Caspian, I was wrong, you are right. I am stupid, you are clever. You're a genius, really," he adds as he gracefully slides out of the car.

"You also have an ego too big, your head might explode, Prince Caspian," I mutter.

"Hey! I heard that!" comes his exclamation from outside the car.

Serena giggles. "As if he ever experienced traveling on commercial airlines." She rolls her eyes.

*   *   *

379

I was introduced to the flight crew, who I can tell are all werewolves. Caspian flirts with our two flight attendants, Anna and Yuliya with familiarity. Both girls blush with pleasure at his attention.

The interior of the aircraft is as luxurious and lavish as our house. The six cream leather seating at the front are plush and comfortable, so is the sofa behind them.

For the first hour of the flight, I was wide awake with excitement.

"We're starting your education on Russia with food," states Constantine.

"Perfect! I love food!" I exclaim, almost clapping my hands.

"I know." He grins.

Our flight attendants serve us breakfast not long after.

Breakfast consists of syrniki, a type of cottage cheese dumplings which are served with sour cream and jam, pancakes with minced meat fillings also served with sour cream, morning kasha, in this case, a bowl of buckwheat porridge with milk, and some fruits.

Constantine explains to me about the food, while I stuff my face with them. I love syrniki, and the pancake is awesome. I wasn't sure about the buckwheat porridge at first, but it's surprisingly pretty good.

Serena and Lazarus disappear right after breakfast. They've probably gone to bed.

I have a good view of the sunrise above the clouds and keep struggling to keep my eyes open.

After my third cup of tea and a hundredth yawn, Constantine pulls me up to my feet and walk me to the back of the plane.

"Off to bed with you," he says.

"But I've slept like ten hundred hours already," I mumble stubbornly. *Fuzzy slippers!* Ten hundred hours? I didn't mean to say that. I swear my brain stops working when I'm tired. That, or bad math skills.

"Ten hundred hours, huh?" His mouth curls up into a smile and his eyes alight with mirth. "Your body is repairing itself. You need a lot of rest, sunshine."

Caspian is already sprawled on the sofa, sleeping soundly. A blanket is nicely spread over him. His long legs are dangling slightly out at the end, but he looks comfortable enough.

Constantine walks me all the way to the back and slides open a door to a bedroom. The room isn't big, but the bed looks really comfortable. It carries the same plush cream, white and black decor as the front cabin. The lights are dimmed, and the windows are drawn.

"Come on, sweetheart. Let's sleep ten hundred and seven hours more," he murmurs against my forehead as he tugs me closer to him. He wraps his arms securely around me as we lie in bed. Warm and comfortable. Huh, what do you know, I think I'm in love with this bed too.

*   *   *

We are met with five lycans dressed in black fighting gears in a private lounge as soon as we arrive at Vnukovo Airport. They all look tough and formidable. Constantine introduces me to the leader of the group, Darius, who seems to be a close friend of theirs. He's as tall as the three but even bulkier than Lazarus. His blond hair is almost white and is swept neatly back. He seems very intimidating. His pale blue eyes are almost as pale as Constantine's. I sense warmth, strength, honor, and loyalty in him.

"So, finally I get to meet Constantine's mate. I'm sorry about what happened, but I'm glad that you're doing very well." He smiles, offering me his hand. His English is thick with the Russian accent. He will be traveling with us to track down Milan who is now meeting with the rebel group leader. They are believed to be in a werewolf pack territory suspected of supporting the rebels.

"It's nice to meet you too," I reply, taking his hand.

I climb in a big black Hummer-like vehicle that is waiting for us. Darius is driving, with Caspian sitting beside him. I sit next to Constantine in the second row, while Lazarus and Serena sit behind us. We're traveling with three other cars behind us.

"There will be an army of werewolves in that territory. There are also six lycans that we know of who are going to fight us in there," says Constantine. "You've been hurt...badly, just yesterday. I'd rather you sit in the car with two of our men..."

"No! Costa!!! Seriously???" I almost yell. Not only he wants me to hide in the car, but he's also going to assign babysitters for me too?

I can see Darius's amused eyes glancing at us in the review mirror. Caspian hides his snickers behind fake coughs.

"Listen, sunshine, we'll bring Milan to you, I promise. I know your lycan wouldn't be satisfied until you can exact revenge, but let us deal with..."

"No, you didn't hear me when I told you we're together forever," I interrupt him. I touch his ring, and he sighs in defeat. I know he's worried about me, but I'm not a helpless little girl who's going to gnaw on my fingernails waiting in the car while my mate and my pack are out there fighting the bad guys. No, thanks. I'll fight next to my mate and my pack.

"Okay...but you're staying close to me. At all times." He relents reluctantly. He brings my hand up to his lips and kisses my ring finger. "I'm going to put that ring back on your finger," he vows.

*   *   *

Just like all the other lycans that I know, Darius drives very fast. It takes over an hour drive to get to our destination. We're driving into a territory that belongs to a werewolf pack called Krasnyy Volk Pack.

It must be close to midnight by now. It is dark, and all I can see are trees around us.

Darius had briefed us on our strategy during the drive. It sounds pretty simple to me. The palace task force is already in place, just waiting for our signal. They are to take care of the fleeing rebels, and also to take the women and children to safety.

Our job is to go into the very center of it. We are to deal with the rebels and the lycans. I'm making it my personal mission to hunt Milan down. I'm going to make sure that she's not getting away this time. Ezra's hunger for her blood is a constant twinge in my consciousness. It's like an itch you can't scratch. It won't go away until she is gone.

Once we entered their territory, I'm sure they are all alerted of our arrival. Four cars with all lycans in them wouldn't go unnoticed.

"They know we're here now. We have to act fast," says Darius. He then barks orders into his radio in Russian. The cars behind us suddenly swerve into different directions.

Constantine squeezes my hand. I look up and our gaze locked. I know he's worried about me, I can feel it, but I'm telling him with my eyes not to worry. Despite what happened yesterday, I'm not made of glass.

I look at my pack mates, Serena, Lazarus, and Caspian. We have all phased halfway into our lycans. Our senses are sharper. We are ready.

CHAPTER XLIV
Of an Angel and Monsters

As soon as Darius stops the car, we jump out like the car was on fire.

All of them move so gracefully and quietly. Any sounds they make blend in with the whispering of the wind and the rustling of the leaves. I try to do the same as I climb up the nearest tree, then transfer from one tree to another. I don't know why I'm so comfortable being up on a tree. I might have a monkey ninja DNA or something.

From up here, I have a clear vantage point of everything around me. I can see the building that Milan and five other lycans are supposed to be in. We're approaching it from the back. It's a two-story building. The top level is totally dark, while there are lights in a few rooms on the ground level. Everything seems so quiet right now and it doesn't feel right. I know beyond doubt that they're waiting for us.

I know Constantine is just below me. I make sure not to stray too far from him, and he makes sure that I'm within his sight.

I know exactly where everyone is, except for Darius. For such a big guy, he moves like a shadow. I wouldn't want him as our enemy. I'm glad he's on our side.

I can see one of the cars that was behind us speeding past the front of the building. Suddenly, I hear a howling signal from the pack warriors. Seemingly like hundreds of werewolf warriors jump out from their hiding. Three of them jump right onto the moving car, pulling the doors right out of their hinges.

The uneasy silence of the night is now broken with the sound of the screeching tires, metal crashing against metal, chaotic growling, screaming and howling.

I'm about to spring over to help the two lycans that I know are in that car when I feel Constantine's hand grab me around my waist.

"They don't need our help, sunshine," he whispers into my ear. "We have bigger fish to fry."

I lean into his warmth and the safety of his arms for a little bit. To say that I'm not apprehensive and nervous would be a lie. My heart is beating much faster than usual. My stomach is clenching. However, those are also due to some strange excitement building.

"Here they come," he murmurs before he presses his lips and nose to my neck and breathes in deeply. Adrenaline is already coursing through my body.

I see movements down below. A few tall figures are coming out of the house through the back door. I count five of them. I see Lazarus rushing to the front with Caspian and Serena not far behind him. Suddenly, I see Darius jumping down from the rooftop.

Inhuman growls and snarls fill the air.

"Stay close to me, my love," Constantine says, then he jumps to meet our enemy.

I climb lower. My eyes are scanning around. I'm looking for only one lycan—Milan. She is not among those lycans down there.

My eyes fall on my mate who is fighting a big blond male lycan. They are both in their full lycan state. They both look menacingly dangerous, circling each other. Already, their clothes are in tatters. Constantine's black leather jacket is gone. There's not much left of the white shirt he put on this morning.

My eyes seem to be transfixed on my mate who moves with graceful aggression. His every step is smooth and calculative. I fight the impulse to jump and push him out of the way when the other lycan lurches at him with claws fully extended.

Constantine dodges out of the way at the very last minute. All I can see is the razor-sharp nails whizzed by dangerously close over his head as he crouches down. He swiftly rolls over to land gracefully back on his feet. He's unharmed, his opponent, however, staggers to the ground, clutching his stomach. Blood is seeping out between his fingers. I know my mate is fast, but I didn't see him striking out at all. He's too fast for me to see him lacerating his opponent's abs with his claws.

I hear the howling sound, and I see more werewolves coming this way.

Caspian is fighting with a lycan the size of Darius. The other lycan's size is intimidating, but Caspian is cunning and elusive. He is very aggressive and vicious when he finds an opening for an attack.

Lazarus and Serena are fighting with their back against each other. Their movement in synch with one another and that only comes from training and being together for decades.

A werewolf army descends on us, and I'm about to jump down when I sense movements in the form of heat from the corner of my eyes. My eyes zoom in on it; very clever swift movements that are meant to fool the eyes in the dark. *Milan.* She's careful to move in the shadows, but I can still make out the outline of her body. There's no mistaking it. I know that silhouette of hers anywhere. My eyes focus unwaveringly on it. I'm scared that if I missed a beat, I would lose her. She's moving away fast. Oh, no, bitch! You're going nowhere but hell.

I hop from one tree to another, making as little noise as possible. When I reach my intended target, I let go of the branch, propel myself forward and land on my all fours right in front of her.

I have the satisfaction of seeing the shock on her face. She blinks as if she could hardly believe her eyes. Then the shock turns into a hateful smirk.

"I thought I sent you to the pit of hell yesterday." She sneers. "I see you survived. I didn't know you're a masochist, though. Are you here to be sent back to hell?"

"I'm here to drag you to hell with me." I sneer back, standing up.

She's about to open her big mouth again when I leap forward with my claws aiming for her chest. I want her beating heart in my hand. She dodges away in time, but my claws manage to drag bloody graze marks on her flawless cheek.

She touches her cheek and yells, "Bitch!" I can see my ring on her finger, and I want that ring back!

This time she attacks first. Her foot landed on my chest, and I land on the ground a few feet away. She jumps on me before I could get back up and sinks her claws into my right arm, while the other tries to grab me by the throat. I smack the heel of my palm under her chin and pull my foot back, kicking her in the stomach, sending her reeling back. Her long nails scrape across my arm. Suddenly, I can feel the familiar awful throbbing pain.

"What did you do?" I hiss even though I already knew the answer.

"I dipped my fingernails in venom." She grins. Her sharp white teeth glisten in the moonlight. How stupid of me. I should have known she would have a trick up her sleeves.

The scratches from her nails on my arm burns. I surreptitiously survey our surrounding as we circle each other. All of a sudden she barges again, this time her poisonous fingernails are clawing for my heart. I leap away, but she manages to grab my shirt, tearing it to bits. I spring up fast to grab onto a tree behind her with one hand. Before she knows what's happening, I drop down, planting my feet on her back. I wrap one arm around her neck, while the other hand grabs onto her hair. I grip tightly, like pulling on a reign while I'm straddling her from behind. She growls furiously as she reaches up and her fingers grip both my arms, digging into my flesh. I can feel the poison of her claws. I feel it burn. I feel my arms weaken. I don't have much strength to choke her with my arm, so I lean down and sink my teeth into the scruff of her neck.

She screeches loudly. Her grip on my arms tighten, and I bite down harder and shake my head violently. I pull back up with a chunk of her flesh in my mouth. Blood sputters out of the wound. I spit it out as she falls on her knees. Both my arms are on fire, and I'm starting to see dark haze swirling in my eyes for a while. She makes a move to get out from under me, and I sink my teeth and canines into her shoulder in desperation. I am not letting her go. Her grip on my arms loosens until she lets them go completely by the time I sink my teeth in deeper.

"Viktor!" she suddenly calls out weakly.

I suddenly notice a lycan standing in front of us. He stalks closer. I know I have no chance of winning the fight with this Viktor. My arms are burning and pretty useless now. That's why I'm using my sharp teeth. I know he's going to kill me. No matter what happens, I'm not letting Milan go. I'm going to do as much damage to her as I can.

He grabs my shoulders to pull me off Milan, but I just growl and clamp my jaw harder. NO! I'm not letting go! I feel the bones and flesh separated in my jaws as he tugs me hard and flings me back like a ragdoll. My back hits a tree with a crack. My arms hurt. My back and my neck hurt. My head, I'm not even sure what's wrong with my head, but blood is trickling down my temple. Everything hurts, but I'm feeling victorious. My front is completely drenched in Milan's blood. Her shoulder is still clamped in my jaws. I bit her arm right off its socket. Her blood is dripping out of my mouth as I let her arm drop and roll down on the forest floor.

Her loud piercing cry is seriously hurting my ears as she thrashes about on the ground. One arm is still attached to her.

Unfortunately, that's the arm that still has my ring. I spit her blood out and hiss furiously. Damn, wrong arm!

The other lycan, Viktor, doesn't seem to pay much attention to her scream and suffering. His eyes are focused on me. His face is austere and forbidding. I bet he's a good poker player. I open my bloody mouth and bare my teeth to him. I can tell this Viktor guy has no sense of humor.

He reaches for me, and I duck down, trying to evade his grip, but I'm not fast enough. He is so big...and with no sense of humor, and he's going to tear me to pieces.

*   *   *

A loud fierce growl reverberates through the air just before a set of sharp claws wraps themselves around Viktor's chin, pulling Viktor off of me. Viktor's head is being pulled back, leaving his neck arching backward as far as it can go. One clean swipe of another set of claws on his throat and his neck is ripped wide open. His skin is torn out like ribbons, and he makes a sickening gurgling sound as his blood splatters everywhere.

Constantine.

He looks like a terrifying avenging angel. Blood splattered across his naked upper torso. Dark veins protruding and snaking around his bulging muscles. His black eyes are wild and vicious. His lips are slightly parted in a snarl, baring his sharp teeth and canines. For a few seconds, Viktor is writhing on the ground with blood gurgling from his neck. Then he's struggling to get up on his feet again, his hands are clamped around his neck, trying to hold it in place. Lycans recover fast, but he's no match for a very angry mate. Constantine tears through him again without missing a beat. I turn my face away from the spraying blood.

My arms are still burning, my eyes are seeking out Milan. She's crawling on her stomach with one arm, trying to get away. As soon as she sees me crawling after her, her eyes widen. My gaze turns hungry as I stare at her other hand. I want that ring back.

"Hello again, Milan," says Caspian. He's stepping right in front of her with a wide menacing smile on his face. Lazarus and Serena are just a step or two behind him.

Two strong hands on my upper arms pull me up to my feet.

"What did she do to you?" My mate hisses as he picks up my hand to inspect my still bleeding arm. Viktor's body is lying broken on the ground. His vertebrae are torn out and lay in several broken pieces in a dark puddle of blood. I can't see his head anywhere.

"She has the poison in her nails," I answer. It's painful but not nearly as bad as the hell that I went through last night. I can ride this one out, I think...then I see that dark haze appearing in my eyes again. Constantine wraps his arms around me to stop me from falling. He lets out a string of expletives in Russian.

None of the rebel lycans were spared, except for one. The unlucky one. He was taken to the palace to be interrogated and most probably tortured.

Darius and his men left to let us deal with Milan. We can either bring her back to the palace to stand trial and be prosecuted, or we can be the judge and jury and prosecute her ourselves. We earned that right since she tried to kill me and that could've caused direct and dire consequences on Constantine as my mate as well as to all my pack members. This is how justice works in the lycan world.

Torn limbs and dead bodies are everywhere. The sickening stench of death permeates the air. The "cleaning crew" will arrive soon to burn the bodies and clear the area. It will be as if nothing gruesome ever happened here.

Milan is on her knees. Blood has stopped pouring out from the stump that was her arm. Her designer dress is gone. She has nothing but mud and blood covering her body.

Caspian is standing behind her. The rest of us are standing right in front of her, blocking her in.

"Constantine? You would kill me? You would kill me over this...this...lowly mutt?" Her eyes flash hatred as she glares at me. She then turns her attention back to Constantine. Her eyes are big and pleading as she stares up at him.

"*Закрой свой рот, сука!* (Shut your mouth, bitch!)" snaps Constantine. "That's my mate you're talking about. You almost killed my mate. My mate!"

"But I can be your mate! Constantine, *Я люблю тебя* (I love you)!"

"But I feel nothing but disgust and hatred for you. You tried to destroy the one I love," he hisses. His sinister black eyes glisten eerily. His voice is gravelly and threatening. His canines gleam in the moonlight. I feel his burning fury.

The four lycans are now staring at the kneeling Milan with a bloodthirsty look in their eyes. I grin at her and lick my lips hungrily myself. I want blood. I'm thirsty for her blood...and her pain. The four of them move in closer. Their fingers are twitching like they're itching to crush her right away.

"NO! STOP!!!" I hiss out.

Four sets of cold black eyes like polished onyx stare back at me incredulously.

"You want to spare her after what she did to you?" growls Lazarus in disbelieve.

"She won't stop until she kills you," snarls Caspian. "We have to end her. Now!"

I look at Milan who sits kneeling on the ground. She's looking up at me in disbelief, relief...and some disdain. I understand that look. She can't believe her luck. She thinks I am stupid, weak, and naive.

"We can't let her go free," growls Constantine. His jaw is clenched tight. I can feel his mounting frustration, his burning rage, and his need to get rid of her. I can feel his blood thirst for what she did to me. "I need to end her."

"Don't kill her," I interrupt him. I bare my sharp teeth and canines at her in a semblance of a smile. "Not yet...I want my ring back before things get messy." Boy, my voice sure sounds strange.

Constantine kneels down and pulls the ring roughly off her finger as she struggles to keep it.

"And another thing," I add. Time to deliver just as I planned it. "She killed Antonia."

Loud fierce growls and hisses rumble out like a volcano eruption from all the lycans.

"Make it painful. Make it as painful as possible. Finish her off," I utter while I stare fixedly into her eyes and smile. I had been waiting patiently for this moment. I want them to know she killed Antonia just before they rip her apart. I want them to be filled with nothing but hatred and fury for her, more so than they already do. I want them to be ravenous anew for her blood. This one is for Antonia.

"*пизда!* (cunt!)" spits Caspian. He grips the hair at the very top of her head and pushes her head back roughly. He's gripping it very hard that she winces. She is now forced to look up at an odd angle. Caspian makes a move to swipe open her throat, but Lazarus puts up a hand to halt him.

"Why?" growls Lazarus.

"Why did I kill her? Because I hated her, obviously. There were always the four of you—Caspian, Constantine, Lazarus, and Antonia. You had no time for anybody else. You gave me no time of the day. She's weak, yet everybody loved her. After she's died, I was finally one of you." Her eyes try to seek out Constantine. "I was there for you, wasn't I? I've been there for you through everything. I can be your mate! I can!!! We have a special bond. I can feel it."

I feel my mate's fury rises with every word she utters, but she keeps talking. He is so furious that I feel my chest bursting into flames from it.

"I'm doing this for you! For us! You'll be the king and I'll be the queen by your side," she says. "We'll rule together. We'll kill anybody that comes between us."

Constantine growls fiercely. His eyes narrow with contempt. He's done listening. One quick powerful swipe and her jaw is severed from the rest of her face and falls with a clack on the bloody muddy ground twenty feet away from where she's kneeling. The gurgling shrieking sound that comes from her throat is sickening to hear, but I want more. I can feel my mate's hunger to do more damage, but he steps back and lets Lazarus step in.

I know Caspian and Lazarus have so much anger to unleash on her too. Even Serena takes her turn. There's a lot of fury in her. She is like a mama bear when it comes to us.

In the end, they pulled her apart till there is nothing recognizable of her left. Lycans are monsters they say. Now I know it's true. I'm one of them. I try to find it in my heart to feel a bit of remorse for what we did to Milan, but I find none.

CHAPTER XLV
Forever Mine

The poison from Milan's nails that had gotten into my system has taken its toll on me. My energy is completely drained out of me after the adrenalin rush of fighting ended. I fell asleep in the car with my head firmly tucked under Constantine's chin and our arms wrapped around each other.

I know we arrived at the palace in the wee hours of the morning, but for the life of me, I couldn't force my heavy eyelids to open. I vaguely aware of being lifted and given a bath by Constantine.

I wake up on the plane feeling clean and fresh, not sticky and gross and covered with blood anymore. My mate is taking good care of me. Right now, he's lying beside me. His arm is wrapped around me tightly, protectively and possessively even in his sleep. I sigh as I look up at him. He looks peaceful and kind of harmless when he's sound asleep.

Harmless. I almost giggle at the word. The word harmless shouldn't be used to describe Constantine. My Constantine. His long sooty lashes fan out against his cheeks. It's funny how his long thick eyelashes never make him look girly or anything. I guess he's too manly to ever look girly. His high-bridged nose is straight and perfect. His lips full, pink and sensual. I know what those lips can do to me.

His lips twitched, and the corners lift up all of a sudden. My eyes move up to look into a pair of bright silver-gray eyes already staring down at me. We just lie there staring into each other's eyes for the longest time. I got lost in his eyes. I can look into his beautiful, unusual pale gray eyes for days and days. He seems as equally lost and mesmerized by my eyes.

Then I feel his fingertips lightly tracing my cheek.

"You have the most amazing eyes, sunshine," he murmurs. "It's like they can't make up their mind what color they want to be, so they take every color they can...gold, green, blue, gray—" His thumb is now tracing my lower lip gently "—and they're mine. You are mine."

"Yours," I say.

"Nobody's taking you away from me."

"Nobody," I agree.

"You're mine forever."

"Forever," I reply.

His lips twitch up again, and a naughty glint enters his eyes.

"And I'm going to eat you up for breakfast."

What? "WHAT?" I nearly jump out of bed.

He laughs, and his hand comes up to pull me back to him.

"Ever heard of the Mile high club, sweetheart?" he whispers wickedly into my ear.

I smacked his chest playfully. I know my cheeks are turning bright red. Curse my pale skin. I wish I could stop blushing. I know how much he enjoys saying outrageous things just to make me blush.

He chuckles, cupping my warm cheek in his hand and says, "I thought I'd take advantage of your agreeable mood today, but I know you're too loud for us to do it here. Everybody on this plane would be able to hear us." There's a hint of challenge in his voice.

"I am not loud!" I protest. Now I'm feeling hot all over. Don't they have air condition on this private plane?

"Oh, wanna try it out?" he lifts an eyebrow up challengingly. "I don't mind," he adds, grinning wide.

I smack his broad chest again before I hide my flaming face against it and he chuckles.

"Why are we going home already? I didn't even get to see the palace you grew up in. I didn't get to see much of Russia!" I try to change the topic. The brief tightening of his hand on my hip tells me that he's aware of what I'm doing.

"I'm sorry about that, sweetheart. You were at the palace, but you were mostly sleeping. King Alexandros and Queen Sophia really wanted to see you, but they understand. They know your body needs to repair itself after having the poison in you. You barely recovered from the last time."

Oh, how embarrassing! I groan and burrow deeper into his chest.

"We have to be back in school for our exams tomorrow."

So many things have happened that I completely forgot about exam week!

"We're going to visit Russia and the palace again. If Caspian doesn't mate with Lady Celeste or someone soon, we'll probably be there for a very long time." He sighs. We'd be there as the king and the queen of the lycans and werewolves. He left that unsaid, but there it is. That, in itself, is a very scary thought. I don't have the slightest clue how to be a queen.

"Sweetheart," he says, lifting a few locks of my hair away from my face. "Don't worry about it. We have the rest of our lives together. I'll take you to see the world. I'll give you anything your heart desires. All you have to do is say it, and I'll give it to you. Just tell me what to do, and I'll do it. You own me."

He lifts my chin up so that I'm looking into his eyes again. Tears well up in my eyes. I love this man with all my heart. I fall deeper and deeper in love with him every day. My heart is brimming with love for him. I don't need to say it. I know he can feel it as I can feel his love for me.

"Will you wear this ring again for me?"He produces the ring out from his pants pocket. "I had it cleaned."

I lift my hand up so that he can slip it on my finger. He raises my hand up to his lips and kisses it.

"I love you," he murmurs before his warm lips find mine. Ripples of pleasure run down my whole body. I open my mouth for his tongue to delve inside, finding my tongue, tangle, and dance together. Teasing and tasting each other. I miss the intoxicated taste of him. My hand goes into his hair while his hand tugs my body to be under his. I love the feeling of his weight over me. I wrap my legs around him as he grinds his lower body against mine. I can feel his straining bulge grinding against my core.

His mouth travels along my jawline and down my neck, kissing, sucking, licking, nipping. When his mouth finds that little spot behind my ear, a little moan escapes my mouth. He quickly covers my mouth with his again.

"Uuummm... not... too... loud... love.." he murmurs between kisses. His voice is husky and so sexy.

How can I be quiet when he's doing things to me? Oh, Constantine.

His hand comes up to cover my mouth as his lips move lower down my body. His other hand slowly pulls my top down while his mouth follows. When his mouth closes over the peak of my breast, I moan aloud despite his hand that's covering my mouth.

He removes his hand, and he pushes up to look into my eyes. His face flushed and his breathing ragged. His hair is all mussed up. Hunger is evident in his eyes.

"Goddess, your moans are sexy and driving me crazy," he groans before he dips his head down to place his magical mouth on my skin again.

Once we started, it's hard to stop. We might or might not have joined the Mile high club.

*   *   *

397

When we emerge from the bedroom later to get ready for the landing, I notice Darius and a couple of other lycans from the task force sitting at the front. Apparently, they're joining us to go back to investigate the involvement of several high ranked werewolves from our pack in my kidnapping.

My first thought is, I didn't know they're coming with us. The second is—cuddly bunnies and fuzzy slippers— I hope they didn't hear anything!

My hope is crushed when Caspian gives us a mischievous look. He smirks knowingly and says, "Painting session in the sky? Damn, I'm jealous!"

Constantine smacks him upside the head while walking past him. I hear Serena giggle while Lazarus clears his throat. The two lycans stare out the window without any expression on their faces. I guess they're trying to be respectful. Darius just gives us a brief nod while a tiny smile is playing on his lips, softening his hard features. His icy blue eyes look amused.

Arrghhh! Kill me now! So I spent the entire flight hiding my face against Constantine's broad chest.

We arrive back late night, Sunday. My family and friends are waiting for us inside the house. My mom, dad, Autumn, Reese, River, Penny and even her parents are here. I've known Penny's parents since I was still in diapers. Constantine had called and asked the caretaker to come and let them in earlier.

I was hugged tightly by everybody. We introduced the three lycans to my family and friends, then they updated us on what had happened here during our absence.

Both Logan's and Mia's bodies were brought back to be buried on Wednesday. Alpha Carrington is crushed. Logan was his only child. Mia's parents are devastated too, especially with the circumstances that lead to her death. The elders refused to let them be buried in the regular higher ranked werewolves cemetery. That's where Logan's long line of Alpha ancestors was buried. That would

398

be the ultimate disgrace to his family and to his memory. That saddens me. I decided that I would go and talk with the elders about it.

I notice Penny is awfully quiet. That doesn't happen very often. She seems distracted.

"Persephone Aspen Ruiz, did you hear a word I was saying?" asks her mom after she didn't answer her mom's question the third time tonight. Penny's smooth tanned cheeks turn bright red, and I notice her glancing very quickly to Darius before her eyes dart away.

This is very new. I've never seen Penny blush before. Blushing is my thing! Something is definitely up.

*   *   *

The mood at school is sober today. The death of Logan and Mia weighs heavily on everyone's mind. I don't see Hunter, Zeke, Caleb or the rest of their group at school. I wonder if they're allowed to take the test separately or later than anyone else. Logan's empty chair during English lit test is a stark reminder that he'll never walk the hallway or sit in that chair ever again. There's a little twinge of pain in my chest. He was after all my born mate.

Penny is quiet today too. I don't think this is caused by Logan's or Mia's passing. She's never fond of the two, especially after Logan rejected me. After my last exam for the day, I can't take it anymore.

"What's up, Penny?"

Her eyes are wide as she stares at me when I pull her aside.

"Nothing's up. Why do you think something is up?" she squeaks.

Now I know something is definitely up. I raise an eyebrow, telling her that I'm not fooled.

"Okay, okay..." She relents, but her eyes are busy scanning the hallway.

"Who are you looking for now?" I ask her, feeling exasperated.

"Your mate...and all the other lycans," she answers.

"They're not here. They still have another exam. Why?"

"Okay then." She sighs with relief. Then she pulls me to sit on the grass outside. The weather is beautiful today. Not many students are around right now.

"Well?" I ask her when she just sits there fidgeting with the strap of her bag.

She puffs out some air, blowing the bangs off her forehead. "Okay...uh..you know that lycan the other night?"

"Which one?"

"Uh...Darius?"

"Okay...what about him?"

She blows her cheeks like a cute chipmunk and raises her face up to look at the sky before she let it go.

"He's..." She stops, then groans, then flops herself to lie on the ground.

"Hot?" I supply. Of course, he's hot, and Penny is boy crazy. Nothing new there.

"Yeah...he's crazy hot...but there's something more." She sighs. "I don't know Gen. When I look into his eyes, I forgot where I was. There's this... magnetic pull. I couldn't stop looking at him, I couldn't think when I was near him, and I can't stop thinking about him. I mean, I know I have a mate out there for me...This is crazy!"

That sounds familiar. I know that feeling. For a minute I just stare at Penny. She's looking up at the sky, watching the clouds drift by. Her silky short, dark hair fans out behind her. There's a dreamy look in her big brown eyes.

"That sexy Russian accent...so so so hot." She sighs under her breath.

Students are rushing out of the entrance. We are no longer alone.

"We need somewhere private to talk, Penny," I tell her.

400

"Genesis," says another voice. Evan. "Can I talk to you for a minute?"

No. "Yeah, sure," I turn to look up at Evan, the new human student that I stumbled upon in the hallway a few weeks ago.

"In private?" he asks.

"Why not here?" another voice drawls out lazily as an arm wrapped itself around my shoulders from behind possessively. Constantine pulls me close as he gives Evan a measured look. Evan is eyeing him the same way.

Penny is eyeing both guys with widening eyes.

Then my mate starts nuzzling my neck. The way he does it shows possessiveness. It shows to everyone looking there should be no doubt that I belong to him.

"Wait. Are you... engaged? Married?" asks Evan, staring at the rings on our fingers, looking baffled.

"Yes," says Constantine, but doesn't elaborate further as he kisses and nips my neck. Goddess! How am I supposed to think when he's doing that?

"Well...okay then," says Evan, seems like he's lost for words. "Don't you think we're too young for that?" he mumbles before he walks away. I feel Constantine's arms tighten around me. I don't expect a human to understand our situation, but I should tell my mate to lay off a little bit. I should be mad for the high-handed way he's handling this. If only my brain isn't all mush right now.

"I love you," he whispers against my neck. Warm lips are teasing my skin. Chills running down my back. Oh, gosh. How can I be mad and stay mad?

EPILOGUE

You know that theory that Serena had about Caspian throwing a dart at a map to decide where to go next? It turns out that her theory is correct. He's deciding where to go and which university to attend, and he's dragging me into it. When I say dragged, I mean he literally and physically dragged me here to do it.

Three years have passed since that incident with Milan. We've traveled the world the first year after high school graduation. The five of us. Sometimes my best friend Penny would join us, and we visited my old pack often. Most of the last two years we spent here in Banehallow Palace, Russia.

Now we're in Caspian's bedchamber in the east wing of the Palace. He has a map of the USA and Canada taped to the wall of his suit.

Caspian's bedchamber is more like a two story suite. Both levels are luxuriously decorated in red, gold, black, white and cream.

The first floor, where we are now in, has sofas and chairs facing a big screen tv with PlayStation, Xbox and all the other latest video game consoles. One wall is dominated entirely by bookcases, filled with books from different times and written in different languages. Contrary to his appearance as a royal brat with no brain, he actually loves to read. He can also speak and read in so many languages. There's a comfortable reading alcove by the big arched window overlooking the garden below. You can only access the second level of his suite through his room. His massive bed is on the second floor, along with a balcony as well as a huge fireplace. No one else is allowed into his private space except for us and his trusted valet.

The Palace has its own media room and a huge library, but I think Caspian likes his privacy. I know there are so many layers to this prince in spite of his playful, bratty, childish manners that he shows to the world.

"Come on, Red, now it's your turn," he urges me. He threw a dart the first time with his eyes closed. It landed in the middle of nowhere with no college nearby. The second time he did it, it landed in the middle of Lake Huron.

"This is stupid, Caspian. Why can't we just pick a good college that offers a good program that we like, apply like normal people do and just go?"

"That's a stupid way to do it. Besides, this is more fun," he disagrees.

Gah! Why do I feel like up is down and down is up when I'm talking to this Lycan Prince?

"Look, the last time I did it, you ended up meeting Constantine. You still think it's stupid?"

"Fine!!!! Give me that thing!" I exclaimed, holding out my hand for the dart.

"Did you ever tell everyone else that this is how you decide they're spending the next few years of their lives? By throwing the dart at the map?" I ask him before I close my eyes.

"Nope! You're the only one I let in on the secret. You should feel honored, Red."

"Yippee!!!" I say flatly, while trying to figure out which way I should point the dart to. Maybe on Caspian's gorgeous forehead. That would end the discussion.

*   *   *

403

Well, we ended up coming to California. The dart had spoken. The dart that I threw landed right on a college town. A community College, no less. Lazarus, Serena, and Constantine were less than impressed when Caspian broke the news to them. We could've gone to an Ivy league university, argued Lazarus. Caspian was adamant that this is the place we should be. Then he accused Lazarus of being a snob. Like I said, up is down and down is up with this prince.

We bought a massive three-story beachfront property. It is on three and a half acres of private land, and the house is even more impressive than the house that we were living in three years ago. It is high-ceilinged and tastefully and lavishly designed. It is sleek and modern with gleaming marble floors. Almost the entire back walls of the main floor are made of glass, showcasing the outside view with its two-tier waterfall swimming pools and a hot tub facing our private beach. Caspian picked the house, of course.

Caspian also claimed the whole third floor for himself, which we don't mind at all. Who needs that much space anyway? Well, Caspian, obviously. I teased him that he needed the space to store all his shoe collection. I was only half kidding too because he has more shoes than I do.

Constantine and Lazarus decided not to attend the college with us. They're still living with us, just not attending the college. They manage a lot of business and palace matters from home. Serena and I weren't that interested in the college either, but Caspian somehow managed to guilt trip us both to join him.

I actually feel bad for Caspian. The last two years we spent in Russia, I've come to know his mother, Queen Sophia. She's very nice to us all, but her relationship with Caspian is very strained. Queen Sophia is a very authoritative figure. A formidable lady behind that sweet motherly smile. She wants Caspian to mate with Lady Celeste. I don't know how long Caspian would be able to fight his mother on that. He had another massive blow up with the queen a few months ago, and King Alexandros agreed to let

Caspian attend university in North America or Europe. I think that's what Caspian really wanted. He might have even planned this. I wouldn't put that past that devious mind of his. He chose North America, which I don't mind. I get to see my family and werewolf friends more often.

Well, as for the news from back home, a lot had happened within the stretch of three years.

Alpha Carrington is no longer the alpha. They can't find enough evidence to convict Alpha Carrington of having anything to do with my kidnapping. However, he stepped down not long after the incident. Beta Stevens took over from then on since Alpha Carrington has no son to replace him. Logan was his only child.

Hunter became the new Alpha of Shadow Geirolf Pack after he finally found his mate last year. Autumn. That's right! My sister Autumn is the new Luna of the pack! It's hard to believe, not to mention very worrisome when I first heard the news. She's doing a great job at it though. I'm very proud of my little sister. I am happy for them both too. I'm happy Autumn found herself a good mate. I approve of Hunter one hundred percent.

No wonder Hunter thought he was in love with me. I look a lot like my sister...or rather, my sister looks a lot like me. We probably smell a lot alike too. I'm just a bit worried for Hunter because my sister is a handful and a bit crazy sometimes.

Reese and River have a daughter now. They named her Piper. She's the most adorable thing ever! She has Reese's golden ringlets, but River's almond-shaped brown eyes.

As for Penny and Darius, well, what can I say? It's obvious that Penny is Darius's erasthai, but they had been doing this dance for three years now. Penny had been trying to get close to him, Darius kept pushing her away. Penny tried to get his attention. He ignored her. Penny kept coming to Banehallow Castle when we were living there in the hope of seeing him and spending time with him. None of us minded her visits. The five of us were rooting for her. She visited the castle so often that she had her own room there. At first, I thought Penny was winning. I saw the way Darius looked at Penny when he thought nobody was watching.

He made it clear from the very beginning that he didn't want her. I feel bad for my friend. It must've been painful for her.

Penny tried hard to win his heart. Three years. Three *effing* years. He showed her in every way possible that he didn't need or want her. From blatantly ignoring her to parading other women in front of her.

Finally, she admitted defeat. Nobody could stand offering her heart, laying it open at his feet only to have it stepped upon and trampled on over and over again.

I would've cut off his balls and feed them to the ducks if I could, but Constantine asked me to stay out of it. Besides, he's a very intimidating skilled fighter. *Fuzzy slippers!* I think he can shrink my head to the size of a walnut just by staring at it.

When it comes down to it, I didn't think he could stand it if somebody else would come along and claimed Penny. Lycans are very possessive. Darius is no exception.

Anyway, Penny is living here with us at the moment. She's attending college with us. She says there's nothing else she'd rather be doing anyway. She's going to go all out and experience full college experience, whatever that means. I'm just glad to have my besties with me.

*   *   *

Caspian and I just finished our last class for today. We make our way across campus to meet up with Penny and Serena at Club Espresso Degree. It's Caspian's favorite place to go to on campus for coffee, smoothies, and lunch. We didn't use to come here often, but I find us going there more and more lately.

I see people straining their necks to look at us as we enter the restaurant. Some do double takes. No matter where we go, people always look. Mostly out of curiosity. A lot out of lust. Many in awe. Some out of jealousy and envy. I'm okay with it now. I understand we stand out in the crowd, especially among the humans. They mostly don't know what to make of us.

Humans sense our power, but they don't understand, or rather don't rely much on their basic animal instinct that warns them to stay away from danger. They are attracted to our beautiful human forms.

In our lycan state, we are the stuff that nightmares are made of. Not only do we look like monsters, our moral compass changed along with our appearances. We kill brutally and without mercy when we feel that we are wronged or one of us is threatened. There will be no regrets even after we have changed back into our human form.

I see girls staring at Caspian with blatant interest and lust. He looks bored. There's this haughty, aloof expression on his gorgeous face as if everyone in the room is beneath him. That doesn't help, really. I think a lot of girls find this very hot. Some might even find it a challenge they can't resist. When he sees a few girls who have gathered enough courage getting ready to approach him, he just grabs my shoulders and tugs me under his arm. He told Constantine he's looking out for me, but I think he's just using me, or sometimes Serena and Penny as his shields so that human girls don't get too close. Even that doesn't work sometimes.

Serena and Penny are waiting for us at a table by the window. A group of guys at a neighboring table is eyeing them with interest.

"Hey, you two!" greets Serena, giving us a big smile. Penny gives us a little wave while furiously typing something on her phone.

"Hey!" Caspian and I reply at the same time.

"We already got you two your shakes," says Serena, sliding two Super sized plastic cups of smoothies. Caspian's favorite is Super Caja, with Caja, banana, strawberries, flax seed, yogurt, acai or some healthy crap like that. Mine is Mango Sunrise, a combination of mango, strawberries, vanilla, and yogurt.

I take a sip. "Ummm... yummy! Thanks." I grin up at her.

"You wanna order a sandwich or something to take home?" I ask her.

"Nope! I want to try food made by that new cook Caspian hired yesterday," she answers, deadpan.

"This should be good," mutters Penny.

Caspian flashes them a big devilish grin.

Oh uh, I don't like that grin. "I hope we won't go to bed hungry or have to order pizza or Chinese again tonight," I tell them. We've been surviving on Pizza and Chinese takeout for dinner for the last few days. The last cook he hired had big boobs, which has nothing to do with her job description. When I said big, I mean REALLY big. Penny called them bazooka cannons. They reminded me of overblown balloons. But hey, if she could carry those babies around, who am I to judge? Oooppss! Back to the topic. What I wanted to say was, our cook really can't cook!

Lazarus fired her yesterday morning after she burnt the toaster trying to make toast. It's a mystery to me how she managed that feat—burned the toaster. I guess that's the last one out of her many mishaps in the kitchen.

So, yeah, we're still looking for a good cook, or rather, Caspian keeps hiring them, and we keep firing them. I wish we still had Duncan to cook for us. Duncan is working on opening his own restaurant soon, which is the reason why he turned down our generous offer to move to California.

"Hi, would you like to order anything?" comes a breathy flirty voice of a waitress before we stand up to leave. The top few buttons of her shirt are undone. In fact, so many of them are undone that her black lacy bra is showing.

"Nope, we're good," answers Penny.

"You're Caspian, right? I'm Jenna. We're in Gothic Architecture and Art class together," she adds quickly over Penny, completely ignoring her. "Would you like me to do anything for you? Anything at all?"

Serena raises an eyebrow, Penny rolls her eyes and I hold in a smirk.

"Well, Jenna...can you bark like a dog for me?" asks Caspian, looking serious.

"Excuse me? Err...sorry, what?" the waitress asks, looking confused.

"Never mind. We're leaving," says Caspian looking bored now.

I grab my smoothie and move out of the chair. "Let's go then." I can't wait to see my mate. I missed him the whole day today.

The waitress, Jenna, is still standing there, staring at us in confusion. Poor girl.

"Come on, Beany Penny." Caspian drawls.

Penny winces at his nickname for her, then she gives him the meanest scowl. That doesn't affect him at all. As soon as she stands up, he curves his arm around her neck, making her scowl even more.

Caspian really knows how to push her button. Well, he's an expert at pushing everyone's button. Even the forever serene Serena would lose it once in a while because of him.

When we reach the road where we left the car this morning, I can feel the excitement and feel his eyes on me. Constantine! He's here. I look around and spot him leaning against his jeep next to where Caspian's car is parked. He looks so hot with his white t-shirt that follows every curve of his broad muscled chest and flat abs. Dark jeans that hug his long sinewy legs.

His dark silky hair as messy as usual. He has sunglasses on, but as soon as I smile at him, he lifts it up to reveal his beautiful light silver-gray eyes. His lips curve up slowly into a sexy smile.

My heart goes into overdrive as usual when he's around. Oh, be still my poor heart.

"OMG! I think my panties just melted," says one girl to her friends. They are staring at my mate with their backs to us.

"Wow!" Breathes another.

"Well, yeah… he's smiling this way," declares another. "I call dibs. You bitches stay here while I go talk to him."

"Wait a minute, you can't call dibs! I saw him first!" exclaims the first girl. She pulls her friend who's about to sashay towards Constantine back behind her.

Caspian grins at me.

"Stupid hoes," mutters Penny, scowling.

"Go get your man, tiger," whispers Serena in my ear.

We walk past the three fighting girls. My eyes glued to my mate who's smiling wider as I get closer. My breath hitches in my chest as I look at my beautiful mate. The love in his eyes and in his heart is all consuming. I love this man with all my heart and soul. I belong to him completely.

"Hello, sweetheart," he murmurs as he grabs my waist possessively and tugs me to him. His lips swoop down to capture mine. My hand goes up to hold him at the nape his neck.

His lips are firm and warm yet velvet soft. They're coaxing mine to open so his tongue can delve inside and explore my mouth and my tongue. My heart picks up the beat and an explosion of heat and fireworks burst all over my skin. I missed him so much. I'd gone without this for so long. Five long freaking hours!

"Ummm...you taste like strawberry and mango, and you...yummy," he mumbles against my lips. "I can't wait to taste the rest of you." He trails his mouth across my jaw and down to my neck, sucking me there. If he doesn't stop now, we might end up getting arrested for public indecency.

"Continue this at home, you two. We don't get paid to make porn in public!" yells Caspian.

Constantine flips him the bird, though he pulls back a bit. I lift my cup of smoothie to his lips so he can take a sip.

410

"What are you doing here? We're on our way home," I ask him.

"I missed you. Can't stand waiting for you at home any longer, this is torture, sweetheart. It felt like forever. We've gotta do something about this." He sighs. "And I hate the way those guys are looking at my mate," he growls. "Maybe I should attend classes here too, so you won't be away from me for that long...and so I can pound those pricks who.."

"Just stop talking and kiss me again," I tell him as I sink my fingers in his thick luxurious hair, tug his head down and plant his lips on mine. He's so hot when he's jealous.

Serena and Penny ride with Caspian, while I go home with Constantine.

He holds my hand all the way home. His eyes slide to me every now and then like he can't keep his eyes off of me. Once in a while, he raises my hand to his lips. It's always been like this every time we're in the car together.

We've hardly ever been apart these last three years. Today is the second time we're away from each other that long since I started college. He really is a part of me. My other half. I know I would gladly leave this world if he's not in it.

As soon as we get home, I enter the kitchen to see a human cook, wearing nothing but a g-string and an apron. Her ample and generous bosom is spilling over the top and the sides of the apron.

Cuddly bunnies and fuzzy slippers! Does she really need to prepare our food wearing those?

The busty cook looks like she's busy on the stove, but as soon as Lazarus walks to the fridge to fill up his drinks, she presses her body up against his, effectively trapping him against the kitchen counter. Lazarus isn't looking very amused.

"I can get that for you." She smiles flirtatiously up at him. He pushes her back, trying not to be too rough.

I could almost see smoke coming out of Serena's ears. "Caspiaaaan!!!" she yells loudly, making the human jump.

411

"I'm going to kill that prince. I swear it," she growls, advancing towards the woman who seems quite oblivious that her life could be in danger if she doesn't back off soon.

Penny snickers and makes a quick exit to her room.

I try to hide my smile behind my hands. I'd probably have pulled that bitch by the hair if it was Constantine she was pressing herself up against instead of Lazarus.

We know our men can't mate with those humans or werewolves without hurting or killing them, but that doesn't stop us from getting jealous. Like our men, we are very territorial and possessive.

All of a sudden I feel two strong arms wrapped around my middle from behind.

"Let's get out of here, sunshine," whispers Constantine in my ear. "I see a war coming," he continues. His voice is filled with humor.

I giggle as he gathers me closer and lifts me up while nibbling my ear.

"We'll be in our room for our painting session!" he announces as he carries me up the stairs. I smack his muscled arm and he laughs.

Constantine closes the door to our bedroom with his foot, then he drops me in the middle of the bed. In a flash, he is on top of me. His hand is pinning my hands down above my head. His body is pinning my body down. There's a wicked smile playing on his lips. "I love you," I whisper.

His eyes soften as he stares down at me. "I love you too, my sunshine, more than words can say," he whispers back. "I belong to you, heart, body, and soul."

I look up at him and smile.

He raises his eyebrows. "Now it's your turn to say it."

"Say what?"I pretend not to understand. Then I giggle as I wiggle my body underneath him. Delicious thrill course through my body. His gray eyes smolder. A hungry look crosses his gorgeous face.

"Naughty minx. You're going to be punished for teasing me like that."

"Ooohh...I can't wait! Punish me, my prince. Wait, what's the punishment this time?"

"The punishment is, you are going to be my dinner, appetizer, main course, and dessert. Now prepare to be properly devoured, my love," he growls sexily in my ear, and he proceeds to do just that.

THE END

Can't get enough of Genesis and Constantine? Make sure you sign up for the author's blog to find out more about them!

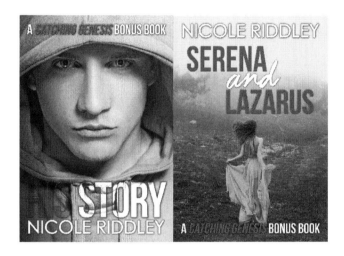

Get these two bonus chapters when you sign up at nicole-riddley.awesomethors.org.

Do you like werewolf stories?
Here are samples of other stories
you might enjoy!

MY SECOND CHANCE MATE

ANNA GONZALES

CHAPTER ONE
Rejected but Moving On

HARMONY

Waking up in the morning has never been easy for me and now it feels as if there's no point in doing it at all. I didn't always feel this way. I used to love life. I enjoyed hanging out with friends and even going to school. That changed the day I met my mate. What is a mate? It's supposed to be the best part of being a werewolf, which is what I am. We are born in human form and can transform into a wolf at the age of twelve. From that point on, it's a waiting game until we find our mate. A mate is a special someone who completes you; the one you was made for and vice versa. I should be happy to have found mine. Unfortunately, my story is unique and I don't mean that in a good way.

*   *   *

One Year Ago . . .

I met him at the age of sixteen. He was everything I could've hoped for. Seventeen years old, 6"1', gorgeous gray eyes, dark black hair, nicely tanned skin, washboard abs, and strong long legs. Perfect, right? I thought so too. We found each other outside the airport baggage claim area. Our eyes met and it was electrifying. We moved towards one another as if pulled by some force until we were only a foot away.

"Mate," we both whispered. He reached out to touch my cheek and I leant into his palm. It felt right; like home. I was so happy that I closed my eyes to savor the moment when he suddenly tensed and dropped his hand. I opened my eyes to ask what was wrong just as he took a big step back. I stared at him in confusion and was about to ask what made him move away when the sound of a familiar voice made the words freeze on my lips.

"Babe, I see you've met my sister. Isn't she adorable?" My older sister, Megan, gushed as she gave me her usual too-tight, can't breathe type of hug.

"Did you say babe?" I asked.

"Yes, silly! Aiden, you didn't introduce yourself?" She laughed while playfully swatting his chest. "Harmony, meet the best thing to come out of this whole mandatory wolf camp that mom and dad sent me to. My boyfriend, Aiden James," she announced happily while grabbing his arm.

My wolf growled at the sight of her touching my mate, but I couldn't say anything right now. I love my sister. She's my best friend and she looked so happy. I couldn't do anything to ruin that. Don't get me wrong; I had some serious questions to ask but I would get my answers when the time was right. Even if I had to tie Aiden to a chair to do it. There was a satisfactory rumble from my wolf just by picturing it. I couldn't believe that, out of all people my sister could have met at this camp, she had to meet and fall in love with the one wolf meant for me.

The camp they attended was a first of it's kind. It was created for two types of wolves. The first was for someone like Aiden, a future alpha. These types of wolves would one day be the leaders of their pack and had to be taught to control their added power and authority so that it wouldn't be misused. The second was for wolves born from two werewolf parents who both carry the recessive gene. It causes their child to be born completely human, and my sister was one of those children. The whole thing was complicated enough as it is, and finding out I was the mate of a future alpha my sister was currently dating only added to the complication.

Aiden and I quickly exchanged hellos as if the spine tingling encounter between us never happened. We grabbed their bags and headed to the car. The ride was uncomfortable mainly because the love birds decided to share the back seat and cuddle. I exchanged looks with Aiden a couple times in the mirror, and though he would smile at my sister, the looks he gave me seemed sad and resigned. His mood confused me but I expected to get an explanation soon.

We made it to our pack house where they were having a big barbeque to welcome my sister and Aiden back. Aiden is the only nephew of our alpha, and because our alpha's mate is human, she could not conceive a child. Our law states that the next male in line would be the alpha's younger brother, Aiden's dad. However, he was killed by rogues when Aiden was thirteen so by law, Aiden is the next heir. It is strange that we never had the opportunity to meet before but that's due to the fact that Aiden's mother took him back to her pack shortly after his father's death. She was unable to deal with the memories of her lost mate that surrounded her wherever she went. Her story was sad and was still used today to teach young pups the ups and downs of mating.

After about an hour into the barbeque, my sister made a run to the store with our mom, and it finally gave me a chance to get Aiden alone. I dragged him to a clearing, a little far down from our pack house, and laid above him.

"So, what are we going to do? I love my sister to death but we're mates. We can't deny that. I don't want to hurt her but the pull I feel for you is so strong I can't ignore it," I started rambling.

"I can," he said.

I continued, not quite hearing him. "I mean, I know this is going to be difficult and create a lot of drama but I'm so happy I've found you a—"

He cut me off and repeated those two words, loud enough so I could hear them. "I can."

"You can? Can what?" I asked, confused.

"I can ignore it. This pull between us," he stated. He proceeded to rip my heart out of my chest with the rest of his words. "I never had a choice in many things in my life. I didn't choose to lose my dad, or have to leave my pack, or be put into the role of alpha but I chose your sister. I fell in love with her all on my own with no influence from anyone. I refuse to change how I feel just because my wolf wants me to. I want to be with the one I love because I say so and not because a bond is forcing me to."

I stared at him. I was shocked and hurt. "Are you saying what I'm thinking? Are you rejecting our bond?"

He sighed. "Look, I don't want to hurt you, Harmony. I spent time with your sister, and I got to know her and fell in love all on my own. If I'm with you, it's not by choice anymore but by fate. I refuse to let fate control anything else in my life. I'm sorry but that's just how it has to be."

To say I was hurt was an understatement. What came next was just anger. "You refuse? What about me? Do you know how long I've dreamed of meeting my mate and finally feeling the love only he can give me? Only you can give me? And now you tell me I can never feel that because fate has dealt you a cruel hand and you're rebelling? And so I'm the one who has to pay for your misfortune? I have never done anything in my sixteen years of life to deserve that, but does it matter to you? Obviously not!" I cried out.

"Look, Harmony. I—"

"No, you look. I'm sorry you had to go through all that but that's what I can be here for. I can help heal the pain you've been through and support you through the role that was forced onto you. No one will be able to understand you like I, your mate, can. Let me do this for you. For us," I pleaded.

"I just can't, Harmony. I've already chosen the future I want, and that future is with your sister," he replied firmly.

"What about our bond? It's going to be hard to fight it. My wolf is trying to get through, and I'm sure so is yours. How are you going to deny him?" I questioned.

Nothing. And I meant nothing could have saved me from the pain his answer caused. "Well, I'll fight him off until I completely mate with Megan. Once I mark her, he will be easier to control, and as more time passes, our bond will eventually weaken."

"True, but you forgot one important detail. Or maybe it's not so important to you since you won't be affected but what happens to the rejected mate, Aiden? What will happen to me? Let me remind you, being that I don't have a choice in the rejection," I lashed out in anger, "my wolf will weaken. When you mark Megan, I will feel as if my chest has been ripped open. You will have your love for Megan to help get you through the weakened bond, but I won't be able to find another wolf mate since we are only given one in our lifetime. Even though the bond will deteriorate, I will still hurt every day. I will have to see you together and be reminded of my rejection time and time again. Is that really what you want for me? I know you feel something for me. I saw it at the airport. Are you absolutely sure this is what you want to do?"

"It's what I want," he whispered. "I've thought about this my whole life."

I tried one last plea. "What about kids, Aiden? Megan is human. You won't be able to have a pup with her. How will you carry on your alpha line?"

"I'll deal with that when the problem arises."

"So you'll give up your mate and any future blood children just to spite fate?" I asked, hurt and shocked.

He nodded. "Yes. I'm really sorry. I just can't be with you." There was a hint of sadness in his voice.

"It's not that you can't. You just chose not to," I whispered in defeat. "So you're finally getting to choose for yourself, and that choice forces me into a life of pain and misery," I said as I looked him in the eyes. I thought I saw some indecision and pain, but it was quickly replaced by resignation and determination. I looked away as the tears started to fall. "Fine." I turned back to face him. "I will accept your rejection of the bond but only because like a mate should; I only want your happiness. You see, that's what mates are supposed to do: Protect each other, care for one another, and put each other first. I will endure the pain of the future for you, and I hope that it haunts you every night while you live your happily ever after with my sister." And with that said, I shifted into my light brown wolf and ran further into the darkness of the woods.

*　　　*　　　*

Shaking my head of the unwanted memories, I think about my life since then. I haven't done anything drastic to my appearance. I still wear my brown hair long and straight, no contacts cover my light green eyes, my full lips are still only covered in clear lip gloss, and I haven't changed from skinnys and tanks to ripped jeans and grungy t-shirts. No, the only change is my attitude. The sweet carefree nature is gone. I now know how real life can be and it isn't a fairytale. My enthusiasm for life is gone. When you look into my eyes, you'll see emptiness that hides the constant pain.

I no longer live with my pack. Six months after my rejection, Aiden marked my sister and the pain was unbearable. I couldn't be around him and see him happy anymore. Yes, there were times when I was near him and could feel his wolf fighting for control but Aiden always pushed him back. I begged my parents to let me leave the pack and join my maternal aunt's pack— Her mate's pack in Hawaii, to be specific. My parents didn't understand why at first because I never told anyone about my rejection. I made up the excuse of it being hard to be around Aiden and Megan knowing I haven't found my mate yet. At least it was half true.

That's where I am now. A new pack, a new school, and hopefully, a new life. I should have an optimistic attitude, but I no longer have the illusion of happily ever after. Hope is something I seriously lack in the present. There is one good thing to come from all this.

"Harmony, get your lazy ass up so we can get to school. I don't want to miss all the fresh meat awaiting me. My game is on fire today. Just don't stare too hard at me 'cause you might be blinded by all this hotness."

There it is. My cousin Jared. He's the only one who knows about my rejection because, unlike my aunt and uncle, I can't hide the pain from him. He knows me too well, and it took all of my wolf strength to stop him from jumping on a plane to beat the crap out of Aiden. It's good though because he constantly takes my mind off of things with his crazy man whorish ways and wise remarks. His friends are awesome too. And are total eye candies. A few tried hitting on me when I was first introduced to the pack, but Jared gave all them death glares. He warned his player friends that I was completely hands off unless any of them were planning on putting a ring on my finger. I laughed at all the deathly ill expressions in the room after that announcement. Commitment is equal to a bad case of crabs in their minds. I can't wait 'til they meet their mates. It'll be fun watching them get tamed.

I get dressed in some black skinnys and an off-shoulder white top with a black tank underneath. I put my hair in a loose bun, gloss my lips, and slip into a pair of black gladiator sandals. As I'm tucking a fly away hair behind my ear, the opening of the front door announces Jace, Nate, and Brad's arrival. I make my way to their voices and find them in the kitchen as usual.

"Bro, I'm telling you. This year we're gonna score so much pu—"

"Lady in the room!" I shout, interrupting what I'm sure was gonna be one of Nate's more colorful terms for *vajayjay*.

"Right. Sorry, Harm. As I was saying, we're gonna score so much chicks because we're now seniors," Nate corrects himself excitedly.

"Well, I know I will, but I'm not too sure about you ugly mutts. Just don't stand too close to me and you'll have a chance since my sex appeal is just too massive," Jared boasts, a l in his usual arrogant self.

"Really, Jared? I know what's massive about you, and it's not your sex appeal or your weiner. Don't try to deny it. Our moms showered us together when we were little, and if I remember correctly, which I do, it was very, very, very tiny," I say, making sure I emphasized the size with my thumb and pointer fingers.

"Hey, that's because I haven't changed yet. Trust me. Massive isn't even a big enough word to describe it now," he argues, a tiny bit offended.

I cringe. "First of all, gross. And second, your ego is the only thing that's massive. I'm worried if you don't bring it down you might not be able to fit your fat head out the door."

"She's right. Besides, we all know my sexiness outshines all of you," Brad informs them.

"No way. I score the most ass . . . I mean chicks every year," Jace argues.

"That's only cause you don't have standards and will screw anything with two sets of lips," says Nate with a raised brow.

This sets off a whole new conversation about what's doable and what's not, followed by pushing and headlocks. These boys are too much and, even though I'm not excited about the day ahead, it promises to be entertaining.

If you enjoyed this sample, look for
My Second Chance Mate
on Amazon.

MATED TO THE ALPHA KING
JENNISE K

PROLOGUE

Dear Reader,

It is with great pleasure that I present to you a brief introduction to the new world you have decided to enter, a new life you have decided to live. Let it be that it will only last for some chapters, but I hope you enjoy it until it lasts.

Let me introduce myself first.

Hi, I am Theia Anderson. I am just like any one of you, human, alive, and breathing. (Unless you are a zombie, in which case I am not, and I especially do not have brains!)

Just putting it out there!

I am eighteen, and currently a senior in Rosenberg High. (I'm what they call a nerd. But let us face it. Nerds nowadays are hot!) I have also only recently moved from the sunny state of California to a city called Peidmond, just beside Seattle. Needless to say, it rains here a lot.

When I moved here, I imagined finally living in a cold state and thought that it would be an amazing experience. Although, the fact that it was in the middle of the year, and I would have to settle in as the "new girl" was very well placed in my mind.

New friends, new teachers, a new environment— everything was new. But that all was well-known and understood. I had expected those.

However, what I certainly didn't expect was to meet the man who owns the castle I gazed upon from my window every morning and night. Yes, a castle…A castle I am now living in.

This is my story. A story I am now willing to share but only if you can keep a secret.

Do you remember the stories your grandma used to tell you every night about cursed beasts, village beauties, girls in red capes, and wolves in disguises?

Well, maybe, just maybe…they actually do happen. Maybe beasts do exist.

They do. I would know. I am bound to one.

Whom, you may ask?

Well, I am mated to the Alpha King.

How?

You will see.

You will live through it with me.

I hope you enjoy the ride.

Best wishes,
Theia

CHAPTER ONE

Done finally!

Packing had never been my forte. In fact, I absolutely detested packing. Maybe it was because the amount of books and other things I possessed seemed impossible to place in tons of boxes.

Slapping duct tape across the box, I picked up a marker and marked it as Theia's Books #3.

When the box was pushed aside carefully, I finally let out a sigh of relief as I wiped away a layer of sweat that had accumulated on my forehead. I lived in the warm state of California. It was summer. So naturally, the heat was killing me.

A single thing one should always know about me—I was not much for heat.

When my dad came home one afternoon and declared that we were moving from California to a cold city just near the outskirts of Seattle called Peidmond, I was actually very excited.

Well, that was until I realized that I had to attend a new high school in the middle of the year and leave my best friend, Casey, behind. And since it was senior year, with prom and all, well, it sucked.

Had I been in my old school, Stinson High, I would have at least had my best friend to accompany me. The thought of being home, all alone on prom, only helped me sweat more.

We were a small family—my dad, Arthur Anderson, a professor of history and literature; my mom, Maia Anderson, a designer and entrepreneur; and me, Theia, currently a senior student in high school and hoping to become a criminologist or psychologist—whatever came first. I also had a very strange fascination with history.

I guess Dad's genes rubbed off on me that way.

Another soft huff of sigh left me as I lazily picked myself off the floor and dragged myself towards the bathroom. I only had two hours before we were to load everything and leave, and I knew, in this heat, I would need every minute of it.

Minutes later, as I stood under my cool shower and slowly observed my bathroom for the last time, I let a few stray tears flow with the water as I washed the tiny ache in my chest away.

It seemed like a day had passed when I found myself scrubbed and fresh, walking out into my bedroom in a towel.

A loud yelp left my lips when I suddenly found myself on the floor and a heavy weight on me.

"Don't go!" Casey cried hysterically against me. I would have cried too, but the fact that I was currently sprawled on the floor with a towel on and my hundred-something-pound best friend was on top of me was a little suffocating. Especially in my part, I was merely five feet after all.

"Need…to…breathe, Casey!" I managed to gasp as I writhed under her, trying to escape her deadly grip. Immediately, Casey stilled above me.

"Oh, I'm sorry!" She apologized hurriedly, blushing beet red as she got off me, and stood. She gave me her hand and helped me stand up.

On my feet, I sighed as I brought her in for a hug. "We will talk every night on Skype or FaceTime, and then there is Messenger! We will always talk. It'll be like I'm not even away, I promise." I assured her as I pulled away. Losing my towel, I pulled on my clothes.

Casey sighed a little heavy and a little scared. "What if we don't?"

I smiled a small, broken smile. My hand found Casey's again, and I gave it a comforting squeeze. "No matter what happens, whether we talk every day or not at all for months, when we do talk or meet, we will always be the same best friends."

A small tear dropped down Casey's cheeks, and she nodded, chuckling.

"You better tell me everything when you get there!" she blurted out, smiling a bit as she folded and placed my towel inside a plastic before packing it into my suitcase. My room was nearly empty. It was literally stripped bare except for the built-in bookshelves and a few boxes and suitcases that were still lying around waiting to be hurled into the moving truck.

Smiling, I nodded and pulled Casey in for a final hug. "We'll visit each other during breaks. I'll miss you, you know."

Casey nodded. "I'll miss you too, Thi."

The loud stomping noises alerted us both of someone coming up the stairs, and soon enough, there was a knock on the door. "Theia, are you done?"

"Yeah, Dad, come in!" I replied as I picked up my jacket—just in case it got cold—and slipped into my flip-flops, which seemed like an irrational choice considering the two contrasted each other, but I wouldn't need my shoes in the car, anyway. I'd probably just tuck them under me throughout the ride.

The door opened instantly and in walked my dad with two bulky men. Smiling at me softly, they strode towards the boxes and picked them up.

Again, Casey and I stood in my empty room—a room we had dozens of sleepovers in, a room we played doll in, a room we gossiped, planned, and plotted in, and a room we did our homework and fangirling in. I sighed.

"I think we should go now…"

"Uh-huh."

Casey and I walked downstairs hand in hand. I took a deep breath as I stood in the living room.

The place had a lot of my memories. I grew up in this area. Well, that was until I turned sixteen and got the television setup in my own room. My eyes were closed. I let out a deep breath and whispered, "I'll miss you, home. Goodbye."

"Theia, sweetie!"

My mom's voice rang out to me like a fire truck's siren. I instantly opened my eyes and walked out of the threshold, letting Dad lock the door and hand over the keys to our real estate agent, who had managed to sell our home for a very, very reasonable amount.

The day outside was bright and happy, vibrant and warm, yet the heat suddenly didn't bother me anymore. I looked around my neighborhood and smiled. I would be taking all the good memories as I went. But as much as I was sad, truth be told, I was also secretly excited.

I didn't know what it was, but I felt like something was waiting for me in Peidmond. An adventure was waiting to be lived—maybe a mystery waiting to be unraveled. The little knowledge about the new feeling in me was all the more alluring, and somehow, secretly, I couldn't wait to reach Peidmond.

"Bye, Cas. I'll call you when I reach there okay!" I muttered, suddenly holding back my tears as I was pulled into a hug.

"Uh-huh, we will always talk! And if we can't, we will at least message when we can." Casey assured me as she hugged me back.

Smiling slightly, I pulled out of the hug and with a final wave, climbed into our SUV, watching my best friend stand in my yard and my neighborhood for the last time as my dad drove off.

It felt like I was leaving a part of me here. But then again, I was going whole.

**

"Are you excited, darling?"

Mom suddenly asked me, cutting the silence that had been building up since we left seven hours ago. The ride from California to Peidmond was fifteen hours and thirteen minutes, and already in these seven hours, we had stopped twice to fuel up the SUV and buy some snacks for along the way.

"Yeah, Mom, are you?" I murmured back, knowing well that both my parents were extremely excited for this "new chapter" in their life. Dad would not stop talking about the amount of brilliant literature his new university had, not to mention the immense raise in wage and position. He was ecstatic. For Mom, her boutiques and salons around California were still running. And although she would have to fly back and forth occasionally, her excitement with opening a new boutique and salon in Peidmond was especially overwhelming.

"Oh, I am so excited!" She squealed, clapping her hands together before turning towards Dad and placing a loving kiss on his cheek.

It was normal for me to witness their weird romance, so I just rolled my eyes and looked at the passing views.

"The new house is bigger, Theia." Dad chuckled and looked at me from the review mirror.

I knew he was trying to make me feel better about moving, leaving my old friends and life behind, so I just grinned at Dad and spoke the first thing I thought would make him worry less. "I get the room with the best view!"

Dad chuckled and nodded, making my grin widen. It was not hard to notice that I was a papa's girl. And with me being the only child, he doted on me. I was his little Fuzzybottom—not that my bottom was fuzzy, but just because—well, he was my hero.

"One of the best things about the house is that it has great views all around the rooms. But you'll receive the one with the best view, we promise. We should be settled by tomorrow. Hopefully, the day after, you and I could go shopping!" Mom said as she turned to look at me. Not excited at all, I somehow managed to produce a fake smile and plaster it across my face.

Nobody messed with Mom when it came to shopping. Nobody!

Once her attention was elsewhere, I turned around to see how far off our moving truck was behind us. Before turning around, I brought out a book from my backpack and plugged my earbuds into my iPod before playing "Davy Jones Music Box and the Rainy Mood." Somehow, the rumbles of thunder together with the soft tunes created a more reading mood for me. Shoving the iPod inside my pants pocket, I flipped through the pages of my newest read, Indiscretions, slumped back into a more comfortable position and began journeying once again into a different time and a whole different world—this time, into the world of Lord Lockwood.

***

"Thi, we are here!"

I mumbled a few incoherent words before turning in my bed. Need sleep.

"Thi, wake up!" Dad's voice urged before I was shaken on the shoulder and lightly tapped on my face. What the heck?

"Alright, alright!" I grumbled as I sat up on my bed and peeped my eye open.

I gasped. My face becoming warmer by the second as I finally realized that I was in our SUV and a couple of people were staring at me, smiling like a bunch of weirdos. My folks included.

My cheeks burned as my eyes rested on a blond-haired guy smirking at me, an axe in his hand as he rested it on his shoulder.

What was he? A huntsman? I rolled my eyes in my mind as I pushed any budding crush away. I was more of a Beauty and the Beast girl, anyway.

Finally managing to look away, I smiled at the rest of the folks smiling at me, two slightly elder couples.

"Oh, she's so beautiful!" The red-headed one gushed as I shoved my iPod and book into my backpack and got out of the SUV.

"Thanks," I mumbled back, knowing full well that the blond was still staring and smirking at me.

"Hello, dear. Welcome to Peidmond! I'm Jane, and this here is my son, Alex, and my husband, Hugh. We live just there beside your house. That one there is Mary and her husband, Grant. They have a son too, Matthew. He is good friends with Alex here," Jane told me excitedly, and I smiled back, brightly mirroring her excitement.

"It's nice to meet you all. I am really excited to be here," I replied back happily as I extended my hand towards each one of them, shaking their hands softly but waving awkwardly at the smirking blond, Alex.

That boy seemed as beautiful as he seemed arrogant. But then, arrogance trumped beauty any day.

My new home stood tall and proud—red bricks and a posh-looking French door. It seemed to have at least three floors, including the small attic on the third floor. Even the front yard seemed beautifully cultivated. I waited for Jane and Mary to start talking to Mom and Hugh and Grant to start helping my dad and the movers place all our stuff into the house before picking up one of my smaller book boxes. I made a run for it.

Making a dash into the house as quickly as I could, I stopped only to grab Dad and drag him away, begging him to show me my room.

He grinned excitedly and exchanged a knowing look with both Hugh and Grant who led me upstairs until we came to a stop on the very end of the hallway. He unlocked the room and opened the doors, motioning me to walk in.

I walked in and froze.

There, in front of me was the most amazing view of a castle perched on a mountain, surrounded by pine trees and fog.

Beyond it, I could see water, maybe a lake. Maybe a sea…It was actually hard to say through the fog.

I turned around, already readying myself to leap on Dad but frowned when I noticed that I was now alone in my room. The blond Alex was standing in the doorway with the usual smirk on his face and his axe missing.

I frowned. The urge of just smacking his smirk away seemed quite strong now, and it would be easy too.

"That is the Castle Dovelore, owned by His Grace, Alexander Whitlock. 'His Grace' because some say his grandfather was a duke, and that has now been passed over to him. He is also very rich if the castle isn't proof enough. But not by heritage, most of it is self-made and all. We are supposed to visit that castle this year, you know. Mr. Whitlock is providing one lucky student with a full-time scholarship to any university he or she wishes to attend and another lucky student a chance to stay in his castle for the breaks with the full usage of his library and a full tour around the castle if he or she wanted to, that is," Blond spoke, but his gaze did not once shift from the castle, which although looked quite brooding, looked equally inviting as if charming me into visiting. There definitely was something about that castle.

Suddenly very curious, I turned towards Blond and asked, "What would you like?"

He turned his attention towards me, and for the first time since the fifteen minutes that we had known each other, he smiled at me—a real smile.

"Although the most brilliant of literature are available in the castle library and I would love to roam the dungeons and secret pathways where the pirates were slain and beasts held hostage, I want the scholarship." I nodded and turned back to look at the castle.

What beasts was Blond talking about?

The feeling of my feet pushing itself forward registered slowly before I found myself staring at the castle and my hands, sliding the window open.

Is someone living there right now? How many rooms can there be?

I swept my gaze along the windows of the castle but stalled when I saw someone staring back at me. It seemed a he. His bulky built made sure of showing no confusion even if he was so, so far away. It was quite distinguishable that he was wearing a white shirt, but that was all that could be made sense of. The rest was a blur.

"Hey, Blond, come here!" I whispered, motioning Blond to move forward.

"Blond?" he asked quite confusedly and sounding outraged as he made his way to me.

The man was still staring. His stare seemed so intense it made hairs stand at the back of my neck. I turned towards Blond, wishing he could see the strange man just as I did. Castles were always haunted. But the one I would see day and night could not possibly be haunted, could it?

"Can you see the man?"

"What man? I see no man," he whispered back, scrunching his eyes as he looked in the direction of the castle.

I turned towards the castle, and the man was gone.

"He was just there! I promise!"

He looked at me frowning for a second before his smile came back.

"I can help you decorate your room." He offered, looking as if he really were interested in sorting out my mess.

I smiled as I brushed a stray of brown hair behind my ear, silently thanking God for his sudden offer to decorate my bedroom. It would have taken me all day and night, otherwise.

"Let's do this."

If you enjoyed this sample, look for
Mated to the Alpha King
on Amazon.

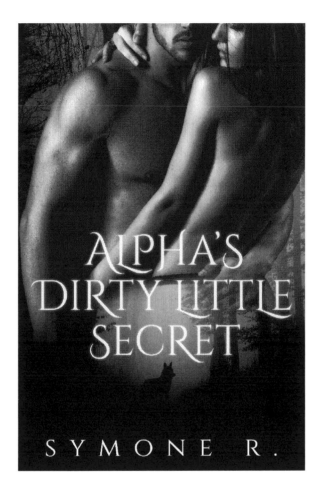

CHAPTER I

AMIRA

Gazing at the several unknown faces, I began to feel as if I was living in the shadows once again. I was left bearing a secret that made me feel like I was living in a lie.

Innocent humans watched as our college professor continued to lecture about Accounting and Finance. I looked to my left; beside me was a girl. Her blonde hair was draped over her brown eyes as she continued to scribble insignificant pictures on her notebook. What amazed me the most was how unaware she was of the nonhuman creature seated only inches away from her.

She sighed. My useful heightened senses allowed me to listen to her heartbeat and breathing that would accelerate every time the professor searched for a student to answer a simple question. Her heart rate would regulate once the professor called someone else. She slouched in her chair, her eyes occasionally wandering off from her work to a boy sitting in the far corner of the room.

"Amira? Are you paying attention?" I looked to my right, finding the eyes of my friend, Eric.

Eric and I have been friends since we were thirteen. Six years later, we were still going strong. We had a lot of classes together over the years, so our friendship continued to grow. However, despite us being friends, I could never find it in myself to tell him who I really was. Or should I say, *what* I was.

"Yeah…no," I admitted before we both shared a low snicker.

"Eric, you know I got all of this stuff already," I reassured him, slouching down in my chair.

I was known to be very intelligent in school. Unlike most, it was very easy for me to remember and comprehend any given task. This skill has been very helpful to me.

"Well, then, if it's so damn easy for you, you can teach it all to me because I'm lost as hell." Eric sighed. His eyes narrowed in on the textbook in front of him as I chuckled at him.

"Okay, ladies and gentlemen, class dismissed," the teacher announced as she wrapped up her lecture. I stood from my desk. Students began gathering their things before everyone scrambled out of the door.

"So, lunch on me today?" Eric offered.

"No, sorry. I have to help my mom prepare for this dinner we are having tomorrow. Just a few out-of-town guests." I sighed heavily.

"Okay, cool. Well, I'll text you tonight?"

"Sure."

*   *   *

The appetizing smell of food danced its way around me, clouding my nasal passages with the mouth-watering aroma of my mother's home-cooked meal.

I walked into the kitchen to see my mother running back and forth. She was cutting vegetables, stirring food in the pots, and measuring the temperature of whatever she was roasting in the oven.

"Mom, is it this serious?" She was acting as if the president was stopping by for dinner.

"Yes, sweetie. This is when you'll see your new alpha for the first time." My mother was more cheerful than the rest of us were.

It was amusing how my mother cared about the alpha's arrival more than the actual werewolves that lived here. I expected her to feel uncaring about his presence as if he was just another regular visitor, her being a human and all.

I guess being married to and being the mother of a werewolf really had her interested in the supernatural world. Unlike her, I couldn't care less about the werewolf society. I found human life to be much better. Accepting. I enjoyed not living under the command and authority of some male who was determined to show his dominance over everyone because of a title.

That was why I loved living in the city. Majority of our pack, including the alpha and beta, lived far out in the country somewhere.

Honestly, that's how I liked it. I loved being away from the group who allowed their title to get to their overgrown skull.

I preferred the distance. However, my father seemed to not feel the same way I do. Recently, he had invited the previous alpha and luna, and their son—the new alpha—over for dinner. Only my father could ruin such a beautiful thing.

"But Mom, they aren't coming until tomorrow," I reminded her again.

"I know, I know, but I prefer to get things done now."

I sighed. Looking over everything, I could see how she had handled things.

"You seem to have everything done." The chicken was roasting in the oven; the vegetables were boiling in the pots; and she seemed to be starting on dessert. "Call me if you need anything then."

I snatched up my bag from the kitchen counter. Reaching into the cupboard, I pulled a granola bar from the box before I left the kitchen.

I silently cursed my mother and father again. I don't even know why I have to be here. If I could, I would disappear before the guests even made it to town. Sadly, my father requested that I should be present for the attendees.

Why did I seem so against the presence of the new alpha? I would say our past was just a tiny piece of the reason that I wanted to disappear. Even though my mother said it's the first time meeting the new alpha, it's actually not. We had already met before he had taken over the title, alpha.

When I was about eight years old, my father and I would visit the main pack house for some business. Since my father was one of the strongest warriors of our pack, the previous alpha would need him by his side during decision-making.

That's when I had first met eleven-year-old Xavier, the soon-to-be alpha.

My father said—to keep us busy and out of their hair while he helped the alpha—Xavier and I should go play, and we did. Honestly, I thought Xavier was cute. I was actually very fond of him. Stupidly, I asked him if he felt the same way. Let's just say it was not the answer I hoped for.

To impress his friends, who were the children of other higher ranked members, he knocked me off the swing. I remembered crying on the ground as he and the other kids laughed before they left me soaking in my own tears.

That fucking bitch.

Yes, I knew that it happened many years ago, but for some reason, I just couldn't forget and forgive. I guess I just didn't take rejection or embarrassment too well. I still don't.

Luckily, after that, I never saw him again, and I was perfectly fine with it.

I quickly shook the thoughts off before I disappeared into the bathroom.

I stood in front of the mirror in my room after I finished taking a shower. I ran my hands down my hips as I stared at my reflection. I adored my frame. I didn't consider myself fit or slim like the other female werewolves I had encountered. Other she-wolves had a fit and athletic physique, the type of body that would look exceptional in anything. I, on the other hand, did not have that. I was a curvaceous woman—full breasts, thick hips and thighs without such a slim waist. I would always assure myself that I would soon diet. At least, after I finish off the pizza I was enjoying.

I began to smile. My full pink lips looked well with my silky smooth skin and brown eyes.

I pulled out my blow dryer and started drying my shoulder-length black hair. When my hair was already dry, I pinned it up and leaped into my bed. Turning my television on, I searched through various channels until I finally landed on a show I could finish my night with.

*   *   *

Wrapped up in my comforter, I felt at ease. No classes. No early morning wake-up calls. Just the perfect time to oversleep.

"Amira, wake up. Let's go the mall." I heard my mother's all too familiar voice as she pushed through my bedroom door.

"No, thank you," I rolled away from her. "It's too early."

"Too early? It's 12:30 in the afternoon. Now, get your butt up."

I turned to my mother and an annoyed snarl escaped me. She narrowed her eyes and shot me a warning glare before walking away. It was a warning, convincing me that her wrath was more powerful than my teeth.

"Make it an hour, or I'm coming back."

"Fine." I sighed.

I stayed in bed for another fifteen minutes; I just did not want to get up. Mustering up some energy, I swung my legs and sat up from the bed. Tired and drained, I dragged myself to my bathroom.

After finishing my routine, I picked up my bag and made my way downstairs.

"Hey, Dad," I greeted my father as I walked into the kitchen. He glanced up from his paper to meet my gaze.

"Hey, where are you two headed?"

"She's dragging me to the mall." I slipped into a chair beside him. I reached for his paper and pulled the comic section from the crumbled pile.

"Oh, good luck." I could sense the humor in his comment.

My father knew how things went when it involved accompanying my mother to the mall. He had found a way to get out of it. During their mall trips, he would make her shopping experience hell. He complained, dragged his feet, and gave opinions my mother found useless. Occasionally, he would become 'ill' during their mall runs.

I could only admire his tactics for escaping.

"Okay, sweetie, I'm ready."

"Okay." I sighed and stood up from my chair.

I followed my mother out to the car and got in. I slumped down in my seat as I listened to the vehicle's engine roar to life from under the hood. I slipped my earbuds on and drifted into my own thoughts the entire ride.

$$*\qquad*\qquad*$$

We roamed the mall for hours, not looking for a specific item. My mother just wanted to buy random things. With the help of my complaints, my mother wrapped up her shopping journey, and we finally left the mall.

"Sweetie, can you tell your father to come help with the bags?" I scowled at her. *What am I? A personal beeper?*

Reaching into our mind link, I urged for his assistance. A few seconds later, my father emerged from the front entrance. He grabbed my mother's bag, refusing to have her carry her own.

He should have joined us in our mall run then. With his petty whining, I would have been home already.

By the time we arrived home, I made my way to the kitchen and walked over to the refrigerator, pulling a bottle of water from the shelf. As I turned to leave, I witnessed my parents sharing an intimate kiss in the living room. "We all have rooms for that, people."

"Sorry, honey." My mother's cheeks flushed red as she pulled away from my father.

"You will understand once you find your mate," my father explained.

A mate. To us werewolves, our mate would be someone the moon goddess has blessed us with. A mate would be someone we plan to spend the rest of eternity with.

Love. A destined bond that was almost unavoidable and hard to break. My mother and father were mates. He shared his secret with her, and she accepted his life and him as well.

However, some weren't that blessed. Some were cursed. Some were given a mate who could be careless, cold-blooded, and downright disgraceful.

There could be some who don't want a mate. Some who would rather remain unrestricted than fall into the spell of the mate bond.

Rejection. Some would rather reject their mate; it's their way of freeing themselves from the world they consider a prison. However, it's not always accepted by the other. The rejected mate may not fully accept it, leaving them with a broken heart and the feeling of desertion. Some would begin to feel as though it's their own actions that caused the rejection, and feel self-loathe and hatred for their wolves. Finally, another dangerous aspect was pain, hatred, and even suicidal ideation.

Honestly, I didn't care about finding my mate. I didn't want to find some wolf who probably believed that I my only purpose was to bear his children and sleep with him. A man who would probably only use me as his chew toy. I couldn't allow someone to have so much control over me, so much power. And then give me so much heartache.

"No, thank you on the mate thing, Dad." A waved my hands frantically. I didn't want that curse.

"Honey, go, get dressed. Our guests should be arriving in about an hour." My mom pressed.

Shifting my eyes toward my father, I shot him a venomous glare once again.

"Oh, honey, you will love them. They are nice people, so relax."

Disagreeing with him, I picked up the small bags I had gotten from the mall and ran up to my room to prepare for an unwanted arrival.

If you enjoyed this sample, look for
Alpha's Dirty Little Secret
on Amazon.

ACKNOWLEDGEMENTS

I would like to thank my mother and father for their endless love and unshakable belief in the existence of my questionable intelligence.

My brothers and sisters for their endless teasing,

I know there are encouragements in there somewhere.

Adam and Milla for cheering me on to finish this book and listening to my endless chattering and crazy ideas.

You two are my inspiration.

My beautiful and fabulous Wattpad readers everywhere, you guys are my best cheerleaders.

Last but not least, my wonderful and patient editor, Precious and awesome agent, AJ.

AUTHOR'S NOTE

Thank you so much for reading *Catching Genesis*! I can't express how grateful I am for reading something that was once just a thought inside my head.

Please feel free to send me an email. Just know that my publisher filters these emails. Good news is always welcome.
nicole_riddley@awesomeauthors.org

Sign up for my blog for updates and freebies!
nicole-riddley.awesomeauthors.org

One last thing: I'd love to hear your thoughts on the book. Please leave a review on Amazon or Goodreads because I just love reading your comments and getting to know you!

Can't wait to hear from you!

Nicole Riddley

ABOUT THE AUTHOR

Nicole Riddley lives in Ontario Canada. She likes to travel, swim, read, write, paint, draw and take pictures in her spare time. She takes thousands of pictures every time she travels.

She loves drawing portraits of people that tell stories. She loves coloring outside the lines.

Printed in Great Britain
by Amazon